Between the Lies

Susan Schussler

ISBN: 0989033325
ISBN 13: 9780989033329
Library of Congress Control Number: 2015944757
Rocky Shore Media LLC, St. Paul, Minnesota

CONTENTS

LIES

We all tell them—little white ones, ones of omission, giant jawbreakers that are impossible to swallow, ones where only our best friends know the truth, and others that cover realities too dark to share.

Chapter One

Sarah

The text read, Call me when U have time 2 talk—ASAP. Sarah pressed send and set her phone on the table next to the couch. She curled up her legs next to her and opened her laptop. The text was to her best friend and someday sister-in-law, Jessica. The "someday" came from the fact that Sarah's brother, Jeff, and Jessica had been talking about getting married for almost a year now, and Jeff still hadn't given her a ring. He was waiting for just the right moment to make it official. This detail had put the slightest rift in Sarah and Jessica's relationship. Not that anything could ruin their friendship. They had been best friends since middle school, and their friendship could withstand much worse. Sarah knew Jessica's ring was a sore point, so she tried to avoid mentioning engagement rings or wedding plans when talking to her, though this was getting more and more difficult to do.

Sarah missed Jessica. She missed all her friends. It seemed like so long since she had seen them. Several months had passed since Sarah left her family and friends back in the Midwest for her new life in Los Angeles. When she made the choice to leave, she hadn't really known what to expect once she got to California. All she really knew was that she couldn't live apart from Will any longer. Being with him was the only thing that mattered. She still called him Will sometimes, though lately she had gotten used to calling him Jon. It was just easier. No one knew him by his nickname except his good friends, and they weren't around that often. She equated it to adopting an accent. The people she interacted with every day called him Jon, and she picked it up like a drawl or Valley speak. Besides, she was tired of explaining who Will was as he stood next to her laughing.

She logged on to the Internet while she waited for Jessica's response. She buzzed through a gossip site's pictures of her movie star fiancé coming out of a hotel, followed by Natalie Lipka. The caption read, *Boys will be boys.*

She knew Jon had gone to dinner with the gorgeous Ukrainian actress as part of a business meeting for an upcoming film, but why did it have to be at that particular hotel? The Hotel Freemont was known for celebrity hookups, and the photos of them walking out separately and then getting into the same car just made them look guiltier. Sarah knew it was just dinner, but she also knew she would have to explain the pictures to her family and friends—like so many pictures before—and this week the whole world would think Jon was cheating.

At least it wasn't Mia Thompson. A picture of Jon with his ex would take much longer than a week to blow over, and it would drive Sarah crazy. She could imagine Mia staring back with her "I've got a secret, and you're so screwed" expression. Mia made her completely irrational. She didn't know how to explain it. Maybe it was the way Mia carried herself around Jon, as if she owned him, or maybe it was that the fans hadn't fully accepted Sarah and still wanted Jon and Mia together. Sarah could put up with any other woman flirting with Jon, but if Mia was in the same room, sirens blared in her head.

She took a deep breath and glanced at her phone—nothing yet. She still had time. She maneuvered her way to the one site where she wasn't supposed to go. She couldn't save the site on her desktop or in her favorites because he would see it, so she made the extra effort to key in the address by hand. Then she typed in the user ID and password she remembered from when the account had been set up. A smile spread across her face as she caught up on the site's activity. He had been to the Mall of America and rode the roller coaster last week. He took the light-rail train to Nicollet Mall in downtown Minneapolis and bought some tulips from the Danish vendor who always gabbed too much. Sarah could almost smell the flowers. And last night, he ate dinner at Sarah's parents' house. The picture of him sitting at the table with her mom and dad made Sarah laugh.

Just then, Sarah's favorite song began to blare from the table next to her—or it used to be her favorite, until she set it as a ringtone. She picked up the phone and slid her finger across the touch screen.

"What's up? You haven't been abducted, have you?" Jessica's voice rang with mockery.

"No, not this week," Sarah said with a chuckle. "I see William was at my parents' for dinner last night."

"Well, you know how much he likes your mom's lasagna."

"No. Jon really likes my mom's lasagna. Plastic dolls that look like him don't eat, but I liked the picture with Mom and Dad. I miss you guys. I miss school. I even miss our old, run-down rental house. Do you want to go out for drinks on Friday? You can bring the doll."

"Are you going to be in town?"

"No, I wish! I won't be home until graduation. Jon has a bunch of commitments, and you know how he is about me traveling by myself."

"I don't blame him, Sarah. Look at all the garbage that has happened to you, and that was before you announced the engagement."

"Well, it's not like him being with me makes it any easier to travel. He's always recognized. It takes twice as long as it should to go anywhere. At least I can slip in and out under the radar usually—not yesterday, though. Some idiot followed me all day long when I was meeting with the wedding planner." Sarah caught herself. She'd almost started talking about the wedding, and she had told herself she wasn't going to do that.

"That's exactly why he's so worried about you. There are crazies everywhere. He feels responsible for you being in danger all the time."

"It was just paparazzi. I'm not in danger. It's not like I'm ever alone, anyway. We have a whole team of security now, not just Sam. I mean, I can't even use the bathroom by myself."

"Ew, too much information."

"No, I just mean there's always someone standing outside the door, as if I'm going to be knifed in the bathroom stall or something."

"He's just worried about you."

"Shut up! You're supposed to be on my side."

"I am on your side, but I think Jon's right. You need to be cautious—at least until after the wedding. I read somewhere that the pop star Fretti got into her car one day and some psycho fan was waiting in her backseat with duct tape. If her boyfriend hadn't been three cars down and heard her scream, who knows what would have happened?"

"I'm not a pop star, and you know that ninety percent of what you read about celebrities is fake, right?"

"Yeah, but I saw her talk about it in an interview, too. I know you would like to deny it, but most gossip is spawned by seeds in the real world."

"You've been cyberstalking us with my mom, haven't you?" Sarah could tell by Jessica's tone that she was holding back.

"Your mom isn't that bad, and yes, I see her all the time. She's worried about you."

"Did she see the pictures of Jon with Natalie?"

"Yeah," Jessica said in a subdued voice.

"You think that's why I called, don't you? He's not cheating on me. It was just a couple of business dinners. That's all. There were a bunch of people with them. They're going to be doing a film together."

"So, what's up, then?"

"I don't know. I'm bored—or lonely?" Sarah declared, not really sure what she was feeling.

"I know you and Jon go out all the time. I see you on Celebrity News every other night. The press wants more public displays of affection, by the way, just in case no one has told you."

"We really don't go out much because Jon is always mobbed. We definitely don't go out as much as I did back home, and I'm not PDAing on camera just so the press can dissect our every lip and hand movement. I love Jon, but I just need to hang out with the girls once in a while."

"No girls in California?"

"No, I just don't have any friends—not that I trust, anyway. Everyone acts like my best friend, but it's just because of Jon. I can talk to Leslie, but I never know how much is filtering back to Jon. Not that I keep secrets from him," Sarah assured. "But it's girl stuff, and his cousin shares everything with him."

"So come for a visit. Bring a bodyguard."

"Actually, I was wondering if you, Alli, and Megan could come out to LA for the weekend. I'll send you the plane tickets, and you can stay at the house with us."

"So you and Jon stopped arguing about money, then?"

"Yeah, I caved."

"So did he give you a credit card or something?"

"Yep, but that's not all. Jon added my name to all his bank accounts, and I added him to mine—like that mattered. It almost killed his accountant. The accountant wanted to set up an expense account for me like Leslie's, but Jon said no. He says we're equal partners, and we need to mesh our lives completely. He doesn't want me to have to ask him for money, so I have full access. He says that I just have to accept that I don't really have an income right now, and since we're getting married, I have to get used to sharing. Besides, I know I'll never make as much money as he does, and everything is so expensive out here. He keeps telling me to stop worrying about money and just enjoy life. He's been bugging me to have you guys out. So what do you say?"

"I'm up for it, but let me ask Megan and Alli," said Jessica. "Sarah is on the phone and wants to know if we can come out to the coast for the weekend—on Jon's dime."

"Are you kidding? Yeah! I'm there," answered Megan. Sarah could hear her clearly in the background.

"Let me talk to Sarah." Alli grabbed the phone from Jessica. "Sarah, what's wrong?"

"Nothing is wrong. I just miss you guys."

"So, you gave up on the money thing?"

"It was futile. Can you come on Friday after class? We could go to the beach or just hang out at the pool. It's in the seventies and sunny. And the shopping is unbelievable."

"That sounds great. I think it was twenty-six this morning when I caught the bus. I had to wear mittens and my winter jacket. I'm putting you on speaker, OK?"

"Megan, you have the last class at two thirty, right?"

"No, I dropped that class. I didn't need it. Besides, I hate having class on Fridays, and the TA was a douche," admitted Megan.

"All teaching assistants are douches," Jessica proclaimed, and Sarah could hear the smile on her face.

"Hey!" Alli protested.

"Alli is dating her TA from organic chemistry. He's Indian," revealed Jessica.

"I'm pretty sure TAs aren't supposed to date undergrads. How did that happen?" asked Sarah.

"We're not dating, and he's not from India—his parents are."

"You meet him for coffee almost every day, and he calls you all the time. Most TAs don't do that, especially when you're not in their class anymore," Megan remarked.

"Well, at least I'm not back together with a guy I've been avoiding for four years," Alli stated.

Sarah groaned. "Please don't tell me you're back together with Chase. Megan, what are you thinking?" She got up and started pacing through the house. She couldn't believe Jessica and Alli could let this happen.

"We're not back together. We were just catching up," claimed Megan.

"Yeah. I thought you said you would only meet with him in public. Your room with the door closed is not public," Alli snapped.

"Megan, how many times did you say never again? You can't get back with Chase. You promised," said Sarah.

"I'm not. I was tempted, but I'm not."

"Really? You've already given him more chances than you should give any guy. He's going to hurt you again," Sarah said.

"It's not the same."

"Just be careful. He's your kryptonite," Sarah warned, exasperated. She pulled her long, dark hair into a loose bundle at her neck before sitting down at the kitchen table. She looked out into the courtyard at the shimmering pool, trying to figure out why Megan would even go near Chase after all the crap he had put her through.

The courtyard was blissful with stone paths methodically designed to look natural as they weaved their trails from one gathering spot to another. Jon's parents purchased the house when Jon was eight. Jon's dad had received a large monetary payout from a big studio movie he directed at the time and put almost all of his earnings toward the purchase and remodel of the house. The entire estate was gorgeous, but Sarah's favorite place was the courtyard.

She thought about her life back home. It still snowed this time of year in Minnesota—not that often, but she could remember at least a couple of big snowstorms in April in her twenty-one years. Her life was so different now, but part of her wished it wasn't.

"It's a good thing you guys are getting away for the weekend. It sounds like all hell is breaking loose there," she said.

"I can't wait to tell you everything. We can be at the airport any time after two on Friday, our time," said Jessica.

"Great, I'll get it all set up and get back to you this afternoon," said Sarah. She listened to her old housemates chatter about what they were going to wear on the trip and what they needed to pack. She liked to hear them interact. It made her feel like she was back at home.

As she listened, she looked up to see Jonathan crossing the courtyard from the main house. He had been working out with his personal trainer for the last ninety minutes in the main house's weight room. He wore athletic shorts with no shirt and had a white towel draped over his shoulders. His dark hair curled up in its damp state, and he pushed it out of his eyes as he passed the pool's diving board. His well-defined muscles glistened with sweat, and Sarah forgot she was on the phone for a second as she watched him. His ice-blue eyes brightened when they met hers through the glass french doors, and when he opened the door, a warm breeze blew in with just a hint of the fragrant orange blossoms from the trees up on the hill.

Sarah held her hand over the mouthpiece for a second and mouthed, "It's the girls."

Jonathan leaned into the phone and said, "Hi, ladies," before touching his lips gently to Sarah's neck just below her left ear—her favorite spot.

Sarah chuckled as Jon continued to kiss her. "Jon says hi."

The girls all responded in unison. "Hey, Jon."

"So I'll talk to you guys soon." They said their good-byes, and Sarah set her phone on the table as she turned to Jon. "You are very distracting."

He smiled his perfect smile, revealing the single dimple on his right cheek. "Want to hit the pool? The water is warm, and I didn't see anyone at the gate."

"There are no paparazzi outside?"

Jon shook his head. "No one's at the main house, either. I'm going to rinse off and grab my trunks."

Sarah needed to line up the flight for her friends before she went swimming, so she was going to call Jon's assistant first for some help. "OK, I'll meet you out there after I call Leslie."

"In your bikini?" he pleaded with wide eyes. "Please?"

Sarah hadn't worn her bikini since the car accident that almost took her life. She didn't feel comfortable showing the ugly scars on her abdomen. She scrunched her nose and scowled just a little. "Not yet."

This wasn't the first time Jonathan had specifically asked her to wear her bikini and she refused. He sighed and walked into the living room without another word.

Jonathan

Jon knew that she was still self-conscious about the scars. He wished she wasn't. He felt responsible for the accident that had disfigured her, and it hurt him to see her so insecure.

He made his way toward the bedroom to change and paused when he saw her silver laptop open on the couch. Colorful bubbles danced across the screen, but he could see the website behind them. He stared at it a moment, picking it up to get a closer look. His engagement photo was clearly visible on the wall in the dining room at Sarah's parents' house. With his hands fisting tighter on either side of the keyboard, it took all his restraint not to smash the computer against the wall.

He and Sarah had talked about this. With all the trouble they had been having with their personal life being leaked to the press, why would she log on to this site? It was known for how easy it was to hack. And why was their engagement photo in the background? That was just asking for trouble. He almost called for Sarah to explain, but instead, he squished his eyes together and took a deep breath. He knew she missed her friends, and he felt guilty for stealing her from them. He set the laptop back on the couch, then clicked on the red box with the X in the corner of the screen to close the site before heading out of the room.

Chapter Two

Jonathan

Jonathan spun his chair to the side to catch a better look at the monitor in the main house's security office. The large flat-screen was divided into sixteen different camera views. He clicked the computer keyboard nervously to enlarge each view one at a time. A couple of paparazzi were in cars outside the gate. *Click.* The white van that always seemed to be on the street strategically blocking the camera's line of sight. *Click.* The front door of the main house: clear. *Click.* The front of the guesthouse: clear. *Click.* Inside the rock wall's left side: clear. *Click.* Right side: clear. *Click.* The pergola by the pool: he stared at the monitor a second and toggled the buttons to zoom in on Sarah's face. She was laughing as she visited with Leslie. *God, she looked beautiful.* Her dark hair shimmered as she turned to look up at the camera. He must have moved the camera with his adjustments. Her green eyes penetrated him as if she could see him. Then Leslie said something, and her attention returned to the magazine on the table. Jonathan strummed his fingers as he watched her on the large screen.

"What does it mean?" he asked.

"Nothing. It means nothing, Jon. Don't even think about it," said Isaac.

"Then why are you all here?" Jonathan turned to meet his agent's eyes. He knew Isaac was lying.

"It's not something you should worry about. You getting all upset isn't going to help."

"It's easy to ignore the threats, pretend they're not real," contradicted Sam. "That just makes them more dangerous."

"Jonathan gets threats all the time."

Jon turned to spy on Sarah again as he listened to his head of security and his agent argue. Then he clicked the monitor back to the split screen view of all the cameras before asking, "What makes this one different?" He spread the three typed letters out in front of him next to the keyboard and examined the pictures on each.

"It's the same person who sent the one in January. The print's the same. The way the pictures are inserted is the same. Even some of the wording is the same. But Isaac let everyone in his office handle the letter before we could get any prints off it. He even tossed the envelope. There's not much left for us to work with," stated Sam.

"That's the girl's job. She opens the mail. Sam, are we going to start with this again? I can't change it now. Get over it."

"I just don't want any more stupid mistakes," Sam boomed in his intimidating voice.

"Maybe you should send over one of your militia to open the mail. I'm sure they would do a much better job." Isaac glanced over to Craig and Raul when he said the word *militia*.

"Just stop. What does it mean?" Jon asked again, rubbing his fingertips across his forehead.

"It means that it may be time to get the FBI involved," stated Sam.

"That's just going to bring the press in, Jon, and open it up to all kinds of crazy copycats." Isaac folded his hands behind his head as he leaned back in his chair.

Jonathan looked to Sam for confirmation.

"That can happen," Sam admitted. "But this guy most likely means what he says, and that's why we're all here. Raul and Craig have experience with terroristic threats from their special ops duty, but it's different stateside. The FBI has teams of people that work on this kind of crap every day."

Jon looked to Raul and Craig and asked, "What do you think?" His two new security members were both former special ops marines. They handled situations very differently than Sam with his police background, and Jon valued their opinions, too.

"The guy wouldn't have been so specific if he didn't plan to follow through," answered Raul with a slight tinge of a Puerto Rican accent.

"I'm not going to let anyone hurt Sarah," stated Jon.

"Nobody wants that, Jon," added Isaac.

"The notes weren't explicit. It may not be Sarah at all. The guy could mean you," stated Sam.

"So we talk to the FBI and then what?" Jon made the decision. He couldn't sit around any longer waiting for something to happen.

"Then they tell us what to do. They'll keep it quiet if needed," Sam answered.

"Could the letters be related to the recent leaks to the press?" asked Jon.

Sam shrugged. "Hard to tell."

"OK. Is there anything else I should know?" Jon turned back to the security monitor.

"No. I'll keep you updated," stated Sam.

With his heart still in his throat, Jon rose and turned toward the door. He needed some time to calm down before he faced Sarah. "I need a drink." Jon nodded toward his agent, and Isaac followed him out of the room and down the hall. The bar in the media room was stocked, and Jon spotted his dad's scotch decanter right away.

"Scotch OK?" he asked as he took out two lowball glasses and set them on the wooden bar top. A knot grew in his stomach, just like the one that had been there the last time he drank scotch. It had been years. Jon opened the icemaker and scooped a couple of cubes into each glass with his hand.

As he poured the amber liquid, filling the glasses half-full, Isaac asked, "When did you start drinking scotch?"

"Shortly after the accident. I used to drink my dad's scotch just to piss him off. He already hated me for killing Jack. Back then I figured it couldn't hurt our relationship, so what the hell. This won't bother Dad now. I'll replace it." He handed Isaac a glass.

"The problem with the stalker isn't that bad. This kind of thing happens all the time. You can't take on every crazy out there." Isaac took a sip, keeping his eyes pinned on him.

Jon brought his glass to his lips, tilting it to let the golden liquid warm the back of his throat. A slow burn traveled downward as he swallowed. He remembered it tasting better. He rested the tumbler against his temple. The cool glass felt better than the burn on his throat. "The last time I drank it was that week you tracked me down in Atlantic City, remember?"

Isaac nodded again. "You haven't spoken of Atlantic City in almost four years. What's on your mind?"

Jon pushed his hands through his dark hair and inhaled deeply. "Not my best moment."

"Not your best, Jon."

He emptied his glass in one gulp and met Isaac's eyes. "I don't ever want my life to be in that place again."

"It won't happen. We won't let it."

"Can you guarantee that? Because that's what I want. I want a guarantee that Sarah's not going to get hurt because of me. Or my mom. My dad. Leslie. Remi. You. I want a guarantee that I won't kill someone I care about."

"What do you want me to say?" Isaac looked up from his drink. "I personally guarantee that no one will get hurt." He stared at Jon with a somber expression.

Jon shook his head. There were no guarantees in life. "You are so full of crap."

"But my crap smells like gardenias."

Jon chuckled, still shaking his head. Isaac had always been there for him. He was more than his agent—he could always depend on Isaac to get him through. Sure he was arrogant and pushy, but he always had Jon's back. He had been at Jon's side from the beginning, and that type of loyalty was hard to find. "Are you sure you don't want to be in the wedding? You should be."

"Nah. That group of rock stars you have standing up with you would be too humbled by this handsome face. They wouldn't be able to handle me upstaging them."

"You're probably right." Jon got up and poured himself another drink. "You want a refill? We may as well get our fill if I have to replace it anyway."

"No, thanks." Isaac took out his phone and began typing.

"Got a hot date tonight?" Isaac was always on the phone, but he didn't usually text.

"No, but I did score a date with Lizbeth Hanson next week," he answered as he shoved his phone back into his jacket pocket.

"You better not screw that up. Her dad will blackball us." Isaac's love life was a welcomed distraction.

"Oh…I think you are a big enough star to hold your own against Mr.

Moneybags. Besides, I heard she hates her daddy. She sided with her mother in the divorce."

"Just play nice with her. I don't need any more enemies." He definitely had enough enemies.

"You know me. I'm all about nice when it comes to women." Isaac laughed like he didn't believe his own words.

"Hey, Jon." Leslie walked into the room and balanced on the arm of Jon's chair as she grabbed the tumbler from his hand. "Zander's scotch. You live dangerously." She smiled and downed the rest of the amber liquid before setting the empty glass on the table next to her. Her face twisted with a bitter pucker.

A snorted laugh broke from Jon's lips. "Enjoy that, did you?"

"I guess it's an acquired taste," Leslie said, looking to Isaac.

"You can't say she doesn't know how to take charge."

Leslie narrowed her eyes at Isaac, and Jon wondered what his comment meant. *Was Leslie who he texted?* He watched the two as some kind of unspoken conversation passed between them. "What was that?" Jon asked. "What's going on between you two?"

"In his dreams," answered Leslie as she flopped onto the leather couch.

"They're good dreams, Leslie. You'd like them." Isaac broke out laughing. "Do you want the details?"

"No." She turned quickly from Isaac to Jon. "We're just concerned about you. I left Sarah with a couple of tabloids to check out, and her friends should be here soon. I didn't mention your meeting, but you have to tell her at some point."

"I know. I just don't want to ruin her weekend." He struggled with telling her. Sarah always believed the best in others and knowing about the stalker would change that. He didn't want her to become cynical about something she had no control over. Yet, he didn't want her to get hurt. He had hurt her enough.

Sarah

Sarah couldn't wait for her friends to arrive. Sam sent a car service to pick up the girls from the airport, and they would be arriving any minute. Having a whole weekend to spend with her best friends would be unbelievable. They always made her feel at home, normal. Her friends knew all about her. She wouldn't need to put on a show for them. They wouldn't judge her for what she wore or how much she ate. They wouldn't care if she drank through a straw or ran her fingers through her hair when she got nervous. They never called her on petty junk, like her socks not being the right shade of pink to match her blouse. She couldn't wait to spend the entire weekend with them.

Sarah pushed aside the magazines that Leslie had showed her and opened her journal. She paged through the last three months. This book was almost full. She would need to replace it in a few days. She paused on an entry from three weeks ago, written in red pen. The bright color screamed from the pages. She didn't usually use red, but it reflected her mood the day she wrote it—the day after she and Jon had met up with Mia Thompson at a charity event for a battered women's foundation. She knew Mia would be at the event, but she didn't realize how Jon's ex would enrage her.

Mia kept joking that Sarah must be pregnant. But it was more of a jab than a lighthearted ribbing, and Sarah felt that she was implying that the only reason Jon would marry her was if he had knocked her up. It irritated Sarah to her core, but that wasn't the worst part. Mia acted like Sarah was invisible, never acknowledging her existence, only talking to Jon, and then, when Jon got hung up in a conversation with some big producer, Mia swung around to attack Sarah, with full knowledge that he wouldn't hear her.

"Jon and I have a connection, a bond, that can't be broken. We've known each other a long time, and I understand him in ways you never will. Hollywood seeps into all aspects of our lives and if you are not part of it, you will never understand Jon. Just keep that in mind when you plan your future with him. He will never be yours completely."

"Really? Because I'm the one he's marrying." Sarah tried to keep her voice calm and emotionless. *This woman was impossible.* Mia and Jon's relationship ended two years ago and yet she felt entitled to him?

"Oh, I doubt that you will last long enough to make that happen."

Sarah gasped. She couldn't believe that she was having this conversation with her and Jon was oblivious to it. She smiled, waving her left hand in front of Mia's face as she glared at her. She wasn't going to listen to her. She already had enough insecurities about Hollywood. Sarah quickly maneuvered herself back to Jonathan's side and stuck there like glue the rest of the evening, not even acknowledging Mia again. She felt bad that she had stooped to that level. It wasn't her. She tried to live in a better world. Sarah wasn't usually affected by what other's said, but Mia burrowed under her skin like no other person she had ever met.

Sarah hadn't told Jon about it that day. She didn't want him to say something to his ex and give her the satisfaction of knowing how much she was irritating her. But the next day when she was writing about it in her journal, Jonathan sat down next to her. She was tense from the memory of the previous day and when he gently tucked a strand of hair behind her ear, she exhaled loudly. She didn't realize she was holding her breath. He gazed at her with curious eyes as she closed her journal. She definitely didn't want him to read her entry.

"So…" he said with a questioning expression.

"What?"

"Are you going to tell me what happened between you and Mia yesterday?"

Sarah's head dropped against the back of her chair in exasperation. She couldn't believe that woman complained about her to Jon. "What did she say?"

A smile grew on his face. She knew her tone had given away exactly what she was trying to hide.

"Sarah, I haven't talked to Mia, but if you want me to, I will." He chuckled, and she scowled. That was the last thing she wanted.

"Why do you think something happened then?"

He turned on his iPad and set it on top of her journal. "The tabloids seem to think that you two were catfighting yesterday. There are about thirty articles that go into great detail about a big blowout you and Mia had. Did I miss something?" Sarah looked down at the tablet on the table in front of her, and of course the picture was of her waving her ring hand in front of Mia's face—Sarah's hand positioned to be practically giving her the finger, with Mia in mid eye roll.

"Sorry." Sarah didn't want to look like the crazy girlfriend.

"Don't be. This kind of press can't hurt. Remi sent me the link. She wants me to get you and Mia out together more often."

"Remi is a sadist. How could she wish that woman on anyone?"

Jon laughed. "She's not that bad."

"Your publicist's not, but Mia, she's horrible."

He leaned in closer and wove his fingers through Sarah's hair. He nudged her head to the side to open up access to the tender skin of her neck as he whispered, "I chose you. You're the one I love." Then he placed featherlight kisses down her neck.

$$\backsim$$

Sarah smiled, savoring the memory of the rest of that afternoon and how Jon made her completely forget about Mia that day. When she opened her eyes from her daydream, her friends were walking out the door into the courtyard toward her. She jumped to her feet and ran to them, pulling Jessica into her arms first.

"I can't believe you're here," she squealed as her friend's arms enveloped her.

"Oh my god, Sarah! Are you kidding me? Look at this place. We're never leaving. I can't believe you live here," said Megan. Sarah smiled and pulled Alli and Megan into her arms with Jessica in a giant group hug.

"I live in *that* house." She pointed to the guesthouse. "You guys came in through Jon's parent's house. Ours is not as impressive."

"Still, all you need is a Greek god to share your bed. Oh…that's right. You have that too," added Megan.

"He's a demigod, a half-blood." Sarah laughed. "But don't call him that to his face. That's just a character he plays and lately he's been a little sensitive about being objectified. How was your flight?"

"We rode in first class—freaking fantastic," said Megan.

"So you liked it?"

"Yes," said Jessica.

Sarah led them into the guesthouse, and they plopped their bags on the living room floor. "I can't believe you're here," she said again. "Let's go back outside. I can show you the house later. Tell me everything that's happening back in Minnesota."

They headed back outside and quickly fell deeply into conversation as Sarah mixed up a blender full of margaritas.

Jessica thumbed through one of the magazines that Leslie had left. "Don't kill me, but I've seen this one already. There's a picture of you and Jon on the cutest couples page. Did you see it?" She opened it to the article near the back. "See?" Jessica flipped it around so everyone could view it.

"Aw. Aren't you two cute?" cooed Megan mockingly.

"Shut up," said Sarah.

"How do you deal with all the pictures that are taken? You have no privacy," Alli asked pulling the magazine closer so she could get a better look.

"You remember how I used to fight with my mother when she would put a new picture of me on her website or up at the photography studio. I think it was the world's way of preparing me so I would be able to deal with my life with Jon. I don't really have a choice about it. What can I do but accept it?"

"How very mature of you," stated Megan, and everyone laughed.

"So why are we really here?" asked Jessica.

"What do you mean? I miss you guys. I just want to feel normal. I always feel like I'm just frosting."

Her friends looked at her confused. "Frosting?" questioned Alli.

"Yeah, like I'm just extra, to make it sweeter."

"What are you talking about, girl?" asked Megan, before taking a sip of her drink.

"See, that's what I love about you guys. You get me." Sarah chuckled sarcastically, and the girls all laughed. "I mean…it's like…Jon is this god, and I'm just arm candy—no brain, not important—just there to make him a little prettier."

"Is that how Jon makes you feel?" asked Jessica with a scowl.

"No, not at all! Jon treats me like a goddess. He always makes me feel special."

"If it's not Jon, then why do you care?" asked Megan.

"I don't know…It just bugs me sometimes, and I want to be just me. I'm just me when I'm with you guys, not Jon's fiancé."

"You flew us across the country so you can feel like *us*?" Alli summarized. "That's sad."

"I just need a dose of reality…And…" Sarah paused, hesitating. "And Margala Gaunechi won't trust anyone else's measurements, so you guys all have to be measured tomorrow or there will be no bridesmaids dresses," she spewed out quickly hoping to avoid her friends' backlash.

"You're kidding, right? I wanted to lose ten pounds before the wedding," said Jessica.

"You don't need to lose ten pounds. Besides, it's just the initial fitting, so she can get started on the dresses. They can always be taken in. It has to be done," stated Sarah.

"After the dress fittings, I vote we go shopping," declared Alli with a grin.

Her wavy red hair in a ponytail high on her head swung as she spoke.

"You always vote for shopping. I want to go to the beach…see some sites—maybe meet some celebrities," confessed Jessica.

"Yeah, like Jake Gorgeous-Body," added Megan.

"Talk about eye candy. I could lick…I mean…look at him all day." Jessica raised her eyebrows with a smile, and the girls all laughed.

"You know, Jake Gorboni is a friend of Jon's. They work out together sometimes. He seems nice. Jon could call him and see if he could meet us at the club tonight. Though, I think Jon said something about him filming in Tennessee."

"Really? You've met Jake Gorgeous-Body and you didn't tell us?" accused Megan.

"Yes," said Sarah, looking at them as if to say it's no big deal. "He's just a guy. He was here a month ago for a barbeque. I made my fajitas. It's my fallback meal." She smiled at them knowing that's what they would be eating tonight. "I think he sat in the chair Alli is sitting in."

Alli smiled and rubbed her back against the chair, as if a part of Jake would rub off on her.

"I guess everyone else seems like just a guy next to Jonathan," claimed Megan.

"You know, it's not healthy to idolize people. They'll never live up to your expectations when you meet them. You'll always be disappointed," lectured Sarah.

"Just because you have Jon doesn't mean the rest of us have to settle for Jeff's." Megan collapsed against the back of her chair as if she was giving up.

"Hey!" Jessica shot Megan a death glare. "I'm getting tired of this."

Megan always seemed to make fun of Jeff. Years ago, she'd made a move on him without success and since then she never missed an opportunity to make a jab.

"Sorry. It's just a habit," proclaimed Megan.

Sarah rolled her eyes and said, "Did you even hear a word I said?"

"Yeah, but I want someone hot, charming, and perfect like Jon, too," admitted Megan.

"Jon's not perfect, believe me," said Sarah, though he was closer than any man she had ever dated. She wondered what had changed in Megan since she had last seen her. Megan never wanted more than a superficial relationship. "So what's going on with you and Chase? I thought you were over him."

"I ran into him at the coffee shop, and we just started talking. I think he's grown up a lot since high school. He seems to be getting his act together."

"Really?" Sarah asked in a sarcastic tone.

Megan met her eyes with sincerity and stated, "He stopped using and has been clean for two and a half years. He and a friend started their own business and it's really taking off. They design video games."

"He definitely knows how to play video games," declared Jessica.

"No, I'm serious. You know the app Mad Moronic Monkeys? They're the ones that designed it."

"No way! He's such a liar," proclaimed Jessica, shaking her head.

"They did. His name is on the credits," assured Megan.

"I have that on my phone," admitted Sarah, holding her phone up and waving it back and forth. She pulled up the app and clicked on the credits. Sure enough, his name was there. Sarah passed her phone to Jessica.

"I told you…he's turning his life around." Megan smiled and smugly crossed her long legs in front of her.

"Has he figured out how to treat women, though?" asked Jessica.

"He paid for dinner the other night, and I'm not getting back together with him. I'm just happy for him," proclaimed Megan.

"You went out to dinner?" asked Sarah.

"Megan, what the hell." Jessica took a sip of her drink and continued, "You said you weren't going to go out with him."

Megan sighed. "I really think he's changed."

"Guys don't change," lectured Jessica. "If he's trying to convince you he's changed, he's just playing you. Again."

"He was totally toxic for you. Do you remember? 'Cause we all do. You are so much healthier without him," stated Sarah. Sarah remembered an incident when Chase had disappeared without a call or a text. After two weeks of Megan and all of her friends searching for him he showed up at the theater where Megan worked acting like he had just seen everyone that morning.

"You're not fooling me, Megan. I saw how you were looking at him the other day. You're already back with him. You need to end it before you get dragged in any deeper. Toxic!" emphasized Alli, rolling her eyes.

"We just talked," Megan said.

"Who else have you met and not told us about?" asked Jessica, turning to Sarah.

Sarah knew she was trying to make Megan more comfortable. Jessica always tried to smooth over conflict.

"I don't know. I've met a lot of people. They're just people," she tried to convince her friends. Jessica furrowed her brow, and Sarah added, "I'm sure we'll run into some celebrities tonight if Jon is with us…And don't act starstruck and ask anyone for their autograph. It ends up feeling creepy and ruins the entire night."

"Have you done that before?" asked Alli.

"No…but once I had to sit all night at a table with a girl who told me she sleeps with a body pillow that has Jon's entire body silk-screened on it, and if that wasn't bad enough, she said she had a picture of him in his underwear on her bathroom mirror. It was kind of a conversation stopper. I just didn't know what to say to her after that. It's best to act like it's no big deal to be sitting next to them—trust me, otherwise it gets weird."

"So we treat them like any other sausage we meet at the bar?" asked Megan.

"You are so gross. Treat them like you would treat one of your friends. It's more comfortable that way, and they are more likely to have a conversation with you. They might act all cocky and confident, but they're the same scared little boys we have at home," answered Sarah.

As Sarah wrapped up her lecture, the girls glanced up to see Leslie walking into the courtyard from the main house. She stood over six feet tall with her four-inch heels and was thin, like all women in California seemed to be. She was dressed impeccably in jeans, a bright yellow blouse, and a fitted jacket. Her long, straight, blond hair was loosely tied in a fancy knot on the back of her head, and it looked both casual and elegant at the same time. When she reached the group, Sarah introduced her. They all had heard so much about each other that she effortlessly joined the conversation.

"Leslie, Sarah says you're not really Jonathan's assistant; you're her personal stylist," said Alli.

Sarah smiled sheepishly at Leslie. Leslie was an amazing shopper.

"Do you think I could pick your brain tomorrow when we go shopping," added Alli, generating a laugh from Jessica and Megan.

"We didn't decide on shopping for sure," stated Megan.

"You know we're going to end up shopping," added Jessica. "Don't fight it. She will make our lives miserable if we don't."

Leslie looked to Alli. "I don't mind giving my opinion when we're shopping."

"Did you see Jon? He's not hiding from the estrogen out here, is he?" asked Sarah.

"No. I don't think he's hiding. He and Isaac were drinking Zander's scotch."

"Isaac is here?" Sarah moaned. "Why is *he* here?"

Leslie pressed her lips together, hesitating. "I'm not sure."

"Jon doesn't usually drink scotch. Were they celebrating or commiserating?"

"They were laughing when I walked in. Can I get one of those?" Leslie asked, pointing to Alli's margarita.

Sarah reached back and grabbed a glass off the bar. "Do you want salt?"

Leslie shook her head, so Sarah passed her an unsalted glass before settling back in her chair. Another thirty minutes passed with conversations about dating and Leslie's nonexistent love life, until Jon walked out to join them.

"Hi, ladies." Jon smiled a gorgeous smile as he approached. It was more public than the heart-stopping one he reserved just for her, but still breath-stealing. His hands grasped Sarah's shoulders as he bent down and whispered in her ear, "Sorry I got held up, beautiful." He kissed the shell of her ear and a shiver shot through her.

"What did Isaac want?" she asked.

"Nothing important." He grabbed a chair, pulled it next to Sarah's, and asked, "Are you all ready for a weekend in Hollywood?"

Chapter Three

Sarah

When Jon, Sam, and the girls stepped out of the black stretch SUV onto the sidewalk in front of the club, Sarah could feel the excitement of the photographers ignite. "Jonathan…Jonathan!" the paparazzi shouted, hoping to be the first to get a good shot. Jonathan never went clubbing, and Sarah knew his picture, at this club, would bring top dollar.

Quickly the energy spread to the fifty or so people waiting behind the rope barrier that zigzagged in front of the club. The women in the crowd squealed as they glimpsed Jon, and he smiled, holding up a hand in a motionless wave, leading the group to the bouncer's station by the front door. Seeing Jon the bouncer immediately opened the gold velvet rope barrier and secured a bright gold wristband to an arm of each one in the group. Then a shorter, bulky man escorted the group past the guard stationed at the bottom of the stairs and up to the VIP area on the second floor. The girls marveled at the crowd as they scaled the snaking steps, which allowed a clear view of the multilevel dance floor and the DJ's booth. Anticipation bubbled as the girls rose on the steps, chatting wildly as they climbed.

The bouncer led them to a sitting area in the middle of the VIP section. It overlooked the dance floor and was very visible, so all could spy Jonathan at the club. Usually Jon would asked to be moved to a more private table, but Sarah knew he would put up with it for her friends' sake. The group slid in around the large U-shaped black leather sofa that surrounded a glass coffee table. Embedded in the center of the glass tabletop in glowing florescent pink was the word *it*. The word was visible as they sat down and then faded to black. With no lights the table looked like clear glass. There was no sign of any lighting mechanism. About thirty seconds elapsed and a neon blue light reappeared shining the same two-letter word. As the word slowly bounced around the tabletop, Jon chuckled, noting the table they were assigned. Sarah had even heard about the "IT Table." Jon's publicist, Remi, had gossiped about it. The table was given to the biggest star in the club, and Sarah knew Remi would have been pissed if he hadn't been seated there.

Jon explained the significance of the table assignment to the group, and they all joked it was Sarah that made their status substantial enough to warrant such prestige. They were laughing about what Sarah had to do to get such a status when a stunning, leggy brunette who Sarah loathed slithered onto the couch next to Jon.

She bumped shoulders with him and said, "Hey, big guy." She beamed at him with a wink, like they shared an inside joke. "I never thought I would run into you tonight. I could never get you to come here, and I thought you'd given up clubbing altogether."

"Well, it's a special occasion. We have some friends in town, and we want them to get the full star treatment."

"Hello, Sarah," she said with a look that indicated there was a bad taste in her mouth.

"It's good to see you again," lied Sarah with a weak smile, doing her best to be friendly. "Mia, this is Jessica, Megan, and Alli. Everyone this is Mia

Thompson." Sarah looked around the table, making eye contact briefly with each one of her friends before her eyes met Jon's. He wrapped his hand around Sarah's and she knew he could read her mind.

He chose me, he chose me, Sarah repeated in her head. She wasn't going to let Mia intimidate her tonight. With the support of her friends at her side, that was not going to happen.

The girls exchanged niceties, before Jon's ex asked, "How are the wedding plans coming? Am I going to get an invite?"

Sarah couldn't believe it. Mia actually acknowledged they were getting married. Wow. Jon must have talked to her about how she acted at the benefit. But when, and what else did they talk about? And how often did they talk? Sarah started to feel that nasty jealousy building. *Why couldn't she get past Jon's history with Mia?*

Jon paused for a moment and then said, "I don't know. It's pretty exclusive. Of course you're invited." He chuckled as he gently squeezed Sarah's hand, silently apologizing for his words, or maybe he was telling Sarah to let it go. She wasn't sure.

A server, dressed in black, suddenly appeared eager to take their drink order. "Welcome, Mr. Williams, Ms. Thompson. My name is Reanna, and I will be your server tonight. Are you ready to order?" Of course the waitress didn't address Sarah. She wasn't a celebrity.

"Reanna, what's your recommendation for these stunning women tonight?" asked Jon.

"We have a great pomegranate martini. Our Flaming Joe is popular…and the Chameleon's Tear is to die for," she announced in a perky voice, doting on Jon.

"Get the Chameleon's Tear. It *is* to die for," interjected Mia.

"Let's start with six of those and a Heineken." Jon looked around the table to make sure the drink order was acceptable, and everyone nodded except Mia.

She spoke up, "Oh…make that five…I'd like a cranberry-Seven."

As the server left, Jon's eyes lit with amusement. "Wow…did you finally join AA?"

"Very funny. Actually," she looked around the table at the chatting group next to Jon and admitted almost proudly, "I'm pregnant."

Sarah watched as Jon's face paled and then he scanned the area as if he was worried that the whole world just heard her announcement. "Wow, how'd that happen?"

"Jon, I'm pretty sure you know how it works," said Mia. She rolled her eyes at him and added, "You're so paranoid. It's way too loud in here for anyone to hear."

"Who's the dad? Anyone I know?" Jon asked.

Sarah acted like she was listening to Leslie at the far end of the table, but she wasn't. She knew it had to be someone well known. Mia never dated anyone who wasn't highly visible.

"It's complicated. I haven't told him yet."

"He deserves to know." Jon squeezed Sarah's hand again. She didn't know what it meant. Was he trying to comfort her? Did he know she was listening, or was he just nervous?

"He's with someone else," Mia admitted.

"How far along are you?" Jon's thumb started to rub across Sarah's wrist.

"Far enough that it won't be a secret much longer." Mia looked down to the front of her dress and back up with a vulnerable expression.

Sarah didn't think Mia was ever vulnerable. She had never seen that side of her before.

"Well…you should tell him soon then." Jon put his arm around Mia's shoulder and pulled her in for a one-armed hug. His other hand curled tighter around Sarah's and when his eyes met Sarah's, he smiled at her with a look of reassurance. She regarded him questioningly. Jon returned an expression of "I'll tell you later," and Sarah squeezed his hand gently to acknowledge what he communicated.

The waitress came with the drinks. The Chameleon's Tear was clear liquid with swirls of red and milky white, garnished with a long, half-inch-wide coconut shaving curled over the lip of the large martini glasses. Jon pulled his arm off Mia to sip his beer. He let go of Sarah's hand and wrapped his arm around her shoulder. Lovingly pulling her in next to him, he playfully pecked her cheek, and she smiled at his uncharacteristic public show of affection.

"This is to die for, and it's not too sweet," admitted Jessica. "Do you know what's in it, Mia?"

"Vodka. Lots of vodka and some kind of designer rum. I'm not sure what the red swirl is. And be careful, because the alcohol sneaks up on you. I have to get going." She leaned into Jon's ear, and Sarah couldn't hear what she said. She smiled with a nauseated look and then recomposed herself. "Kiera is going to wonder where I am. Thanks, Jon," Mia announced, scooping up her drink and then vanishing into the crowd as quickly as she had appeared.

"At least she left," stated Sarah before taking a long draw from her glass. "We're not really inviting her to our wedding, are we?" It was her day after all. Why should she have to endure Mia?

"She's not that bad." That seemed to be his canned answer when it came to Mia. Jon smiled at Sarah.

She looked back. "You can't be serious. Have you met her?"

"Will it hurt to invite her?" Jon asked. "She probably won't even come. She just wants to be invited." He looked into Sarah's eyes with his most irresistible expression and added, "If you don't want to, we don't have to...but she is my friend. Besides, there will be so many people at our small wedding," he smiled at her, "that we probably won't even see her. And she'll never forgive me if I don't invite her after I said I would." He paused, as if waiting for her to respond, but when she didn't, he continued, "We should go to lunch with her sometime, just the three of us. You'll like her once you get to know her…I promise." He kissed the top of her head and pleaded, "Please don't get all quiet. We're celebrating tonight."

Sarah took another sip of her drink and looked at him. "Out to lunch, right…not at the house? I don't want to see how comfortable she is at our house."

He whispered in her ear, "I love you."

She smiled at him and said, "You better." She couldn't stomach the idea of Jon's ex coming to the wedding, but somehow knowing Mia was pregnant with another man's baby made it easier to swallow. She looked around the club in the direction Mia disappeared as she thought about how this news would change the dynamics of Mia's hold on Jon.

Just then, a man's voice boomed from behind the group. "Jon, I didn't expect to see you out clubbing. I thought you avoided the limelight. Sarah. Leslie."

The girls looked up over their shoulders to see a broad-shouldered, muscular man with brown, buzz-cut hair and big brown eyes. His nose was a bit too large and crooked, as if it had been broken, but his body was like a giant, 250-pound work of art.

"Jake, I thought you were filming in Tennessee?" questioned Jon.

"We wrapped on Tuesday." Jake made eye contact with both Alli and Jessica and smiled an alluring smile. Then he pointed an index finger at each of them and motioned for them to move apart, as if he was parting the Red Sea with his fingers. They made room for him, and he jumped over the back of the couch. Settling between them, he wrapped an arm around each of the girls. "So, Leslie, anyone special in your life?"

"Not since Nak. Why?" She looked at Jake suspiciously.

"Just wondering. You know you ruined him, right?"

"I did not. The breakup was mutual." She scowled at him and then explained to everyone, "Daniel Nackerson and I dated for about a year and a half, if you can call it dating. We were both so busy that we hardly ever saw each other. He was always away filming when I was in town, and he was off when Jon was filming, so we never had time for a relationship. I don't date actors anymore because of it."

"You wrecked him. He's no fun to take clubbing anymore. He misses you too much," stated Jake. Then he ran his fingers through Alli's hair and, focusing his attention to her, added, "You have beautiful hair. What's your name?"

"Alli Cole," she said with a grin.

"Hi, I'm Jake Gorboni. You're not an actress, are you?"

"No," she smiled at him, "I'm studying to be a doctor, or at least I will be in the fall."

"Impressive. You're one of Sarah's smart friends I've heard about? Jon, the wedding's not this weekend, is it?"

"I don't have any dumb friends." Sarah laughed under her breath, but only the girls in the group caught her joke.

"No. It's not this weekend," added Jon. "You'll get an invitation. We can't talk about it here, though—too many ears."

"Jake, these are my very best friends from Minnesota—Jessica, Megan, and you've met Alli," declared Sarah. She smiled at her friends. *Hadn't they just been talking about meeting Jake Gorgeous-Body this afternoon? And now here they were chatting with him.* Sarah was impressed none of her friends was drooling.

"Brains and beauty—that's new," Jake stated, looking Alli up and down flirtatiously.

"Jake, what did Nak tell you?" Leslie interrupted in an irritated voice.

"I don't know. Why don't you ask him? He's over at the bar with Liam and Jon's bodyguard waiting for a signal from you to come over. He wanted me to make sure it was OK with you. I told him I'd ask, if he grew a pair." Jake laughed.

"What the…Liam's here?" Jon looked over at the bar and signaled for the guys to come over. The two men headed toward the group. Liam was tall and thin but muscular, like a soccer player, with a golden-brown tan. His hair was short and sandy blond, and his face had a serious expression even when he smiled. Daniel was a little shorter with dark hair, about as dark as Sarah's hair. He had olive skin and a well-groomed five o'clock shadow. His black high-style glasses accented his deep, penetrating brown eyes.

"Thanks for asking, Jon!" exclaimed Leslie sarcastically.

"Like you'd say no." He chuckled as the guys approached. "Hey, Liam. Nak. What's up?"

"Will-Man, what are you doing here?" asked Liam as he fist-bumped Jon. Liam was one of Jon's good friends, prefame, who still called him Will. He and Nak planted their bodies in the two squat, oversized chairs facing the U-shaped couch.

"The girlfriends are here from Minnesota," said Jon. Then, spotting the waitress, he waved and added, "Another round."

"Sarah…your friends are here? I've heard a lot about you women. Nick's going to be bummed he missed you," Liam said, implying more than was spoken.

Nick was another of Jon's good friends from school and had a whoring reputation with women. He was the lead singer of a band called EXpireD, and Sarah and her friends had actually met him backstage, before the concert where Jon and Sarah met in person for the first time. Sarah noted Leslie and Nak were already in quiet conversation at the other end of the couch, so she introduced her friends to Liam and then added, "They've been told to stay clear of Nick."

"And you let Jake that close to them?" questioned Liam with a raised eyebrow.

"Jake, you're not going to defile any of Sarah's friends, are you?" Jon chuckled.

"Not unless they say please," answered Jake with a leer. Then in one smooth motion he pulled Alli onto his lap, leaned over, and kissed Megan's cheek. Next, he turned the other direction, caught a very surprised Jessica on the lips with a kiss, and then proceeded back to Alli's lips.

"Careful, you don't know where those lips have been. Jake is not a good choice for nice Midwestern girls like you," proclaimed Liam, and everyone laughed.

"Grrrrr," Jake growled at Liam and then helped Alli get seated back on the couch.

"You know, we actually have brains and can make decisions for ourselves. We're the whole package, not the mindless plastic chicks you're used to," declared Megan with a chuckle.

She didn't seem starstruck at all, though Sarah knew it was an act.

"And that's why we love you," proclaimed Jon. "Right, guys?" He squeezed Sarah closer and kissed the top of her head, as Reanna approached with the drinks. The server was able to figure out what the guys were drinking with just a glance, and she brought them refills as well.

"Honestly, ladies, I was just trying to give you a heads up," said Liam. "Jake's a player. You need to stay clear of what he's selling. I'm worried just seeing how close he's sitting."

"You're just jealous I got the last spot on the couch," proclaimed Jake.

"No you didn't, dickwad," challenged Nak, finally joining the conversation. Everyone looked over to see him squashed on the end of the couch, his arm draped over Leslie's shoulder. He looked relaxed, like nothing was out of the ordinary, but there was excitement in his eyes. Sarah hadn't noticed him move. It must have happened when the waitress distracted everyone. Leslie's face exuded apprehension, but her hand intertwined with his, so she couldn't be too worried.

"I swear I showered," claimed Liam.

Just then two girls, identical twins, with short, blond hair in pin curls, approached Liam from behind. One put her hands up to cover his eyes and said, "Guess who. No peeking."

"Kiss me. I'll figure it out." He leaned his head back, and she pressed her lips into his, still covering his eyes. They kissed for several seconds before he broke it off and said, "Nope. Still can't tell. I guess you'll have to sleep with me. I promise I won't peek."

The twin removed her hands from his eyes and smacked him on the shoulder. "It's me, silly."

"Oh. Hi, Tara. Hi, Tina," he said nonchalantly.

"Don't sound so excited to see us," said Tina.

"Who's the player now?" boomed Jake before smiling and downing his beer.

"Come dance with us?" pleaded Tara.

The twins talked to Liam for about ten minutes while the rest of the group chatted about Jake's filming in Tennessee, then the blondes headed off toward the dance floor without Liam. Once they left, Liam admitted, "I'm starting to get bored clubbing. It's always the same." He looked at Jon. Then, making eye contact with Megan, he said, "Hey, blond chick with the brain, I need some air. Will you walk with me?"

"Her name is Megan," said Jon.

"Sorry. Megan, would you come with me to get some air? I need someone to buffer," asked Liam.

"Sure," agreed Megan as she rose off the couch. She climbed past Leslie and Nak to join his side.

He grabbed her hand and said, "I may have to kiss you, just to throw off the wolves. Is that OK?" He smiled and pulled off his innocent expression.

"Yeah…whatever," answered Megan, looking over to Sarah with wide eyes.

Sarah was impressed Megan seemed so calm. She had talked to her friends about Liam, and they admitted they sometimes watched his cable TV show. Liam's character exuded sex and was a self-centered, egotistical ass. He wasn't that way in real life, though. He was a decent guy. On second thought, maybe it was just Jessica she had told about Liam and that's why Megan was so calm.

As Megan and Liam disappeared into the crowd, Jessica asked Sarah, "You're just going to let Megan walk off with him?"

Jon answered, "She's an adult. Besides, Liam's not going to do anything. He just needs a woman with him to keep the other women away. Why do you think Jake hunkered down on the middle of the couch? He just wanted to keep the vamps at bay." He looked over and Jake nodded an affirmation. "That's why celebrities have entourages."

"Beards—really?" Jessica chuckled.

"Yeah, why do you think I hung out with Mia all the time? It wasn't her perky, press-seeking personality. Say that three times without vomiting. It kept the women off me, or at least it helped minimize the problem."

They talked, interrupted by wave after wave of people stopping by to make their mark with Jonathan or Jake. Some Sarah knew her friends would recognize and others they wouldn't. She tried to introduce the ones she'd met, but most were people that she had never seen before.

"Do you guys come here all the time? You seem to know everyone," asked Jessica when there was a lull in the visitors.

"The last time I was here was with Jack and his girlfriend Camille, the night he died." Jon whispered the last part of the sentence.

Sarah squeezed his hand, knowing how hard that memory was for Jon to recall. He rarely talked about that night, but she'd heard the story. It was Jon's first real exposure to the frenzied antics of the photographers. He mentioned how happy the attention seemed to make Jack and Camille and how his reaction was just the opposite that night as if he could predict something was about to go wrong.

Just then, three girls approached the table. They were giggling as they surrounded the open end of the U-shaped couch. The brunette spoke up, "Hey, Jonathan. Hi, Jake. Do you remember me, Jake? I was in *The Summer Killing* with you. I played Candice."

"Oh, yeah…hi. Aneika, right?" said Jake without much conviction.

The girl acted elated that he remembered her, and it seemed to give her confidence to continue. She introduced her friends and tried desperately to make small talk. Sarah had dealt with people coming up to Jon so many times trying to initiate meaningful conversations, but today it irritated her. Pink's song "Stupid Girls" came to her mind as she watched the girls toss their hair flirtatiously, trying to catch Jon and Jake's attention. Sarah just wanted to visit with her and Jon's friends. Tired of listening to the mindless gibberish spewing from the girls' mouths, she asked, "Does anyone else need to use the ladies' room?" She looked over at her friends as she emptied her martini glass. She didn't want to leave her drink unattended when she left the table.

"Yeah, count me in," said Jessica, before she downed her drink as well.

"Me too," added Alli.

Jon declared, "Well…*I'm* going with you."

"To the ladies' room?" questioned Jessica.

"Yep," he answered without hesitation and stood offering a hand to Sarah. She stumbled just a little when she rose, and Jon caught her with his hand on her waist. Mia had been right about the Chameleon's Tear sneaking up. When Sarah stood, the room started to sway.

Jake glared at Jon, and Sarah knew it was for leaving him with the three mindless girls. Then he turned and said, "Alli, you don't have to go, do you?" looking deeply into her eyes.

Alli stood up and leaned over Jake, putting one hand on each of his broad shoulders. Inches from his face, she said, "Don't worry, Gorgeous-Body. I won't be long," and she kissed him on the cheek.

Wrapping one thick arm around her waist and his fingers of the other hand curling around the nape of her neck, he pulled her in for a kiss. Their lips locked. They kissed ardently for several seconds, as everyone stared, before Jake broke it off and said, "Hurry back, honey."

Jon walked the girls to the VIP bathrooms as Sam followed a few feet behind. The girls were loud and animated when they left him outside the ladies' room door, but once inside, Sarah looked at them and motioned to lock their lips shut. They stood in line quietly waiting for stalls to open. When they're needs were taken care of, they met up at the long mirror to freshen up their hair and makeup. The crowd of women they had waited behind had cleared out, so Sarah and her friends forgot about not talking.

"What kind of alternate universe do you live in, Sarah?" asked Jessica.

"It's just another day in my cracked life," she smiled, quoting Jon. "Alli, you called him Gorgeous-Body to his face. You're not supposed to do that—not to his face." Sarah shook her head as she spoke and stopped it with her hands as the room began to spin.

"Crap! I did, didn't I?" Alli said with a slight slur.

"And then you made out with him," giggled Jessica. "You made out with Jake Gorgeous-Body."

"Oh man, what if Neil finds out?" A puzzled expression brushed across Alli's face.

"I thought you weren't dating the teaching assistant," Jessica stated.

"I'm not...really. I don't know what it is. We haven't defined it," admitted Alli.

"Then there's no problem," announced Jessica. "What happens in LA stays in LA."

"Except for...for you," stated Sarah, turning to Jessica. "Because, you know...Jeff is my brother." She smiled apologetically. "I bet Jeff would hate seeing Jake's arm around you."

"Nah, but the kiss on the lips would piss him off. Nobody is going to tell him though." She looked to Sarah, and Sarah smiled. "Let's show him what a good time we're having," Jessica chuckled. Pulling a nine-inch action figure of Jon's character Perseus out of her purse, Jessica declared, "It's OK. No one will see us in here if we take the picture quickly. Besides, we have to get a picture of William with us at the club. It's too bad Megan isn't here."

The girls huddled together with the doll as Jessica snapped the picture in the mirror. The acid etching of the club's name on the mirror was proof of their whereabouts. As Jessica crammed the action figure back into her bag, Sarah admitted, "Jon would kill me if he knew I let you post a selfie of me on that web page." He'd been so sensitive about her social media posts lately. He said nothing had changed, but she was certain something had, at least since January.

"We should probably get going. I bet Jon's climbing the walls wondering what's taking us so long. Men don't understand the social aspect of the ladies' room. They just want to get in and out as fast as they can so they don't see another guy with his zipper down."

Out in the club, the lights flashed pink and purple strobes. The music thumped with the lights and vibrated through the floor and walls. Jon was waiting right outside the restroom entrance, leaning against the wall talking to Sam and several other people. When Sarah's eyes met Jon's, she could tell he was anxious. He excused himself to join her. She intertwined her fingers with his and smiled apologetically at him. "We're fine," she declared. He took a deep breath to relax and mock scowled at her. Sarah asked, "Have you seen Megan and Liam?"

"Don't worry. I'm sure they're around. We are not going looking for them, though." Jon nodded toward the stairway leading into the throngs of craziness. Sarah agreed. A small part of her wished she and the girls could head down to the dance floor with or without Jon, but she knew what Jon's reaction to the suggestion would be and she didn't want to see his eyes light with panic.

They made their way back to the table and broke out laughing when they eyed Jake, exasperation on his face. Jake sat on the couch surrounded by seven chatting, giggly women. He looked bored. He wasn't talking to any of them, and he had three full beers sitting in front of him on the table, while he clinched one almost-empty beer in his hand. Leslie and Nak were nowhere to be seen.

"Ladies, you have to clear out. My friends are back," announced Jake to the group.

"Even me?" questioned the little blonde next to him.

"Yeah, everyone has to go. My Alli gets vicious when she's jealous—the nails come out. You don't want to go there—trust me," Jake smiled at Alli, raising one eyebrow.

After the girls vacated the couch, Jake reached for Alli's hand and pulled her up next to him. Jessica slid onto the couch next to Alli, and Jake motioned for her to sit on his other side. Jessica just smiled, shaking her head as he wrapped his arm around her.

"Gorgeous-Body, huh?" he asked the group.

Alli smiled at him and nodded.

"What happened to Leslie?" inquired Jessica.

"Nak said something about driving out to Malibu. I wasn't going to argue. It's the first time I've seen him smile in months," answered Jake.

"Oh no! Leslie's supposed to come with us to get fitted for her dress tomorrow," declared Sarah.

"You know better than anyone you can't fight true love. It's futile," proclaimed Jon with a grin. "She'll make the fitting." He stared into Sarah's eyes.

"Stop looking at me like that," she blushed.

"I was just thinking about the rain," he admitted, and she blushed even more.

"It's not going to rain," scoffed Jake. "This is Southern California, and we're in the middle of a drought. You really should keep up on current events." Then he broke out into some song that was a billion years old about it never raining in Southern California, and everyone started laughing.

Sarah could have explained Jon's comment, but she wanted to keep that part of their lives private, so she didn't say anything. She knew Jon was thinking about the first time she told him she loved him. It was at her parents' lake cabin in the middle of a summer rainstorm. They had spent the whole evening making love. "Rain" was their personal code word for blocking everyone else out. It brought them back to the lake together and no one else mattered.

An hour passed as the group discussed what was happening back in Minnesota. Alli was excited about starting medical school at the University of Minnesota in the fall. She had just gotten her acceptance letter. Jessica admitted she and Jeff had gone shopping for engagement rings. While Jessica described her future ring and Jeff's relief at finding one she loved, six more people stopped by the table to say hi to Jonathan and Jake.

Finally Jon spoke up, "Anyone else ready to go?"

"We can't leave Megan," declared Sarah.

"Text her. If she doesn't respond, we'll hunt her and Liam down," said Jon lightheartedly.

"I'm sure they didn't get far. Nak was our ride," admitted Jake.

"You can catch a ride with us. We just have to call our driver," proposed Jon.

"Great," said Jake. Then he turned to Alli with a devilish smile and offered, "You can get off at my place if you want."

"No, she can't, Jake," declared Sarah in a firm voice as she sent the text to Megan. She looked up with a scowl. "We have dress fittings tomorrow, and all my friends are coming home with me tonight." She was starting to panic at the thought of her friends missing the fitting. She didn't know when they could do it if they missed their appointment tomorrow.

"Sorry, Bridezilla. I didn't know," claimed Jake with a wary look on his face.

"Yeah, don't mess with my wedding or you'll suffer my wrath." Sarah twisted her face into a fake sneer and everyone at the table laughed.

Her phone vibrated and she flipped it over to read the text. "Megan and Liam will be back in a couple of minutes," she said as she looked over at Jessica, who was grinning back at her.

Soon, Liam and Megan returned to the table, and the group got ready to meet the car Jon called. They made their way toward the exit, and Sarah could see the giant, black SUV parked along the curb. The sidewalk looked clear until they stepped out the door. Then the paparazzi quickly swarmed, filling the empty space between the group and the car. Sarah gripped Jon's hand tightly as he maneuvered their way through the crowd. The rest of the group followed. She knew the paparazzi were the worst part of Jon's job, and she hated that he had to deal with them.

The photographers engulfed the group, separating them into pairs and blocking their access to the vehicle. There were at least thirty of them. The cameras clicked like castanets with blinding flashes. When Sam's intimidation couldn't even get the photographers to move, Jon spoke up, "Guys, can you let us through, please?"

"When's the wedding, Jonathan? Come on, tell us," a paparazzo yelled. "We won't tell anyone, promise."

Sarah worried this was too reminiscent of the night Jack died. His thumb began rubbing across her wrist. He was nervous. She rested her head on his shoulder, hoping it would bring him comfort.

Someone in the crowd yelled above the others, "Jon, is this the first time you've been to Club Priela since your brother's death? I was here that night. Sorry about what happened, man. That guy was such an idiot." The crowd went silent for about two beats.

Jon said, "Yeah…thanks. Can you let us through?"

"I'm going to grab a couple of those bouncers over there. This is ridiculous.

We shouldn't even have to ask," Sam stated, heading for the bouncers' station.

Jon pulled Sarah in closer, wrapping his arm around her, as the paparazzi discussed the night of Jack's death with each other. Jon hadn't been to this club since that night. Sarah's friends wanted to see the infamous club. Sarah told them no, but Jon said it would be all right. He said it was completely remodeled. Everything was different except for the sidewalk full of paparazzi. It was public domain, and the club couldn't limit them. Sarah knew neither Jon nor Sam could get physical with the vultures or it would be all over the press, so they all stood and waited.

Then Jake spoke up, "All right, if we give you something you can sell, will you let us through?" He held up his hand to catch everyone's attention. Then he wrapped his arm around Alli and planted his lips on hers. He ran his hand down her leg and pulled her knee up to hug his thigh as he dipped her backward—still kissing. The camera flashes popped liked there was one continual spotlight. Jake righted Alli and broke off the kiss with a smile. "Guys?"

Sam and a couple of enormous bouncers from the bar pushed their way toward the group and the vehicle. The paparazzi cleared a small path for Jon's group as they called Jon, Jake, and Liam's names, trying to salvage a perfect shot as each loaded into the SUV. Sam closed the door, jumped into the front seat, and instructed the driver to move out slowly. Lenses clacked against the windows as camera flashes blinded the vehicle's occupants. Everyone settled and eventually found a seat, though Alli was practically on Jake's lap.

As the driver slowly pulled away from the curb, Sarah scowled at Alli, shaking her head gloomily. "Do you realize what you just did?"

"It was just a kiss, Sarah," answered Alli.

"No, it wasn't. Jake just ruined your life, and you let him," she exclaimed. Jon looked at her questioningly as if to say, "Do you really feel that way." When Sarah's eyes met his, she knew how her words must have sounded to Jon. "I don't mean ruined," she stammered. "I mean…complicated, definitely complicated it. In a couple of hours, those pictures are going to hit the Internet, and everyone you know will see you kissing Jake—everyone. I'm sure they are already uploading them."

Alli's jaw dropped. "Wow…I didn't really think about that," said Alli with a suddenly wary look.

"What—do you have a boyfriend back home or something?" questioned Jake. "Don't worry; he'll get over it." He chuckled.

"I don't have a boyfriend…exactly," admitted Alli.

"Then, what's the problem?" asked Jake defensively. "I'm not diseased or anything. Most women would pay to have me kiss them, especially in public. What the hell?"

"It's not that I didn't enjoy kissing you," admitted Alli with a giggle, "but we saw what happened to Sarah when Jon entered her life. It was kind of a train wreck. No offense, Jon. I know this is just a one-night thing with you, Jake… but I don't have room in my life for complications—not now, not ever. What if someday someone posts the picture in the hospital I'm working in or…what if my patients see it? I'll lose all my credibility as a doctor. All anyone will see is a bimbo kissing the movie star."

"Not if you're a plastic surgeon," added Liam with a grin.

"Yeah, you should be a plastic surgeon. The pictures could actually help your credibility," added Megan, "and you could help us out when we start getting wrinkles. Botox party, anyone?" Everyone laughed, even Alli.

"Mr. Williams, where do you want me to head from here? There are two vehicles following us, but I can probably lose them if needed," stated the driver.

"Hey, guys, you want to come back to the house?" questioned Jon. "It's early and we've already done enough damage in the press."

"Sure," replied Liam.

"Why not? Alli said I only have the one night with her after all," responded Jake.

Jon yelled up to the driver, "Let's head back to the house."

Sarah

Back at the house, the group settled in the courtyard chairs under the pergola by the pool. Jon got out glasses and whiskey. He lined up shots for everyone. Sarah knew Jon preferred to drink beer, but the whiskey was a ritual that he and his buddies held, and they always drank it when they were together out of the public eye. She watched him take his first sip and laughed inside when his eyes squinted closed as if it tasted like paint thinner. Then he knocked it back, slamming the glass to the table as if it had been a race.

The girls downed their shots and quickly decided they were in dire need of food.

"I'll make something," Jon volunteered. "You enjoy your friends while they're here."

"Chicken curry?" yelled Liam as Jon headed to the house.

"Not tonight. You'll be lucky if you get chips and salsa."

Jon disappeared into the house, and the group settled in around the table. When he returned fifteen minutes later, he had a platter filled with fresh bruschetta. The toasted bread circles topped with chopped tomatoes and fresh mozzarella smelled of garlic and basil.

"Do you have a hot Italian servant locked up somewhere?" asked Jake. "Because I'd like to borrow her next weekend when my dad is in town. These are great—as good as my madre's." He took another off the plate and popped it into his mouth.

"Nope, just me," answered Jon.

"Are you sure Sarah didn't make these?" Jake grabbed three more off the platter as Liam pulled the platter away and set it in front of Megan.

"You're done, mama's boy. Get your Italian grandmother to make them if you want more." Liam slid one into his mouth.

"Jon, what can't you do?" asked Jessica.

Jon smiled his killer smile and admitted, "I had to make these once for a role. An Italian chef taught me. I spent three days working with him."

Within minutes, the plate of food was empty, and Liam asked, "Now that we're fed, anyone up for swimming?" He tugged on Megan's arm, pulling her toward the pool. "You don't need a suit. We're all friends here."

Jon cleared his throat, and Liam immediately dropped his hold on her. Facing the group Liam added, "Anyone?"

"Hell yes. I'll go swimming," boomed Jake as he stood up and started stripping off his clothes.

Sarah knew the lack of modesty Jon's friends possessed and decided to head them off. "No commando. The paparazzi sometimes climb the wall. You never know who is watching, so leave something on. There was some guy sitting on the wall with a giant lens a month ago, probably photographing one of us in the shower. Luckily Sam and Craig were here."

"Anything you say, Sarah. It is your house…I mean Jon's parent's house,"

Liam teased with a smile as he unbuttoned his shirt and slid it off his shoulders.

"You had to go there, didn't you?" accused Jon. "Sarah and I are going to find our own place. We've been looking."

As Sarah and her friends headed toward the house to get into their suits Jon called, "Bikinis!"

"Or nothing. You can decide," chimed Jake as he splashed into the water wearing his boxers.

"My vote's nothing," yelled Liam as he dove into the pool.

When the women returned, Jon asked, "Sarah, where's your bikini?" He sat on a chair under the pergola sporting the pair of old swim trunks he kept in the pool house.

Sarah wore a short swim dress with separate bottoms. "I just…I like this suit better," she stammered. "It's a two-piece," she smiled and lifted her suit to show her navel. "See?" she said, cocking her head playfully.

He scowled at her. "Come here," he said sweetly. He pulled her down on his lap and wrapped his arms around her. He kissed the back of her neck as his fingers found her stomach under her suit. He trailed them up her abdomen until he reached her scars and then ran his fingertips over the tops. He knew her body so well like he had memorized it. She turned her head to look at him, wondering what he was doing. It wasn't odd for him to touch her scars and he often kissed them, but he didn't usually touch her in front of other people.

"Guys, can you even see the tiny scars that prevent my beautiful fiancé from wearing a bikini?" he asked as he lifted her suit to expose the top of her stomach.

Sarah quickly extricated herself from his lap, pulling her top down as she widened the distance between her and Jon. She glowered at him. "Cut it out," she uttered softly in a hurt voice. *Why would he bring attention to them?*

He got up and wrapped his arms around her again. "I'm sorry," he whispered in her ear. "You don't know how beautiful you are, do you? Why do you let some stupid little lines that no one but you sees bother you so much? It's been over four months since the accident. No one can see them."

She shook her head at him and scowled. "No, you're wrong," she said, staring him down.

"I'm not." He hugged her tighter and rubbed her back gently trying to comfort her. He kissed the top of Sarah's head and said, "Come on. Let's swim." They walked slowly toward the others. When they got close to the water's edge, they sat down next to each other, dangling their feet in the water. Alli sat down on Sarah's other side.

"Are you OK?" she asked.

"Yeah...You?

"Yeah. I guess we'll just have to see what happens," Alli said, turning up one corner of her mouth with a quick smile.

Jon got up and kissed the top of Sarah's head before walking toward the bar. Sarah knew that he was giving her time to talk to Alli.

"So, do you like him? I mean...is there potential for you two?" Sarah questioned.

Alli glanced at Jake, who was across the pool talking to Liam and Jessica. He stood in the water up to his waist. "You mean...if he wasn't a movie star?"

"No. I mean even if he is."

"No. It's purely physical. Look at him. He's Jake Gorgeous-Body...so not my type. He's a really good kisser. Wow, he's good." She rolled her eyes. "And way more experienced than I will ever be. I'm enjoying it while I can."

"The chemistry is there, though," claimed Sarah. For a brief second Sarah daydreamed about a perfect world where all her friends moved out to Hollywood and married Jon's friends. She knew it was ridiculous to even think it, but in her mind that would be a utopia.

"He's hot," admitted Alli, "but I could never give up my dreams for a man like you did."

Sarah looked at her questioningly. She didn't realize Alli thought that of her. "I guess my dreams changed when I met Jon."

"I never would have believed you would change so much for a guy. You were always so strong. You never needed anyone and now you seem so... vulnerable." She smiled at Sarah.

OK, filterless Alli. Sarah didn't care for Alli when she turned her mouth filter off.

"I don't know. I guess I used to be so afraid of being hurt that I never let anyone get close. Then I met Jon, and he showed me so much love I had to let him in. When you let your guard down, there is some level of vulnerability that comes with that."

"Do you miss your life back home?"

"Every day. Especially my friends, but I can't imagine my life without Jon."

"Oh…But you can imagine your life without us? Thanks," said Alli.

"It's different. Someday you'll meet your Jonathan and the choice will be made for you. When it is right, there's really no other decision."

"I don't know if that will ever happen, but if I do meet someone who changes my life, I hope it's not until I'm done with med school. My life doesn't have room for a relationship for a while."

"You know, I'm still looking for a job. I just don't want to start before the wedding. And I didn't give up my dreams. I'm still writing. I've really enjoyed writing the screenplay for my final school credits, and I got that short story published last year." Sarah was feeling a little defensive about Alli's attitude. "But I would give up writing in a heartbeat if I had to choose between it and Jon. He would win easily."

Just then Jon approached with his one dimple denting his cheek, and she knew he had caught her last sentence. He crouched next to Sarah and handed the girls each a beer. "I can get you something else, if you like."

51

"No, this is great. Thanks," said Sarah before kissing his cheek. She knew he really wasn't trying to make fun of her earlier. She wished she could wear her bikini again for Jon—for herself—but she didn't want to have her belly blown up on a colored spread of a tabloid with the headline: CELEBRITY'S WIVES WHO SHOULD RETHINK THEIR BIKINIS.

He bumped shoulders with her and the bottles in his arms clattered. "I better deliver the rest," he said as he stood.

"I hope I'm wrong about the pictures," professed Sarah.

"Me too. Maybe no one will recognize me?"

"Yeah, that worked so well for me, right? I didn't realize anyone knew who I was. It's amazing how many people recognize you when you're with someone famous," said Sarah.

"I could be lucky."

"So what is your teaching assistant like?"

"Neil? He's hardly mine…but he's the opposite of that," she said, looking over at Jake, who was staring back at her with a devilish look. When their eyes met, she stuck her tongue out at him.

"In what way?" asked Sarah.

"Neil is really smart and very methodical in everything he does, which I like because I know what to expect, but he's not at all spontaneous. I mean…we make plans to meet—never for dinner though—and he's never mentioned the word *date*. I think that would be too much of a commitment."

"Have you kissed him?"

"No."

"But there's chemistry?"

"There's something. Neil is really sweet and funny, but he doesn't take control like Jake. I'll probably have to be the one to make the first move." She chuckled. "I don't know what he'll think when he sees me kissing Jake."

"Maybe he'll surprise you and ask you out on a proper date." Sarah smiled.

"Or maybe I'll never hear from him again."

"You don't seem too attached to him. Will it matter?"

"Like I said—I don't really have time for a relationship now anyway, so it wouldn't change much," declared Alli. "I worry more about what my parents are going to say."

"Your parents are going to flip out," Sarah proclaimed.

"I know. You don't know how lucky you are to have sane parents."

Suddenly Jake appeared in the water in front of them. "Hey, we're wasting time. Remember we only have the one night together," he said with a look Sarah had never seen on his face before. "Come on." He motioned for Alli to climb onto his shoulders as he crouched in front of her. She wrapped her legs over his shoulders, and he lifted her off the pool's edge. Sarah watched as she struggled to gain her balance while Jake's thick arms wrapped around her legs to secure her, before he carried her away.

Jon's eyes met Sarah's with a questioning look. Then he reached toward her, wrapped his arms around her neck, and with his eyebrows raised, asked, "Hey, beautiful. You want to make out?"

She chuckled and gave him a kiss. He looked so sweet and innocent, like making out in front of everyone was the most normal thing to do.

After swimming, the group gathered under the pergola. Sarah grabbed some blankets from the house and passed them out. The air temperature was cooling, but everyone was enjoying the poolside atmosphere. Jon turned on some music and made sure there was plenty to drink. They all chatted for a couple more hours. It was somewhere around four o'clock in the morning when Sarah started to struggle to stay awake.

Chapter Five

Sarah

Sarah awoke to a loud thud followed by a clanging noise. The sound pinged in her head like the old radiator in her freshman dorm pushing water through corroded pipes. She glanced to Jon to see if the sound was coming from her brain or an outside source. One of his eyes peered at her with a questioning look.

"Sarah, we have that fitting," blared a woman's voice from the other side of the door.

Slowly she stretched her neck to locate her phone on the bedside table. It was almost nine o'clock. She stumbled out of bed and pulled open the door. Looking down, she spotted the offending noisemaking bangles on Leslie's wrist. "I'm glad you're here," she mumbled. *Funny, she didn't remember eating paste last night. Why was her tongue sticking to her teeth?*

"Malibu isn't that far. I'd never miss the fitting," proclaimed Leslie, exuding sunshine. "Good morning, Jon. Looks like I missed a party last night. There are beer bottles all over the courtyard."

"It wasn't a party," Jon grumbled as he sat up. "You should have been here, though. So the Nak is back, huh?"

"Yeah, I guess."

The bed gravity pulled on Sarah, and she face-planted back onto her pillow. Leslie was a bit too cheery for this early.

"Sarah, you've got to get ready. The car is coming at ten thirty."

"You hit the shower, and I'll make some omelets for everyone," said Jon, slipping on a pair of jeans and a T-shirt.

"Coffee?" pleaded Sarah, raising her head the best she could.

"Of course. A giant mug just for you." He offered his hand to help her off the bed, his grip strong and comforting.

When Sarah got out of the shower, her friends were gathered in her room, talking about the previous night in a hushed tone.

Jessica had showered and was completely ready to go, but the other two looked like they just rolled out of bed. Megan was wearing sleep shorts and a tank top, but definitely hadn't showered yet. Her hair was mussed and wild, sticking up on one side. Alli was still in her swimsuit but sported Jake's oversized button-down shirt as a cover-up.

Sarah pulled out the black-and-white sundress with turquoise accents and laid it on the bed. It was one of her favorites, and she couldn't wait for her friends to see it.

"Is this a Michael Tarnell purse? I was going to ask you last night," questioned Alli, picking up Sarah's purse from the bed next to her dress. She could always spot a designer handbag.

Sarah pulled her robe from the back of the door and slipped it over her shoulders just in case more people joined them in the bedroom. "I don't know. Check the label. Jon's mother gave it to me as a welcome-to-Hollywood present when I moved," answered Sarah.

"I don't need to check the label. I can spot one of these from a mile away," Alli said as she checked the label. "It is. I can't believe you have a Michael Tarnell purse. I've always wanted one, but they're super expensive."

"It's my favorite. It goes with everything," Sarah claimed. She finally had an idea what to get her bridesmaids for their wedding thank-you gifts. She bent over, flipping her head upside down, and began brushing out her hair before drying it. *Boom, boom*, drummed the pounding in her upside-down head. Sarah decided to pull her hair back in a ponytail instead.

She smiled when she heard the knock on the door. It was good she had put on the robe. Jon opened it slowly, presenting them with a large wooden tray. The aroma of fresh-brewed coffee swirled around the room. Perched on the tray were four hefty mugs of coffee, a carton of flavored creamer and a bottle of ibuprofen. "To help with the hangovers," he said as his eyes raked over her open robe.

"Jon, you're too perky. Why aren't you hungover?" asked Megan.

"I'm a lot bigger than any of you, and I don't drink much when I go out. The press would be all over it if I did, and besides someone had to watch out for the crazies."

That's why Sam was with them. Jon was so paranoid. Sarah opened the ibuprofen, took two out, and passed the bottle to Megan. Then she grabbed her favorite pink mug off the tray. Jon had already mixed in the creamer. He knew her so well. Though Sarah usually drank her coffee black, she always added cream when she had any sign of a hangover. It helped settle her stomach somehow. She sipped it to swallow the pills. It was hot and scorched the back of her throat just a little as it went down.

"Better?" asked Jon as he tucked a loose strand of her hair behind her ear.

"Much…Thanks."

"Can I talk to you in the hall for a second?" He touched her elbow and motioned toward the door.

She set her mug back on the tray, and as she followed him out, she wondered what had happened that he couldn't talk about in front of her friends. But once in the hall, his lips crushed hers with an unexpected fury. He pressed her to the wall with one knee wedged between hers as his hands slid under her robe and smoothed across her lace bra. The kiss was slow and deep and hungry, and it made Sarah want to drag him down the hall to the music room. When the kiss finally broke, Jon pulled back and said, "You can't walk around like that, looking so sexy and expect me not to react."

"Tease," she proclaimed as she pulled the front of her robe closed and fastened the belt.

Jon peeked his head back in the bedroom door. "The omelets are ready for anyone who's hungry." Then he kissed her one more time before heading toward the stairs.

"What was that about?" asked Jessica, when Sarah walked into the room.

"I don't know," she said, but she was sure they could tell by the blush on her cheeks what took place in the hallway.

Sarah and Jessica headed down to get the omelets while they were hot, leaving Megan and Alli to finish getting ready. Jake and Liam were sitting quietly eating at the table under the pergola when Sarah and Jessica arrived. Both guys looked tired. Leslie was sitting at the bar with her iPad out, working unobtrusively away from the group, or maybe she was messaging Nak. The beer bottles had been picked up, and there were no signs of last night's party except a pile of folded blankets on one of the deck chairs. Not much was said when Jessica and Sarah sat down at the table. They quietly greeted everyone and filled their plates.

Soon Megan and Alli joined the meal and Sarah was surprised by the silence of the group. No one seemed to want to talk about the previous night. It was almost as if they were purposely holding their tongues. Sarah smiled at Jessica. She could tell she was thinking the same thing. Then Sarah looked up to see another familiar face coming across the courtyard and her stomach dropped.

"Jon, what are you doing today?" she asked.

He got a devious smile on his face and said, "I thought the guys and I would hang out here. Maybe play video games or work out to get rid of last night's beer."

"I didn't realize video games and weights were so dangerous." She said it to make her point, but she knew Jon was expecting Sam to go with her and her friends. She didn't want his protection today. She just wanted to have some private time with the girls. Jon seemed to be more and more persistent about her bringing security everywhere she went and she hated it.

"Sam," Jon greeted. "Actually Sam called me this morning wondering if he could come into work. I think he just needed to get away from the kids. How could I deny a face like that?" Jon joked while Sam mockingly glowered at him with his most intimidating face. "I told him he could go to the fitting and shopping with you."

"You were just being helpful, so he could get away from the kids, huh?"

"Of course, beautiful," he placated. He smiled at her and addressed the group, "Sarah thinks I'm overly protective of her. You would think that with all that has happened to her in the last year, she would welcome some security, but obviously she doesn't understand how important she is to me."

She sighed, shaking her head. He was too smooth. She couldn't get mad at him. He always knew what to say to make her do what he wanted. She loved that he knew her so well, but she also hated it. Though she was starting to get used to having security in tow, it still made her uncomfortable talking girl talk in front of Sam. "I guess we better go," she said, getting up. Then she rested her forehead against Jon's and looked into his eyes. "You worry too much," she whispered and kissed him on the lips.

"Stay safe," he said, and she could see the love in his gorgeous blue eyes.

Everyone said their good-byes and within a couple of minutes, the girls and

Sam were loading into the black SUV and on their way to the fitting. "Leslie, what did you end up doing last night?" Sarah asked as they settled in the car.

"We just drove out to Malibu and walked on the beach—nothing as exciting as your gathering by the sounds of it. We talked and…I guess…we're going to try to make it work. We are really good together, and I miss him. It will be a scheduling nightmare, but that's what I do best, right? Nak is going to try to schedule his projects when I'm busy so that we can have our free time together."

"What I know of Nak, you two belong together," Sarah said with a smile.

"Daniel said he could come to Cannes with us in May and has most of the summer off. Jon only has the wedding this summer, so hopefully Nak and I will get to spend some time together."

"Sarah, you're going to France? I'm so jealous," declared Megan.

Sarah hadn't mentioned it to her friends. She was starting to feel like she was boasting every time she mentioned her trips or famous people she met. It wasn't that she was keeping it from them, but she didn't want to make a big deal about it.

"Yeah…one of Jon's films is showing at the festival. He filmed it years ago, but they never found a distributor for it. It's an indie film without big studio backing. I'm pretty sure Jon's name is what is moving it forward now," said Sarah. "I'm excited to go. It will be the first time I've ever left the country."

The car arrived at a stark white building with a large picture window in the front. In the windows stood several all-white, headless manikins dressed in elaborate, full-length black gowns. Above the entrance hung a large sign branded with a single scripted letter *m* in bright pink and outlined in gold.

Inside Sarah introduced her friends to the squat Italian woman with black hair twisted on the back of her head. The woman sized up the girls as she walked a circle around them. She pointed to Megan and said in a thick Italian accent, "You first." Then she led the girls into a smaller private room and asked them to strip down to their undergarments. She said that she didn't want to get the measurements wrong because of a belt or a bulky pair of shorts. As they stripped down, Sarah gave them an apologetic look.

After the measurements were gathered and the girls were dressed, Margala's assistant addressed Sarah, "We'll need an actual fitting with everyone once the dresses are complete. It will have to be at least a couple of weeks before the wedding. Do you want to schedule it now since everyone is here?"

Sarah nodded, looking at her friends, and they all pulled out their cell phones to check their calendars. Leslie took out her tablet and clicked on the calendar app. Sarah glanced over Leslie's shoulder, knowing Leslie's calendar was more accurate than hers and that Leslie probably knew Sarah's schedule better than she did.

She stared at the screen for a second, not understanding one of its entries: SARAH/DR. KRAVITZ 1:00 THURSDAY. Sarah withdrew from Leslie's side and clicked on the calendar on her phone as she contemplated the appointment. She had met with a couple of doctors since she moved to California. She had follow-up visits from her accident just to make sure she was healing correctly, and then after she was abducted in January, Jon insisted she get checked out completely to assure none of her old wounds had opened up internally. Sarah racked her brain. She didn't recognize this doctor's name. She was sure of that. Then she remembered a conversation she and Jon had a couple of weeks ago. They discussed how Sarah needed to find an OB/GYN in California, before they started their family. But it was just in passing, they hadn't really discussed it.

"Oh god..." she mumbled to herself. Did Jon want her to get pregnant right away—on the honeymoon? She knew he wanted kids, but they hadn't talked about when they would start. Sarah wasn't sure if she was ready to be a mother yet. *I'm only twenty-one*, she thought. She glanced up to see everyone looking at her.

"What's wrong, Sarah?" asked Jessica.

"Nothing," she assured, shaking her head. "I'll tell you in the car." She would have to wait to ask Leslie about it. She didn't want to bring it up in front of the dressmakers. The group found a weekend in June, after graduation, which would work for all, and Leslie said she would order the plane tickets for the trip. Sarah thanked her for her help and they said their good-byes to the dress designer. Sam looked bored seated in the chair outside the fitting room, and Sarah jokingly questioned him, "Did you have to shoot anyone while we were in there?"

Sam stretched his arms out in front of him with interlocked fingers. As he stood up, his knuckles cracked a rhythmic song and he smiled at Sarah. "I like my workdays boring. Don't worry about my entertainment, Sarah. You know me. I'm amused just knowing how much my presence irritates you."

Sarah didn't hate Sam. She liked him. He was never afraid to put the problem out into the open and make a joke about it. "Honestly, it's not you. You're family. I just hate being a prisoner, and I like to be alone sometimes," she assured.

"Well…you're marrying the wrong man then. Jon will never let you be alone, not anymore," he said.

Even after a journalist obsessed with Jon abducted Sarah in January, he hadn't been so zealous about having constant security. *What had changed?*

"I know, but I love him, so what can I do?" She smiled at Sam as he held the door open for the group to file out onto the sidewalk.

Once inside the car, Sarah had to ask Leslie about Thursday's appointment. She wanted to be prepared when she talked to Jon, and she knew her friends would support her. She needed their advice if the doctor was the kind of doctor she suspected. "Leslie, I didn't know I had a doctor's appointment on Thursday. Am I terminal?" she asked, trying to make a joke, but it came out sounding nervous.

"Oh gosh…I thought Jon discussed it with you. I made the appointment over a month ago." Leslie looked at her warily, and Sarah shook her head. "Dr. Kravitz is really hard to get into, but he was willing to fit you in because of Jon. He's the best in his field. Jon wanted to make sure you had a chance to meet with the doctor before your honeymoon."

There was the confirmation. Clearly Jon had been planning this long before their talk. "A month? You've known for a month and you didn't say anything... really? I thought you were my friend."

"I'm sorry. I thought you and Jon had talked about it."

"We did. I just didn't realize how serious he was."

"Jon has been talking to me about making this appointment since you moved here. I think he is pretty serious about it."

"Wow, that long? I guess I need to talk to him." She smiled uncomfortably at Leslie. She knew Jon talked to Leslie about almost everything, but she hoped their sex life was off limits. "You know too much," she added.

"I think I know Jon better than he knows himself."

"If that's true, Leslie, then answer this: How badly does Jon want kids?"

"Well," she paused as if considering whether she should extend her opinion or not, "I think, if Jon had his way, you two would be married by now and you'd already be pregnant."

"Oh..." Sarah gulped.

"Sarah, you look a little green," said Alli, and all of Sarah's friends laughed.

"No...really...I'm all right. I've always known Jon wanted kids. I want kids."

"You sound like you're trying to convince yourself," accused Jessica, and all of Sarah's friends laughed again.

"I'm not. I love Jon. Of course we want kids," declared Sarah.

"Jon will be ecstatic to hear that. I think he's been afraid you two weren't on the same page," acknowledged Leslie.

Sarah gulped again and looked warily at her friends.

"Well, maybe not the exact same page," Leslie chuckled.

"Don't say anything. I'm ready, or I will be."

"Damn…where is your backbone, Sarah?" questioned Megan.

"I told you she's changed," declared Alli to the group. "Sarah does everything Jon wants. She's lost herself." She turned to Sarah and asked, "What did he do with our friend? Tell us where she is?"

"Shut up. I haven't changed. We want kids—both of us. What are we waiting for, anyway?" Sarah tried to convince her friends. "Jon's babies will be adorable. A thousand women would kill to have Jon's baby. Literally kill."

"Yeah, like Mia Thompson," commented Megan. The look on Sarah's face must have revealed her thoughts because Megan apologized. "Sorry. Really I am. But I saw how she was eyeing Jon. She *so* wants him still."

"So I'm not imagining it. Jon doesn't see it, but she definitely wants him, right?" asked Sarah. Jon always denied that Mia still had feelings for him, but Sarah could tell. Mia wanted him back.

"She might have some strange media-oriented attachment to Jon, but Jon doesn't feel anything for her," added Leslie, and Sarah wondered if every thought in her head was visible on her face.

"Then why does he let her walk all over him? It's like she's got some kind of hold on him. He invited her to our wedding…Really, who does that?" she declared.

"Sarah, you don't burn bridges. Hollywood is very incestuous. Jon may have to work with her again," proclaimed Leslie.

"I would kill him if he ever accepted a role opposite Mia again. It's bad enough they have a history together and a movie to immortalize it. There is no way I will ever let him do another movie with her."

"That's the Sarah I know and love," declared Megan.

"Sarah, you don't have to worry about Mia and Jon. You should have seen Jon when he got back from that first week in Minnesota with you. He was crazy in love—seriously crazy. He couldn't stop talking about you. I remember Remi asked me to "misplace" his wallet and passport, just to keep him from flying to see you that next weekend. Don't be jealous. He was never like that with Mia," said Leslie. She turned to Sarah's friends and added, "She was afraid he would run off and elope."

"Why would she think that?" questioned Jessica.

"Because Jon kept telling everyone he was going to elope with Sarah," declared Leslie. "Remember, Sam?"

"Yeah," he admitted without adding to the discussion. He was always more cautious about sharing when Jon wasn't around.

"He asked Sam to drive him cross-country because he couldn't find his license," Leslie admitted. "Sam finally talked him out of it. It took some convincing though. He found his IDs a few days before we left for Greece, and then he immediately flew up to see you. We were all afraid he would return married. I expected you to be on the plane to Greece with us at the very least," confessed Leslie.

Sarah remembered back to Jon's visit. She couldn't forget the look of disappointment on Jon's face when he found out she didn't have a passport. Jon never mentioned eloping that weekend, and it surprised Sarah to hear this revelation. "I wish we had eloped. It would have been a lot easier than planning this wedding," stated Sarah, laying her head on Jessica's shoulder. Leslie's words felt reassuring, and Sarah knew she just needed to forget about the psycho woman wanting her fiancé. *Jon chose me*, she reminded herself.

The car pulled up next to the famous Chinese theatre on Hollywood Boulevard so they could play tourists for lunch. The handprints from the *Twilight* and *Harry Potter* actors caught everyone's attention right away, and they all crowded around to get pictures. They spent a half hour walking around putting their hands and feet in the cement prints of the movie stars. Sarah laughed at how giddy her friends were looking at the signatures and prints of the celebrities. She had never really connected before that this was the same way people felt about Jon. Even Leslie seemed to enjoy the childishness of their visit and admitted she had never played the tourist in Hollywood before today.

Sarah hadn't forgotten about the constant observation she was under. She felt Sam's eyes flick to her every few minutes. She knew he was trying to give her space without actually giving her space, and she realized he was close enough to hear her conversation, but he made it look like he wasn't listening. She watched Sam scan the foreyard for "threats." She followed his gaze. Near the theatre entrance, seven sightseers snapped pictures of each other in front of the displays. It was a big group, but they looked harmless. Against the far wall of the court, a young couple clung to each other as they looked around not completely interested in the exhibits. They were kissing now. Sam continued his search, but Sarah could tell he hadn't ruled out the kissing twosome, because his eyes grazed them as he continued his search. A gray-haired couple chased two small boys back and forth through the center of the foreyard—not a threat. That's when Sarah spotted them. Sam had seen them too, the group of five teenage girls with cell phones in their hands walking right for them. Sarah knew they were trouble because Sam shortened the gap between himself and Sarah's group. He turned in his threatening way to face the teenage girls as they approached.

"You're that bodyguard, aren't you? Hey, Brea, it's Jonathan Williams's bodyguard."

"Where is he? Is Jonathan here?" a blond girl squealed as the group encompassed Sam.

"I think you've mistaken me for someone else," claimed Sam in his deep voice as his eyes skimmed over the tops of their heads. Sarah's friends stopped and turned to see what was causing the commotion, but Sarah tried to get them to turn back around.

"We're not mistaken. We know who you are. You're always with him, on the red carpet, at the airport, even on set," declared the blonde named Brea as she fiddled with her phone and held it up in front of her. She must have flashed a picture of Sam on her phone. "So…is he here?" The girls all smiled smugly and crossed their arms.

"Nope…It's my day off."

Sarah wasn't going to interfere. Sam obviously had a plan.

As the girls turned and panned the area for Jonathan, one of the teens declared, "He's got to be here somewhere." Then they strolled confidently toward Sarah with Sam following.

"Sarah…Sarah…Where's Jonathan? Is he here?" they called to her as if they were old friends.

"Oh, sorry, girls…he's not with us today."

"Aw…" they sulked.

"He'll be so disappointed that he missed you," claimed Sarah. "You're real fans—I can tell—and he loves his fans." She wasn't lying. Jon always said his fans were what kept him employed. He always made time for them.

"You're so nice. I can see why Jonathan loves you," declared a girl with a head full of dark braids. "The way he looks at you. Everyone can see how much he loves you. When he kissed you on the red carpet at the Academy Awards, I just about died."

Sarah smiled.

"What's it like to kiss him?" asked one of the blond girls.

"It's great. He's a really good kisser," Sarah chuckled, and all of her friends started laughing.

"Hmmm…" a couple of the girls crooned at the same time.

"You're so lucky," gushed the brunette. "Can we see your ring?" she asked.

Sarah held out her hand as they swarmed to admire the ring. "It's so beautiful," proclaimed one of the blondes.

"We can't wait until the wedding. It's so exciting. I'm glad it's you and not Mia Thompson. You're much nicer," said the other blonde.

"Yeah, she totally blew us off when we ran into her last year. She's such a beeoch. I bet your dress will be gorgeous," stated Brea. Then she turned, staring wide-eyed at Alli, and questioned, "Aren't you the girl that was kissing Jake Gorboni last night in front of Club Priela?" She manipulated her phone again and flashed them a picture of the kiss.

Sarah and her friends stared at it a moment and then they all turned toward Alli, who admitted, "I guess that's why my mom called…twenty-seven times in the last two hours. I had my phone on vibrate. Its battery finally died…I wasn't going to answer it."

Sarah turned to the teenage girls and stated, "It was so nice to meet you, but my friends and I have to go." She turned to Brea and added, "If you write down your address and all your names, I'll have Jon autograph five pictures, one for each of you, and I'll mail them to you myself." She smiled at them. She felt very comfortable with these girls, and for the first time, she realized why Jon loved his fans so much. It was as if her whole mindset changed. Sure they were pushy and nosy, but they seemed to truly care about Jon, totally vested in his happiness. They had opened their hearts and made him, made her, a part of their lives. No wonder Jon made his fans a priority. It wasn't a show. Sarah finally understood.

The girl quickly jotted down the information on a small scrap of paper and handed it to Sarah. Sarah carefully tucked the paper into a zippered pocket in her purse. She didn't want to lose it and disappoint the fans.

"Can we get a picture with you?" someone asked, and Sarah nodded.

After the photo, the girls said their good-byes and seemed truly sad their conversation had to end.

As Sarah and her friends made their way out onto Hollywood Boulevard, Jessica spoke up, "Wow, Sarah. When did you become such a politician? You were so good with them."

"They were sweet, weren't they?" she stated, feeling a sense of peace in understanding.

"Yeah, in a bratty, nosy, little sister sort of way," admitted Megan.

They walked while glancing at the stars outlined in bronze that trailed the boulevard, until Sarah dragged her friends up the tall white steps and through the doors that led into another courtyard. She declared, "You have to see the white elephants. Jon took me here before we announced the engagement and we made it through without being recognized. It was so cool. It's a must-see—very touristy." As they gaped at the overwhelmingly white courtyard, they debated how to deal with Alli's parents.

"I can call them if you want," stated Sarah, feeling a little responsible for her problem.

"No…they are always overreacting. I want them to sweat a bit," answered Alli.

"It's up to you, but I'm sure your mom is just worried about you. She probably thinks you're dead in a back alley somewhere, and you know she's going to call Kate. My mom will be calling me any minute. They have their networks to get information."

"Tell Kate I went home with Jake and you haven't seen me since last night."

"I'm not telling my mom that. She'd never believe that I let you do that,"

"You may as well have," she admitted, looking up with a not-so-innocent expression.

"I knew it," proclaimed Jessica, pointing her index finger at Alli.

"Tell me you wouldn't, if Jeff wasn't in the picture…Tell me you wouldn't. He's Jake Gorgeous-Body. And his body *is* gorgeous. All of it." A huge smile took over Alli's face. "Like I'm going to let that opportunity walk away without grabbing it."

Jessica cleared her throat and turned to Megan. "And you?" she questioned. Megan shook her head, and Jessica asked, "Are you sure?"

Megan chuckled, "Yeah, I think I would remember. We just talked."

"Sure you did," proclaimed Alli sarcastically.

"OK...We didn't just talk, but we didn't..." she trailed off. Everyone looked at her doubtfully. "We didn't."

Then Sarah's phone vibrated. She looked at it and laughed. "It's Kate." She slid her finger across the touch screen and said, "Hi, Mom." She explained to Kate that Alli's phone battery had died and they hadn't checked the Internet this morning, because they had to get to the dress fitting. She asked her to call Alli's mom for them and let her know that Alli was all right. Alli couldn't call her right now, because they were in a very public place with lots of ears to overhear any phone conversations. It wouldn't be a good idea for Alli to try to explain last night right now, but she would call her mom as soon as they got back to the house. Sarah thanked her mom for her help and got off the line. "I think Kate has it under control for now," she said to her friends, as she tucked the phone back into her purse.

"I'm not calling them," stated Alli.

Sarah rolled her eyes at Alli. She thought that postponing the conversation with Alli's parents was a mistake, but they weren't her parents, so how could she judge? She put her arm around Alli's shoulder and said, "It will all work out. Let's go shopping. Do you want affordable or ridiculously expensive? It's your choice."

"Ridiculously expensive, of course. We have affordable at home," she answered.

"Unlike the rest of us, she has her mommy's credit cards," razzed Megan.

Leslie spoke up, "I know of a couple boutiques that we should visit before we head to Beverly Hills. It will be worth our time, I promise, and you'll be able to afford the clothes." They all agreed, and Sam called the car to come pick them up.

Chapter Six

Sarah

By the time they got back to the house, the girls were exhausted, and they all quickly collapsed with their hauls on the living room furniture. Sarah was elated that she was spending time with her friends. It was as if they had gone back in time. It had been so long. So much had happened in the last year, but today felt like no time had passed at all. They giggled as they kicked off their shoes. They were starving, but no one had enough energy to care.

Jon wove his fingers with Sarah's as he sat down next to her. "What are your plans tonight?" he asked casually.

Sarah could tell he was fishing for information. She knew what he was thinking and placated him. "We'll be here when you get back." She smiled at him. He wrinkled his brow, and she added, "We're too tired to go anywhere." She didn't want him to worry. Besides, they would be fine even if they went out.

Not long after Jon left, the girls started to get their second wind. They had spent an hour in the hot tub reminiscing about college parties, and then decided they either had to eat sandwiches or go out for some food. Sarah could tell the girls had already decided they wanted to go out. "Why don't we just get dressed? I know this place we can go not too far from here." She was nervous about going out at all. She had told Jon they would stay home. He would freak out if he came home and they weren't there. But if they went somewhere close, they could be back before he ever found out they left. By the time they were ready to go, it was nearly eight thirty, and Jon probably wouldn't be home for two more hours. They could eat in that time.

The girls piled into the car, and Sarah backed it out of the garage, the new car smell filling her lungs. She really hadn't had much chance to drive her car. She could count the times she had taken it out on one hand. Jon usually insisted that they take his SUV. It blended in with every other BMW, big and black with dark tinted windows, just like every other nonhybrid vehicle on the road. She stopped in the long drive before the gate and pushed the button to lower the roof. The air was refreshing. Jon never wanted the top down. He preferred his privacy. *But why have a convertible if you're not going to put the top down?* Sarah pushed the remote for the gate, and the heavy metal door began to pull open. Cameras started clicking as she pulled out onto the street. She forgot about the paparazzi. There were only two, but still, they were there.

"Smile for the cameras, ladies." All the girls smiled and waved, before they took off down the street and out of the neighborhood. *So much for Jon not knowing.* "I'm so tired of the vultures," Sarah complained. "I don't know how they get some of the information that they know. I swear there's a spy in our house."

"I think I would be completely creeped out if there were people stalking me all the time," said Jessica. "I mean, this is fun for a weekend, but I can't imagine dealing with it every time I went out."

"You don't seem to let it bother you, Sarah," added Alli.

"Thanks. I'm trying. I don't really have a choice."

When they arrived at the restaurant, Sarah found a parking spot on the street. She put the top back up, before heading inside. The pub-like atmosphere was teaming with untapped energy, and they were seated in a booth across from the long wooden bar. She and Jon had been there a couple of times and no one had bothered them. The girls ordered, and had gotten their meal before they noticed the two cameras pressed up against the window, pointing right at them. Just as the paparazzi were discovered, two guys walked up to the table. They were decent looking and brought drinks. The short, blond surfer type asked, "We're looking for some help with body shots at the back of the bar. Are you interested?"

"Sorry, not tonight, guys. We're just trying to grab some food." Sarah was trying to be polite.

"Are you sure? I promise it will be a good time," said the guy with the long dark hair pulled back in a ponytail.

"She's not allowed to have a good time," said Megan. "She's engaged."

"You're not married yet," said the blond guy, pushing his hair out of his eyes and spying Sarah's left hand. He took a swig of his drink and set it down on their table. "That's a big ring. He must have little-man syndrome."

Sarah hid her hand on her lap and started to wish one of her big strong bodyguards was there to get rid of these guys. "No, not his issue."

"Well, he's not here and you're not married yet. Come live a little before you're locked up for good," said the dark-haired guy with a grinding laugh.

"It's only body shots," Megan said, chuckling, and Sarah knew she was just egging the guys on.

"You go right ahead, Megan. But keep in mind anything you do in here is going to be on the Internet in a couple of minutes." Sarah pointed to the window.

"What, are you actresses or something?" asked the blond.

"Nope. I think they have us confused with somebody else," admitted

Jessica.

"They called me Ashley Tyler. It's a stretch, but I suppose anyone with blond hair and long legs could be mistaken for her." Megan held her leg out and lifted her heel into the air.

As the guys gawked at Megan's flawless legs, a third guy joined the group. He stood by the table and asked, "Are you going to do shots with us, or what?"

"Sorry, we don't want our moms to see," stated Alli as she pointed to the paparazzi, and all the girls began to laugh. The irony of last night's photos and Alli's parents hung in the air.

"So who are you?" the new guy asked.

"They claim the paps are targeting them by mistake," the blond guy announced.

"I'm going to ask them." The new guy set his drink on the table and went outside to talk to the photographers.

When the guy returned, he said, "They want to know if you and Jonathan Williams broke off your engagement."

Sarah knew what the headline would be tomorrow. *Jonathan's fiancé partying with friends post breakup.* She placed her hand on the table and twisted her ring. "Nope, still engaged." She smiled at her friends.

"They also want to know who your friends are. They swore one of you was making out with Jake Gorboni last night and another was with Liam Nordstrom. So who are you? Do you have some new reality show coming out?"

"Yeah, like the *Real Coeds of Beverly Hills*. We want to be on your show," stated the blond.

"Honestly, we're just friends, and it's girls night. We came for the food," admitted Sarah.

"Come on, girls. Now we're intrigued. You have to tell us more," the new guy declared. "The paps want me to report back to them."

"Tell them to go screw themselves," said Megan.

"Just do a couple of body shots. It's not going to hurt anyone," said the blond.

"Sorry, we really just want to eat," Sarah said as politely as she could muster.

"Come on." The third guy held his hands in front of his face as if praying.

"Can you leave us alone? We're not interested," added Alli.

The third guy moved closer to Sarah, making eye contact with her. "Please? They told me they would pay me a hundred bucks if I got you to do body shots or if I kissed you."

"Are you serious?" asked Megan.

"The paps are awful. They might give you a hundred dollars, but they'd be making twenty times that or more," said Sarah to the third guy. She was getting used to the paparazzi's antics. "Can you just let us eat? They just want to use you to make up a story to make it look like I'm cheating on my fiancé."

"I wouldn't mind being used," said the blond guy, putting his hands on the table and leaning in toward Sarah.

"Well I would," said Sarah, pulling away from his invasion into her personal space.

"Just back off. We're not going to do body shots. Leave us alone," added Jessica.

One of the guys said, "Yeah. No problem, bitches," as they all walked away.

Well at least no rude gestures that could make the headlines were exchanged.

They were on their way home when he called. Jon could have sent a text, but he usually called Sarah since her abduction in January just to hear her voice, and she understood. Guilt filled her when she heard the worry in his voice, but they were hungry, and nothing happened to them. He was waiting for them when they got home and even though she could tell he was mad, he wrapped his arms lovingly around her as if he was relieved.

Chapter Seven

Jonathan

After Jon and Sarah returned from dropping their friends off at the airport, he could feel the change in Sarah's mood. Gloom hung on her face. He hated to see her depressed. He watched as she picked up her journal and collapsed on the far end of the couch. She tucked her legs up next to her and opened the book. Approaching her, he leaned over and kissed the top of her head. Her eyes met his, and he smiled sympathetically at her. "We'll see them soon, just a couple of weeks."

"I know," she said with no enthusiasm.

"Did you have fun last night? The tabloids have you cheating on me."

"Yeah. Did you see the picture of me doing that guy right there on the bar?"

Jon chuckled. "Saw it. It made me hard." At least she had a sense of humor about it. He gently trailed his finger down her cheek. *Why was she being so reckless?* "I wish you would have brought Craig with you. He was at the house."

"When did we start twenty-four-hour security?"

"I want someone here with you when I'm not home. I'm surprised I haven't done it until now. It's not a big deal. Just bring someone with you next time you leave the house. I don't want you by yourself." Craig had called him when he wasn't able to track Sarah down and Jon cut his meeting short. He hadn't told her that though. His thoughts kept drifting to his dead brother and then back to the stalker. He didn't know what he would do if anything happened to Sarah.

"Afraid I'll do another guy on the bar?"

"Yep. Totally jealous." He was trying not to make a big deal about it but still get his message across. The stalker was a real threat that couldn't be ignored.

"I wasn't alone. The girls were with me."

She wasn't getting it. Maybe he should just tell her about the stalker. But she'd been through so much already because of him, how could he put her through more? "I'm going for a drive. Will you come with me?"

"Are you scared to leave me alone at the house?"

"No. I just want to share something with you." He could tell her about the stalker, about how oddly specific the notes had been, and about the tabloid picture of Sarah and him that was embedded in the last one. *Shit*. How could he tell her? He couldn't even think about it. He had enough baggage to deal with today. The stalker would have to wait. He shook his head trying to clear his thoughts as she rose, grabbing her purse and phone. She followed him into the kitchen and watched him while he grabbed an imported beer from the fridge.

"A beer for the road? I'm pretty sure the highway patrol frowns on that."

"You'll see." He stuffed it into his jacket pocket and reached for her hand. He weaved his fingers between hers and took a deep breath. He could do this. It would be a lot easier with her at his side.

Silence filled the car for most of the ride. Sarah must have been waiting for his explanation, but the lump in his throat prevented him from talking. He didn't know what to tell her about where they were going. She'd see soon enough anyway. He slowed near the gate opening and turned onto the narrow road.

Sarah turned to him with questioning eyes.

When his eyes met hers, he nodded. "It's his birthday."

The car followed the pavement around and around as if it knew exactly where to go, until the grassy hill came into view. Jon shifted the car into park and took a deep breath. Sarah placed her hand on his knee and tenderly kissed his cheek.

"Let's go wish him a happy birthday." She opened her door and turned to him. The corners of his lips turned up just a little as he opened his door. She was so much stronger than him. She met him by the front of the car and wove her fingers through his. He glanced up the hill, letting go of her hand and curling his arm around her waist to pull her closer—her warmth giving him courage. "I've only brought beer once before. I know you're not really supposed to drink in a cemetery, but Jack enjoyed a good pilsner. His first birthday after the accident I just couldn't face the reality and I didn't come. I felt too guilty. But I haven't missed one since."

"It wasn't your fault."

He stopped and turned to her, placing a hand on each of her shoulders. "It was, Sarah. I made the choice to veer into oncoming traffic. I know I was trying to avoid killing the paparazzo on the road, but it was still my decision. And my actions killed my brother. It is my fault he's dead."

"You were only nineteen. It was an accident."

He shook his head, knowing she was just trying to comfort him, and he started walking again, returning his hand to her waist. "I've been coming here a lot more since I met you. I slip away sometimes just to clear my head." They climbed the hill, and he spotted the black onyx stone in the ground. A fresh single red rose lay across the stone, and Jon wondered if his mother had stopped here earlier in the day or if Jack still had fans after almost five years in the ground. "As long as I can sneak past the paparazzi at the house, no one bothers me here."

Sarah sat down on the ground next to the gravestone, more comfortable in a cemetery than he expected. She skimmed her finger lightly over the inscribed name. *Jackson Alexander Williams*. Tears pooled in the corners of her eyes, and Jon swallowed hard, fighting back the emotion he felt having her here. He sat next to her on the grass and pulled the beer out of his pocket, setting it on the onyx stone. He twisted the cap off and held it up for a toast. "Happy birthday, Jack." He took a swig and handed it to Sarah.

"Happy birthday, Jack," Sarah repeated, before taking a drink and handing it back to him.

Jon guzzled half the contents of the bottle. Then, feeling Sarah's eyes on him, he glanced up. A single tear dripped down her cheek, and he wiped it away with his thumb. "Don't cry, beautiful. We're celebrating his life, not his death. I had nineteen years with him, and I'm thankful for that." He pulled her against his chest and smoothed his hand up and down her back, as more tears leaked from her eyes. "Honestly, it took me a long time before I could come back here and face what I had done. That whole first year after his death I was such a mess. I didn't even want to accept his death let alone that I had caused it. Now I've got you, and we're sharing a beer with him. I've come a long way."

"You never really talk about the year after the accident. What happened that was so awful?"

He forgot Sarah didn't follow the tabloids back then. If she had she wouldn't have to ask. "A lot happened. It's not important now. If it was, I would tell you."

"You know that I can find it on the Internet."

"I know. But you won't." He downed another gulp and handed the bottle to Sarah.

She smiled and asked, "What's your favorite memory of Jack."

He glanced across the grounds as several cars slowed to pass each other on the narrow street below the hill. "I have so many great memories of him. He bitched out my dad for me when I wanted to quit acting. It was great; my dad was pissed at both of us." He paused, searching his brain for a better story. He knew which one he needed to share to show what kind of person Jack was. "And Liam had this huge party once. Well…he always had a party when his parents were out of town, but this one was epic."

"Did you just say epic?"

"Yeah. OK? But we were sixteen and it *was* epic. There were hundreds of people there, everyone we knew, and it was completely out of control. Jack had already made a name for himself in film by eighteen and of course every girl in the place was vying for him. He was out by the pool when he noticed a couple of drunks throwing Liam's dog in the water. The little white puffball, all of twelve pounds wet, was scared out of its mind. It was the kind of dog that peed if you bent down to pet it. I'm pretty sure it was on doggy Prozac. Anyway, the idiots were trying to impress girls by tormenting it. Jack excused himself from the group of girls that surrounded him and confronted the guys, just as they started feeding it beer. Jack ordered them to give him the dog. He had this really deep voice. I can still hear him saying it."

"So did the guys give him the dog?" asked Sarah.

"No. One of them tossed it into the air over his shoulder. Luckily it landed in the water. Jack didn't engage in fights. He had a career to protect. So he pushed the guys in the pool, clothes, phones, and all. He fished the dog out and carried it around the rest of the night, then took it home and kept it until right before Liam's parents came home. I think he was scared Liam was going to have another party. Jack was always rooting for the underdog. Did you know he saved two kids from the backseat of a car that was on fire on the interstate? He was a superhero."

"Sounds like he knew what was important in life."

"Yep. He always had my back. I was never as good as him. I don't know how many times I've heard, 'It should have been you.' And it should have been. I know that. I was a fuckup, and he was a better person than me."

Jon took another drink and passed the bottle back to Sarah. He knew Sarah's silence meant she was searching for the right words, deliberate and well constructed.

"I'm glad it wasn't you," she muttered so softly that Jon had to lean in to hear her.

"You are one of a few," he said, covering her hand with his.

"That's not true. You have millions of fans that worship you."

"And if I wasn't here, they would cyberstalk someone else." He knew she couldn't argue with that. She lay back on the grass with a defeated groan and pulled him down next to her. He propped himself on his elbow as he turned to face her. "Why are you so comfortable here? You act like we're having a picnic. Most girls would be crawling out of their skin sitting in the grass of a graveyard."

She turned on her side to face him. "I have graveyard experience."

He lifted his eyebrow questioningly.

"Well, when I was eleven, a boy moved in on our street, Tyler Rainer. He was twelve, but mature for a boy, and super cute."

"Was he?" Jon reached out and tucked a strand of hair behind her ear. "How cute was he?"

"He was so cute that I used to ride my bike back and forth in front of his house for hours." She laughed and Jon knew it was his expression that brought it on. "Blond hair, big brown eyes, very buff for a twelve-year-old."

"How does this relate to a cemetery?"

"I'm getting to that." She paused and jokingly told him with her eyes to be patient. "One day he was out on his bike waiting for me. He asked me if I wanted to race, and we raced to the end of the block. I let him win because he was so cute."

"Oh, you're one of those kind of girls. That makes sense." He couldn't stop teasing her.

"Would you listen? It was summer, so we met up on our bikes every day after that. Sometimes we would stop and get an ice cream cone, but usually we just rode. One day he turned into the cemetery that we always rode past and parked his bike. He seemed out of breath and at the time I thought that maybe he had asthma. He grabbed my hand and led me to the top of a hill before sitting down. I didn't care where we were because he was holding my hand."

"And he was super cute," Jon added.

"Exactly. We talked for a while, and then he said something like, 'It's nice here, right?' To which I responded, 'I guess, if you like dead people,' and he laughed and laughed. Then he leaned in and kissed me. My first kiss." She paused with a thoughtful look. "He died a few weeks later of some kind of cancer. I never found out what kind. And he was buried in the cemetery near where we first kissed. I found out later that he had moved to our street because his grandparents were trying to get custody of him. His parents' religion didn't allow him to get treatment for his disease and his grandparents wanted him to get treatment. His parents were hiding him from them. I felt bad that he never told me. We didn't really know each other that well because all we really did was ride bikes, and I felt guilty about that. I wanted to know him better, and I wanted him to know me better. I used to go to the cemetery to talk to him after he passed. He was always a good listener. Is that weird?"

"Is it weird that we're sharing a beer with my dead brother?"

They laughed as they sat up. Sarah took another drink of the beer and held it out to Jon. He shook his head and motioned for her to dump some on the grass. Laughter bubbled up from each of them again at the ridiculousness of feeding the grass, but a desperate, piercing scream broke it.

"Charlie! Stop!"

A young mother frantically struggled to unbuckle an infant from a car seat as her toddler took off running across the grounds. Jon jumped to his feet and sprinted to catch the child before it reached the narrow road on the other side.

"Gotcha," he said as he scooped the boy into his arms. The boy giggled as if it was a game, and Jon started laughing at the infectious smile on the toddler's face. *He was so adorable.* Jon turned, walking back toward the mother as Sarah joined his side.

"I want one of these." He tickled the boy's tummy, which brought on a string of giggles. He couldn't wait to start a family with Sarah. *Maybe their children would have Sarah's laugh.*

Sarah shook her head in amusement.

"Isn't he cute? How could you not want one of these?" Jon held the dark-haired boy out in front of Sarah and raised his eyebrows questioningly. Sarah smiled as he tucked the child back in his arms. The boy's mother met up with them quickly as they reached the halfway mark between the two roads.

"Thank you so much. I'm still trying to figure out how to manage two kids," she said, stuffing her keys, phone, and a pacifier into her bag. "I guess I need to unbuckle the baby before Charlie." Settling the newborn in one arm, she looked up and her eyes widened. "You're...You're Jonathan Williams."

Jon smiled. "You must be Charlie's mom."

"I can't believe you caught him. He's so fast. He always takes off running. I should have known better. Thank you so much."

Jon slid the boy to the ground, hanging on to his hand so he wouldn't take off again. Bending down, he said, "Don't give your mom any more trouble, Charlie." The toddler looked at Jon trying to fake a serious expression before breaking out in giggles again.

"You're so good with him. You definitely should have one of your own." The woman's eyes scanned Sarah as she added, "You are, right?"

He saw how Sarah tensed at her words. "Someday," he said. "Well, we should get going." He placed the boy's hand in the woman's so he wouldn't take off running again and said, "Be good, Charlie." The woman thanked him again as he and Sarah turned toward Jack's stone. "My pleasure," said Jon.

When they were out of hearing distance, Sarah asked, "Do I have a baby bump?" She spun sideways as they walked, flattening her sundress over her stomach. "I'm going to have to work harder at Pilates."

Jon grabbed her from behind and wrapped his arms around her. His hand splaying across her stomach as he pulled her against him. "I wouldn't mind if there was. I'd love it," he whispered centimeters from her ear. He felt a shiver rake through her body before she wiggled out of his grasp. Her expression said, "You're crazy." He grabbed her hand.

"I'm not crazy, Sarah. You would look so hot with my baby growing inside you."

"Oh my god! Did you just say that?"

"What? You would." He released her and bent down to pick up the empty beer bottle.

"Should we even be talking about this in a cemetery?"

"Are you afraid the dead people will hear us?"

"No," she answered, though she said it as if she didn't want to admit the answer was yes. "We're not even married yet."

He knew she wanted to wait until they were married, but he also knew life was too short to worry about social etiquette. Jack's death had taught him that. He wished they could sneak off and get married. It would be easier. And faster. He couldn't wait to move forward in their life together. "You're right," he agreed. "But it won't stop me from dreaming about it."

"Shut up." She playfully hit his abdomen with the back of her hand. "You'd think you were sex-starved."

She wasn't taking him seriously, but he was serious. He wanted to live for the now. He'd known her for a year, and she'd already been in a car accident and been abducted by a crazed lunatic. He didn't want to wait, but he'd planted the seed in her brain, and he would let it germinate before bringing up children again.

When they reached his BMW, he opened her door and waited for her to settle in her seat before kissing her cheek. "You know I love you, right?"

She smiled and nodded. He could tell she understood his need for the declaration. It was just something he had to say. In the cemetery where his brother lay, it hung in the air: *life can change in an instant.*

Chapter Eight

Sarah

Sarah stared out the window at the setting sun as Jon drove out through the cemetery gates. She hadn't thought about Tyler Rainer in a long time. She hadn't sat in a cemetery for a long time either. It had been ten years since Tyler's death, and he hadn't crossed her mind much in the last five. She had no pictures, and she didn't even remember much about what he looked like, other than his hair color and the fact that she thought he was cute. She remembered being so mad at him for not telling her about the cancer. Then she felt guilty for being mad at him. She felt guilty for not getting him treatment—not that an eleven-year-old girl could do anything. In reality she probably didn't even know him until it was too late to save him, and he never told her he was sick. She didn't know until he had stopped showing up to ride bikes and she knocked on his door to find out why. She thought he was just blowing her off, and she wanted him to explain. It wasn't like they were dating. They mostly just rode bikes. Even though they had only kissed the one time, she thought she deserved an explanation.

Tyler's mom was the one who told her he was dying. Tyler refused to see her after that, and Sarah remembered feeling utterly helpless and guilty. She knew her experience with Tyler made her understand Jon's feelings about Jack's death just a little better. Her loss was nowhere near the loss Jon felt, but it still gave her understanding.

She bent forward and turned the music down so Jon could hear her. "You're not so different from Jack after all."

He glanced at her with one eyebrow raised as he did when he was trying to figure out what she was thinking.

"You rescued that toddler from certain peril just like Jack rescued Liam's dog and the kids in the burning car. You're cut from the same cloth." When his smile met her eyes, she knew her words had made the impact she wanted.

"Charlie would have been fine, but thanks," he said, reaching out to touch her cheek. "You seem pretty quiet. Are you OK?"

"Just a little tired." She didn't know what more to say.

When she got home, she told Jonathan that she wasn't feeling well and wanted to get to bed early. She wasn't sure if it was the emotions the cemetery visit uncovered or if she was getting sick, but she was drained. She brushed her teeth, washed her face, and curled up with her favorite pillow on the bed.

Within minutes she fell asleep, but it was not restful. She tossed and turned as images flashed in her mind—Tyler's twelve-year-old body lying in a casket. She was kissing him for the first time on the lawn of the cemetery. Then, she and Jon were in the cemetery and Jon was kissing Sarah's rounded pregnant belly—his breath warming her skin. Hmm. Jon was kneeling in front of Mia, talking softly to the baby growing in her stomach as her fingers tangled in his hair. Arrgh. Sarah was eleven again. She and Tyler were riding their bikes, laughing, and then a car came out of nowhere. The driver was taking pictures of them and no matter how fast they rode, they couldn't get away. Sarah looked over and now it was Jon on the bike next to her and Mia was driving the car. The scene morphed again showing Jon and Mia lying on a bed, while a little boy with a single dimple on his right cheek jumped on the pillows between them. "Catch me, Daddy. Catch me." The little boy giggled as Jon's arm wrapped around him, pulling him to his chest.

Sarah awoke with a shiver. She sat up and brushed the hair out of her eyes, waiting for her heartbeat to slow. There was no way she was going back to sleep. She slid her feet to the floor and started for the stairs, but she stopped when she heard Jonathan's voice. She had on a tank top and sleep shorts, and she wasn't going to change. If someone was here this late, it had to be someone they knew, but her hair was probably a disaster. She bent over, running her fingers through her hair to straighten it and then flipped it back as she stood upright.

"Why would I do that?"

She couldn't help eavesdropping, but when no one answered Jon's question, Sarah realized he was on the phone.

"Mia, she's smart. She'll realize that the second she finds out you're pregnant." She froze midstep. *What the hell?*

"No. That's not fair to her." His pause stretched long, and Sarah wished she could hear what Mia was saying. The house was quiet, no music blaring and no TV spewing commercials in the background. Sarah tried to calm her breathing—afraid Jon would hear her.

"If that's what you want."

"It can't be that hard. You're not even showing."

He laughed.

"I didn't see a baby bump. You looked stunning as ever the other night. I don't know why you are so worked up about it."

Jon tapped a foot on the floor.

"I've got to go. Warn me before you send out any press releases."

Sarah waited until she was sure that Jon was off the phone before moving off the top step. Her heart hammered against her chest wall again. She only heard half the conversation. *Maybe it wasn't what it seemed.* Maybe she wasn't the "she" Jon was talking about. She closed her eyes, recalling the words Jon had spoken, not wanting to follow where her mind was pushing her. She needed time to process the phone call, so she quietly snuck back to her bed and texted Jessica, making sure she closed the door behind her.

Sarah: *R U home?*

Jessica: *The flight got in early. Crazy drama happening downstairs with Alli's parents. I'm hiding in my room.*

Sarah: *I get that. Just overheard Jon talking to Mia. I was supposed to be sleeping.*

Jessica: *What did she want?*

Sarah: *I only caught the end. Something about notifying Jon before sending out press releases about her pregnancy.*

Jessica: *What???*

Sarah: *She told him at the club that she's pregnant. I heard her. I don't think they know I know.*

Jessica: *I'm calling you!!!*

Sarah answered it the second Jessica's picture flashed on the screen.

"What the hell? Why didn't you say something when we were there?" Jessica huffed, and Sarah imagined her scowling with her arms crossed.

"I didn't think it was any of my business."

"Not your business? Is it Jon's business?"

"No! Jon wouldn't cheat on me." She exhaled defensively and flopped her head against the pillow. In her heart she didn't believe he would cheat. That didn't prevent her mind from going there, though. "We went to visit his brother's grave today and when we got home, I was emotionally exhausted because I was thinking about Tyler Rainer. I guess going to the cemetery just made me think about him. So I laid down for a little bit and had this dream about Mia."

"Oh. Are you OK? What happened?"

"I don't even remember exactly. Somehow, it transformed into a dream about Jon being the father of Mia's baby and when I woke up, he was talking to her on the phone. He told her to let him know before she sent out any press releases about the pregnancy."

"Why was he talking to her? And why would he care when it's leaked to the press?"

"I don't know what to think. I mean, I get why he wants to know. If she doesn't come clean about who the father is, then the press will assume it's Jon's—and knowing her, that's the game she'll play."

"Did she tell Jon at the club who the father is?"

Sarah thought about the conversation at the club. "She didn't ID him. Jon asked, and she didn't tell him *he* was the father."

"Jon asked if he was the father?"

"No. He asked who the father was."

"Then, this is good news. Now she'll stop trying to bed your fiancé. I mean she can't keep trying if she's as big as a house, right?"

"I guess. Except I'm pretty sure she will look great no matter how pregnant she is, and she knows Jon really wants kids."

"He wants kids with you, but that doesn't mean he wants some other man's kids. It's like a survival of the species thing. No matter how sophisticated they dress, men are still Neanderthals. They want to pass their genes on."

"He wants kids now, though. I'm pretty sure that appointment Leslie scheduled for me is with a gynecologist."

"You guys are getting married. Maybe he's just tired of wearing a condom and wants you to check out your options. Seriously? Men hate those things. I'm surprised he's been so patient. Stop worrying about Mia. She's no longer a problem. And take full advantage of her mistake."

"How?"

"The next time you see Mia, make sure you are wearing the skimpiest, most-formfitting clothes you own. As she's growing bigger with some unknown man's baby, you will still be your hot little self. You can torture her for months. I know it's petty, but she's been such a bitch to you—she deserves some payback."

Sarah smiled. "Gloating? It's tempting. You always know how to make me feel better. Thanks."

"Anytime."

"Can you do me a favor? Don't mention the pregnancy to anyone else."

"Of course. My lips are zipped."

"Thanks." As she set her phone down, she emptied the air from her lungs. *Jon is not the father.* What was she thinking? She must have been messed up by the cemetery visit. She needed to talk to him about the doctor's appointment and figure out where his mind was. Did he want her to get pregnant or just get on birth control?

As she descended the stairs, she could see Jon sprawled on the couch with his arms crossed over his face and one foot planted on the floor. His phone rested next to him on the ottoman. He looked like he was sleeping. So peaceful.

She quietly snuck into the kitchen and found a glass in the cupboard to push against the ice dispenser. The cubes clattered to the bottom, louder than she expected, and she pulled back, switching to water. She didn't want to wake him if he was sleeping. The water cooled her parched throat as she gazed out at the courtyard. Her friends were just there that morning and now it seemed so empty. She felt his eyes penetrate her before he spoke.

"Are you feeling better?" He hung back tentatively in the doorway with his hands grasping the top of the arched entrance.

She took a sip of water. "A little." Watching his reflection in the glass, convinced if her eyes met his he would be able to read her mind, she tried to compose herself. "I guess if I still feel sick on Thursday, I'll ask the doctor to do some tests. She didn't really plan on asking the doctor anything, but she wanted to bring up the appointment.

He entered the kitchen and leaned against the granite countertop next to her. "So Leslie told you about the appointment and you're OK with it?"

"I wish you had asked me before you made it. I mean, I *am* the one being examined." She understood he wanted children, but to make an appointment for her with an OB/GYN without even talking to her—that was a bit too much.

"I was going to tell you about the appointment, but it never seemed the right time. Besides, after this weekend…you have to agree that it's the right thing to do." He ran his fingers gently through her hair and gazed into her eyes as if waiting for her to agree.

She shook his hand off and abruptly pulled away. "This weekend?" she shrilled. "You mean with Mia? Well, there you go…the press is going to say the baby is yours. You may as well claim it now." She walked backward toward the staircase. "Problem solved. You don't even need me." Then she turned and sprinted up the stairs, slamming the bedroom door behind her.

Jonathan

Holy shit. Jon stood near the counter contemplating whether he should follow her or let her calm down first. He had never seen Sarah blow up like that. Obviously she was fuming about the appointment and knew about the pregnancy too. He didn't realize Sarah had paid attention to his conversation with Mia at the club. Clearly she had. He took a deep breath before heading up the steps two at a time. Gently closing the bedroom door behind him, he slid to the floor with his back against the exit, quietly waiting for her to look up. When she didn't, he said, "Sarah, I'm sorry I made the appointment without asking you, but you really haven't been open to talking about it."

"And all that matters is what you want, right?" she mumbled into her pillow.

"What? I just want you to be happy."

She lifted her head and stared at the wall, not turning to look at him. "Jon, I know you want to have a baby, but I don't know if I'm ready to have kids yet."

He cocked his head, staring at her. He didn't understand this conversation at all, but he knew he needed to sort it out. He thought about her last statement. *Was she worried about what the press would say?* "Is that what you're worried about? Just because Mia is having a baby doesn't mean you have to. I don't care what the press says." He climbed onto the bed next to her. "I can wait until you're ready." He wrapped his arm around her and whispered as he kissed the back of her neck, "I'm ready whenever you are—just so you know." He kissed her neck again. He could feel the tension leaving her body as his fingers smoothed over her shoulder.

She flipped over to face him and said, "I'll go to the appointment. It can't hurt to go, but no promises beyond that."

The smell of cherry blossoms and vanilla from her hair hit his nose, and he didn't want to argue anymore.

"We'll just see what the doctor says." He covered her lips with his and gently coaxed a kiss from her. When he pulled back, he whispered, "Maybe you can wear a bikini on our honeymoon." His lips met hers as one of his hands found its way to the scars on the top of her abdomen.

When his finger traced the slightly raised line on her skin, she lurched up, asking, "Dr. Kravitz is a plastic surgeon, isn't he?"

He pulled her back down next to him. "Yeah…the best in the country. Isn't that what we're arguing about?" He propped his head up on his elbow and looked at her curiously, hoping for some clarity into her mood.

"We're not arguing," she said decisively as she started unbuttoning his shirt. "I don't have a problem with Dr. Kravitz." Her hands slipped inside so softly against his chest. He leaned down to brush his lips to her temple.

"Honestly, I don't even notice the scars. You will always be the most beautiful woman in the world." He ran his fingers through her hair. "But they seem to bother you, and I will do anything to make you happy."

94

"OK. Just stop talking and kiss me."

Jon laughed, shrugging out of his shirt, then pulled her on top of him and stretched up to meet her lips. He didn't know what she was thinking, but she seemed to have gotten over it. Jack's birthday, his conversation with Mia, the stalker, and Sarah's mood had all taken their toll on his ability to think clearly. And then there was the issue with Cannes. He really wished he could find a way out of going there altogether.

Sarah's lips were soft and sweet. He pulled her in closer. All he wanted to do right now was lose himself in the woman he loved and forget about the rest of the world. He knew not all his problems would go away if he ignored them, but at this moment he couldn't handle anything else.

Chapter Nine

Sarah

On Thursday, when Jon and Sarah arrived at Dr. Kravitz's office, they were surprised to see a photographer waiting for them in front of the nondescript medical building. There was no one at the house when they left, so they didn't think they'd been followed. It was as if the press knew about Sarah's appointment. The photographer snapped pictures of them as they entered the building's door. As he followed Jon and Sarah to the elevator, he asked, "Getting some plastic surgery before the wedding, huh? Getting rid of those scars from your accident, or are you really getting a boob job?"

Sarah looked at Jon in horror. *How could he know that?* There were many different doctors in the building. He couldn't possibly know where they were going, and how did he know about her scars.

Jon whispered in her ear, "Don't react. That's what he wants."

Sarah closed her eyes and tried to calm herself, but she knew it was too late. The paparazzo already got the shot.

The atmosphere inside the doctor's office was serene and helped Sarah calm her breathing. The waiting room was decorated like a private library with dark, wooden bookshelves, and dim lighting. The receptionist greeted them from behind a simple wooden table as they entered and led them back immediately to an examination room. Inside the room Sarah pulled the curtain around the small changing area and unbuttoned her blouse. She pulled off her bra and slipped on the white cotton robe like she was instructed to do. She was nervous the doctor might recommend surgery. She didn't really want to have surgery again. She was also a little apprehensive to have a doctor evaluating her body—a doctor who specialized in beautiful bodies, beautiful Hollywood bodies. It was a bit daunting. She looked nervously at Jon as she opened the curtain, and he smiled back at her.

A man in his early forties knocked before entering the room, wearing dark purple scrubs with designer running shoes. His dark hair was slicked back and perfectly styled. He got down to business right away. And as he stepped closer to Sarah, she could smell the clean scent of his cologne. Sarah realized she was the only one in the room who could be improved by plastic surgery.

"So let's see those scars, Sarah." He directed her to open her robe.

His fingers were cold against her skin as he examined her side. Sarah felt very exposed standing in front of a complete stranger in the open robe, and she shivered a little as he touched her.

"Well…these don't look bad at all. The surgeon did a decent job. There's just this one small pucker. It's mostly flat, so I don't think it will be too much trouble to get rid of these scars completely. We'll take some pictures here, and I'll show you the results you can expect on the computer." The doctor took out a small camera and snapped several close-up shots of Sarah's scars. "I think we can take care of this with just one session of dermabrasion and a topical."

Sarah wrapped her arms around herself, closing her robe tightly. She felt just a little violated, like she was a piece of meat being evaluated by a butcher. It was just a feeling she'd gotten from the doctor. She looked warily at Jon, and he returned his best reassuring expression.

The pictures loaded wirelessly onto the computer, and Dr. Kravitz manipulated a flat rubber pad with his finger to produce several before and after picture sets. "As you can see, the scars won't disappear completely, but they won't be visible either," the doctor confidently stated as he turned to Jon. "We can squeeze the treatment in next week, for ample healing time." Then he turned to Sarah and added, "And if you like, we could help you fill out your wedding dress a little better. You could go up a cup size or even two. Augmentation is outpatient surgery. It's very fast. We could do them both at the same time."

"No!" Jon stated firmly. "No."

The doctor nodded and added, "I just wanted her to know that if she has ever thought about it, now would be a good time."

Jon shook his head.

"I don't even get a say in this?" Sarah joked, shaking her head.

"No…we're getting married. The girls are joint property. Changes to them have to be approved by the board," he added with a chuckle. "You're naturally beautiful."

Even though she loved Jon's affirmation and she joked about the augmentation, the surgeon's comment damaged her, just a little. She had always thought she was adequately blessed on top, not as blessed as Jessica but still enough there not to need a boob job. This one conversation changed that.

After the appointment Jon and Sarah took the elevator back down to the lobby of the building. Jon reminded her that the photographer would probably be waiting for them. In the elevator he asked if he could get something out of Sarah's purse. He located her phone and plugged in the earbuds. She watched him as he manipulated it to a loud song by his favorite band and handed it to her. "Here, put these on, then you don't have to hear the idiot on the sidewalk."

Of course, the paparazzo was there waiting for them when they exited the building. Jon was right about the EXpireD song blocking the man's voice completely. When they got to the BMW in the parking ramp, they collapsed into the bucket seats and finally relaxed behind the dark tinted windows. Jon pulled the car out onto the street before he reached over and pulled one earbud from Sarah's ear. He glanced warily at her as he drove.

"How did he know we would be there?" questioned Sarah. "Does Dr. Kravitz publish his appointment schedule?"

"I'm sure he's very discrete. His business depends on it. It's more likely someone overheard someone talking about the appointment."

"I haven't told anyone except the girls in Minnesota and my mom. None of them would say anything."

Jon pulled the BMW to the curb along the busy street and shifted it into park. He turned to her with cynicism. "Was it published on that website you're always visiting?"

"Jon...I..."

"Don't try to deny it. I saw it on your computer last week. Our engagement photo was hanging on the wall in your parents' dining room. Someone sees that, and then you log on—boom...they find a path into your computer. I'm surprised that photo hasn't been leaked to the press."

"It can't be that easy to hack into someone's computer."

"Last year teenagers hacked into one of the big studio's computers and stole movie footage before a film was released. The teens did it just for fun. They didn't even sell it. If teens can do that, hacking into your computer wouldn't be difficult at all."

"No one has access to that site. The only people who know about it are my college roommates and my brother."

"Sarah, any obsessed fan would recognize your friends, especially after the media frenzy that followed their visit over the week. All a fan would need to do is find out one of their names. We both know their pictures were all over the Internet this week, and the Connect-Me website is always getting hacked. This is exactly why I asked you to stay off those sites. Why is it so hard to keep that one little promise?"

Sarah sat sulking, silenced by Jon's words. She didn't know how to respond. She knew he was right, but she was homesick. Her friends kept her grounded. She missed her freedom to do what she wanted. She could come up with a million excuses, but she knew none of them mattered. She had promised she would stay off those sites and she hadn't. "I'm sorry." She looked apologetically at him.

They sat in silence for several minutes until Jon announced, "I guess we just have to move forward from here. Talk to your friends. Tell them what's happening. Ask them to be extra careful not to post any pictures or personal information about us on the Internet—not any."

"There was a picture posted this week with me in it. It was at Club Priela in the ladies' room with William. My ring was in the picture. I'm sorry—I know it makes me more easily recognized."

"You and the doll?" Jon fumed. Sarah could see it on his face.

"Action figure," she corrected, trying to lighten his mood.

"Tell Jessica to take it off. Call her right now," he insisted. He brought his hands up to his temples as if he had a pounding headache.

Sarah took out her phone and made the call. She explained how the paparazzi seemed to know their every move, how a photographer was waiting for them at Chico's Grill on Tuesday in Santa Monica, when they met with Jon's publicist for lunch, and then again today at the plastic surgeon's office. With the phone in her hand, she met Jon's gaze and apologized with her eyes before he shifted the car into drive. Sarah continued to explain to Jessica how she and Jon were worried about the posts on the Connect-Me website and how she thought it would be best if any pictures or posts with connections to her were removed. Sarah told her it would probably be best if they didn't post on it for a while as well. She asked her to explain the situation to the others.

Jessica admitted she, Alli, and Megan had posted at least five more pictures since the weekend and Sarah was in all of them. She agreed to take them all down right away. Then Jessica caught Sarah up on the drama that is now Alli's life. Alli's parents were horrified by the kiss pictures and were waiting at the rental house when Jeff dropped off everyone from the airport on Sunday. They wanted Alli to move home so she could focus on her studies, but Jessica thought that it was just so they could keep Alli from doing anything more to damage her chances of getting into medical school.

"Apparently, even if you've been accepted into the program, they can still kick you out for behavior unbecoming of a med student. Who knew?" Jessica laughed. "Her parents have threatened to make her pay for her own education."

"She said that would happen."

"There was no harm done. So there are pictures of her kissing a movie star outside an LA club—there are far worse things on the Internet. Seriously, her parents are way overanalyzing our weekend."

"That's her mom's specialty, right?"

"Alli agreed to go home on the weekends, but refused to commute to class."

"Well, at least she's standing up for herself a little," stated Sarah. "Get ready for Crazy Alli, though. She always kind of goes off the deep end when her parents tighten the reigns."

"I guess I don't understand the whole rebelling-against-my-parents thing," stated Jessica. "I never really had anything to rebel against. I think after my dad moved out, I was too worried about my mom to do anything to hurt her, and she was reasonable."

"I think that's half the problem. Alli has never been allowed to make her own mistakes. Her parents never gave her a chance and now that she's an adult, they're still trying to control her. I hope I'm never like that to my kids," declared Sarah. Jon glanced at Sarah for a second with a raised eyebrow.

"So have you and Jon talked any more about having kids?"

"Not yet, but I'm sure we'll talk soon." Sarah looked at Jon cautiously, not really knowing what the outcome of that conversation would be.

"Did you see the picture on the Fizzy Pop website of Jon and Mia from last weekend?" asked Jessica.

"Are you fifteen? What are you doing on that website?" questioned Sarah.

"I was just googling pictures from the weekend and there it was…a picture of Jon with his arm around Mia. It was at the table with all of us, but you were totally cropped out. There was a big article about how Jon has been cheating for months and finally broke off the engagement to get back together with his one true love, Mia Thompson."

"Can you imagine what they're going to say when it comes out that she's pregnant?" This wasn't the first time she had heard stories about Jon and Mia getting back together. She hoped that by the time the pregnancy news broke she would be better at dealing with the gossip about her fiancé and his ex-girlfriend.

Jon cleared his throat loudly and turned to Sarah with a glare of disapproval.

Sarah covered the phone's mic and declared, "She already knows. I'm not spreading rumors."

"Maybe she'll figure out who the father is before it comes out in the press," added Jessica.

"She knows who the father is. He just doesn't know he's a father yet," explained Sarah. "Hey, Jess, can I call you back? Jon is burning me with his eyes and it's really not safe because he's supposed to be driving. I'll talk to you when we get home, OK?" When she got off the phone, she turned to Jon and said, "I'm not spreading gossip. Mia confessed at the club. Jessica was right there and besides, everything I said was true."

"You don't like it when you're the one being talked about, do you?" he asked.

"It's just Mia. She drives me crazy, and I need to talk to someone about it. My friends are my therapists."

"She wouldn't bother you so much if you got to know her. I'm going to set up that lunch with her that we talked about."

Sarah grumbled under her breath but nodded. "Did you see the article about you leaving me to get back together with her? There were pictures and everything." She grabbed the handle above the door as the car sped around the corner a little too fast.

She could tell Jon was letting his frustration control the accelerator. "Yeah, Remi mentioned it yesterday. That's why I hate going to public clubs. Everyone has a cell phone camera, and they can make up any lie they want about you," he admitted.

"Can't we sue them?"

"It's not worth it, Sarah. It just brings more attention to their site and encourages them to do it again. They always word the articles to limit their culpability. If they say that a source told them, then they're not responsible for its validity. They're reporting hearsay. It's best to just ignore it. Don't engage the trolls. Trust me."

When they returned home, Sarah called Jessica to complete their conversation away from Jon's prying ears.

Chapter Ten

Sarah

Something Jessica said bothered Sarah. "Are you sure it's not Jon's baby? I mean, they used to go out." At the time, Jessica sounded like she was just joking, but it still burrowed into Sarah, like a sliver just beneath the surface.

"No. Jon would have had to cheat on me. We've been exclusive since July." Sarah tried to shrug it off. Though exclusive since July wasn't exactly true. She trusted Jon. But the idea about the baby being his had been festering since the night at the club.

There was just something about Jon's reaction when Mia told him about the baby that bothered her. The way the color drained from his face when Mia uttered the words, "I'm pregnant," haunted Sarah. What was it that he had asked? Sarah thought back. She remembered it so clearly that night. The wording was awkward, she recalled. "Who's the father? Anyone I know?" It was as if Jon was probing, unsure. And Mia's response, which was clear in Sarah's mind, "He's with someone else." Jon was with someone else.

He wouldn't cheat, she tried to reassure herself. But what if he didn't think he was cheating? What if it was when they were on their break? They took a break from each other when they couldn't physically be together. How long ago was that? Sarah counted back on her fingers—March, February, January, December, November, October, September. Seven months—could Mia be seven months pregnant?

Sarah had heard of a girl in her high school that kept her entire pregnancy hidden from her parents. They brought her to the hospital complaining of stomach cramps and she had a baby. That may have been an urban legend, though. She didn't actually know the girl. Mia didn't look pregnant, but she was wearing baggy clothes, baggy for her anyway. Sarah remembered how her cousin Ronnie complained when she was pregnant with Lilly that pregnancy wasn't really nine months. It was ten. "Forty weeks with four weeks in a month—you do the math," Ronnie had said. Maybe Mia still had three months left.

As Sarah fretted over Mia's due date, she thought about the fact that Jon hadn't come out and said he wasn't the father. He hadn't talked about it at all.

As she pondered, she opened her laptop and booted it up. She should just ask Jon point-blank. "Are you the father of Mia's baby?" It would hurt him though. She knew it would hurt him. She didn't want to hurt Jon—if he wasn't the father. If he *was* the father, he would be in big trouble. *Oh, crap*! What if he really had sex with her and she's carrying his baby. What then? Was that what she had over him?

She clicked on the icon on her computer and the search engine appeared. Sarah typed in "Mia Thompson." She wanted to see who the press had caught with her in the last year. And there it was—the picture Jessica mentioned. Jon and Mia were sitting at the "it" table at Club Priela. By the looks of the picture, Jon and Mia were back together. Sarah shook her head in disbelief. She continued down the screen. Mia's next movie comes out in a month—*Illicit Black*. It must be about sex.

She pulled it up on IMDb. Sarah opened her journal. She was going to make a list of possible baby daddies, just to calm her nerves, and she knew looking at Mia's costars from her last movie was a logical place to start. Sarah scanned down the cast list. Jason Sanchez—he looked too old to be a love interest, in his late fifties at least. She skipped his name. Martin Cross—he was good looking, but was he famous enough? She knew Mia's appetite for fame. She clicked on his page and noted Mia had done another movie with him three years ago. He was a possibility. Maybe she had a prior relationship with him. She wrote his name down in her journal and then clicked the *back* button.

When the movie's page reappeared, she continued down the cast list. Tom Fallston—wow! He's definitely famous enough. She added his name to her journal page without any further investigating. Peter Jason—not as famous as Tom, but he definitely had a reputation for clubbing with the ladies. Sarah added his name too. She continued down the list, writing down the names that might be relevant, until she felt this source was exhausted. She gathered six names just from this movie alone, and then she returned to her original search.

Sarah wanted to see if any of these guys were spotted with Mia in the last six months, but there was nothing obvious to link them to her here, so Sarah brought up the Fizzy Pop website. It was all teen gossip on Fizzy Pop, but she was getting desperate. She typed "Mia Thompson" in the page's search box and waited for the gossip to come up. There was the Club Priela picture again, with an article about how Jon and Mia were getting back together. Sarah did her best to ignore it. She panned down the articles about Mia. There were a couple of pictures of her at different clubs. Mia Thompson and Kiera Hanks surrounded by some guys not on Sarah's list. Sarah added the names. She clicked on the next page of articles and added the names she found there too. Then she clicked on the subsequent page and scanned it. So far none of Mia's costars were photographed with her at the clubs or events she attended. The articles on this page dated back to January, and Sarah figured she may as well go all the way back to September—the break—as long as she'd come this far, so she continued.

As she browsed down the page, Sarah started doubting she would get any useful information from this website. Then she saw it: a series of pictures with an article titled "Jonathan Williams's Closest Friends Welcome Mia Thompson into Their Tight-Knit Family." *Sources tell us Jonathan is going to pop the question over the holidays, and Jonathan's bros couldn't be more thrilled.*

There was a picture of Jonathan walking out of the posh Beverly Hills jewelry store where he bought Sarah's ring. Then there were a series of three dark and grainy pictures inside a sushi bar. They were all candid shots, probably taken without the group of friends' knowledge. Sarah read the tag under the first photo—*Nick Reyes and Hayden Nappo from EXpireD console bad boy Jonathan Williams on his pending engagement.* And sure enough there in the picture was what looked like the three of them laughing with drinks in their hands. The second shot was tagged, *Chris Hanson from Invasion and Liam Nordstrom buy a round for the group.* This picture expanded, showing two more figures with the first three. They looked like they were all enjoying the evening, and Liam was handing out shots from the bar. The third picture was of Mia standing between Nick and Jonathan. Jon and Nick's arms were around her waist.

She felt as if she'd been stabbed in the forehead with an ice pick. She hadn't expected this. Jon and Mia were out together in December. It was the night before her car accident. *How could he not tell her that Mia was with them?* He had told her about "the night out with the guys" that he had when he got back from filming in New Zealand. Jon had slept all day and then had gone out to a sushi bar for dinner and drinks. He had admitted a couple of times how guilty he felt that he didn't spend the night with Sarah. If he had just flown to Minnesota instead of spending the night with the boys, maybe she wouldn't have been in the accident, he'd lamented. Sarah started to wonder if that was the real reason Jon felt so guilty. She clutched her head in her hands in frustration as she stared at the web page. This wasn't helping. Sarah wanted to exonerate Jon, not convict him. Why would he keep that from her?

No wonder everyone in Hollywood had a therapist. Sarah needed to talk this through with someone—not Jon. He had already kept it from her. She needed some time to help her plan out what she was going to say to him. Sarah knew Jessica always believed the worst of men. It stemmed from her dad's infidelity, and she would tell Sarah to leave him before he could hurt her. Too late. She just wouldn't understand how hard it would be to leave him. Alli wouldn't be compassionate at all. She never really got that attached to guys.

Sarah knew that from past experience. She wouldn't be any help. But Megan, she would understand. Megan had been hopelessly in love with Chase in high school. Even though she caught him cheating on her, she couldn't seem to give him up. Megan could relate to this—on so many levels. So Sarah took out her phone and called Megan.

"Hey, girl, what's up?" Megan questioned.

Sarah hesitated for just a second and then admitted, "I just need to talk to someone. I'm feeling sorry for myself and need someone to pull me out of this pity party." She knew Megan would be straightforward and not just tell her what she wanted to hear.

"What's going on? Did Jon buy you another sports car and you donated it to charity behind his back? I'm sure if we put our heads together, we can come up with a good cover story. He'll never know," Megan chuckled.

"Very funny. You know Jon gives to charities all the time. We've attended six different events since January," Sarah proclaimed. "My problem isn't trying to lie to Jon—which is impossible, by the way. It's figuring out if he's been lying to me."

"Wow…what's he done?"

"I don't know if he's done anything, but he hasn't denied it either."

"A hint?"

"Mia. She's pregnant and—"

"So you think that Jon could be the baby daddy?" Megan interrupted.

"I don't know. He wants me to get to know her better, like we're going to need to learn to get along, and he acts different around her. There's a feeling I get when she's around, like she knows something I'm not privy to. I feel like I'm out of the loop."

"How does he act?"

"Like he's waiting for her to say something that he's going to have to explain. He's nervous, but yet smooth enough that no one else notices—except I notice. I know him so well that I can tell when he's anxious. When he worries his right eyebrow raises just a little higher than the left one. It's barely noticeable, and if he's holding my hand, he rubs his thumb over the top of my wrist, back and forth really slowly. It's totally unconscious. He doesn't realize he's doing it."

"So he's nervous? Maybe he's afraid she'll be her bitch-self and offend you. If you haven't noticed, he seems kind of protective of you."

"That's not all. He's never denied the baby is his."

"How dare *he*. It's his for sure, then."

"Don't mock me," Sarah said with desperation in her voice. She knew Megan was just trying to lighten her mood, but it didn't make her feel better.

"I'm just trying to look at it from all sides. Maybe he doesn't think he needs to deny it. Just because he hasn't told you that it's not his doesn't mean it is his."

"That's not all…I came across some pictures of him and his friends at a bar in December."

"So? We went out to the bar in December. That's not a crime. Did he lie to you about it?"

"A lie of omission. He told me about it, but he didn't tell me that Mia was there."

"Were they making out in the picture?"

"No. But she was there and his arm was around her. And I know what you're going to say. He and his friends always have their arms around someone. It's just who they are, but her? He should never put his arm around her."

"Did you ask him about it?"

"No, I just saw it before I called."

"So why are you talking to me and not him?" Megan's voice softened calmingly.

"Because what if I ask him," she said hesitantly, "and he admits the baby could be his. I don't think he would lie about it." She took a deep breath and continued, "I really don't want to hear that he cheated on me, especially with her."

"Plausible deniability. Happy are the clueless!" Megan announced. "You love him, right?"

"More than I thought was possible."

"So what would change if it was his baby?"

"You know I have trust issues. If he cheated, how could I ever trust him again?"

"Would you stop loving him?"

"No."

"You can learn to trust again. It just takes time," declared Megan.

"I don't know if...*I can.*"

"Mia having his baby won't change your feelings. People make mistakes. You're still going to love him. It's hard to let that go. Trust me, I know. If you can accept the fact that he's human and not perfect, then you can't let one little mistake ruin your life."

"It's not a little mistake."

"If you give him up, she wins. I saw how much she wants him. He loves you so much. Everyone can see it. The way his eyes follow you in a room—it's like he doesn't see anyone else. No one else exists. If the baby is his, it's probably because she drugged him or something in a last-ditch effort to entrap him. You said she's manipulative. She has to have access to drugs. Hell, there were two girls passing out ecstasy and some designer drug in the corner of the ladies' room at Club Priela when I was in there—right in front of the attendant. I'm sure she could get anything she wanted. Do you want Mia to win?"

"If it is his, she wins...even if I don't leave him. She wins because she'll always have her claws in him. They'll always share the child."

"She doesn't win Jon unless you leave him. You heard what Leslie said—that he's never felt for Mia what he feels for you, remember? He loves *you*, so she doesn't win."

"I lose either way."

"Damn it! Stop with the pity party. You still have Jon. That's more than most people have. He's human. Accept it or be unhappy for the rest of your life. It's your choice."

"You're right," Sarah whispered. "I know you're right. I hope it's not his...I know it takes two, but...I hate Mia."

Megan chuckled. "Forgiveness is easier when you have something to focus your hate on...trust me," Megan proclaimed. Her voice got softer on the phone and she added, "Yes...I *am* talking about you, and you're almost forgiven."

Sarah heard a man's voice and asked, "Are you talking to me or someone else?"

"Chase just walked in. Don't get all bent out of shape, Sarah. We're just friends," announced Megan. "We're just friends," she said again firmer.

Somehow Sarah didn't think Megan was talking to her anymore. "I better go," she paused, wishing Chase hadn't come in. "Be strong and don't let Chase back in," she reminded Megan.

"Talk to Jon and let me know, OK? Talk to you later, Sarah."

So her choices were either to leave Jon and live unhappily ever after or forgive him. Was Megan right? Could Mia have gotten pregnant on purpose to entrap Jon? She would have had to. Jon always wore a condom—always. He never slipped up. Sarah hadn't thought about that before. Either the baby wasn't Jon's, or Mia found a way to get around Jon's condom fixation. The cheating was another issue. Sarah never thought she could forgive a man for cheating—not since her high school boyfriend of two years cheated. Cheating was her deal-breaker. That was the one act she always held as unforgivable.

As she closed her laptop, she crushed her eyes together unable to accept that Jon might have cheated. She didn't think she could be happy without him. Could she let it go, just this one time? She hoped it never came down to forgiveness—that she was just overreacting, overthinking. Maybe it wasn't even an issue. Sarah wondered whether Mia's baby would even matter when she and Jon had their own baby. Maybe they *should* have a baby right away.

Chapter Eleven

Sarah

Jon was asleep by the time Sarah went to bed last night—just as Sarah had hoped—and he was up working out when she awoke. She wasn't really trying to avoid him. She just didn't know how to approach the subject of Mia's baby, and until she had that figured out, she thought she should stay clear of confrontations with him.

Sarah spent the morning, so far, putting the final touches on her school project—the screenplay she was writing to complete the credits she needed for graduation. Without her high school advanced placement and the college in the school's classes, she would have had another year to complete her double major. She was lucky. She had already finished a couple of smaller projects online that her faculty advisor requested, but this project was huge. She wasn't sure she would ever complete it. She had been working on the screenplay since January and was finally ready to submit it for grading. She had poured so much of herself into the manuscript that she really felt relieved it was finally done. She uploaded the file onto her professor's web page and smiled. Her faculty advisor had already approved its draft, so Sarah knew it would get her a passing grade. All she had to do now was wait for graduation.

She knew Liam was at the house. She had heard him come in. He had been at his parents' house, a few streets over, visiting with them in the morning.

The low growling of the drill caught Sarah's attention, and she peeked her head into the music room to see what was making the noise. Jon and Liam were chatting quietly in the music room. Liam was sitting on the mustard-colored sofa examining Jon's birthday present from Sarah—a vintage electric guitar that once belonged to Terence Halverson, Jon's favorite classic rocker. Jon had seen him once in concert when he was ten, and the musician had been Jon's favorite guitarist ever since. The guitar was the one Terence played at a famous show in New York City. Jon was affixing a hook to the wall with an electric drill. The specialized hook allowed him to display his prized guitar with the rest of his collection on the wall.

"Hey, Sarah," Liam greeted when he spotted her in the doorway. She smiled and waved. She was in a better mood than when she awoke. She felt like the weight of the last four years of school was no longer crushing her, and she couldn't wait to share the good news with her friends and family.

Jon paused from his work and looked up to meet her eyes. "Did you get it sent off?" he asked, but the smile on his face said he knew she did.

"Yep...no problems. I'm all done. I can't believe it. All I have to do is show up with my gown to the ceremony."

"I knew you could do it. We'll have to find some time to celebrate tonight." He raised his eyebrows, and she could read his mind about how he wanted to celebrate.

Liam cleared his throat loudly and glanced at Jon.

Jon's smile faded and he added, "Liam wants to talk to you about something." Sarah looked over to him questioningly.

"What's up with your friend Megan?" asked Liam.

She didn't understand the question. "Why? Do you want her phone number? She's not great at showing her emotions, but she really is a sweet person once you get to know her." The thought of Liam being interested in Megan thrilled her, and Megan would be so excited.

"Actually, she gave me her phone number," he admitted as he looked over at Jon with an apologetic expression.

What? Sarah looked at him with surprise. Megan hadn't said anything to her about Liam. Why would she keep that a secret?

"Have you called her?" Megan usually would have shared something like that. Sarah had heard the story about Jon lecturing his groomsmen months ago to stay away from Sarah's friends at the wedding. He said they were family, like Leslie, and off limits. It made sense now. That was why Megan and Liam had been acting so standoffish the morning after they met, at least in front of Jon.

"Well, you and Jon always play up how trustworthy your friends are and lately I haven't felt like I could trust anyone. So when we hit it off on her visit, I called her and confided in her about some family problems." He shook his head in frustration, like he regretted what he had done. "My eighteen-year-old brother has been doing drugs for about a year, designer stuff mostly, some coke. We tried to get him into treatment, but he wouldn't go. It's been getting pretty bad lately. He's been stealing from my parents, stealing from me. He literally lost his car. He couldn't remember where he parked it. My folks and I were planning an intervention for him. It was supposed to be on Tuesday, but over the weekend it came out in the press that we were planning it and he took off. Nobody knows where he is."

"Oh…that's awful, Liam."

"I told Megan about our plans. She could relate to my situation. She said she had some boyfriend in high school that was using and that she had planned an intervention for him. She told me she ended up giving him an ultimatum—drugs or her—and she had to leave him because he wouldn't stop using. She said it was one of the hardest things she'd ever done. Was that even true?"

"Yeah…that was true. She dated him for three years and ended up walking away from the relationship."

"I felt like I could trust her. I thought she was safe, but some of what I told her came out in the tabloids."

"She wouldn't sell you out. That's not her at all," declared Sarah.

"I don't know if it was her, but I didn't tell anyone other than her and Jon about the intervention, so it's one of the two," he accused, looking to Jon. "My parents haven't told a soul. They're way too embarrassed by the situation. Jon says you've been having some problems with the paparazzi. They seem to know your every move, right? I just thought our problems might be related, that's all."

"I really can't believe Megan would sell us out. Could someone have hacked your phone?" she asked. She couldn't fathom any of her friends going to the tabloids.

"I thought of that too, so I had mine checked out. It was clean," Liam confessed. "I just thought you should know."

"Maybe it's Jon's phone?" she suggested, struggling to make sense of this information.

"Jon and I talked at the house here, not on the phone. I guess your house could be bugged."

"I'm sure it wasn't Megan, but I'll talk to her."

"Sam is bringing a guy over in an hour or so to sweep the entire property for bugs and check out the computers and phones as well," interjected Jon. "I thought it would be best to get everything checked out before we accuse anyone of anything."

∽

Soon after Liam left, Sam and Craig showed up with a couple of casually dressed men pulling a small black suitcase. They opened the bag and pulled out a metal device about the size of a cell phone with a long cord that looked like a small microphone. Sarah didn't want to watch. She was torn. Part of her wanted them to find some sort of surveillance device in the house to exonerate her friend, so she could be comfortable trusting the ones she had always trusted in the past. The other part of her was worried that there was a surveillance device in the house and every conversation, every intimate moment between her and Jon, had been recorded. She couldn't decide which one was the worst scenario. Not really wanting to know the answer, Sarah grabbed her journal and headed for the courtyard, but before she reached the kitchen door, Sam stopped her.

"I need your computer and your cell phone. We're going to change the passwords on all your Internet accounts, too. We can't leave anything to chance, Sarah. We have to be very thorough, or we'll continue to have problems," lectured Sam.

Sarah retrieved her computer and handed it over with her phone, just as Jon entered the kitchen. "They haven't found anything so far," Jon admitted as he approached them. Sarah looked up, her face twisting with apprehension.

"Whatever happens, it will all work out. It always does," Jon soothed, wrapping his arm around her shoulder.

She rested her head against his chest and said, "I know. I just don't want to believe one of my friends could betray us like that. What if it is Megan, then what?"

Sam spoke up, "Sarah, if nothing pans out at the house, then we'll feed your friend some mild misinformation and see if it comes out in the press. If it does then we'll know it's her. If not, we'll keep searching."

"I don't want to think about it," Sarah admitted as she left Jon's side and walked out into her happy place, the courtyard. She looked up toward the sky with her eyes closed, letting the sun warm her face, then settled in a chair under the pergola and took a deep breath. She opened her journal, but couldn't concentrate enough to write a sentence. Instead she tapped the pen nervously against the page, strewing pockmarks across the paper. She didn't know how she would even approach a conversation with Megan, or any of her friends, about selling secrets. They had talked about it before, but she never considered any of them to be the culprits. They all had joked about it. It couldn't be any of them. There had to be some other explanation.

After about twenty minutes, Jon joined Sarah in the courtyard. He sat down next to her without a word. Pointing to her peppered journal page, he said, "That's not how dot to dot works." He gestured for her pen. She passed it to him with a serious air, and he drew an elaborate smiley face on the page connecting the dots. "See?" He raised an eyebrow and grinned back at her. Then he nudged his chair closer to hers and wrapped his arms around her.

He pulled her against his chest, and she asked, "They didn't find anything, did they?"

"No, but that doesn't mean the Internet accounts weren't hacked. We'll change all the account passwords before we accuse anyone of anything." He paused and took a deep breath. "But honestly, if she and Liam spoke on the phone, changing our passwords won't make a difference. We didn't even know they were talking to each other."

"Do you think she's leaked our wedding information to the paparazzi?" she earnestly asked, wanting to know Jon's honest opinion.

"We may just have to accept the facts. This kind of betrayal happens all the time," he acknowledged.

She nuzzled against him. She didn't like what he was saying, but she needed him. She couldn't deny it. Being next to him comforted her. Sarah peered under his arm toward the glass door of the kitchen. Sam and Craig were standing behind a man who had Sarah's laptop in front of him on the kitchen table. "Don't they need my passwords?" she questioned.

"I gave Sam most of them. The ones I knew." He smiled at her. "He may have to ask for a couple. He's going to pick the new ones so none of your friends can guess them and you can't give them out."

"How am I going to remember them?"

"Write them in here. No one who knows you would ever touch your journal," he said pointing to the book on the table.

She pulled back and looked at him with a pouty face. She didn't want to change her passwords. Had it really come to this? Keeping secrets from her best friends—the friends she had shared everything with her entire life. The same friends she confided in about Jon. "Then what? What happens now?" she whispered. She had just spoken to Megan about Mia's pregnancy. Would that come out in the tabloids next?

"I've been through this before. The faster we act on our suspicions, the better off we'll be. I think we need to confront Megan today. Whether she leaked it intentionally or not, it started with her. I can call her if you want."

"No, I want to do it."

It wasn't that she wanted to do it. She just didn't want Jon unleashing on Megan and Megan firing back at Jon. She spotted the large digital clock on the bar. "Is that time right?" she asked, though she knew it was. "I've got to go. I need some time to think about what to say. I'm going to Pilates class to clear my head." She had almost forgotten about her class. "There is a six-hour cancelation policy. The instructor is really strict. She likes her class full, and I just secured my spot. If I don't show up, I'll get knocked back onto the waiting list. I'll never get back into her class." She stood up and headed toward the kitchen door.

"Craig can go with you. I'm sure Sam can handle this on his own," he stated, as he followed her toward the house.

She opened the kitchen door and turned to him.

"No, Jon, I'm going by myself. I need to be alone. I never get to drive anymore. It's just Pilates class. No one knows who I am unless I'm with you." That was usually true, not always, but usually.

The group of men around the computer looked up in silent concern.

"Sarah, that was before…" Jon started to say, his voice slightly raised.

"I don't care. I'm going alone," she snapped as she walked swiftly through the kitchen. She needed some space. It wasn't just the leak and her total lack of privacy. It was the whole Mia pregnancy, too. She needed to think, away from Jon's network of spies.

She changed, pulled her hair into a ponytail on the back of her head, and trotted back down stairs in yoga pants, a tank top, and her bright green cross-trainers. She looked around the kitchen. Craig was missing, and it didn't take more than a beat to figure out Jon's plan. "You can call Craig and tell him not to follow me, please."

"Take your phone at least. It's ready." Jon handed her the phone and Sarah slipped it into her bag.

Why was he so calm? Normally he would put up more of a fight. Sarah wondered if he finally was seeing her point of view, giving her the space she needed. Security tagging along really wasn't the issue, but it was one she could control. She just had so much pressure on her—the wedding, the paparazzi, Mia, and now Megan. She needed the privacy to pull all her thoughts together.

"Bye." She kissed Jon on the cheek and left through the garage. As she settled into the bucket seat, she pushed the button to retract the roof. She was going to take full advantage of not having anyone to tell her what to do. When she reached the half-open gate, she smiled. Craig's blue car was on the other side driving in. She waved at him as she pulled out onto the street.

Outside the gate she cranked her music up and tried to clear her mind. Mia's smug face kept popping into her head, though. It must have been the Ashley Tyler song blabbering about betrayal through the car's speakers. *How fitting*, Sarah thought.

Sarah

By the time the Pilates class ended, most of Sarah's worries had been filed away—at least for the moment. She was completely centered now, and her "powerhouse" muscles burned more than she wanted to admit. She had struggled with flow today, and the instructor had come over several times trying to help her make her positions.

She rolled off her mat and reached for her bag. Pulling her towel out, she wiped her face and cringed when she heard the instructor call her name. She looked up to see Cami motioning for her to come to the front of the room. She had never asked to talk to her after class before.

"I'm sorry, Cami. I know I was off today. I'm usually better. I can do better. My head is just messed up, and I really needed to get centered. Please don't kick me out of your class. I wasn't a complete disaster by the end."

"I'm not going to kick you out of my class, Sarah. I just wanted you to know that there is a guy out in the hall asking for you."

Sarah stretched up onto her tiptoes to spy through the small window in the door. "Crap!" Craig sat on a bench in the hall.

"Let me guess. Your distraction?"

"Not really, but part of it." Sarah crinkled her face with embarrassment.

"You can go out through my office if you want to avoid him."

"It doesn't matter. He probably has LoJack on my car."

"Come on." Cami pulled Sarah into her office. "Let's go grab a juice. Maybe he'll give up if he finds the studio empty."

"Sounds good." Sarah smiled. *Serves him right*, she thought. She followed Cami out a back door to a sporty, silver Audi parked by the curb and got in the passenger side. "I can't believe he followed me," she muttered, gazing over her shoulder to make sure Craig wasn't out on the curb watching her leave. Why couldn't Jon just let her have an hour at Pilates alone? That's all she was asking for, just an hour.

"I don't think he's following us. What's his story anyway?" asked Cami, glancing in the rearview mirror.

"I don't really want to talk about it. I'm overreacting. It's nothing really. I just want to make him sweat a bit."

"I'm all for torturing men. They get what they deserve—I always say. So how do you like LA? You're new to town, aren't you?"

"Yes. I moved here from Minneapolis a few months ago. How did you know that?"

"Your motivation on your application. You wrote that you wanted a way to stay in shape because you used to jog, but you couldn't jog now that you were in Los Angeles."

Sarah sighed with relief. She was worried that she was in the car with one of Jon's stalker fans.

"And I saw it in the tabloids," Cami added.

Sarah dropped her head back against the seat. *Was she still so naive to think that people didn't know who she was?* "I was hoping you didn't know who I was. At least you're honest."

"Don't worry, Sarah. I used to date an A-list actor. The paparazzi followed us around and never gave us peace. I hate the press as much as you. If there was a plague that only infected paparazzi, I would risk my life to steal it from the CDC and plant it in their camp. They are such vultures. I would never sell you out."

"I'm just so used to everyone pretending around me, hoping to get close to Jon. It's exhausting."

"I'm not like that. What you see is what you get with me, and believe me, I have no interest in actors anymore. That ship has sailed. So why are you hiding from the bodyguard."

"Oh my god. Am I that transparent?" Sarah shook her head in disgust.

"You kind of are. The guy was too fit to be a bouncer, and I know he's not your boyfriend. I made an educated guess."

"I just get overwhelmed sometimes. I never have any privacy anymore. I used to do everything myself and now I'm never alone."

"It's hard to adjust to LA. And dealing with that celebrity garbage must be a nightmare. It took me two years of living here before I felt comfortable. I moved here from Michigan when I was eighteen—fresh out of high school. I wanted to be an actress, like every other teen that comes here. I struggled for a while. I even lived in my car for a month before I got a job at a fitness center. I ran auditions and picked up a second job waitressing so I could pay rent.

"My mom died when I was ten and by the time I was eighteen, my dad had started a new family, of which I was never really a member. I didn't want to ask him for help, and I'm not sure he would have helped me even if I had asked. He didn't put up much of a fight when I left."

"But you're so successful now. You own your own studio and the only way to get into one of the classes you teach is if someone dies or moves away. Everyone knows you're the best."

Cami laughed. "I don't know about that. But I have come a long way from living in my car." She pulled the Audi up to the curb and shifted it into park. "Have you ever been to Caboose Juice?"

Sarah shook her head.

"It will be your new favorite. Trust me—it's that good."

She followed Cami into the building, expecting to find a train theme inside. Instead, large colorful photos of fully clothed backsides of men, women, and children stared back at her from the walls. The butts ranged from obese to extremely fit, and the sight of them made Sarah chuckle.

"I know…very motivating, right?" said Cami. "And the juice is amazing. Everything is made fresh. Try the kale-strawberry flirt. It will give you tons of energy."

They ordered their juices and sat at a table away from the door. "So tell me how you became the owner of a Pilates studio."

"I really enjoyed my job at the fitness center and trained with a woman who really knew Pilates. She taught me much of what I know, and I took over for her when she retired. I really wanted to be an actress, though, so I kept going on auditions as well. Eventually, I got a big movie deal and I had to give up my classes."

The server brought their drinks, and Sarah took a long draw from her glass. "This is so good. You were totally right about this place becoming my favorite."

"I come here all the time," admitted Cami.

Sarah smiled. It felt so normal, being here with Cami. Even when her friends came, she didn't feel completely normal. Sitting here with Cami, having easy conversation without everyone staring at her, relaxed her. "Acting isn't as glamorous as everyone thinks, is it?"

"I didn't give up acting because I didn't like it. I loved acting, but I was in a car accident and it really messed me up. It left me with a concussion and a huge scar that runs all the way down my leg. After the accident I couldn't concentrate. I couldn't remember my lines. My short-term memory was permanently damaged, and the doctor's say I may never get it back. I can't act anymore. And the scar took away my confidence. It's hideous. I'm too self-conscious to parade around naked, like is expected of an actress. So after I got my settlement from the insurance company, I bought the studio."

"That's awful, but at least you have the studio."

"It's a totally different life than I expected, but I'm not living in my car."

"I understand the whole self-conscious thing about your scar. I was in a car accident in December and ended up having to have surgery. It was laparoscopic surgery but still left a couple of horrible scars. I went to the plastic surgeon to get the scars removed just this week, though, and I think I might be able to get back into a bikini again after everything heals. That's the plan anyway." Suddenly Sarah's scars seemed insignificant. At least she could cover them up easily. "Have you had a plastic surgeon look at your scar?"

"No. My insurance won't cover plastic surgery, and I don't have the money. It doesn't bother me at the studio, so what's the point? Is the accident why your boyfriend sent the bodyguard?"

"Part of it," Sarah admitted. "The crash was caused by a stalking paparazzo of sorts, but I think the constant surveillance is a result of me being abducted in January. The combination of the two really sent Jon over the edge. He's super protective of me."

"You don't seem traumatized at all by what happened to you. Why aren't you traumatized? I would never leave the house again."

"I was in a coma for the first one, and for the second I was drugged up and shoved into the trunk of a car. I don't remember either of them. I try not to think about them because I can't change what happened, so what's the point? It really wrecked Jon, though. It would kill him if anything ever happened to me."

"Sounds like your attitude is healthier than his and he needs to take a chill pill. He never lets you out of his sight, does he?" Cami pointed across the restaurant to a table, where Craig sat.

Sarah grunted when she saw him. "Damn it. How did he find me?"

"My guess is that the LoJack is on your phone, not your car. I think you need to have a talk with your famous boyfriend and tell him you want some freedom."

"I think you're right. Do you mind if we go?"

∽

By the time Sarah got home, she was seething. "Jon!" she called as she entered the house. "We need to talk."

Jon plopped down on the couch. "OK. Let's talk."

Sarah stood in front of him with her arms crossed. "You put LoJack on my phone."

"Technically it's not LoJack. It's just a stalker app."

"You admit it?"

"Yes, I admit it. It's for security. It's not because I don't trust you. It's on my phone, too."

"But you had Craig follow me after you agreed you wouldn't."

"I never agreed he wouldn't. I just told you to take your phone." He held his ground as he stared back at her. "Don't you get it? There are crazy people everywhere. I'm not going to let anyone hurt you again."

"Great. So you'll be able to find my dead carcass as long as the crazy doesn't throw my phone in the trash."

"Why would you say something like that? Now I have that visual in my head. That is never going to happen, Sarah, because you aren't going anywhere without a bodyguard ever again."

He practically yelled the last sentence, and it made Sarah want to walk out of the room, but the tormented look on Jon's face stopped her.

128

"I'm not trying to hurt you." She collapsed on the couch next to him, and he turned to face her.

"Then why would you get in a car with a stranger?"

"She's not a stranger. She's my Pilates instructor, and she owns the studio. She's not just a plastic bimbo off the street. I've been to her class three times, and she's very professional. She comes highly recommended. And she's the first person I've met in LA who was interested in me and not my relationship with you."

"Just bring one of the guys with you next time. That's all I'm saying."

"Whatever. I need a shower." She stood up and began walking toward the stairs without looking back.

Jon waited until she was in the shower before he came in to finish their conversation. He leaned against the door, watching her.

"Now I can't even take a shower by myself?"

"Sarah, this is our life. You have to accept it because it is not going away. Sam and the guys are not spying on you. They don't give me verbal reports about what you did at the Caboose Juice. They are just there to keep you safe and make our lives easier. You can ignore them and they will eventually blend into the scenery. I'll tell them that's what you want and that's what will happen."

She drenched her face under the spray of the shower and turned her back to Jon's gaze. She could tell he wasn't going to leave, so she rinsed her hair and then reached for her towel. When she stepped out, she looked into his blue eyes and knew she shouldn't be arguing about this. It's not that she cared that he knew she went for juice after her workout; it was that she needed time to be herself and not on show. She grabbed another towel off the shelf and wrapped it around her head.

"I'll try. I just need time alone sometimes."

"I know of this secluded resort we could go to—just you and me." He stood up and smiled at her.

"Tomorrow?"

His arms slid around her and he leaned down to kiss her. "If that's what you want."

His lips brushed hers, soft with just the perfect amount of pressure, and when his tongue slid into her mouth, he lifted her, wrapping her legs around him as he spun and pressed her against the door. He pulled back to stare into her eyes and asked, "Should I set it up? We can skip Cannes for all I care. Let's just skip the festival."

He looked so sincere, like he would give up anything just to make her happy.

"No. We can't skip Cannes. Maybe we can do it when we get back…But we can't because we have the wedding…and the *Demigod Forbidden* promotion… and then you start filming again. Maybe we can do it in January?"

"I love you, Sarah. We can find some time for ourselves before the wedding and then we have the entire honeymoon." His lips perused her neck as he tugged at the towel wrapped around her.

She stiffened and grabbed his hand to stop him.

"Are Sam and the guys coming on our honeymoon?"

He pulled away slightly and moved his hand back to her thigh. He pressed his forehead against hers and looked into her eyes. "You won't even know they're there, I promise."

She slid her legs to the floor and kissed his cheek. "I need to call Megan before it gets too late."

He shook his head as if he couldn't believe she just said that. He backed away, putting his hands up in defeat, and she slipped out the door to get dressed.

❧

Sarah found her way downstairs to make her first phone call just as Leslie was coming in the door. "Will you tell your cousin I want to be alone with him on our honeymoon?"

Leslie looked at her with a confused expression. "I'm not going on your honeymoon. Jon, what is she talking about?"

Jon followed Sarah down the stairs and grasped Sarah's shoulders, gently holding her in place as he explained. "She's worried we won't have any privacy because Sam and the guys are going to be there."

"Sam and I have both walked in on you—how many times now? I can't even keep track anymore. Honestly, there's nothing more for either of us to see. You two are like horny little rabbits."

"Not this week, and don't say 'little' when you're talking about me in that way," Jon muttered under his breath.

Sarah rewarded him with an elbow in the gut. "That must have been some other girl with Jon, not me, because Sam has never walked in on us." She remembered Leslie walking in on them once, but never Sam.

"He has, Sarah, and I think Raul has, too. Last week he came into the main house with the prettiest shade of blush on his face. He wouldn't tell me why, but he told me not to bug you two for at least thirty minutes."

"No." Sarah turned and hid her face against Jon's chest.

"It's OK, Sarah. It's a hazard of their job. They're used to it. They could have it much worse—we're fairly tame. Don't let it bother you. It doesn't bother me." Jon pulled her against him and began caressing her back.

"You're used to showing everyone your goods. You strip down to nothing in front of a hundred people. The people who have seen me naked are very limited and I'd like to keep it that way."

He smiled. "Me too. But it's not a big deal. It's not like they stand and watch. They'd be fired—they know that." Jon looked her in the eyes for several seconds and then whispered in her ear, "I love that you only want to show *me* your bits, and I will try harder to keep our private time private, OK? You're right. You are mine and mine alone."

They stood in silence several seconds until Leslie cleared her throat and said, "Still here. And I could use some help with the swag boxes in my car." She walked toward the door.

Jon pulled back. "Sarah has a call to make, but I can help you." He kissed the corner of Sarah's mouth as he turned to follow Leslie outside.

Chapter Thirteen

Sarah

Sarah called Jessica first to explore the possible alternative explanations for the leaks. Jessica would tell her what she needed to know before she accused Megan of anything. The conversations started out with a catch-up on the week's events. Jessica had gotten an A on her nursing clinical final and was excited because Jeff was taking her out for a fancy dinner on Saturday to celebrate. She was convinced the grade was just an excuse so Jeff could officially propose. He had bought the ring, but he hadn't showed it to her yet.

Alli wasn't seeing the teaching assistant anymore. He saw the kiss pictures and couldn't believe she would kiss someone else while they were dating. Alli explained to him that she didn't even know they were dating at the time, since they never discussed it. It was an ugly argument according to Alli. The good news was that every male at the university saw the kiss picture and now she had more attention than she wanted. Alli was eating it up and acting more like Megan than herself.

Then there was Megan. Chase had been at the rental house four times in the last week. Jessica was afraid Megan and Chase would be getting back together soon if they weren't already together. She was sure of it, and she wanted Sarah to talk to Megan about what was going on with Chase. Sarah was the only person Megan ever listened to when Chase was involved.

"You have to talk some sense into her and remind her about the hell he put her through," exclaimed Jessica. "I've tried, and it's like she doesn't even hear me."

"I'll do what I can," she said, knowing that the accusations she was going to make would probably just push Megan closer to Chase. She hesitated for a second. "Did you know Jon's friend Liam and Megan kept in touch? Liam mentioned it earlier today."

"Yeah…She texted me right after he called her the first time. She was so excited. It's too bad he doesn't live here. He's probably the one guy that would stand a chance against Chase."

"She never told me. Why would she keep that from me?"

"There was something about Jon not wanting his groomsmen hooking up with any of us, because he didn't want any awkwardness between the two groups. I'm surprised Liam let it slip. Megan said he felt really bad about it because Jon rarely asks for anything," Jessica stated. "Did everything turn out all right with his brother's intervention?"

"You knew about that?"

"Megan was all bent out of shape about it. I think she only told Alli and me, though. She just needed some people to hash it over with. She couldn't talk to Chase about it. She felt really bad for Liam. He and his brother used to be really close. I think him talking about it stirred up all the bad memories about Chase…not enough for her to stop seeing him though."

"Did she tell you over the phone or at the house?"

"I think it was on the phone. Why?"

"Don't…tell…*anyone*," she enunciated slowly and clearly. "Liam thinks

Megan leaked the story about his brother's intervention to the tabloids. No one but Megan and Jon knew about it and the story came out in the press over the weekend."

"She wouldn't do that. She likes Liam."

"That's what I said, but Jon and Liam are convinced it had to be her. If she told you over the phone, though, maybe her phone is bugged."

"Bugged? Really? Can you say delusions of grandeur?"

"Jess, today two guys swept my house and the courtyard for electronic listening devices while a third guy dissected my computer, Jon's computer, his iPad, my phone, Jon's phone. We changed all our Internet account passwords. I don't even know how to sign on and get my e-mail anymore. It took all afternoon. They swept everything so we could eliminate every other possibility for the leak besides Megan and now I'm supposed to talk to Megan to see if she'll admit to leaking it."

"You think that maybe it's her phone?" Jessica asked, her tone changed.

"I just can't accept the alternative. You guys are all I have. I've cut everyone else out of my life. I don't have any other friends, not anymore." Sarah was feeling a little sorry for herself. She chose Jon over her friends. She chose Jon over her freedom to be alone. She knew he was worth it, but she still mourned her losses, and Mia's pregnancy still hung unrevealed.

"Megan would never sell you out, Sarah. Talk to her. I'm sure it wasn't her. Chase left about a half hour ago. Give her a call…and don't forget to tell her to lose the ex-boy toy."

Sarah chuckled. Jessica always made her feel better.

"I'll do my best," she promised. She looked at her computer and the password list on the table trying to gather courage. She knew she and Jon couldn't go on like this any longer. Someone was leaking information to the press. The leaks had to stop. If it was one of her friends, she was sure it was unintentional.

She met Jon coming out of the office, and without a word he followed her into the living room. He was wearing a new pair of dark sunglasses, probably swag from the boxes in Leslie's car, and she couldn't see his icy blue eyes. She rolled her eyes at him as she sat down on the couch and tucked her legs up next to her. Then she took a deep breath and made the call.

"Oh, Sarah, I'm so glad you called. I need some advice." Megan continued without letting Sarah talk, "Chase was just here, and he wants to get back together. He told me that he never stopped loving me—that we could make it work now. What do I do with that?"

This was the last thing Sarah wanted to do—give dating advice to Megan. She wanted to talk about the leak. She wanted Megan to reassure her that she would never do anything to hurt her. She thought a few seconds and declared, "You know you can't get back together with him, right? I mean, you know that or you wouldn't be asking *me* for advice. He's never treated you well. Even before he started using drugs, he treated you like you were a second-class citizen."

Sarah got up off the couch and glanced at Jon, who was sitting next to her, reading. His dark Ray-Bans now perched on the top of his head. She knew he was sitting close so he could eavesdrop on her conversation. She strode into the kitchen as she listened to Megan's response.

"I know," Megan admitted slowly. "He just seems so different now though, like he's really trying. Did you know he bought me a new phone? It's totally loaded. It has everything. He just gave it to me as a gift—not to say he was sorry and he didn't expect anything in return. He never would have done something like that before. I really think he's sincere."

"He gave you a phone?" Sarah questioned. In her mind this explained everything. "I bet it *was* totally loaded," she stated cynically as she filled a glass with ice water.

"Wasn't it sweet? So un-Chase. I priced it out, and he had to have paid close to eight hundred for it. I told you he's changed." Megan didn't pick up on Sarah's tone.

"When did he give it to you?"

"Right after we got back from your place. He just showed up with the new one. It had a red bow on it…a bow." She emphasized the last part.

Sarah paused for a couple of seconds as she took a goblet out of the cupboard and filled it with water. She didn't know how to tell Megan that Chase hadn't changed. He was still the same scheming and insincere guy he had always been.

"You know…I talked to Liam today. He told me you two have been keeping in touch." She walked into the living room and slouched back into the spot she had vacated. She took a sip of her water before setting it on the large wooden tray on the ottoman in front of her.

"He told you? He's really great. I wish he lived here," Megan paused. "Is he mad at me?"

"Is there a reason why he should be mad at you?" Sarah asked.

"No, but I called him twice and he hasn't called me back. Did he say anything?"

"Megan, he thinks you leaked the story about his brother's intervention to the press. He only told you and Jon and it came out on Friday on *Celebrity Daily*. After the story broke, his brother disappeared."

"What? Did they find him?"

"No…He's still missing."

"Well…Jon's got a lot of explaining to do, because I didn't tell any vultures anything. You told Liam it wasn't me, right?"

"I tried, but…" Sarah stuttered. "They can't figure out how else it could have leaked."

"They? Jon believes it too? I would never do that. You know I would never—"

"You wouldn't, but the Chase I used to know would. That perfect phone he gave you probably has a stalker app that gives him access to everything you say and text and your e-mail."

Megan was silent for several seconds. "Damn him...Always the user. Why do I let him do this to me over and over? I can't believe I trusted him again. I let him back in my life and he does this to me? I bet Liam will never talk to me again."

"So you didn't tell anyone about Liam's brother?"

"No...just Jessica and Alli...and *they* wouldn't tell anyone. I can't believe I fell for his BS. I am *so* going to tell him where to shove his phone. I should have done it as soon as I noticed him downloading my contact list. I'm going to kill him."

Sarah was feeling bad that it was sort of her fault that Megan would be losing her dream phone, so she said, "Hey, Jon and I will replace it. Just tell us what you want and we'll send you a new one." She wanted to feel secure when she spoke to her friends again, and if Chase had given her the phone, he had to be the source of the leak. Sarah stretched her leg out and tapped her foot against Jon's knee. He was pretending to read, but she could tell he was listening to her conversation.

He smiled without looking up from his screenplay.

"That's OK. I still have my old phone. I'll just switch it back. It would be weird having you buy me a new one."

As Sarah wrapped up the call with Megan, she bubbled with relief. She felt so different from this afternoon. She had a complete mood transfusion in one phone call. Sarah noticed Jon staring and smiled hugely back at him. When she was off the phone, she climbed onto his lap and kissed him. Gaping at him, she stated, "I told you it wasn't her."

"I think we still need to test her after she gets the new phone, just to make sure...before we completely trust her again," Jon announced.

"You'll see...it wasn't her."

Jon smiled, his dimple pulling into his right cheek. "I hope you're right," he declared. "So what should we let slip?"

"I don't know…We could tell her we bought a puppy."

"How is that scandalous?"

"A purebred puppy from a breeder. She knows my parents would kill me. With my dad being a vet, and my parents volunteering at the animal shelter, they would disown me if we got a dog that wasn't a rescue dog. The story is benign enough that it won't hurt us, yet personal enough that the press would print it. It's not like we're actually going to adopt a purebred, so all we have to do is deny it. If it doesn't come out in the press—which it won't—then I'll just tell her we changed our mind or that the breeder took it back because there was a problem."

"When did you become such a good liar?"

"Should I become an actor?" she retorted sarcastically. She smiled wryly at him. "I'll tell her in person when we're home to rule out the phone, too."

"Don't get mad at me," he looked at her with knitted eyebrows and sternly continued, "but you really scared me today. I know you're planning to go shopping tomorrow, and I want to go with you."

"No," she said blatantly, glaring at him.

"But—"

"I won't get anything done if you come with me," she interrupted. "The paparazzi and fans will be all over us. I have a million places to go and it's the only day I can do it. There is no way you're coming."

"Then Raul is going with you." He glared her down. "It's not like it's a new request…same old-same old. I just want you to accept it, without argument."

"He'll die of boredom."

"I'll make sure I write a nice note to his mother then," Jon declared with a chuckle. "If you're sure you don't want me to come shopping with you, then I'm having lunch with Isaac."

"You just wanted to get out of lunch with Isaac, didn't you?" She bumped shoulders with Jon.

"No…I want to go to lunch with him. If we don't get lunch together tomorrow, he'll sit next to me on the plane and talk business the entire flight to France."

"Oh, joy!"

"Isaac is a good guy. He built my career from nothing. He works hard."

"I thought you were the one standing in the ice-cold fake rain for five days to get ten minutes of *Demigod Forbidden* footage last fall?"

He smiled his crooked smile and added, "He's a great negotiator. Trust me. He earns his money. He and Remi have kept me on the right track for five years. He got us backdoor rights on *The Demigod*, and that's unheard of in the industry for an unknown actor. He's worth his weight in gold." He stretched his arm around her shoulder, and Sarah could tell his mood shifted slightly. "I just want to keep you safe. I'm not asking much."

"OK…Raul and I will go shopping," she said comically in a Valley voice.

Chapter Fourteen

Jonathan

"Everything is ready for Sarah's surprise, right?" Jon asked as he and Leslie left the restaurant after lunch with Isaac and headed to his car. Leslie pointed out the guy in a hoodie lurking by the curb near the valet desk, and they held silent. Jon handed a generous tip to the driver and climbed into the car.

As she buckled her seatbelt, Leslie stated, "The furniture came last week. The fridge is stocked. Everything is ready, and she's going to love it. What girl wouldn't die to get a house for her college graduation?"

"Are you sure it's not a dump?" He started the engine and turned down the radio. There's got to be something wrong with it. A million five can barely buy a guesthouse here. The neighborhood looked OK?"

"You saw the video I took. It's gorgeous. Houses are just cheaper there. All the inspections came out perfect. It's almost identical to that one she loved in Calabasas, and it's only about a thousand square feet smaller. She's going to flip out when she sees it."

"The security is all set up?"

"It came with the house. I don't think you can even see the house from the road. It's completely gated, like Fort Knox." She paused as she studied his face. "Did you tell Sarah about the stalker yet?"

Jon closed his eyes as he shook his head. He'd been meaning to tell Sarah. He had. He just hadn't found the right moment. He knew that after he told her, she would wish he hadn't. That was what Mia had said anyway. And she was probably right. Mia had dealt with her share of stalkers. The last one was some college dropout who began showing up at every event Mia was scheduled to attend. The stalker was so adamant that he convinced a security guard to let him into a private party where he continued to pretend he was Mia's date. When she confronted him, he acted as if she was the one who was crazy. She filed a restraining order against him, but it didn't seem to stop him from showing his face in the periphery every once in a while.

Jon's stalkers, like Mia's, had always been crazed fans. They fantasized about relationships or hookups. No one had ever wanted to hurt him before. And the last letter had mentioned Sarah. He would die if anything ever happened to her. The stalker could be anywhere, and Jon needed to make sure she was safe wherever she went. Sam would make sure the house's security was stringent, but not until they arrived. "You showed Sam the video of the security room?"

"Yes. He said it was first-rate. He's already got it interfacing with the computer system here."

"Good." Maybe he could keep Sarah innocent about the stalker a little longer. He wouldn't have to tell her until after they got back home from Cannes. She could enjoy her graduation unspoiled by the threats. The new house would give them a place to hide close to Sarah's parents.

Her parents knew about the house. Sarah's mom was the one who told him about the property. The six thousand square foot house, nestled in the middle of a thirty-acre wooded lot had sat empty for two years. Built by some corporate CEO and abandoned before it was ever used, the house had all kinds of amenities that he and Sarah had talked about—a pool, a media room, an exercise room, plenty of bedrooms, and a big chef's kitchen. Those were all the amenities they searched for in the LA area. The only amenity they hadn't discussed was being close to her parents. Owning a house twenty minutes from them didn't mean that they would be raising their children in Minnesota, and Jon had tried to stress that point with Sarah's folks. But they probably heard what they wanted to hear, because they seemed a lot more accepting of Jon after the purchase was made.

He and Sarah would still need a house in LA, but this house gave them options, and it was so cheap he couldn't pass it up. Nondisclosure agreements had been signed by all parties involved with the sale and set up of the house, except Sarah's parents of course, but they promised to keep quiet about it. Jon had talked to Sarah's father, David, a few days ago, and he had assured him that no one in the family besides he and Kate, Sarah's mother, knew about the house. They had gone and looked at the property while Leslie was in town and absolutely loved it.

Jon was excited to finally have their approval about something, anything. Sarah's parents hadn't been thrilled when Sarah agreed to move to LA with him after the engagement, and they had been pretty vocal about how selfish they thought he was for asking Sarah to do so. It was selfish of him, and he knew it. He didn't mean to steal their daughter, and Jon understood why they were angry. It was a loss to them seeing their only daughter moving across the country. Loss, he understood. Sarah had been furious at them for their reaction at first, but he recognized their thinking and couldn't be angry at them. He had learned the stages quickly after Jack's accident and waited as they made their way through their loss. He knew it was time to make amends with them, and the house was part of that amends. It was mostly for Sarah and Jon, but a tiny bit of the purchase was to help heal the relationship with Sarah's parents.

The plan was for Jon and Sarah to spend one night at her parent's house. Then the next day they would go for a drive and stumble upon the property by accident. Sam would punch in the code at the gate while Jon distracted Sarah, and they would pull up at the new house. Jon would make a big deal about asking the owners if they were willing to sell. He would ring the doorbell over and over, convincing Sarah that he was going to buy it for her. Once Sarah was completely mortified by Jon's actions, he would hand her the key and congratulate her on completing her degree. It would be before her actual graduation. But since they had to leave for France shortly after the ceremony, it would have to be early.

Sarah

Sarah couldn't wait to get back to Minnesota. There was something about the place she grew up that would always be home. Besides, her mom and dad seemed to be coming to terms with her decision to leave school and live with Jonathan in California. They had stopped nagging her about it anyway. Her dad hadn't even mentioned school the last time she talked to him. She would be seeing them tomorrow, but today she needed to make sure her parents had gotten the e-mail she sent them with her and Jon's itinerary. She wanted to be able to spend as much time as she could with her family and friends, but her mom seemed to be scheduling get-togethers without telling her about them. Jeff had sent her a warning text about it. Sarah pulled out her phone and dialed her mother's cell.

"Hi, sweetie. Is Jon treating you right?"

"Of course." She lay down on the bed next to her open suitcase, which was almost packed. "I just wanted to let you know I e-mailed the final flight information to you. You don't mind picking us up at the airport?"

"No. We can't wait to see you. You've been away so long."

"It's just so much easier and quicker for you to get us than waiting for a car. Are you sure it won't be too much trouble for us to stay at the house?"

"No trouble at all, honey."

"Sam will be with us, too."

"I know. Your father was going to make Jonathan stay in Jeff's room so Sam could have the guest room, but I convinced him he was being ridiculous.

'Not under my roof,'" she said, capturing the essence of Sarah's father's voice. "He knows you don't have separate bedrooms in Los Angeles. Anyway, it took some convincing, but he came around. You and Jon will be in your old room, and Sam will be in the guest room."

"Thanks, Mom. I'm glad you understand. Jeff said you had planned a graduation party with all the aunts and uncles. You know we are leaving the day of graduation, right?"

"Yes. I got your e-mail. I was planning the party for the Sunday before."

"OK. Is there anything else happening at home?" Sarah wanted to know if Jeff had proposed to Jessica yet. Jessica thought he was going to propose over the weekend, but she hadn't mentioned it again, and Sarah was afraid to ask her. She thought about asking Jeff, but her mom would know.

"The studio has been crazy busy. We're booked out into the fall already. It seems like every weekend is packed through the summer. I don't know when your father and I will make it up to the lake this year."

Sarah sat up on the bed and started fiddling with the contents in her suitcase. "The dock is in, right?" She and Jon planned on trying to recreate last summer's getaway at the cabin while they were home, and she didn't want to have everyone up at the same time to put the dock and boatlift in the water.

"Jeff and your dad got it in a couple of weeks ago. If you and Jon want to use it while you're here, it's ready."

"We're planning on it. I miss you guys so much. Is there any good news you haven't told me?"

"I don't know if I would call it good news, but Hilary Anderson is pregnant again. It won't interfere with your wedding, though. She's not due until November. Your father says she wants to take three months off from the clinic again, so the holidays may be a bit hectic. Your father will be putting in all kinds of hours."

"It seems like Dr. Anderson just had a baby."

"She must want them spaced close together. Her daughter is a year old already," said her mom.

It wasn't exactly what Sarah wanted to talk about, but she thought it could be useful. "Mom, how would you feel if Jon and I had a baby?"

"Oh, Sarah. You're not pregnant, are you?"

Sarah couldn't tell if her mom was excited or disappointed. "No. I'm not pregnant."

"Oh thank god. They keep coming out with the breaking news of your pregnancy in the tabloids, so I've been waiting to see if it was true."

"You should know me better than that, and why didn't you just ask me?"

"I know how much you hate the tabloids. I didn't want to admit I was buying them."

"You can look at the rags, just don't believe them. So…what would you think if we had kids right away?"

"How do *you* feel about it, Sarah? You sound apprehensive."

"I don't know. Jon wants kids, like yesterday. He wants to be a young dad."

"Well, don't let him bully you into doing something you're not ready for. You shouldn't have a baby until *you* are ready. You have enough issues adjusting to Hollywood, and having a new marriage will be hard enough. You don't need to add more stress to the equation."

"He's not bullying me. I just know what he wants, and I don't know what I want."

"I don't think you should start a new marriage with the stress of a pregnancy, honey. You think he's overprotective of you now? Just wait until you're carrying his child. You'll have a bodyguard with you whenever you leave the house."

Sarah didn't have the strength to tell her mom that was already happening, so she stayed silent. *How much more restrictive would her life become?* She hadn't thought of that.

146

"And who's going to take care of the child while he's off traveling the world filming and promoting his movies? You. You're the one who will be stuck at home. You can't drag a child around the world with you."

"I know actors that do, Mom. There are tons of them."

"Well…It's not good for them. Children need consistency. They need to know what to expect when they wake up in the morning. I think you need to take some time to be a couple before you add a child into the mix. You're still young. You have another fifteen years to have kids. You shouldn't rush into anything."

"I don't know what I want. I know I want kids, but I never thought I would be having them before I turned twenty-five. I mean, I was planning on going to grad school. I never thought I wouldn't have to go, but now I'm just confused about what to do."

"You can still go to grad school. They have schools in California."

"I know, but I'm not sure that's what I want to do anymore. There are so many opportunities that weren't there a year ago. I never thought I could write a screenplay. I really enjoyed it. I can write whatever I want. There are endless possibilities. And after I've chucked out a few scripts, maybe one will be good enough to make into a movie. I hated the internship at the web magazine last summer. There is no follow-through with a job like that, no plot. I wasn't allowed to be creative. If I'm working from home, it makes sense to start our family. But how do I know if I'm ready?"

"You're never ready until it happens, but I think you should wait, Sarah. It's your body. You're the one that decides when to have children. Jon doesn't get to make this decision."

"We're going to make the decision together, Mom."

"Don't let him pressure you into doing something you're not ready for."

"You just said I'll never be ready until it happens."

"Just weigh your options. I'm going to make an appointment with Dr.

Johana for you when you're home. I'm sure she'll get you in. I just did a complete layout for her high school senior. Most people schedule portraits in the fall and she needed a rush job before graduation. She owes me. You can talk to her, and she can tell you what your choices are, OK?"

"OK. Thanks. I'll see you tomorrow. Mom?" She had almost forgotten.

"Yes."

"Did Jeff propose yet?"

"Not yet."

"Thanks. I just had to know. Bye."

Sarah ended the call frustrated with her brother's lack of initiative, excited about using the cabin, and a little relieved about the doctor's appointment. It would be good to see a doctor. Jon probably *was* sick of using condoms. And she would definitely feel better about getting pregnant if she knew her body was working properly. Her mom was right. She needed to know all her options.

Chapter Fifteen

Jonathan

Jonathan's jaw twitched. The thought of going to the airport tensed his whole body. It was hard to avoid the paparazzi at LAX, and with someone feeding them his schedule, he was sure the press would be waiting for them. He knew it was time they stopped flying on commercial flights, but flying privately made him feel like a sellout. He flew in chartered jets all the time. They would be taking one to Cannes, but when it was just Sarah and him, it seemed wasteful to take up an entire plane.

The paparazzi weren't the only problem with going to LAX. The stalker was still out there and a bigger threat than any guy with a camera. Jon knew they needed to be extra vigilant in such a chaotic place as the airport, especially since he had no idea who the stalker was.

He loaded the bags into the back of Leslie's car and headed back into the house. All they were waiting for was Sarah. She had been bouncing around the house all morning, and he could tell she was excited. She hadn't been home since December, and he knew she missed her parents. Sarah's parent's house would surely be stalked. The fans had been outside the house a couple of times when it was rumored he was in town. That was why Sarah's graduation present was so perfect.

He grinned at Sarah as she came down the stairs. She had her carry-on bag draped over her shoulder and her phone in her hand. The earbuds were already plugged in, staged to ignore the paparazzi. Her hair was pulled back in a ponytail on the back of her head. She had on jeans, and one of his vintage T-shirts tied at her waist with a lavender-colored hoodie. She looked so relaxed compared to how he was feeling. She was glowing. "You ready?" he asked.

"I can't wait. My mom is making lasagna for dinner. She knows how much you love it," she announced with a huge grin.

"That sounds great," he smiled at her enthusiasm. He wasn't going to crush her good mood by reminding her about their problems, so he did his best to suppress his nerves. He hadn't told her about the stalker yet. And, honestly, part of him didn't want to tell her. It was like telling her about Santa Claus. Once it was shared, innocence was lost. She would never be able to walk into a crowd without fear. He poked his head around the corner into the kitchen. "We're ready in here. Should we head out?" he asked, making eye contact with Sam. Sam returned a skeptical look. "She's got her music ready. What more can we do?" questioned Jon.

Sarah called from the living room, "I'm not wearing my earbuds at the airport. It's for the plane. I want to hear what those idiots have to say. I'm so over being afraid of them."

Facing Sam and Leslie, Jon silently mouthed a curse word. He didn't want Sarah to know he was struggling with this. He didn't want her to deal with the paparazzi at all. He looked over his shoulder at Sarah. Her expression was resolute. "Let's go," he announced with a glance back at Sam. Then they piled into the car—Sam and Leslie in the front, and Sarah and Jon in the backseat.

Jon didn't mention the paparazzi the entire ride until they approached the loading zone at the airport, where ten to fifteen stood watching, expecting, on the sidewalk. "Well, the welcome party is here, right on time," Jon said cynically.

Cameras perked as Sam and Jon popped out of the car before the car stopped. Sarah followed quickly. They didn't want to give the vultures time to react. Leslie had released the trunk before they reached the curb. She stayed in the car, while the other three grabbed luggage and headed for the baggage check-in. The flashes exploded—*click, click, click, click, click, click, click,* and they didn't stop. Jon glanced at Sam as the luggage handler slapped the long, thin tags around each bag's handle. Large black letters publicized MSP on the labels as the handler stacked the luggage.

"You were right. We should have sent the luggage over early," Jon acknowledged. As the group took off toward the gate, the crowd of press swarmed around them, like wet sand filling in a hole when the tide comes in.

"What are your plans in Minnesota? Getting married?" a photographer questioned. *Click, click, click, click*—the cameras kept spluttering. "Jon. Jon. Over here, Jon. Jon."

"So where are you staying? Spending some time with your in-laws?" asked a baby-faced guy with blond hair. He couldn't have been more than eighteen. A shout came from the crowd as the photographers pushed and scrambled to stay in front of Jon, "It's the wedding weekend. Tell us about the wedding. Where are you going for the honeymoon?"

The three remained stone-faced as the group walked quickly toward the security gate. Sam spoke up every once in a while when the paparazzi got too close. "Back up," he commanded in his deep voice. "Out of the way." He put his arm out in front of Jon and Sarah, trying to keep the vultures back, but there were so many pushing to get the perfect shot that they were being overwhelmed. Sam kept changing the direction of their path just to throw the paparazzi off, like a border collie redirecting a flock of sheep. It bought Sarah and Jon just a little space, while the press scurried to catch back up to them.

They were about halfway to the security station when two guys appeared in front of them. They whispered to each other as they strategically maneuvered their way in next to Sarah. They hovered around her, trying to question her. "It's pretty intimidating thinking about Mia getting her claws in your fiancé, isn't it? She's clearly fighting for him. I bet you would do just about anything to keep him, wouldn't you?" the baby-faced blond asked, while the other paparazzo videotaped. Sam stepped in front of Sarah and wrapped his arm back around like a cage to keep the encroaching guy back, clearing a path through the dense press herd.

Sarah squeezed closer to Jon, as a third guy with greasy dark hair in a ponytail stepped up and started to verbally attack Jon. The guy wore a backward Lakers hat and held a camera a foot in front of his chest, glancing at the LCD screen occasionally as he walked. "I heard Mia Thompson wants you back, Jon. I wouldn't mind tapping that, if you know what I mean. I bet your fiancé would do a threesome. She looks like the type. I can record it for you if you need someone." Click, click, click, click.

Jon was losing his composure. His body stiffened and his fist clenched. He wanted so badly to knock the guy to the floor and pummel his face. The guy in front of Sarah was quiet now and had started taking pictures, so Sam moved in front of Jon with the same caging technique he had used to protect Sarah.

The ponytail guy backed off, but now the blond guy moved in on Sarah again, walking backward in front of her. He didn't bother to watch where he was going and kept bumping into other vultures as he rambled. "Is that why you went to the plastic surgeon...to keep your man? Steve over there thinks those are fake," he said, pointing to her chest. "But I told him if someone paid for them, they would make them bigger." He reached out, cupped Sarah's right breast, and squeezed. "I'm right. They're—"

He didn't get to finish his sentence. Jon's fist connected with the guy's jaw with a loud crack. The force of it penetrated every bone in his body. Jon shrugged off his bag and guitar. He needed to hurt this guy. The roar of the blood in his ears silenced the noise around him. The world moved in slow motion. The guy hadn't even hit the ground yet, but he was on his way. Jon sucked in a breath when he felt giant hands grip his shoulders. He turned readying to take another one out. It was Sam. The grip tightened holding him in place. He could see Sam's lips moving but couldn't hear him. He looked over to Sarah, her appalled expression morphed to concern. He looked down at his hand, the pain finally breaking through the thunder in his ears. Blood oozed from a tear in his skin and dripped down between his fingers making them stick together. He lifted his T-shirt, wiping off the blood the best he could.

Jon looked around—the fog in his head starting to clear. The mass had stopped moving. The paparazzi stood silent, except the incessant clicking of the cameras. Sam asked, "Are you all right?" His grasp loosening on Jon's shoulders as his eyes inspected Jon's hand.

Jon nodded and wrapped his pained arm around Sarah's shoulder.

"Good. As much as I would like to join you in bloodying these asses, I don't think it is the best idea."

As Sam backed away, Jon spotted the culprit sprawled on the floor, his legs twisted in an awkward position. With his hand caressing his jaw, the baby-faced guy called to his friend, "Did you get it, Steve?" Then he looked to Jonathan. "You're going to pay, pretty boy. That punch is going to cost you big time. Someone call the cops." He winced as he spoke, and Jon found some satisfaction in his pain.

"You all saw that, right? I was just taking pictures and he goes all postal on me."

"I don't know what made him go off. You were just taking pictures," said the young skinny guy, whose name was apparently Steve. He looked like he was about fifteen, but his voice was deep like a man's.

That was the last straw. Jon was going to take him out, too. He looked at Sam, hoping for the OK, but Sam shook his head. He was on the phone, probably with airport police.

"If you ever touch my wife again, you'll be dealing with more than just a broken jaw, asshole," exclaimed Jon. Jeers rose from the crowd. Click, click, click, click, click…

"It's probably best if you let me handle this, Jon." Sam spoke calmly and concisely

Jon nodded, glaring at the guy on the ground for several seconds. Then he looked over to Sarah. Her arms were wrapped protectively across her chest. She was wearing the dark glasses that used to be on top of her head and had pulled the hood of her sweatshirt up as well. Jon's heart sank. He wished he could keep her safe, but he knew he couldn't. He apologized with his eyes and asked, "Are you all right?"

"I'm fine. He deserved it," she declared, but he could tell she was traumatized. Jon pulled her to him, burying his now-swelling hand in her hair, and kissed her head.

"Should I call Remi?" she whispered. She waited for his nod before she took out her phone to make the call.

Jon glanced around the mob. Several of the paparazzi were uploading their photos onto their phones. *What was taking the police so long?* The security checkpoint sat a mere forty feet away.

Four airport police officers finally surrounded the group, and the person in charge started making demands. "I want all cameras turned off and on the ground," he boomed in a loud voice. "If I find any that are still recording, I will confiscate them and the owner will be arrested for disrupting Homeland Security." His experience showed in his actions. But still most of the photographers slipped away into the crowd and moved to a position on the edge to escape quickly if needed as he spoke. "Who can tell me what's going on?" the officer in charge asked.

The guy on the ground declared, "He broke my jaw. I want him arrested." He dramatically cupped his jaw and cried out in pain.

Sam spoke up, "Lieutenant," he glanced at the man's nametag, "Menendez. We were just trying to catch our flight when that idiot there—"

"He punched me and broke my jaw. We have it on tape," the baby-faced blond interrupted, pointing to the camera in Sam's grasp.

Sam continued, "When that guy there blocked our way and started fondling my client's breast." He gestured toward Sarah as he handed the camera to the officer.

"You're not the one that punched him? It was Mr. Williams?" Officer Menendez questioned. He recognized Jon and seemed to be untangling the incident in his head. "All right, you recorded it?" he questioned the videographer. The officer quickly ran through the footage as he stood in front of the group. Then the lieutenant gathered the licenses of the five people involved. He handed the camera and licenses to another officer and stated, "File this in evidence and copy the IDs." He looked around the growing crowd and announced, "Let's take this somewhere private. Anyone with a video camera needs to follow officer Rodrigues." He pointed to the officer to his right. "Except you." He pointed at the guy whose camera he possessed.

"Come on, Officer. I want my camera back. I was just filming. I wasn't even involved," claimed the mousy-looking man-boy.

"You're coming with me and the rest of the video stars. If I have your license, you're mine." All of the press had vaporized into the bustling airport by this point, even the guy with the Lakers hat, so Officer Rodrigues was left with no one to lead.

"Can we deal with this later? We're going to miss our flight," questioned Sam, though Jon could tell the question was just a formality. They all knew the answer.

"We have to fill out an incident report, and if either of you wants to press charges, we have to take statements. I'm sure he doesn't realize that if he pushes the charges, he will end up with a sexual assault conviction on his record. He obviously hasn't thought it through." He paused and turned to Jon, "I know it's not fair these guys can harass you and you just have to let them, but consider yourself lucky."

"Lucky?" Jon questioned.

The lieutenant glanced over at the paparazzo who was still holding his jaw and stated loudly enough so he could hear, "Yeah…you got to deck the idiot… By the looks of the swelling, you broke his jaw, and it's not going to cost you a thing. No one wants a sexual assault record."

"Well, I don't feel very lucky," uttered Sarah. "I want to punch him. At the very least…I should get to kick him in the groin." She turned and glared at the guy.

"You're right, Sarah, you should get to…I'll hold his arms," Sam said, pinning the guy with a very menacing death stare.

"Officer, did you hear that? They're threatening me," whined the blond.

"So the hundred-and-ten-pound woman is intimidating you now? What about when you groped her, were you scared of her then?" asked Jon. He so wanted to pound him back to the ground.

The lieutenant tapped his ID badge on the access pad next to the door's entrance. The LED turned from red to green and he pulled open the steel-and-glass door. He held it for the group to enter and then led them to a clutch of rooms, motioning for the videographer to sit in the first room and the baby-faced blond in the second. The lieutenant closed the doors to the rooms and addressed Jon in a soft voice, "It looks pretty cut and dried, so I'm going to try to convince this guy not to press charges. If he refuses you're probably going to want your lawyer here." Then he yelled down the hallway to the front desk, "Bloom, bring the guy in room two an ice pack and get someone from the team to come look at his jaw."

"Sure thing, boss," returned from the end of the hall.

He looked down at Jon's hand and asked, "How's your hand?"

"Fine." Jon was lying. He didn't want this to take any longer than it had to. A trip to the ER would add three hours.

The officer turned back to the group and said, "Rodrigues here can get you coffee, if you like. You can make yourselves comfortable in there," pointing to a larger room about halfway down the hall, "and I will see if I can make this go away."

Jon followed Sam and Sarah into the room and closed the door. "The officer must be pretty confident the guy won't press charges or we would be in separate rooms at least until the statements are given," said Sam. "But...he *is* going to press charges. There would be no other reason for doing this. He wants the publicity."

"I shouldn't have hit him. I know I shouldn't have hit him," Jon lamented as he gingerly wrapped his arms around Sarah's waist from behind her. He snuggled next to her ear and whispered, "I'm sorry."

He wasn't apologizing for the actual act of hitting the guy, but for being in the situation in the first place. He could see her emotions catch in her throat as she swallowed hard. She leaned her head back against his shoulder and touched her cheek against him, holding it there as if to gather strength. "I love you, Jonathan Williams...Don't ever be sorry. It was the right thing to do."

"It did feel good. I never get to hit anyone. I've got the 'just missing' down for filming, but it felt really good to make contact on his smug little face. I wanted to disfigure him. It was a setup though. He didn't even pull away." He squeezed her tighter. He hated being manipulated by the paparazzi.

"Is Remi coming?" he asked. He definitely needed her to do her PR magic.

"Yes...She's calling the lawyer," Sarah answered. "I should probably call my parents and let them know we missed our flight." She turned around and met Jon's eyes. *Oh god. What would they think?* He slowly released his hold on her, wishing Sarah didn't need to make the call.

"So now what do we do?" Jonathan asked Sam as he watched Sarah cross to the other side of the room.

"Let's just hope he doesn't press charges." Sam paused. "But he will. Then they'll arrest you for battery. You'll be booked at the Pacific station— fingerprints, mug shots. They'll take your statement and release you on bail. It will take hours. A court date will be set, but by then the charges will probably be dropped. You were clearly defending Sarah. Judges hate the paparazzi wasting court time. We'll need to press the sexual assault charges, though—to emphasize the defense."

Jon glanced up and met Sarah's eyes briefly. Though he had worked to mend his relationship with her parents, he worried what they would say. *Jon needs to protect you better.* What was he thinking going to the airport with only one security guard?" He could practically hear her father's voice.

Sarah sat on the edge of a metal desk turning her back to him. Her arms wrapped tightly around her as she began the call.

"Hi, Dad." Sarah almost sounded perky, but Jon knew it was an act. She paused.

"Actually, Dad…we missed the flight. I was just calling to let you know we won't be in until tomorrow." She paused again.

Sarah's voice started to reverberate, and Jon could tell she was crying. "One of the paparazzi at the airport grabbed me and Jon punched him. Now we're just trying to figure out if the guy is going to press charges."

Another pause. Jon looked down at his hand. The pink skin across his knuckles stretched taught, but there wasn't any fresh blood.

"Dad, there wasn't anything we could do. There were at least thirty of them. Jon was just defending me. He didn't mean to break the guy's jaw."

"It's broken, isn't it?" Sam asked, nodding toward Jon's hand.

"Probably. I'm not dealing with it right now, though." He had broken his hand once before on the set of a movie. It felt about the same.

"I've got to go," said Sarah. "I'll call later when we know more. And tell Mom not to worry."

Jon watched Sarah shove her phone into her purse and wipe her eyes with her middle finger before turning.

"So…what's the plan?" she asked, her arms still wrapped tightly around her chest. Her eyes were red and her makeup blotchy. She had definitely been crying. Jon's hand touched the small of her back and pulled her in. As his fingers grasped her, the tension in his muscles released just a little. She rested her head against his shoulder and took a deep breath, as if she found comfort in his arms as well.

"When they arrest me, Sam's going to take you to a hotel, because we can't go back to the house if we want to avoid the press. I'll meet you there after I make bail and then we'll figure out our new flight plans."

She nodded with understanding. She looked so sad.

"If you have anything in your pockets, you should have Sarah put it in her bag. It will just make it easier if they arrest you, but keep a credit card and your license, when you get it back," declared Sam.

So Jon emptied the change from his pocket out onto the round table they were standing next to and handed Sarah his phone and wallet, minus a credit card. "Don't go rifling through my bag. Your graduation present is in there and I haven't wrapped it."

She smiled, and he ran his fingers through the end of her ponytail. *How could he let this happen?*

Just then the lieutenant entered the room with a younger officer behind him. The lieutenant scratched his head with a look of frustration. He handed back their licenses and stated, "Well, the good news is…the videographer admitted to conspiracy. He admitted he and Mr. Davis planned to provoke you into violence to get a good shot. He wouldn't admit that he knew Davis was going to molest your wife, but just admitting to the conspiracy is a misdemeanor."

Jon looked at Sam, and Sam added, "Five hundred-dollar fine. It's nothing compared to what they can make."

"I think they had a third accomplice with a camera that got the actual sellable material. That's how it usually works. The footage these two clowns got won't get picked up. Since we have the film on record, you can sue anyone who buys it because they deliberately provoked you. The bad news is that Mr. Davis won't drop the battery charges and wants his lawyer before giving his statement. This means I'm going to have to arrest you. It's just a formality," he announced. "You have the right to remain silent. Anything you say can and will be used against you in a court of law. You have the right to meet with an attorney and have one present during questioning. If you are unable to afford an attorney, one will be appointed for you. Do you understand these rights as I have presented them to you?"

"Yes," said Jonathan feeling exasperated. He dug his hands into his jacket pockets and looked toward Sam. He knew his mug shot would get plastered all over the news. Eventually, the story would fade and no one would remember why he was arrested. All they would remember is that he was.

The officer led them into the hallway to a large open room with metal desks. Several of the desks were occupied with officers, and most of them were on the phone with papers in front of them. "Mr. Williams, you can call your lawyer from the phone at that desk over there, if you haven't already called him, and have him meet you at the pacific station." The lieutenant pointed to his right at an open desk. "We'll be heading there next." Jon walked toward the desk and sat down. He called Remi's cell.

"Jon, are you all right? I saw the footage. It's already up. Sarah said the guy grabbed her? That part wasn't visible in what I saw, but...is she OK?" Remi quick-fired questions without waiting for his response in her usual excited fashion.

"As good as she can be," he answered. "They're arresting me and taking me over to the pacific station. Did you get a hold of Jim's office?"

"Yep. He can meet us there within the hour. You and I have some talking to do when I get there, though."

Just what he needed: another person lecturing him. "Get in line, Remi." There was nothing he could do now to change what was already done. "I'll see you in a bit." He hung up the phone and spotted Sarah standing at the edge of the room.

"Sam is giving his statement," announced Sarah. "I guess...I'm next." Her eyes motioned to the room they were in previously.

"Are you going to be all right? I don't want you to do anything you're not comfortable with. I can probably stay while you give your statement. Just for moral support," he stated, touching her shoulder.

She shook her head. "I can handle it. Let's just get it done, so we can get out of here."

Jon looked to the lieutenant and said, "So…"

The lieutenant motioned for him to stand next to him. "Do you have any needles or illicit drugs on your person?" Jon shook his head. "Please pull out the contents of your pockets and set them on this table before Officer Stewart pats you down."

"I don't have anything but these in my pocket," answered Jon as he set his license and credit card on the table.

As the younger officer put on gloves and patted down every surface of Jon's body, he knew Sarah could see the humiliation on his face. He hardened his expression, pretending it was just a roll he was playing. He didn't want her to worry. When the officer was finished patting him down, he physically checked Jon's pockets himself and asked Jon to remove his shoes. After the search the lieutenant called out to the officers in the open bureau and announced they would be leaving. The officers on the phones ended their calls one by one and rose to join Jon's exit entourage. "We'll be exiting to an unmarked car out front. There is already press out there, but we have it under control," announced the lieutenant.

"Where's the groper? He *is* getting arrested too?" questioned Jon.

"He left for the ER about twenty minutes ago, but he'll meet us at the station once he's had medical attention. He is definitely under arrest, and so is his accomplice."

Satisfied with this, Jon said, "I'm ready." He looked over his shoulder at Sarah, needing to know if she would be OK. The corners of her lips turned up, but he could tell it was a mask put on to placate him. This was not fair to her. She didn't deserve any of this. He mouthed, "Stay safe," as the mass of officers with him in the middle started to move down the hallway.

Chapter Sixteen

Sarah

Sarah watched as the mob disappeared down the hall. She looked around the almost-empty office and sat down in the chair outside the room Sam was in. She hoped Jon would be all right. He looked so humiliated. She couldn't believe this was happening to them. She and Jon had put up with so much already.

Who was leaking their personal information? It was as if the mob had been waiting specifically for them. When they got out of the car, she swore someone said, "It's them." Could Chase still be stalking Megan's phone? She knew how manipulative he could be. He probably convinced Megan it wasn't him, and he's still using her phone to track her messages. She would have to be more careful about the information she shared with her friends—all of them. None of them thought anything wrong of sharing information between each other. They had all been so close that it was never a problem before. She turned her phone over in her hand. The thought of calling one of her friends sickened her. She could listen to music and try to drown out the day's events, but she wasn't really in the mood to crank up the tunes. She opened her screen, clicked on the Mad Moronic Monkeys app, and started to build a tower of monkeys. Twenty minutes later when she had moved up five levels, Sam came out of the room laughing and joking with the female officer who was taking his statement.

"That just doesn't sound like Marshall. I can't even imagine him doing that," the officer chuckled.

"You'll have to ask him about the hula skirt. He was quite the dancer ten years ago," declared Sam. He looked puzzled at Sarah and asked, "They left you out here by yourself?" He scowled at the officer. "Let's get your statement done and get out of here. You head in and tell her what happened. I'll call Craig and Raul. I won't go anywhere," he stated.

Sarah went into the room with the officer and left Sam to make the calls. The female officer started by asking her if she would like something to drink. Sarah wasn't thirsty, but the officer brought her a glass of water anyway. She told Sarah they could go as slowly as she needed. She didn't want Sarah to feel uncomfortable. The officer was acting like Sarah had been raped. It surprised her. She had been more upset about Jon getting arrested and about missing their flight than the guy touching her. Truthfully it wasn't the first time some guy she didn't know groped her. She'd gone to enough parties in high school and college to know what to expect from the male species when it's drunk. She was always able to brush it off before, but the more she talked to the officer, the angrier and more disgraced she felt. This guy wasn't drunk. She couldn't believe he could fondle her and then broadcast movies of it all over the world for everyone to see. *How dare he?*

Sarah shared every detail she remembered with the officer. She told the woman how the paparazzo weaseled his way between her and Sam, and how she felt like he had targeted her because it would get the biggest reaction from Jon. She told her about the sneer on the man's face as he reached for her breast. Sarah clinically described exactly how he touched her and the proud expression on his face as he looked toward his buddy afterward. She described how she feared the guy was reaching for her other breast when Jon hit him. She didn't understand why her eyes were welling up, but they were. By the time she finished her statement, the tears were dripping down her face.

The officer handed her a box of tissue and placed her hand on Sarah's shoulder. "I'm not usually like this," Sarah admitted as she blotted under her eyes.

"It's understandable, Sarah. This was not your fault. You need to put the blame on Mr. Davis. He's the one who planned this and did this to you. You were just trying to get to your flight," proclaimed the officer. "You're going to be just fine," she smiled encouragingly at Sarah with the most sincere eyes and touched her shoulder again. Then she stood up and crossed the room to open the door. "Mr. Kachinske, we're done in here. Is your ride on its way?"

"Yes. They should be here soon. I told them to pull into the bay," Sam admitted. Sarah spotted him in the doorway and quickly wiped her eyes again.

Sam looked at her questioningly. "Sarah, are you all right?"

"Don't tell Jon," she pleaded as she tucked the tissue into her jean pocket. "It wasn't his fault and he would just blame himself."

"I won't mention it to him. He'll be fine, you know. He's been dealing with the paparazzi a long time," Sam stated.

She looked up at him with a forced smile and proclaimed, "I know." She took a fresh tissue from the box and wiped her eyes one last time.

"Sarah, I'm sorry I couldn't protect you today."

"There were just too many of them, Sam. No one could."

"So, you won't mind if Craig and Raul come to Minnesota with us?"

She shook her head. "Not after today." She looked up to see Raul's face staring back at her from the doorway. His black hair was buzzed short on the sides with longer curls in an oval shape on the top of his head, like he had forgotten to remove his hat during his haircut.

"Rough day?" Raul asked in his "I'm here to cheer you up" voice.

Sarah nodded and stood up. The men carried all the bags out to the car. As Sarah waited, she found just the right song on her phone for her parade past the press.

But by the time the men returned, Sarah was crying again. She didn't know what was wrong with her. Sam snagged a box of Kleenex off a desk as they passed it and handed it to her.

"I won't let this happen again, Sarah. I am so sorry," Sam apologized again. "Let's wait a few minutes before we head out into the crowd."

He grabbed the baseball cap off Craig's buzzed head and placed it onto Sarah's head. She pulled it down, shielding her eyes.

"Ready?" asked Sam before, he, Craig, Raul, and several police officers escorted Sarah to the waiting car.

Chapter Seventeen

Jonathan

At the police station, the blond female officer pressed Jonathan's fingers against the scanner pads, her touch gentle but firm. One by one, she turned them to get a complete print until all the spots were filled on the computer screen. When she was satisfied with the fingerprints, the officer smiled at Jonathan and said, "Stay right here. I'm going to get you some ice for your hand. You're obviously in pain."

As she made her way out of the room, Jon could hear the two male officers at the back of the room gossiping loudly about the blonde, who had beat out three other female officers for the right to process him. "Akins picked the number that was closest to the one chosen by the lieutenant," one announced.

She glared at the chatty men as she returned with an ice pack. She cracked the pack to activate it and folded it over Jonathan's knuckles. "Is that better?"

Jon nodded. It did help.

"Mug shots are up next," she added. "Just in case you want to fix your hat hair."

"Thanks for the warning," Jonathan stated with a smile. He removed his hat and bent over, shaking his hair out. He ran his fingers through, trying to erase a day's worth of hat-wearing from his hair's memory. He thought about all the other celebrity mug shots he had seen. He didn't want to look as disheveled as them. If his picture was going to be on the cover of every magazine, at least he would look decent. "Do I look all right?" he asked in a self-deprecating tone.

"Yes…You look great," she answered with a dreamy smile. Then she handed him a numbered card and showed him the X to stand on. He handed her the ice pack as he walked to his mark, then rotated to face her and held the numbered card against his chest.

"Higher," she called. Jon inched it up closer to his chin. "Right there," Officer Akins commanded. Jon held still for the flash. "Turn to your right, please," her voice called again. He turned. "Now, to your left." He turned the other direction. When the pictures were done, the officer stated, "Your lawyer is waiting for you, Mr. Williams."

"Call me Jon." He smiled at her and winked. "And thanks for the ice pack." He knew how to work his charm to get others to like him, and right now he could use all the support he could muster.

She smiled and led him through a hallway into a small room. In the room sat his publicist, with her dark, razor-cut hair sticking out in all directions, and Jim Nordstrom, celebrity lawyer, in a gray Armani sports coat. They greeted each other and sat down. Jon had known Liam's dad since high school and had worked with Jim many times before on little problems. Jim knew celebrity issues—one of the best lawyers in Hollywood.

"Did they treat you all right, Jon?" asked Remi. Jon nodded as the officer closed the door. "How many times have I told you not to punch them," she scolded mockingly, and Jon chuckled. It was Remi's catchphrase. Whenever he left on a trip, she would always tell him, "Don't punch any paparazzi."

"He grabbed Sarah's breast. I'm supposed to let that go?" Jon questioned, looking at Jim as he leaned forward in his chair and wrapped his knuckles with the ice pack again.

"Is she all right?" asked Remi with sincere concern.

"She was crying…but I think she's OK."

"Remi showed me the footage," stated Jim.

"I had everyone in the office scour for it, but couldn't find the right angle—nothing showing the guy grabbing Sarah," disclosed Remi.

"We'll keep looking. More is bound to come out. Why don't you just tell me in your words what happened, and I will let you know if you need to change any wording for your statement," Jim declared. So Jon told them the entire story, and Mr. Nordstrom advised him on a few better word choices to emphasize Jon's desperate need to stop the man. "That's just the right amount of emotion. Show them how frustrated you were, but don't let it choke you up, or it could come off as forced or acting."

Jon ran through his story again with the changes. He felt like he was learning lines for a film and the director had just tweaked the script.

Obviously feeling confident, Jon had his lines down after the third run-through, Remi asked, "So you and Sarah did or did not tie the knot? Did you elope?"

"No. Why?" He pulled the ice pack off his hand, letting his knuckles warm.

"So, why did you call her your wife? It was clearly articulated on the video," announced Remi.

"I did?" He tried to remember. "I don't know. I wasn't thinking. It was instinct. I think of her as my wife." Jon began to rage again, thinking about the baby-faced guy. "Seriously, who the hell does he think he is, touching her like that? I should have pummeled him unrecognizable," he roared.

"I think you made your point, Jon. There is no need to disfigure him in front of the cameras," declared Remi. "It wouldn't be good for your image, but now the press mistakenly thinks you're married."

Jim spoke up, "So…I can tell Tyren that there is still a chance she can get you to sign a prenup? She asked me to remind you as I walked out of the office today." Tyren, a lawyer in Jim's firm, specialized in marital contracts. She was also a close friend of Jon's agent, and Jon knew Isaac was the one pushing to get a prenuptial signed.

"I've already told her I don't want one," he clarified. "Isaac is just going to have to let it go." He was getting frustrated with Isaac and really didn't have the patience to talk about this right now.

"Prenups are smart, Jon. A man with your means needs one," Jim added.

"Jim, can we just address today's problems. How is me calling Sarah my wife going to affect anything?"

"Well…you calling her your wife made this little story about a celebrity punching a paparazzo into a worldwide phenomenon. The phones have been buzzing off the hook at the office. Everyone wants to know about the wedding. The media is mad that you got married and they didn't get any pictures. Teenage girls are crying on YouTube. The press is determined to find out every missed detail. You're already trending at number four on the Internet. By ten you'll be number one," bragged Remi.

"So, I just made our paparazzi problem even worse?" he exclaimed. "They're going to be hunting us more than ever. Damn it. I can't seem to do anything right lately. Sarah's going to miss her graduation because of me."

"We'll figure something out. We have to get you out of here first. Are you ready to give your statement?" Remi asked.

"Yeah…I'm ready, but…what do we do about the molester? We can't just let him get away with that. Even if the charges are dropped against me, I want that guy to fry," Jon declared. He knew if the guy didn't get prosecuted, then someone else might try the same act or even worse.

"You're right. We have to jump on that right away. I've already worked up some ideas on it. We will definitely file both a criminal and a civil assault claim, and I think we should file for a restraining order on both of them. It will help

170

emphasize how dangerous you think they are and help you with your case. I'll make sure we have everything needed."

"I don't want them anywhere near us," Jon affirmed, shaking his head. "Let's get this over with."

Jim got up and opened the door. Officer Akins was standing outside, and Jim motioned they were ready. The officer entered holding a laptop and a camera on a tripod. She stated that she would be recording the statement while he spoke. Jim took out a similar recording device and set it on the table next to the officer's. Jon gave his statement. Then the officer asked additional questions, and Jon answered them the best he could. When they were finished, the officer stated, "You need to wait here until the bail hearing. I'll be outside the door if you need me."

"I'll go see what I can do to expedite this," stated Jim as he got up and left the room.

Three hours later, Jon had finally been released and he and Sam were pulling into the parking lot of the hotel where Sarah was hiding out. They had stopped to pick up some burgers and drinks. Remi would meet them in about an hour. She wanted to talk some more about damage control.

Sarah was lying on her stomach on the king-sized bed, looking adorable when Jon stepped into the hotel room. Her hair was wet, as if she had showered, and she was wearing one of his vintage T-shirts. She looked so sweet that it just added to his guilt about the day. Her face lit up when he entered the room, and she rose to greet him. Jon wrapped his arms around her and pressed his body to hers. She was his release. She'd always been. She was the reason he got up in the morning, the reason he lived. Ever since he'd met her, she'd been that for him. He didn't want her to be tortured by his life, but he couldn't live without her.

Craig peeked through the doorway of the adjoining room, just as a bomb blast detonated on the TV in the other room. Jon lifted his chin to acknowledge Craig, and he disappeared back behind the doorway.

He kissed the top of Sarah's head. "Are you all right?"

"Yes, they took really good care of me." She smiled up at him. "Leslie booked a private flight tomorrow. She figured we had enough of the paparazzi. It's at six thirty in the morning. It'll be just the five of us on the plane."

She finally understood. Security was essential.

Her expression turned even more serious. "I talked to your mom. She said there were at least thirty reporters outside the gate an hour ago. Vans with telescoping satellite dishes were lined up all the way down the street."

"This isn't really fair to her either," he asserted.

"We probably can't stay at my parents' house or the rental," Sarah declared. "I suppose we could find a hotel like this and do the vampire thing again."

"Slipping in and out only at night," Jon finished her thought and she nodded. "I've got it covered. We'll have a place to stay." He wanted to bring her comfort without giving away the surprise. He looked her up and down, realizing the shirt she wore came from his bag. He had pictures of the house in his carry-on. "You didn't go snooping through my carry-on, did you?"

"No…Craig got it out for me. You don't mind, do you? The one I was wearing just felt gross after what happened today," she declared.

"I don't mind." Pushing his good hand through her hair, he stared into her eyes. "We better grab some food before it gets cold."

Remi arrived as they were finishing up their burgers. She looked around the room with raised eyebrows. Jon knew what she was thinking and moved quickly to cut her off. "We're in hiding. We're comfortable enough."

Remi turned to Sarah. "Are you all right?" She placed her hand on Sarah's shoulder.

Sarah's lips tightened into a straight line and she admitted, "I'll be all right. Thanks for asking."

Jon noted the difference between what Remi asked and Sarah's answer and frowned. He never wanted her to have to deal with this crap. Protecting her from his life seemed impossible.

Chapter Eighteen

Sarah

The next evening in Minnesota, Sarah stared at Jon in disbelief. His smile reached his gorgeous blue eyes, his expression indicating the complete honesty of what he'd just told her.

"It can't be. Who does that?"

"I did." He licked his perfect lips, and she wanted to kiss him. She pushed up onto her tiptoes, and he bent to meet her mouth.

"I can't believe it. It's beautiful."

"Well, let's take a look before you get too excited." He opened the door, and she followed him inside.

"When did you do this?"

"I signed the papers a month ago. It came partially furnished, but everything is new."

Jon led her up the grand staircase near the entryway straight to the master bedroom. She could hear his sigh of relief as if it was the most important room in the house. He wrapped his arms around her, and she smiled. Her hands pushed under his shirt, and she ran her fingers slowly across his hard abdomen.

Sarah couldn't fathom how he had kept it from her. Who gives someone a *house* for graduation? The idea of it was overwhelming. Jon didn't spend money needlessly, but this was the most lavish gift ever. And the way he tricked her into believing they were trespassing on a complete stranger's property was just mean. He deserved reciprocation. She tackled him to the floor, overpowering him with her tickling fingers. He was so easy to take down when he wasn't expecting her attack.

"Stop, Sarah. Stop. Please, stop," Jon pleaded as he writhed on the floor beneath her. She knew he could easily buck her off, but he never would for fear of hurting her. She paused and let him suck in a breath. She didn't want to be cruel.

"How did you pull this off?" *Damn*. She shouldn't have given him a chance to regroup. Now both her hands were locked in Jon's good hand. His other hand, the one with the brace, caressed her cheek. They had stopped by the vet clinic and x-rayed Jonathan's punching hand on the way to her parent's house. The digital film showed a small fracture in a bone just above Jon's smallest knuckle. Sarah's dad had wrapped it at the clinic and before dinner an orthopedist friend of David's fitted the hand with a plastic air brace. He didn't even charge for the house call or the brace.

"You're ruthless," Jon panted. "Your parents and Leslie helped. Why don't you attack them?"

That explained it. Her parents were in on the surprise. She couldn't understand why they suggested she and Jon go for a drive after dinner. Now it all made sense.

"You like it, right?"

"I love it. Thank you."

He smiled but looked at her warily, as if he was unsure if he could let her hands go or not.

"I won't tickle you anymore," she promised. "Now, anyway."

He sat up, using only his core muscles, no hands, and Sarah ended up on his lap straddling him. When he finally let go of her hands, he kissed her forehead and said, "You worked hard to get your degree. Congratulations, beautiful."

She just couldn't believe he could be so underhanded. How could he have kept all this from her? She kissed him on the lips and clambered back onto her feet. "I want to see the rest." She smiled, straightening her skirt.

The house was gorgeous. With the wood floors throughout the main level, a huge chef's kitchen, and a ginormous outdoor kitchen on the patio, how could Sarah not love it? The wooded property gave them more privacy than Sarah thought possible. The long drive curved around for a half mile from the security gate to the point where the house came into view. It was flawless. The house was really similar to the one in Calabasas that she fell in love with. The only problem with that house was the property. The land was broken up in a strange way and seemed too small for the house and multiple guesthouses. It was also ridiculously expensive.

This house was perfect. Maybe a bit big for the two of them, but there was room for visitors and security. Besides the five bedrooms on the main side of the house, there was a whole separate wing for the security team with bedrooms and living quarters. The idea that this was her graduation present stunned her.

"This is unbelievable," she said as she stared at the fifteen-foot-tall screen in the movie-viewing room. "It's ours, right?"

"Every inch." He kissed her hair and then finished showing her the rest of the house, even though he admitted it was the first time *he* had seen it.

"I have to show you this." He grabbed her hand and led her to a small basketball court in the basement. "It's for the winter, when it's too cold for the kids to play outside." He smiled at her, raising one eyebrow.

"You just wanted somewhere to shoot hoops." She completely shrugged off the kids comment.

"It can be used for other activities." He took out his phone, turned on an Adele song, and set the phone on the floor before pulling her into his arms. He smiled as his casted hand fell to the small of her back. He placed one of her hands on his shoulder and clasped the other with his. "See? It doubles as a dance floor."

Wow, he was a good dancer. He led her around the floor with confident ease, and Sarah felt like a princess in his arms. When the song ended, he spun her around and dipped her almost to the floor before bringing her in for a kiss. He righted her and grasped her hips, pulling her in. His dimple crooned on his face as her hands cupped his strong jaw and pulled him down for another taste.

"We could always put a lock on the door and turn it into a sex dungeon." He looked at her questioningly, but she knew he was joking.

"Sure. Whatever you want."

"OK. I'll order what we need." And they both laughed.

⌒

Jon and Sarah slept in the next morning and then lounged around their new house until almost noon. Kate had scheduled the appointment for Sarah at Dr. Johanna's office at 2:00 p.m., and Sarah mulled over the questions she wanted to cover in the appointment. Raul would go with her, while Jon stayed back at the house. He needed to connect with both his lawyer and Remi to deal with the fallout from his arrest.

Sarah stared at the phone vibrating on the bed. It was the third time Mia had called since Jon got in the shower. She knew she needed to just walk away. It was almost time for her to leave anyway. She kept telling herself that, but for some reason she couldn't walk away. She sat on the bed next to Jon's phone watching Mia's face stare up at her. Why was she torturing herself? She flipped it over so at least she wouldn't have to look at her. A deep breath pushed from her lungs when it finally stopped moving, and she collapsed on the bed wondering about the reason for the call. When the phone went off a fourth time, Sarah reached her limit. She swiped her finger across the screen and said, "Hello."

"Where's Jonathan."

"He's in the shower trying to catch his breath. We just spent the last three hours making love. And oh, it was *so* good. The best he's ever had, he said. But I thought I should give him a chance to recuperate before we start it all again." *Oh my god!* Sarah couldn't believe how long and sharp her talons could grow when Mia was involved.

"Whatever. You know Jonathan and I have a special bond. You will never know him as well as I do. You may think he shares everything with you, but he doesn't. There is no way you can understand the complexity of his life. I bet you don't even know why he won't let you leave the house without a security detail."

"He loves me, that's why."

"So he still hasn't told you about the stalker and the threatening letters, huh? Makes me wonder what else he's not telling you."

"What do you want, Mia?" Sarah was pissed. It made sense. There was a stalker. That's why Jon wouldn't let her be alone. Why would Jon keep that from her? And why would he tell Mia?

"Just tell Jonathan I need to talk to him. And I want to talk in person."

"About what?"

"He'll know. I wouldn't want to share something with you that he doesn't want you to know. Just give him the message."

The line disconnected before Sarah could suck in a breath. *How could Jon have dated that woman?* Sarah sank into her pillow wondering what Mia would be telling Jon and why he had confided in Mia about a stalker and not her. What else hadn't Jon told her? Sarah wondered if the connection Mia was talking about was the baby. If he hadn't fathered her baby, then what could she possibly have over him.

She shook her head trying to clear the thought of Jon sleeping with Mia. Was she just trying to shove a wedge between her and Jon? Jon wouldn't. That woman was evil. She would just have to figure out how to deal with her, ignore Mia's words, and focus on her own life. She peeked her head into the bathroom where Jon was showering.

"I've got to get to my appointment. I'm taking Raul and the rental car. I shouldn't be too long."

"Stay safe. I love you, beautiful."

"Back at ya," she said, closing the door. He loved her. *Would that be enough?*

⌒

Later that afternoon after her appointment, Sarah, Jon, and Sam held a lengthy discussion about what kind of information should be shared with Sarah's friends and family. There had been another leak—a rumor that Jon had purchased a property in Minnesota where they would be holding the wedding. It was misinformation because the wedding wasn't going to be in Minnesota. The article didn't mention any specifics on the house's location and the sale of a house was public record, but Sarah felt as if Jon and Sam were blaming her friends for the leak.

"I think Mia is the one selling our information to the paparazzi."

Jon laughed loud and hardy. Then his eyes met Sarah's and the smile almost wiped from his face. "You're *serious?*"

"You said it yourself. She's the master of press manipulation."

"Sarah." He said it like he was talking to a small child. "Mia is not the one feeding the press. What would her motivation be?"

"To drive me crazy." Her tone said "duh," and she brushed off the scowl he sent her. "She obviously wants you back and thinks the press will push me away."

"Will it?" His expression changed and he studied her face.

"No. Of course not," she said, meeting his gaze. *Way to kick him when he's down.* He already hated what the paparazzi did to her. She could feel Jon's regret in every touch since the airport incident.

He looked over to Sam and then back to Sarah. "Mia didn't even know we were flying out that day. It wasn't her."

"She seems to know more than me. She told me about the stalker and the threatening letters. Why didn't you?" She didn't mean to bring that up right now, but it just came out. She planned to bring it up on the flight home or after graduation. It was too soon after the airport attack to be arguing. It didn't feel right. She didn't want to talk about Mia. She didn't want to think about what Jon was keeping from her.

"Sarah, just tell me what is going on in that head of yours. When did you talk to Mia?"

"She called when you were in the shower this morning. She wants you to talk to her in person."

Jon rolled his eyes and Sarah didn't know if it was in reaction to Mia wanting to see him or her bringing up the stalker. He gently grasped her cheeks in both hands and looked her square in the eye, the glacial color revealing the sincerity.

"Sarah, I didn't want you to have to worry about it."

"Why did you tell her? You told her. And you kept it from me."

His hands slid from her face to her shoulders and hung there as he searched for his words. "Sam and the guys have it under control. You have so much you are dealing with already—the wedding, graduation, Cannes, the paparazzi. Knowing someone is watching you, following you, it can mess you up, make you paranoid."

"Why her, Jon?" Sarah's voice sounded small, like she felt. His eyes were no longer meeting hers, strained with emotion.

"I told her because I knew she would understand. She's been in the same situation before. Maybe not with threatening notes, but she's had several stalkers and I wanted her advice."

The gap between them seemed to grow, though neither of them moved. "Tell me about the notes. I want to know everything."

Jon looked around the room and then tugged her toward the couch. He pulled her onto his lap, making her straddle his legs. He touched his forehead to hers and took a deep breath.

"I was going to tell you about them after Cannes. I just didn't want you worrying. I wanted us to be able to enjoy our trip." He looked at her with sad eyes as he pulled back to see her face. "We've gotten three notes. Each arrived via courier. A different one each time, without a traceable return address. Couriers come in and out of Isaac's office all the time, so the receptionist didn't noticed until it was too late to question the person. But Isaac changed the procedure so the receptionist opens packages as soon as they are delivered now so it won't happen again."

"How do you know that they're from the same person?" Sarah sat back and pulled her hair out of her face so she could see him better. His eyes burned with concern, but his face showed no visible emotion.

"They are worded similarly with pictures off the Internet embedded in a typed page—not quite as creepy as words being cut out and pasted, but still pretty menacing."

"I want to see them."

Jon glanced at Sam and shifted his body just a little, visibly uncomfortable with her request. "We don't have them here."

"Can I see them when we get home?"

"We gave them to the FBI."

She scrambled to her feet and stood in front of him with her arms crossed. "You contacted the FBI and you didn't think that I needed to know?"

"There is nothing we can do about it, so why put it in the front row?"

She didn't know what to say. She shook her head thinking about all the times he had insisted she bring a bodyguard and she thought he was being overzealous. "It would have been easier if you had just told me. It makes me wonder what else you're keeping from me."

Jon glanced in her direction, looking past her into the room beyond, shaking his head. "I'm not..." His injured fist hit the top of his thigh, hard, and he grimaced. "The first one came right after you moved in, before we even announced the engagement. There have been two since then. Each played on my fears and guilt. The first one talked about how I should have died instead of Jack. It went into great detail about his death and how it was my fault. The last one was about you and said that soon I would know the pain of loss, as if I didn't live with it every day."

"What did the one about me say?" She needed to know everything.

"It basically said I was a giant piece of shit and I would ruin your life, like I'd ruined everyone else's around me or something worse would happen."

"Like what?"

"It didn't say." He held out his injured hand and flexed his fingers in and out several times as if feeling pain could change what the note said.

"Does it hurt?" she asked.

He shook his head. "Just a little stiff."

"Don't let this crazy get to you. There are always going to be haters. It is impossible to please everyone. What did the FBI say?" She sat on the couch next to him, watching his face.

"They are going to work up a profile with what they have. We're supposed to meet with them when we get back from Cannes."

"I'm going to be included in that meeting," Sarah demanded.

"OK," he agreed.

She grasped his hand, bringing it to her lips as gently as she could. "We can't let this stalker rule our life. So we live with security 24/7. I wouldn't have minded so much if you had just told me." She kissed his hand again, running her finger slowly over his fingertips. "You need to be honest with me. That's all I ask." She paused. "And tell me before you tell Mia…anything and everything." She wasn't asking that he not talk to Mia again or that he give up his friendship with her. She just wanted to know more than her. That wasn't too much to ask.

He slid his good hand around her waist to pull her closer and said, "I'm not going to let anything happen to you."

She shook her head, realizing he was still stuck on the stalker's note while in her head his telling Mia first was the biggest problem. *Why was he so blind when it came to her?* She wouldn't put it past her to be behind the leaks to the press. Maybe the stalker would get Mia. A smile edged her lips. She could only hope. Sarah knew her mind was going off the deep end. If there wasn't a baby involved, then it would have been all right, but not now. She should just ask Jon if it was his baby before she drove herself insane.

She stared at him for several seconds. What would she do if it was his? She still hadn't figured that out. She couldn't ask him until she knew what to do. Her mother always said, "Don't ask questions if you don't want to hear the answer." They'd been through so much in the past few days, and his head was all messed up with the stalker.

"Is it OK with you if we have a bunch of my relatives over on Sunday? Mom invited some people over for a graduation party, and I think it would be more secluded if we had it here."

"Do we have to?" He looked down at her apologetically. "What if one of them is the stalker?"

"Why would any of my relatives want to hurt us? It's a good thing I'm getting my second degree in psychology, and I can recognize your paranoia as post-traumatic stress disorder." She gave him a look that said "you are so cute."

"It won't be any trouble. Mom ordered the food from an Italian restaurant. All we have to do is open the doors and let people in. You have to admit this house was built for entertaining."

He bent down and groaned against her neck before connecting his lips to her skin. "Everyone will know where we live," he whispered and kissed her again.

"We could make them meet at Mom and Dad's and blindfold them for the ride over. Or…we could make them ride over in a hockey bag in the trunk."

He pulled back with a scowl. "That's not funny, Sarah."

"It *is* funny. You just need to lighten up. It will be fine. You'll see. My family is not known for its stalking tendencies."

"The house is going to end up in the tabloids."

"It's going to end up there anyway. It's one of my friends, right? And they're coming over tonight," she said sarcastically before kissing the side of his head.

"Just be selective with what you share with them. They don't need to know about every doctor's appointment or luncheon on the schedule. Tell them after the fact, not before. Maybe it will slow down the paparazzi's ability to track us."

"I will. It just slips out sometimes, but I'll be careful."

Chapter Nineteen

Sarah

When Sarah's friends came over a couple of hours later, the four girls sat around the pool. They weren't able to swim because the weather wasn't quite warm enough, but they enjoyed just being together. Jon was in the house on the phone with the lawyer, still working through the paparazzi mess they had left in California.

"Did Mia come out with the baby daddy's name? I've been checking the Internet, but the pregnancy still isn't out there," said Jessica, looking toward the house as if expecting Jon to hear her.

"As far as I know, she hasn't," answered Sarah.

"So did you ever ask Jon if it was his?" asked Megan, and Sarah knew what was coming next. Jessica would climb onto her soapbox about cheating men.

"You don't seriously believe that Jon could have fathered Mia's baby?" Jessica stared at her wide-eyed.

"I don't…" Sarah stammered. "I don't think it's his. He's just never denied that it was his. And I don't want to ask because if I ask that means I don't trust him. How can we get married if I don't trust him?"

"Exactly," blurted Jessica. "You can't get married if he is already cheating."

"He's not cheating. I found at least six or seven other guys online that could have fathered it. It just crossed my mind when I found those pictures of her with him from December."

"I saw them. They didn't look so bad. It's not like they were making out," added Alli.

Sarah looked to Alli, knowing Megan had probably told her about the pictures.

"The only reason I have any doubts is because of Mia. She wants Jon. And Jon talks to her. He says they're just friends, but sometimes she knows more than I do about our lives."

"Like what?" asked Jessica.

"Apparently there's a stalker sending threatening letters, and Jon told Mia but didn't tell me. She's the one who told me about it."

"So he's keeping things from you now and you're talking to Mia?" Jessica shook her head in disbelief.

"I didn't want to talk to her. She called while Jon was in the shower. She just kept calling and calling and I was sick of seeing her face light up his phone, so I answered it. I hate that she knew about the stalker and I didn't. It kills me."

"I have a solution. I say you get a hold of Jon's phone and you take a picture of the biggest, grossest pile of feces you can find. Your dad has to have something you can use down at the vet clinic. You replace Mia's contact picture with the poo picture and then every time she calls, Jon will see her for what she really is," added Megan, and they all broke out laughing.

"Seriously, that has to stop. You have to tell Jon he can't talk to his exes anymore, especially her," announced Jessica before taking a sip of her iced tea.

"She's coming to the wedding." Sarah's head hit the back of her chair and she looked up at the budding trees. She did not want Mia at the wedding—not after the way she'd treated her.

"I still think your best revenge is going to be looking hot when she's a beluga whale," said Jessica.

"Maybe you could just forget to mail her invitation," added Alli. "If she doesn't get the invitation, she'll get the hint."

"The wedding planner is getting them out and if I asked for her name to be removed, Jon would find out. I'm just going to ignore her. I'll be fine."

"That's the best attitude. Everyone's attention will be on you and how hot you look in your dress. She won't even be noticed," added Megan.

"Can we see your dress? I can't believe you've kept it from us. You have to at least have pictures," said Alli.

"I have a couple in the house. After all the garbage going on with the leaks and the paparazzi knowing our schedule better than I do, I wasn't going to trust electronics with the picture. Come on. I'll show you." She actually had a picture on her phone, but she didn't want to make it sound as if she didn't trust her friends. "We were completely targeted on our flight home. The paparazzi knew exactly what time to expect us at LAX. It was ridiculous. None of the BS with the guy fondling me would have happened if our flight information hadn't been leaked. And Jon would never have been arrested either."

"I read somewhere that airport personnel and doctor office receptionists get kickbacks from the paparazzi for information," announced Megan.

She was obviously still trying to clear her name.

"I've heard that, too. I just feel like we have this big bull's eye on us all the time. It's draining." That could have been the case. It could have been a combination of people leaking her and Jon's life. She was probably just taking the leaks too personally.

"I can't wait to see your dress. Who's the designer again?" asked Alli.

"Does it matter?" Sarah still didn't want to reveal too much, but Megan was probably right.

Alli looked at her as if she were crazy. Then she shared the look with Megan, and Sarah could tell she wasn't fooling anyone. Her friends knew she was holding back and it was stupid. Why was she doing it? She could trust her friends. She told them the designer, and Alli squealed with delight.

"I love her. She knows just how to balance old world with contemporary styling," Alli declared.

"I know. I love her, too. And she's not so big that everyone has seen all her work. I love the dress. She designed it just for me." It felt good to be able to talk to her friends about the dress. The only other people that Sarah had shown her dress to were Leslie and Jon's mom, Lara. The girls reached the master bedroom. She had stored the pictures in her journal, knowing it was her most protected place. As she dug her journal out of the drawer next to the bed, her friends gawked at her spacious room.

"Your closet is bigger than my bedroom." Jessica twirled around in the center of the room like she was ballroom dancing. "Now you just have to fill it up with clothes."

"If I ever have enough clothes to fill that room, you can shoot me, because I would definitely be mad," Sarah said, laying her journal on the bed and taking out the pictures.

"I could fill it," declared Alli. She took the photo from Sarah. "Oh, Sarah, your dress is gorgeous."

All the girls sat on the bed next to her to glimpse the photos.

"I don't have the right shoes in the picture, and there will be more detail at the hemline, but that's it." She handed it to Alli.

The girls oohed and ahhed over it, and Sarah felt elated. When they were done looking at the photo, Sarah stowed it back in her journal and tucked the book into her nightstand.

"Tell us what really happened at the airport. Your mom said the paparazzo copped a feel?" asked Jessica, leading everyone out of the room. "The Internet didn't mention he groped you."

"He was checking to see if my breasts were real or if I had gotten fake ones at the plastic surgeon. Jon broke his jaw."

"The punch was all over the Net. Is that what happened to Jon's hand?" asked Alli.

"Yeah. The cast is removable, and his hand should be healed by the wedding, so I have no regret there. The guy deserved worse. If I ever see him again, I'm going to kick him so hard his junk falls off."

"I'm surprised Jonathan didn't kill him," stated Megan.

"Sam stopped him, I think. As it is Jon got arrested and now Remi wants us to sell our wedding photos to one of the better tabloids and donate the money to a charity benefiting abused women. She says it would make the right statement by taking the profit away from the vultures and giving it to the victims. Brad and Angelina donated five million from their wedding pictures. I know ours won't be worth that much, but if the money goes to a good cause it will be worth the exposure."

"Did Remi say how much money she expected the pictures to bring in?" asked Alli.

"Maybe a million. It doesn't matter. The pictures will be exclusive. The photographer we hired and my mom will be the only ones with cameras the whole weekend. All electronics have to be surrendered as you board the plane to the island. The luggage will be checked. Anything that has a camera or Internet gets locked up for the weekend. I would suggest not even bringing electronics on the trip."

"Wow. No electronics for the whole weekend. I don't know if I'll be able to go," said Jessica.

"Yeah. That seems a bit harsh. Are you sure you can deal with not having a phone?" asked Megan.

"I'm looking forward to it." Sarah didn't have the heart to tell her friends that she would have her phone but they wouldn't be able to have theirs. It wasn't that she didn't trust them, but yet it was. Still, in the back of her head, she felt something was off with them.

"Your mom is going to take pictures?" asked Alli.

"Kate's going to take candid shots of the reception and the extracurricular activities, like the beach party and parasailing. We wanted someone we could trust, who would be in the thick of everything, and besides, she volunteered. You know how she loves taking pictures. She'll have a camera at the ceremony too, but we didn't want her to miss any of it because her view was blocked by a camera. And this way we'll be able to control the pictures that get released."

"That's so smart. And if you provide the pictures, the fans will be happy. It said on the Internet that you and Jon already got married. Jon called you his wife? Did he, or was that a total lie?" asked Jessica.

"He did. The whole ordeal was like a circus. It was just a reaction. He wasn't giving away a secret wedding or anything."

"You aren't starting your family yet, are you?" added Jessica.

"No. You sound like Kate. I went to the doctor today, though. I haven't made any decisions yet, but I got a prescription, so at least I have that option."

"Even if you wait a couple of years. You'll be way below average. The average age to have a first child is thirty." Megan smiled. "That's so underachieving of you."

"Ha-ha." Sarah rolled her eyes. "What's going on with you? You're not seeing Chase anymore, are you?"

"No. He's called a couple of times, but I haven't seen him since I gave him that phone back. I don't want to deal with him. I can't believe he did that to me," said Megan.

"Did he admit it?" asked Sarah.

"No, but he said something about helping me distance myself from that Hollywood guy."

Sarah turned to her in surprise. So he was the source of the leaks?

"He was talking about Liam, not Jonathan. I don't know what Chase did, but I'm pretty sure he had a stalker app on my phone, and he kept acting all jealous about Liam. As if I even had a chance with him. Chase said something personal about Liam that he wouldn't have known if he hadn't invaded my privacy. He was acting really weird about the whole thing."

"Stay away from him, Megan. He's not worth the trouble," stated Sarah. She didn't want to know the details.

"I know. I'm not going to see him anymore."

The rest of the evening went by quickly. Too soon, the girls piled back into Megan's car and headed back to the house they rented during the school year. Part of Sarah wished she could go with them, just for old time's sake, but the thought of bringing a bodyguard wasn't appealing. It was easier to just have the girls over to her house.

Sarah climbed the grand staircase and found Jon lying in bed, reading on his tablet. As she undressed, she could feel his eyes on her. "The girls have to study for finals. We're not going to get to see them much until next week. Should we go to the lake, or get settled in the new house?"

"I like the cabin idea. Maybe it will rain and the power will go out again." His dimple sunk into his cheek as he smiled. "We can get settled in the house anytime. How much longer will your parent's lake home stay off the media's radar? We should enjoy it while we can."

Sarah frowned as she pulled the covers back and slid into the silky cotton sheets. She had forgotten that the paparazzi were likely to find the cabin. She had always thought it was protected somehow, but it wasn't. It was public record that her family owned it. "I guess we *should* enjoy it while we can."

She rolled over and reached for her phone, which was sitting on the nightstand. She had a couple of commitments while they were in Minnesota, but she didn't think any of them were this first week. She needed to check her calendar. As she grabbed her phone, she bumped her journal and it clattered to the floor. She thought she had put it back in the drawer. *Why was it out?*

"Were you reading my journal?" She leaned over the side of the bed and picked it up.

"No. Do I look that stupid? Don't answer that."

His comment made her chuckle. No, Jon would never touch her journal; she knew that. She must not have put it away. She browsed her calendar, noting nothing was scheduled until the party on Sunday. Then she set her phone on the nightstand and stashed her journal in the drawer before snuggling next to Jon.

"Flip over," he said, and when she did, he wrapped his muscular arm around her waist, spooning against her. *Heaven.* She drew comfort with each expansion and deflation of his chest. There was nothing that could compare to being in Jon's arms.

Chapter Twenty

Sarah

They spent the next two days at the lake. The lake water was like an ice bath and prevented them from swimming or doing any water sports besides boating. Living in California had messed up Sarah's sense of normal. The lake wouldn't be truly warm until the Fourth of July. She hadn't thought this trip through.

Much of their time was spent in front of the TV watching movies, and on the porch overlooking the lake drinking hot chocolate. It wasn't the same as their last trip. Sam and Raul had come with them, making it impossible for Sarah and Jon to recreate last summer's romantic week. But Sarah had accepted their usefulness. If Raul and Craig had been with them at the airport, Jon wouldn't have broken his hand on that paparazzo. And the guy never would have gotten close enough to molest her. She wasn't going to fight Jon about security anymore.

Sunday brought the graduation party with Sarah's relatives and as Sarah suspected, the house was perfect for entertaining. Even with the rain keeping the gathering inside, there was more than enough room in the great room to seat everyone, and the basketball court was great for letting the kids run around, just as Jon had predicted. Sarah's mom had ordered plenty of food, and the relatives were completely enthralled by Jon.

No matter what her fiancé did to make Sarah the center of attention with her relatives, the conversation seemed to rotate back to him. Sarah was getting used to the effect Jon had on a room of people, so it didn't surprise her. She just wished her relatives were different. She helped her mom restock the trays of pasta and bread and talked to her friends and her cousin Ronnie while Jon worked the room.

"How are you doing, honey?" Kate asked, pulling a hot pan of rigatoni out of the oven.

"I'm fine, Mom." Sarah leaned against the granite counter top and pushed a tendril of hair out of her face.

The crowd in the living room burst out laughing, and she could hear Jonathan say, "And that's why I will never go paddle boarding with Jake Gorboni *ever* again." Sarah smiled. She'd heard the story before and it was hilarious. It involved a group of girls that Jake was trying to impress, a school of fish, and Jon's paddle getting broken.

"Jon's got them all in stitches. He's *so* good with a crowd."

"What did you decide at Dr. Johanna's office? You're going to wait, aren't you?" Her mother ignored her comment.

"Mom, you just say that because you don't want to be a grandma in your forties." She spun around and kissed her mom on the cheek.

"Shhh. I'm still thirty-nine." She winked at Sarah and added, "I just want you to think it through before you start a family."

"I know, but it's my and Jon's decision, and we haven't even talked about it."

"Just be smart, Sarah. You've known Jonathan for less than a year. Children

194

complicate a marriage. You can't take them back. Once they are here, they are here forever."

Whoa. Was she really implying that they shouldn't have children because their marriage might not last? Sarah thought her parents were finally over believing that being with Jon wasn't just a childish whim. It almost made her want to pull Jon into the other room and start a family right now just to spite her mother. Sarah took a deep breath as she shook her head in disbelief.

She pulled a loaf of garlic bread out of the oven and dumped it into the empty basket, avoiding looking at her mother. "They're probably out of bread. I better get this out to the table." She crumpled the foil that had covered the bread into a ball and tossed it in the trash without another word before carrying the basket out of the room.

She smiled when Jon's eyes met hers. She couldn't share the conversation she just had. It would crush him. He thought her parents were finally accepting him. *What was their problem?* Was it so hard to believe that a guy like Jonathan would want to marry her? She wondered if her parents believed, like the rest of the world, that he would end up with Mia. Maybe she was the only one delusional enough to believe in fairytales.

༄

The rest of the week sped by in a blur. Sarah spent a couple of days sharing her favorite places in the Twin Cities with Jon. And even though they had two security men with them, Sarah felt as if she and Jon were on a date. No one even approached them at the Minneapolis Sculpture Garden, or when they walked around Lake Calhoun. It was as if they were normal. Or maybe it was just that no one expected them to be there.

That was until graduation day. For some reason, on graduation day, the press was out in full force. Luckily Jon had a plan.

"So which one of you wants to graduate from college?" Jon glanced back and forth between Craig and Raul.

"We already have college degrees. You're the only one in this room without a degree, Jon." Raul's smile warmed the room as Craig and Sam laughed.

"Wrong question. Who wants to graduate tomorrow with Sarah and me?"

"Ohhh." Raul rolled his tongue like a purr in understanding. Sarah had a hard enough time figuring out how he rolled his *r*'s—*h*'s were beyond human capability. "You want to know who is going on the suicide mission with you on the floor of the auditorium in a graduation gown."

Jon nodded.

"I'm in," Raul spoke without even looking to Craig. Sarah knew Raul was better at reading people's body language and facial expressions, while Craig was better at the technical aspect of the job. Craig would never volunteer to be thrown into the mosh pit and Raul enjoyed it.

"I don't need a babysitter. Seriously, I'm not going to get stabbed or abducted on the floor of Mariucci Arena."

"Sarah," Jon said her name as if she was missing the point, "this may be my only chance to graduate from college. Are you going to deny me this opportunity because you think I'm being overprotective? Maybe I just want to wear the hat and gown."

Sarah laughed at the eloquent expression on his face. "Fine."

They arrived at the arena, avoiding the news trucks in the parking lot, and were, for the most part, unnoticed. Jon, Sarah, and Raul wore the graduation gowns that Sarah had picked up at the university's bookstore the previous week. She had ordered hers, but the other two came off the shelf labeled: HEY, STUPID. YOU FORGOT TO ORDER YOUR GOWN. YOU'RE WELCOME! The sign made Sarah chuckle. She was lucky that there were any extras left so close to graduation weekend.

She knew about Jon's plan to participate in the ceremony with her when she picked up the gowns. It would be a lot more fun having Jon next to her than a bunch of strangers. It'd be a riot, like when he showed up at the concert and revealed his true identity to her. But she hadn't realized Jon's strategy was to *protect Sarah at all costs* until Raul called it a suicide mission. Now, as they filled out the name cards that they would hand to the announcer on stage, she wondered if it was the smartest idea. She took a deep breath and glanced over at Jon. Her life would never be dull with him. That was for sure. For as much as he played it cautiously with the press, every once in a while, he would completely jump off the edge—like today.

She could see people doing a double take when they saw her and Jon, but no one approached except a few people she knew—mostly acquaintances, but a few friends. They posed for pictures together like everyone else in the crowd—Jon at her side. He actually looked as if he was enjoying it. Sarah's best friends weren't at her ceremony. Jessica had already had hers, while Megan and Alli would be in the afternoon ceremony. Sarah's parents and her grandmother were up in the stands with Sam watching. She was only allotted the standard five tickets for audience members, and Jeff had declined since he had already sat through Jessica's.

The speeches weren't as boring as Jeff had made them out to be. Maybe the school of liberal arts had better speakers. The monotonous part was waiting to walk across the stage to receive the case for her diploma. The actual document came in the mail after the grades were finalized and all the bills were paid. When the time came and their row stood to follow the line, Jon grabbed her waist, pulling her against him, and whispered in her ear, "I am so proud of you, Sarah Isabella Austin." Kissing her softly on the ear, he released her just as the line began to move.

At the front of the arena, Sarah handed the card with her name written on it to the woman with the mic and after her name was called, she walked across the stage shaking hands with a couple faculty members she didn't know. Then she moved her tassel and posed for a picture before returning to her seat.

That was all?

Sarah hadn't even heard Jon's name announced. He had used the fictitious name of the character she had written for him in her screenplay assignment for school, just in case there was some law forbidding the crashing of graduation ceremonies. He knew how to play the game. If her manuscript ever made it onto film, his name choice today would bring publicity to the flick.

After the ceremony most of the graduates were too wrapped up in their own bubbles to notice Jon, and they made it to the parking lot only being stopped by a couple of groups of people. As they neared the car, though, a news crew spotted them and literally ran to intercept them. Sarah watched as news reporters she respected growing up turned into vultures right before her eyes, asking intrusive questions about his arrest and the wedding.

Jon handled it without too much pain and soon they were back at their house eating a late lunch with Jeff, Jessica, Nana, and Sarah's parents, Kate and David. And then before Sarah knew it, she was leaving for the airport.

Chapter Twenty-One

Sarah

"Trapped on another flight." That's the way Jon had put it. Sarah on the other hand was excited about her first trip out of the United States. Sure, the flight was long, but the Mediterranean was supposed to be breathtaking. The plane was larger than the one they had taken to Minnesota, but there were also more people on it. Leslie, Nak, Isaac, Isaac's assistant, Remi, Remi's assistant, Remi's husband, and two other people who Sarah didn't recognize were already on the flight when it landed in Minnesota to pick them up. Craig and Raul would be heading back to LA on a different flight, but Sam would be joining them on their trip to Cannes.

The plane was beyond luxurious with its leather seats that reclined and the full bar with stools that could seat eight. A couch ran down one side, and chairs facing each other in groups of four lined the other. Everyone greeted them as they entered, hugs and air kisses everywhere. Jon introduced Sarah to the two unknowns. Definitely super models, they stood as tall as Jon, gorgeous in a simplistic way without makeup. Dwarfed by them in beauty and height, Sarah definitely regretted not getting the boob job.

Jon directed her toward a cluster of empty chairs, and Isaac immediately sat down on the other side of the table across from them. It wasn't as private as Sarah hoped. The flight attendant appeared and offered help getting them settled. Once they were seated, she said, "We will be serving dinner shortly after we get in the air. We have a fully stocked bar, and the cabin in the rear of the plane has a bed, if you would like to lie down. My name is Monroe, and I'm here to serve you, Mr. Williams." Sarah was sure she meant "service you," but she let it go.

"Thank you. We'd like some coffee when we're able," Jon stated, and the attendant left with a nod. He was oblivious to the subtle ways women threw themselves at him, or maybe he'd just learned to ignore them.

"Funny, she didn't offer me the bedroom or her services," said Isaac. "If you don't want the room, I'm sure I could find someone to join me in the mile-high club." He looked around the cabin, his eyes pausing on Leslie, then he tipped his head toward the super models.

It sounded like Isaac was already a member of the club, and Sarah wondered if Jon was too. *What if he and Mia joined together?* Jon glanced at Sarah and said, "I think *we'll* be using the bedroom." A wicked smile washed his face, and Sarah couldn't help but blush. Everybody in the plane would know if they disappeared into the bedroom. She really needed to stop worrying about what others thought.

After brunch, Sarah listened to Isaac argue with Jon for a half hour, and it was starting to get old.

"They don't have the script finished yet. But if you sign on, I bet you can make it into whatever you want," Isaac pushed. "All you have to do is say yes. You saw what they're offering, right?"

"I don't care what they're offering. Have you read the book? There are seventeen graphic sex scenes. That's not where I want my career to go. Didn't you hear anything I said the other day at lunch?"

"They want you, Jon, only you. That's why the money is so good. You're perfect for the role. With your name attached, every horny chick in the world will see the film. Hell…guys will drag their girlfriends, wives, *even boyfriends* to the theater, just to get them revved. There will be a damn baby boom. They'll worship you for the god that you are, and you will graciously say 'you're welcome'…for giving them the best sex of their lives. You'll be a fucking hero— Jonathan Williams, sex god."

"It's not happening, Isaac." Jon chuckled. He wasn't buying into what Isaac was selling.

"Did I tell you Armani is doing the wardrobe? And I'm sure I can work it so you take it home."

"Let it go!"

Sarah slipped her earbuds into her ears to block out their conversation with music and opened her e-book. She knew she'd have this book finished by the time they landed. It probably wasn't the best book for her to be reading, though. It was about a woman whose husband had an affair and knocked up his mistress. No, this book was not a good choice.

$\backsim$

By the time everyone in Jon's group made it to their hotel rooms, it had been almost an entire day since they left. Customs ran smoothly, but the crowd of paparazzi outside the hotel was terrible, though not as aggressive as in the States, and there was some misunderstanding about rooms. By the time all the confusion was sorted out and everyone had a hotel room, all Sarah wanted to do was go to bed. As much as she had tried, she couldn't sleep on the flight, not at all, so she was practically asleep on her feet.

It was late afternoon, and Jon had a dinner meeting with the director of a potential movie at seven. Jon really liked the movie's script, but he needed to meet with the director in order to be considered for the role. He assured Sarah she could skip the meeting and get some rest. It would be boring for her anyway. Then they could go out later after the meeting when the nightlife was just starting. She agreed. She wasn't in any state to argue.

When Sarah awoke to the click of the door, it was already dark outside the large patio window. The only light in the room came from the blinking message light on the phone. She smiled up at Jon as he sat down quietly on the bed next to her. "So…how did your meeting go?"

He wrinkled his nose and made a face at her.

"Not well?"

"I don't know. It was just a meet and greet. The filming schedule isn't even close to being set. Who knows when filming is going to start? I don't even know if he really wants me for the part. Isaac thought it went well, but you know how he's always sugarcoating everything. The director seemed pretty quiet."

Sarah knew Jon really wanted this part. In his mind it was the perfect character to transcend him out of the superhero and man-whore roles he'd played in the past—a serious drama where he could keep his clothes on. He was afraid that his image might be too established to get past it, though.

"He wouldn't have wasted his time if he wasn't seriously considering you, and with your charm, how could he resist?"

"Well…I guess we'll know soon enough. Are you ready to go out?"

"Do I look ready?" She scowled sarcastically at him as she ran her fingers through her flattened hair.

"You always look beautiful to me."

She gave him a look of "yeah right."

"I told Leslie that we would meet her and Nak in forty-five minutes. I think Remi and her husband are joining us, too. We won't be out too late tonight. We have photo-calls tomorrow morning and cast forum interviews before lunch on the boat."

"You don't want me there, right?"

"I always want you there, but you don't have to be there. The carpet is just for the cast and the directors. It's just photos with interviews…super boring."

"Good…because I didn't bring a dress for it. I'm going to sleep in and lounge around all morning." She smiled like she couldn't wait.

Jonathan

The next day Jon got up early to prep for the day's events. Once he was showered and his hair was its perfect messed self, he carried his clothes out into the living room. He didn't want to wake Sarah, not yet anyway. He called and ordered breakfast. He'd wake her up when it arrived. He sat down on the couch and slipped on his socks. He slid into his black pants and threaded his belt through the loops. As he dressed, he clicked on the large television to see if he could catch the day's news before his morning with the press. Cannes coverage was on four channels.

When he saw his face fill the television screen, Jon scrambled to turn up the volume. But when he realized it was in French, he clicked a button on the remote and an English translation appeared across the bottom of the screen.

"Williams, the Hollywood heartthrob best known for his role as the demigod Perseus, will have a chance to prove that he's more than just a handsome face with tonight's showing of *Third Rung*. In the film, Williams plays a troubled young man named Jason, who sets a fire that claims his brother's life. To alleviate his guilt, Jason joins the fire department, where he falls in love with the chief's daughter, played by Amy Richardson. Williams's own brother was killed in a car accident in which Jonathan was driving. Since the movie was filmed shortly after his brother's death, critics are interested to see whether Jonathan was able to funnel his real-life tragedy into his acting to pull out a festival win, or if the film will rely on Jonathan's good looks to carry it."

Jon bent down and picked up the remote off the couch to change the channel. "No pressure there," he muttered to himself. He found a channel with world news in English. Then he pulled his T-shirt on over his head and slipped the charcoal-colored button-down over his shoulders. He was straightening his collar when a five-second gossip blurb came on about Mia. *Oh crap. Here we go,* he thought.

"Rumors are circling around this photograph of Mia Thompson, snapped yesterday." The picture showed Mia holding her belly in the typical pregnant mother pose. In the picture she definitely looked pregnant. "Her people will neither confirm nor deny that she is with child." Jonathan clicked off the TV and finished getting dressed. This would make the rest of the trip more complicated.

After the food arrived, Jonathan eased the door to the bedroom open and sat next to Sarah on the bed. She looked so serene. He wondered what the day would bring. Mia's pregnancy wouldn't go unmentioned in the press. He knew that. Maybe it wouldn't be so bad. She hadn't confirmed it yet. And at least they were in France, where the paparazzi laws were a lot stricter. He kissed Sarah on the forehead and whispered, "I love you, beautiful. Stay safe." He just couldn't wake her knowing what she might hear today. She needed to enjoy the tranquility as long as she could.

༄

The photo op with the cast of *Third Rung* went better than Jonathan expected. He hadn't seen most of the members of the cast for years. Cole Hutchins looked the same as he had the last time he saw him at the wrap party, and he connected with him right away to avoid some of the less-favorable people on the carpet. He posed for a few photos with the director, the assistant director, and the producers. Then the cast lined up for their shots, and luckily no one told him where he needed to stand. After the photos, he buzzed through the preliminary interviews without a hitch—not a single mention of Jack or Mia. By the time he headed back to the hotel, he was feeling pretty good about this trip. Maybe he would make it through this premiere after all.

The worst part about the morning was worrying that Sarah would leave the hotel room, but she was still there when he got back. He wasn't going to leave her alone again though. What if the stalker was someone involved with *Third Rung*? Amy Richardson's face popped into his mind. The first note mentioned Jack, and the last time he had seen Amy was the year after Jack's death. His brother was always on his mind then. Amy Richardson. How was Jon going to tell Sarah about her? Sarah was way too trusting, and he was such a lying bastard. He knew he needed to tell her everything, but he just didn't know how.

Chapter Twenty-Two

Sarah

Jon had gotten an invitation for brunch on a yacht owned by a producer friend of his dad's. It was a large, casual affair and many big names in the entertainment business would be there. Jon said it was a good opportunity to network and they had to go. Sarah wore a flirty, burgundy, flared skirt-dress. Jon couldn't seem to keep his hands off her when she tried it on. It quickly became her favorite.

The car pulled up to pier eleven, and the greeter opened the door. The sun was shining, and a breeze blew off the blue water. Lined with boat slips, the long white pier stretched far out into the marina. At the very end of the pier floated a sleek, but mammoth white yacht, filling with guests. Jon gave their names at the check-in table, and then the group followed the crowd to the awaiting boat. They crossed the retractable wooden dock to the yacht's deck and were immediately greeted by a tall, bronzed woman in a skimpy, nude-colored cutout dress. Her clothes made the woman look naked when Sarah squinted. Her long, straight blond hair blew in the breeze, covering her face as she spoke.

"Jonathan," she brushed the hair out of her face and grasped the top of Jon's arm, "you have to come with me. I've been waiting for you. My father wants to make sure he gets a chance to talk to you. He postponed the brunch just for you, since you were flying in so late," she announced as she hooked her arm around Jon's. "Champagne?" she asked, stopping to grab a flute off the tray held by a blonde dressed all in black. She offered it to Jon and took a second for herself, sipping it while the others in the group got theirs. Jon passed his to Sarah and grabbed another off the tray. The woman guided the group up the glossy wood-and-brass stairs to the boat's upper deck. Sarah wasn't sure what to make of her, but she clung to Jon's other arm as they walked. This whole experience seemed surreal. She had been to outrageously decadent affairs before, but somehow this one on the Mediterranean pushed *extravagant* to a whole new level.

"Jonathan…I'm so glad you could come," a raspy voice boomed from a large, casually dressed man with silver hair.

"Uncle Phillip, it's great to see you," stated Jon, shaking the man's hand while hugging him. Sarah knew this man wasn't really his uncle, but Jon had called him that since he was little.

"Where can I get a boat like this?" he asked, stretching his arms out and gawking around the deck. "It's beautiful."

"I've got a guy. I'll give you his card." Phillip turned to the smaller man next to him and stated, "I remember when he was only this tall." He held his hand up about three feet off the ground. "He used to read Scarlet books for hours while his father and I played cards. Scarlet fell in love with him at a very young age." He glanced at Sarah and added, "I hear you're getting married. You just couldn't wait for my Scarlet, huh?"

"I turn eighteen next week," announced the nude blonde as she sipped her champagne and gazed at Jon with fire in her eyes. There was no way she was seventeen.

"Sorry, but I fell in love," declared Jon with a big smile. He introduced

Sarah and the rest of the group and then added, "You'll be coming to the wedding, right? It wouldn't be a party without you."

"Of course...we've got the date saved," assured Phillip, before changing the subject. "I'm hearing great stuff about *Third Rung*. It could win the festival."

"I doubt that, but thanks for the compliment," Jon said in a self-deprecating tone. "Are you coming to the premiere tonight? If you still need tickets, I'm sure we can scrounge some up for you." Jon looked to Isaac.

Isaac affirmed with a nod. "How many do you need?" He reached into his sports coat and pulled out an envelope.

"No, we're all set. Do you need tickets, Talbot?" Phillip questioned. The smaller man next to him made an apologetic face, and Phillip added, "We could use two more."

Isaac opened the envelope, pulled out two tickets, and handed them to Talbot.

The group made small talk with Phillip and the studio executive who was standing with him for several minutes until Phillip stated, "I have some projects I want to discuss with you, Jon, but I want you to get some brunch first. The tenderloin with the horseradish buttermilk sauce is my favorite, but you have to try the salmon crepe, too. When you're finished, we need to talk, and bring Isaac back with you. I'm talking real business." He glanced at Isaac with a smile. "Scarlet can show you around. It was pleasant to meet all of you, especially you, Sarah." Phillip grasped Sarah's hand, bringing it up to his lips, and kissed it. "I am looking forward to your very special day."

"I'm so glad you will be able to attend, Mr. Leighton."

"Please, call me Phillip." He smiled at Sarah. "I can't miss my godson's wedding, can I? We'll see you in a bit, Jonathan."

For all the overindulgence going on around them on the yacht, Uncle Phillip seemed very down-to-earth.

The group followed Scarlet back down to the main deck, where the food tables were scattered in abundance. "See how confident my father is that your movie will win? He always does something elaborate for his top pick." Scarlet pointed to a large ice sculpture shaped like a ladder with *Third Rung* carved across the front. It was three feet tall with a hollow center filled with colossal shrimp. The richly colored crustaceans flowed from the sculpture onto a crystal platter and looked almost as if they were flames lapping up the ladder from within.

"Wow," whispered Sarah into Jon's ear.

"That's Uncle Phillip—never afraid to share his opinion," Jon said matter-of-factly. "The scary part is, he is usually right."

After about forty-five minutes of discovering all the food delicacies on the boat, while Scarlet watched sipping her champagne, the seventeen-year-old pulled on Jon's arm, saying, "My father doesn't like to wait, Jonathan."

Jon kissed Sarah on the cheek, declaring, "I'll be back," in his best Schwarzenegger voice and then left with Isaac, Sam, and Scarlet.

When Jon returned to the table after about an hour, he collapsed into the chair next to Sarah with a look of satisfaction on his face. "I sold it," he announced. The group of friends looked at him with concern. Had he been out in the sun too long? What could he possibly be selling on a yacht in the Mediterranean? Sarah had no idea what he was talking about.

"You sold what?" she questioned, taking a sip of her ice tea.

"Well…it's as good as sold anyway. I think there's going to be a bidding war on it. Not bad for sight unseen, huh?" he continued, obviously pleased with himself.

"What did you sell, Jon?" asked Leslie in a frustrated tone.

"Sarah's screenplay…They loved the idea. They were all very interested."

"Who?" asked Sarah, not quite believing him.

"Two producers and a studio exec—Jason Baltir from *The Expendable*, Nate Jieters from *The Demigod*, and Jerry Gradstein from Plantation Studios. I need to get them each a copy by next week."

She couldn't believe anyone would be interested in her work. She never really thought it would be sold. It was just a school project. A knot twisted in the pit of her stomach. "It's not that good. They're not going to like it once they read it."

"It's brilliant. I've read a lot of scripts, Sarah. Most of them are garbage. I loved yours, and not because you wrote it. It's really well done. They'll love it, too. They'll be fighting over it. You'll see," Jon boasted.

"They are only interested because I'm your fiancé," Sarah claimed.

"I never told them you were the writer. They loved the plot idea. They don't know who wrote it."

"Really?" she asked skeptically. She was feeling a bit more hopeful now. Jon nodded. She paused a second, thinking about what he had said. He was so good at phrasing his words so as not to lie. "You didn't tell them I wrote it, but you promised you'd be in the movie, didn't you?"

"I may have. Come on, the role was written for me. I have to play it."

Sarah shook her head. She had written the role for Jon. She just didn't know he knew it. "You'll be great in it," she admitted with a soft smile. "I just didn't want it to be a condition of the sale."

"So can I introduce you as a writer tonight on the red carpet?" he asked as he pulled her onto his lap.

"Not until we have the check in our hands," she beamed and kissed his cheek.

"You better watch out," announced Leslie as she pointed to her right. On an outcropping of large boulders near the shore, fifteen or so paparazzi were staged with their cameras on tripods. The four-foot-long lenses jetted out over the water, pointing directly at the deck of the yacht. "Your make out session will be all over the weeklies."

He wrapped his arms around Sarah. "Let it. We're celebrating."

"What did your Uncle Phillip want to talk about?" asked Sarah, turning to see his beautiful eyes.

"He has a project he's pulling together. He wanted to know if I would be interested. It sounds huge, but it's at least a couple of years off. He wants to put my name on it in the early stages just to build interest. I can always pull out later if it doesn't go in the right direction."

Jon looked toward Tom Fallston and his harem of women a few tables over. Nak and Leslie had introduced Sarah to him while Jon was talking with Phillip. Tom seemed a bit flirtier after he found out Sarah was Jon's fiancé. She wondered if Jon and Tom had some kind of rivalry. She couldn't read Jon's expression, but he seemed frustrated. Tom was one of the guys who had costarred with Mia and was on the list Sarah had compiled of possible baby daddies. Did Jon know more than he was letting on? Mia had probably shared the daddy's identity with him, and he didn't trust Sarah enough to tell her. She hoped Tom was the father and not Jon.

"Hey, Nak, what are you doing tomorrow morning while we're at the junket?" Jon turned back, seeming to forget about Tom.

"I don't have any solid plans, why?"

"Could you keep Sarah occupied? I don't want her roaming the city by herself."

"As long as it's all right with Leslie, I'm up for anything," Nak proclaimed, raising his eyebrows and winking at Sarah.

Sarah reached out and smacked Nak's knee, almost falling off Jon's lap to make contact. As her sunglasses clattered to the floor, she declared, "That's not what he meant, Daniel!"

Everyone laughed as Nak picked up her sunglasses and handed them back to her. She turned to Jon and vowed, "And I don't need a babysitter!" She stood up, separating herself from his lap. She straightened the bottom of her dress and glared at him as she sat back down in the chair.

"Leslie, Sam, Remi, and I are going to be busy all day. I'd ask Isaac, but I don't really trust him to keep his hands off you. You're going to be so bored sitting around the junket watching journalists file in and ask the same questions over and over. I get bored and I'm on camera," he stated.

"I'll stay at the hotel and watch TV by myself," declared Sarah.

"No, you won't. You'll sneak off. I'll be worried about you the whole afternoon, just like this morning, and all my interviews will suck. You and Nak can hang out at the press junket until you get bored. Then you can go out to grab some lunch, and Nak can make sure you're safe while you're out," stated Jon.

"Whatever," Sarah agreed. She knew the stalker was the motivation behind Jon's insistence, but what kind of person would follow them to France? Besides, she had vowed not to fight him on it anymore.

The rest of the afternoon flew by as the group schmoozed with directors, producers, studio executives, and the few actors who made the cut. Jon was so smooth that the conversations seemed effortless and Sarah didn't feel out of place for the most part. Jon let it slip that Sarah was a writer and claimed he didn't mean to with a wink at Sarah. She could tell he was proud of her, and it felt good. They talked about the wedding a little, very little, but mostly they talked business, and Sarah loved watching Jon in his element.

They left the boat by five o'clock to get ready for the red carpet, and Sarah was exhausted by the time they got back to the hotel. It must have been the salt air and the sun. Sarah laid her clothes out on the bright white duvet that covered the bed. Her long, silver-and-black gown contrasted with the monochromatic scheme of the white room. "I'm going to take a hot bath before I get ready. Why don't you go get some food?"

"OK…What do you want?"

"You know I can't eat before the red carpet. They'll say I have a baby bump."

"It doesn't matter what they say. You've hardly eaten all week. You barely touched your plate at brunch. Starving yourself is crap for your metabolism."

He stood behind her and met her eyes in the mirror. He smirked and wrapped his arms around her. Touching her stomach, he added, "Definitely no baby bump. I could fix that, if you want?" He slid his hand lower, pulling her against him.

She turned around in his arms and kissed his cheek. "Not today…but I'll keep it in mind." She walked into the bathroom and started filling the large soaking tub.

"We can just practice," he called, and then he mumbled something she couldn't hear.

She fought a smile as she peeked out from behind the bathroom door, catching him with her lace bra in his hand. She wondered why he wanted a child so badly. Was it because of Mia? Or maybe he was just being playful. She hoped it was the latter. She closed the door and then checked the water temperature. Perfect. She reached up to release the blind above the window, and with a yank on the string, it dropped to the sill. Sarah pulled her burgundy dress over her head and slipped off her undergarments. She caught her reflection in the mirror. The scars on her trunk were healing. The itching had subsided.

As she sank into the warm water of the deep white tub, she knew she didn't have much time before the woman styling her hair would be at the door. She was so tired. She just wanted to close her eyes for a minute. She didn't know if it was jet lag or the weight of Mia's pregnancy that was making her drag, but she knew she would fall asleep if she let her eyes close.

Tap, tap, tap. "Sarah, Deidra is here," announced Jon through the door.

Startled, Sarah opened her eyes and called back, "I'll be right out." She couldn't believe she let her eyes close. She toweled off and slipped into the long hotel robe. She peeked her head out the door and asked, "Deidra, do you want my hair wet?"

"Yeah, that'll work," replied the auburn-haired woman in jeans and a T-shirt.

An hour later when Deidra packed up her tools, Sarah's hair and makeup looked perfect. Her dark, silken hair flowed long with curled ends, and her makeup was natural but brought out her green eyes. Sarah thanked her, and after Deidra left she looked toward the clothes still lying on the bed. She was still in the robe. Jon stepped in front of her as she reached for her undergarments, blocking her way. He smiled at her and questioned, "So are you ready for some food? We're not leaving until you eat something." Room service had delivered a tray with food and spread it out on the table while Sarah was having her makeup applied.

She looked at him. "Really? I'm not hungry. We ate all afternoon on the boat." She reached around him and grabbed her bra off the duvet, but he snatched it quickly from her hands, looking deeply into her eyes, and stared her down.

"Honestly, that won't look very good with your tux," Sarah said as she reached for it again.

"I'm serious, Sarah," he stated as he walked over to the small table with the bra still in his hand. "You hardly ate anything this afternoon. There's bread, chicken, cheese, and fruit. It's not much, but you're having something or we're not leaving," he demanded.

She picked a grape off the tray and popped it in her mouth. She glared at him. Why was he being so obstinate? "May I have my clothes back?"

He shook his head no and picked up a bite-sized piece of chicken. He held it in front of her nose, pinched between his fingers.

"I hope your hands are clean," she said and then opened her mouth. She knew he wouldn't let it go until she ate something. He had a second and then third piece in front of her face before she had a chance to say any more. "May I have my clothes?"

He tore off a chunk of the baguette and passed it to her. She took a small bite of it and glared at him. He apprehensively handed her the garment in question. She set the rest of the bread on the table, scooped up her clothes from the bed, and walked to the bathroom, not bothering to close the door. She scowled at him while she got dressed. "If I have a baby bump in any pictures, you're going to pay."

He followed her and stood in the doorway fastening his cufflinks. "You have to eat. The press is going to say you're pregnant no matter what. Even if you don't have a baby bump, they'll doctor the pictures. Next week it will be a new story—they'll say you left me for a woman, and then the week after that you'll be pregnant again with an alien baby. You just have to stop worrying about the tabloids and enjoy life. I believe you told me the same exact words last summer."

"I just want to look the best I can. They are always comparing me to Mia, and they already loath me for breaking up the perfect couple. I know I didn't, but the media and the fans want you two together. They hate me."

"You're way more beautiful than Mia. Smarter, sweeter, sexier. Everyone can see that. That's why they're jealous." His eyes swept her body as she slipped into her dress.

"Yeah, I'm sure that's it." She chuckled sarcastically. "Would you zip me up, please?" She turned her back to him.

He leaned down and kissed the small of her back before zipping the gown. She shivered slightly when his lips touched her, and he smiled. "It's good to see I can still affect you."

"I don't think that will ever change."

There was a knock on the door, and Jon grabbed his jacket off the back of the love seat. "Are we ready? We're meeting everyone in the lobby in five minutes." Sarah nodded and grabbed his arm to balance as she slipped on her heels. "Let's head down. I'm sure that's Sam," Jon stated as he reached for the door.

The premiere's red carpet went smoothly, and it wasn't long before everyone was seated inside the theater. From the beginning, the film's cinematography was unbelievable. Sarah didn't remember ever seeing a movie that captured the essence of the 1960s time period with such attention to detail. The use of camera angles alone made the film worth seeing, but the acting was phenomenal as well. During the scene where Jonathan's character admitted to his girlfriend that he started the fire that killed his brother, there wasn't a dry eye in the room. Even Isaac was tearing up. And when the character told her he loved her, the entire theater stood up and cheered. Sarah didn't know if it was normal for standing ovations to occur at premieres. This was her first official one. She leaned into Jon's ear and asked, "Is that normal?"

Jon shook his head with the hugest smile on his face. "It's the first time I've seen it."

"It's great." Wow. The film was phenomenal. Jon was definitely going to get some recognition from his work in it. "You are amazing. You know that," she said as she smiled up at him.

Chapter Twenty-Three

Sarah

The next day Sarah and Nak slipped out of the press junket to grab some coffee. It was only 10:00 a.m. The actual interviews were just getting started, but the setup was delayed, and they had been waiting around since 8:00 a.m. They were out late again last night with the premiere, and Sarah was tired this morning. She still hadn't recovered from her sleep deficit yet. She had gotten a shower but had not gotten coffee, and her head was starting to pound from the lack of caffeine.

On their way to the café, Sarah and Nak ran into a group of people who Nak knew. One was a makeup artist who used to date Liam, and two others were people who Nak had worked with previously. He introduced Sarah, and she listened to the conversation for several minutes, not really having much to add to the exchange.

As Nak stood talking with his friends, Sarah interrupted, "I'm going to grab that table before it's gone. You want a coffee, right?" There was one table left on the sidewalk, and Sarah wanted to be able to sit outside. The view of the beach was so beautiful she couldn't imagine wasting it by being inside. Besides, her head felt as if she wore an invisible vice as a hat and it was being tightened every minute she was caffeine-free.

"Yes, black. I'll be right there."

She smiled at the group and said, "It was nice to meet you."

She made her way to the table and sat down on one of the wrought iron chairs. The server approached her immediately and took her order. As the waitress left, Sarah looked around the cafe. She was right to grab the table. There was a line starting to form by the entrance. She could see Nak still talking to his friends about thirty feet away from her, and every table in the cafe was full.

As she glanced around, she noticed an attractive man in his late twenties sipping coffee and writing in a leather-bound book. She wondered what he was writing about. Her journal was in her bag. She hadn't had much time to write in it since she arrived in France. She had done some journaling on the plane, but she hadn't documented any of her experiences since they landed. She debated whether she would have enough time to do any decent writing before Nak joined her. It was worth a try, she thought. Sarah pulled it out of her purse. If nothing else it would make her look busy. Just as she began to write, a shadow crossed her journal page and she looked up expecting it to be Nak taking the seat across from her. It wasn't Nak. It was the eye-catching man who Sarah had spotted when she first sat down.

He waved his journal in front of his chest and spoke in a thick French accent. "Not many of us still use paper. So you are a writer, too?"

Sarah nodded with a smile as she closed her book.

"Hello, I am Christophe," he said, extending his hand.

She met his hand and shook. "Hi, I'm Sarah."

"So, Sarah, what kind of writer are you? Have you written anything I would have read?" He stared into her eyes.

"I'm still a student," she chuckled. "It's just a journal."

"Only serious writers use real paper and ink. You must be published somewhere."

"Well…" she hesitated, not knowing if she should share anything personal with this stranger. "I wrote a short story that got published in a literary magazine last year," she looked away from his gaze. He was definitely flirting with her. His thick French accent made every word from his mouth sound dirty.

"Really? Which magazine? I bet I have read it. I love short stories."

"*The Tapestry*. Have you heard of it? It's pretty well known in the literary circles in the United States. One of my professors submitted my story, and they published it last April. I was surprised. I didn't think they would ever accept it," she admitted.

"I do not get that periodical, but I will look for it. I bet your story is wonderful," he stated with a grin. Then he said something in French that sounded like he was asking her out.

"I'm sorry. I don't speak French at all," she chuckled. "I've had Spanish as a second language since elementary school, but I still can't speak it," she admitted.

"Venga a pasar el verano conmigo cerca del océano," he stated in Spanish with raised eyebrows.

She chuckled and replied, "Sorry, but my summer is going to be really busy. I said I couldn't speak Spanish. I didn't say I couldn't understand it. How many languages do you speak?" He was definitely flirting.

"Just the three. I understand more than I can speak as well," he chuckled. He folded his fingers on top of his book, which was now lying on the table. "Tell me, Sarah, who is your favorite writer."

"Classic or modern?"

"Classic," he clarified.

She looked down at her journal collecting her thoughts. "I love Guy de Maupassant. I think his writing is intelligent. His take on politics and world economics is still very relevant to the problems in today's society." She looked up expecting his eyes to have glazed over, but he held his receptive look, so she continued. "He doesn't assume the reader is an idiot by explaining every element of the story. He implies much of the details, which allows the reader to use her imagination to fill in the blanks, but yet he is descriptive where he needs to be. He allows the readers to build the story in their minds. I like that." Sarah finished hoping she hadn't lost him in her explanation.

He brought his hand to his chin, and the corner of his lips curled up. "He is one of my favorites as well, very thought provoking—a fellow Frenchman… and racy for his time, no?"

"A little," she agreed with a smile. She hoped she wasn't blushing as the server returned with two mugs of coffee.

The older woman set them down on the table, and Christophe stated with disappointment in his voice, "Oh, you are waiting for someone. I should have known. I noticed your ring, but I was hoping it was a family heirloom."

"No, I'm engaged," Sarah confessed.

"That is a tragedy. All the beautiful ones are always taken," he stated, taking her hand and examining the ring. "You know the emeralds match your eyes," he said, setting her hand back down and looking into her eyes.

"I've been told that." She giggled.

"By your fiancé, I am sure. He is a very lucky man to have found you. Is the wedding soon?" he questioned.

"Later this summer," Sarah stated. She enjoyed talking to this man. He didn't seem to have any clue her fiancé was a famous movie star, and that made her feel normal.

"He should not leave you alone so long. We Frenchmen are very romantic and may steal you away from him," he declared with a smile. Just then Nak approached the table with a look of concern on his face. Christophe excused himself by stating, "Oh, this must be your lucky groom. I best be leaving." He winked at her as he got up from the table. "It was very nice meeting you, Sarah."

He looked forlorn over his shoulder at her as he walked away.

"So, what did the French guy want?" asked Nak as he sat down in the chair across from her. He continued, "Is this mine?" He picked up the coffee and waited for her nod before taking a sip.

"He was just being friendly. He noticed I had a journal," she picked up her book and stuffed it back into her bag. "He had one too, and we were just talking about writing. The French are very assertive. He just sat down and started talking. He didn't seem to know who I am, though. It was very innocent."

"Oh, I'm sure he knew exactly who you are. Don't kid yourself." Nak laughed as he set his coffee down. "This is good." He paused and looked in the direction of the Frenchman's exit. "Jon's going to kill me for letting him near you."

"No, there was no mention of Jon. It was refreshing." She took a sip from her mug.

"Did he tell you he was a journalist for the *Rendezvous*? It's similar to *Vanity Fair*."

Sarah shook her head.

"He interviewed me on my last press tour in London. Christophe, right? He knew I recognized him. That's why he disappeared so quickly…and I'm sure he knows you're engaged to Jon. It's his job. I hope you didn't spill anything vital. He's probably going to interview Jon right now."

"Seriously? I hate it when I read people wrong. I used to be such a good judge of character. Now, it seems like I'm always off."

"It gets easier. Eventually you won't trust anyone."

"How do you live like that? I have to have people I can talk to. I'll go crazy if I can't confide in anyone. This thing with Liam and Megan almost killed me." Liam was his roommate, so he had to have at least heard the story about Megan leaking Liam's secrets to the press.

"I didn't say *I* couldn't trust anyone. My life is very different from Jon's.

No one cares about me. The only time the press ever talks to me is when I have a movie coming out. When people do recognize me in the street, they're like, 'Don't I know you from somewhere?' Or they say, 'You're that guy from that movie, right?' They don't even know my name," he stated. "What you and Jon have to go through blows me away."

"It doesn't seem fair."

"What's not fair about it? Jon makes a lot more money than I do. I'd love to be able to hire Leslie as my assistant, but she's way out of my price range. He *should* have to put up with more."

Sarah drained the last of her coffee from the mug and looked up at Nak. "So it all comes down to money then?"

"Not really. I just like to throw that out there. Jon is really talented. He is much better at talking to the press than I am. I'm a decent actor, but press tours don't do me any favors. I can never think of the right comeback to the interviewer's questions. I always sound like an idiot. Jon is smooth. He always has some funny story to tell the press. He looks like a hero. I'll never be like that."

"He practices. He has his stories all figured out before he goes into the room. And those funny little stories he tells the press are starting to include me." She chuckled. "It's scary. I never know what he's going to share with the world. My mom called me two months ago frantic because she heard I lost my engagement ring. I had only misplaced it…for about five minutes. I was trying to make meatballs, so I took it off because the recipe said to mix the ingredients with your hands and I didn't want it to get all mucked up. After Jon mentioned it in an interview, there were bogus stories all over the Internet that he had to fly some jeweler in from Greece to make a duplicate because I was inconsolable. Jon didn't even buy it in Greece, and I found it right away. It wasn't lost."

"The press eats that up. They love any tidbit into Jon's personal life."

"Yeah, so they can embellish it. I wonder what Christophe is going to say about me."

"Why? What did you talk about?"

"Mostly about my writing, but he was definitely flirting with me."

Nak raised his eyebrows and looked at her questioningly.

"I didn't accept his invitation to spend the summer with him. I thought he was just joking, but he'll probably say I was flirting with him. I wish I'd known he was a reporter."

"We could head back and catch his interview with Jon. We may be able to talk to Jon before the interview and let him know how the guy tricked you."

"No...It would just make Jon upset and probably ruin the rest of his interviews. I'll tell him tonight when he's done with the press. There's nothing I can do to take back what I said anyway. Can we just stay here and enjoy the ocean view for a while?" Sarah flagged the server down and had just asked for some more coffee for her and Nak when Jon's agent pulled a chair up to their table.

Settling comfortably in his chair, he touched the waitress's hand and ordered, "I'll have a Coke." He smiled at Sarah and added, "I didn't think Jon let you out by yourself."

"I'm not by myself, Isaac. Daniel is here with me." She glanced at Nak, annoyed by Isaac's comment.

"Oh...Nak? He's a pussycat. You don't mind if I talk to Sarah, do you?" He turned to Nak and then back to Sarah. "I want to talk to you because I know Jon listens to you."

She looked at him questioningly but held silent.

"Let's face it—this wedding is not good for Jon's career, Sarah."

"Should we cancel it then?" she asked sarcastically, rolling her eyes.

"Oh, that would be great. I knew you would understand."

"Isaac, how is our wedding not good for Jon's career? It's giving him all kinds of press exposure."

"Well, it's not really the wedding. It's you. And I have a list of reasons why, if you have some time." He reached into his suit jacket, unfolded the paper from his pocket, and chuckled. "I don't really have a list written out, but—"

Sarah shook her head and thwarted him. "I know you don't like me, and I know you don't want Jon to get married, but you sought me out to ask me a favor...I'm listening."

"That's not true. I would do anything for you, Sarah."

She interrupted, "Only because Jon loves me." She stared at him and waited for him to continue.

His face turned serious. "Jon has turned down the last four movie offers. I don't understand it. The scripts were decent. The money was there...I think it's because of you."

The server returned with their drinks, and Nak asked her for the bill in French. Sarah smiled at him, impressed, and then turned to address Isaac.

"I don't tell Jon what movies to sign. Maybe it was Leslie. She is in on all of Jon's business decisions." She glanced over to Nak, rolling her eyes again.

"It's you...He didn't want to do the movies because there is too much nudity in them."

She studied Isaac's face and confessed with a serious expression, "I like looking at Jon...naked. He's got the cutest little heart-shaped birthmark right below his right butt cheek. It's really tiny and is always in shadow on camera, but Jon says it was visible in a close-up on the preliminary *Demigod Forbidden* footage. I can't wait to see if it makes the final cut." She knew why Jon had turned the movies down, and it wasn't her fault, so she wanted Isaac to know she couldn't be manipulated.

Nak snickered and turned it into a cough before taking a sip of his coffee.

"You *are* amusing." Isaac smiled snidely at her. "I think he's worried that the sex scenes will upset you. I just want you to tell Jon it's all right with you if he takes on a couple of love scenes here and there. He shouldn't avoid them like the plague. They're what made him a star, and now he just wants to abandon them?"

"Isaac, you know that once Jon gets something into his head, no one can change his mind."

"Just let him know it's OK with you. He listens to you. It is OK, isn't it? You do know it's just acting, right?" he questioned condescendingly.

She furrowed her eyebrows and declared, "I've never told him he can't do love scenes. And I know it's just his job. Jon takes the roles he wants, and right now he wants to find a serious role that shows off his acting ability. He's tired of using his body to sell movies. He wants more. You saw what he can do at the premiere last night. Find him what he wants." She looked at Isaac, who looked like he was in shock, and then she added, "I'm just telling you what Jon told me."

"And I'll find him that perfect script, but he needs to keep his fan base happy by slipping a few sex scenes into the mix. They're his bread and butter. All I'm asking is that you let him know it's all right with you that he does the movies that pay the bills."

"I'll let him know, but I can't promise he'll do them…So, I take it the meet and greet the other night with the director didn't go well?"

"Ehh…It's too early to tell, but I don't know if it's the right role for Jon anyway. I think he can do better."

She smiled, understanding. That was Isaac's way of admitting it hadn't gone well. "We're heading back to the press junket. You're welcome to join us," she said, glancing quickly to Nak and then back to Isaac. She was hoping Isaac would decline her invitation, but she didn't want to be rude. She put spending the afternoon with him on the same level as spending the afternoon locked in a room with a high-pressure car salesman or a rabid pit bull. She knew he was a good agent and looked out for Jon's best interest, but she did not want to hang out with him socially, especially without Jon. She stood up and pushed the heavy chair in to meet the table. The metal scraped against the cement in a loud squeal, and several restaurant patrons looked up startled by the noise. Nak rose too, not bothering with his chair, and set several euros on the table for the waitress.

Isaac sat at the table looking up at Sarah. "Sorry, I have a lunch date, but I'll see you both tonight at the wind down party."

"See you later, Isaac," stated Sarah as she and Nak headed down the sidewalk.

Isaac called after them as they walked away, "Talk to Jon."

They walked about a block before Nak got a big smile on his face and asked, "Does Jon really have a heart-shaped birthmark on his ass?"

"No…I was just messing with Isaac…but I am going to have the best time watching him at the *Demigod* premiere as he scours the screen for that birthmark. If you see me laughing hysterically during the love scenes, you'll know why," she confessed, and they both broke out laughing.

"Oh, he *so* deserved that," proclaimed Nak.

"He did, didn't he? Thanks for the coffee, by the way," Sarah uttered as they crossed the street. "I didn't know you could speak French."

"I am Canadian. We spoke English in Manitoba, but my mother is from Québec. We weren't allowed to speak anything but French at my grandparent's house. My grandparents spoke English too, but they were really strict about the language spoken in their home. I think it was their way of ensuring we learned French."

"Canadian…I knew there was a reason we got along so well. Have you ever brought Leslie up north in the winter?"

"Yeah…she visited for Christmas once."

"I missed winter this year. It was mild and we didn't have much snow before Christmas. Then I moved to LA and it was like winter never came. I think I'm going to miss the snow living in LA."

"You can go to Tahoe or Vail. Doesn't Jon have a condo up there?"

Did Jon have a condo in Colorado? Sarah thought back to how Jon had planned on asking her to marry him in Vail and how his plans got shot down by her car accident. Why would he keep that from her? Maybe Nak was mistaken. She'd just have to add it to the list when she finally found the nerve to ask Jon about Mia's baby.

They walked several more blocks before they spotted the hotel where they had left Jon and Leslie. A large sign sat on a wooden easel outside the entrance announcing the *Third Rung* press junket. On the sign Jon and his costars' faces ghosted out in front of a 1960s red fire engine surrounded by flames. A crowd of people stood outside smoking, and a cloud of gray haze lingered in the air around them. Two men with cameras leaned against one of the posts that held up the blue awning above their heads, and they spoke softly to each other as their eyes followed Sarah and Nak.

Sarah could tell by their gaze that they recognized her and Nak, so she mentally prepared for the attack. She pointed them out to Nak just before the photographers advanced on them and the cameras began to click. Sarah and Nak smiled and waved as they walked into the hotel lobby. The photographers hadn't said anything as they snapped pictures, which helped Sarah feel a little more relaxed.

When they reached the security desk, Sarah set her purse on the table to retrieve her pass. As she pulled it out and slipped it over her head, someone touched her shoulder. She looked up to meet the eyes of the French journalist, Christophe.

"Sarah," he said as he squeezed past her on his way out. His eyes lingered on her in an apologetic way. Sarah didn't know what to think, so she just smiled back. He would write what he wanted anyway.

Once past the security desk, Sarah and Nak made their way down the hallway toward the second security checkpoint. They slipped through the door silently and flattened themselves against the back wall to observe the rest of the interview already in progress. Within twenty seconds Jon's eyes met Sarah's. His whole face brightened and a huge smile grew on his lips.

"How would you compare your character Jason in this film to the character of Perseus in the *Demigod* saga?" asked the journalist next to Jon.

There was a short pause of silence. Jon looked back at the reporter and asked, "I'm sorry. Can you repeat the question?" He smiled back at Sarah as the reporter restated what he had asked. "I think they are both just trying to figure out where their lives are going and how they can make a difference in the world. Jason is so in love with Justine that he is blind to all that is going on around him. Perseus doesn't find true love until the second movie and is more realistic about the evils of the world."

"Which character do you relate to more?" asked the reporter.

"I can definitely relate to Jason. When he realizes his actions put Justine's life in danger and she may die, he felt so helpless. The guilt dragged him down so low that...he would have done anything to switch places with her. It's the worst feeling in the world," he admitted, making eye contact with Sarah for a second before returning his gaze to the reporter.

"You sound like you know that feeling firsthand. Would you share the story with us?"

A quiet voice came from next to the camera, "Quickly, we're almost out of time."

"Where do I start?" Jon pondered. "Last December, my fiancé ended up in a coma after a car accident caused by a paparazzo who was chasing her because of her involvement with me. It was the longest four days of my life...so I can definitely relate to Jason's situation. My life is crazier than fiction." It wasn't the story Sarah expected Jon to share, and it brought up all kinds of feelings as she put herself in Jon's shoes. She expected him to link it to Jack's death, not her accident. She decided Jack's death was probably still too hard for Jon to talk about.

"Time is up," the voice next to the cameraman called.

"I would have loved to continue with this subject matter and I appreciate your openness. It was great visiting again," the interviewer acknowledged.

"Hope your wife is feeling better, Ted," Jon stated, being his normal charismatic self. He must have known the guy. Gosh, he knew a lot of people.

Jonathan

As the interview set was being readied for the next journalist, Jon made his way toward Sarah. When he reached her, he playfully kissed her on the cheek. He felt so relieved to have her close to him again. He had been worried not just about her safety, but also about the questions the press surely asked her. The news about Mia's pregnancy had broken, and the press was full of conjecture. Mia hadn't identified the baby's father, and one journalist blatantly asked Jon if he was the father. Remi called out from off camera, "This is ridiculous…He's not answering that. Keep to the movie, please," so the journalist returned to the proper interview subject matter. Jon knew how much questions about Mia bothered Sarah. Questions about Mia made his very stable girlfriend irrational. He didn't want Sarah harassed, and he expected it was only a matter of time before the press would be swarming.

"How was your morning? Did the paparazzi bother you?" he asked her, watching her face for changes in her expression.

"No," she answered. "There were a couple of photographers outside the front of the hotel, but other than them we didn't run into any. Isaac found us, though. I'll tell you about it later."

No strained expression on her face—she must not have heard the news yet, he thought. Jon still had time to protect her, at least for now. He had a plan, and Leslie was already working on it. All he would have to do was find a secure exit from the building and make sure the last journalist interviewed didn't mention Mia's pregnancy.

"I have to talk to Remi really quickly before the last interview. Stay right here. Don't go anywhere, OK?" he said before kissing her cheek again. He rushed over to Remi and whispered in her ear. Then he pulled his phone out of his back pocket and sent a quick text to Leslie as he slowly walked back to his interviewing seat. The journalist from CA Entertainment entered the room with Remi at her side. Jon made eye contact with Remi, and she nodded slightly. Good. It was all set. He stood up and greeted the journalist, working to smooth over the warning he had Remi impose.

After the interview Jon enlisted Sam to help them escape without running into the paparazzi. Jon knew it would involve going through the kitchen or a service entrance, as it often did. First, Sam cleared the hallway leading to the elevator and they made their way down through the kitchen. It was still lunchtime and the kitchen was in a busy, chaotic state. Flames shot up in a sauté pan as the chef swirled it over an open flame in front of them. They could feel the heat of the flames as they rushed past. The back door was open and they could see the car waiting for them in the alley.

They settled in the car and Sarah look at Jon questioningly. He wove his fingers with hers and smiled back at her with a sigh of relief. She watched his face as he erased his expression and turned on a carefree look.

"So, what was that all about?" she questioned.

"I'm just tired of dealing with the press. I reached my limit and couldn't do any more," he answered. *Was she suspicious already?*

"Where are Leslie and Nak?" Sarah asked.

"Leslie is helping me with a surprise I'm setting up for you," he said, raising his eyebrows and attempting to look innocent. "She'll meet us back at the hotel." Jon was relieved to be past the first line of the press. He knew they could sneak into their hotel without problems. Sam had mapped out the best route the day they arrived. Jon was sure if his plan worked, Sarah would forget all about the Mia gossip. It just wouldn't matter anymore. He smiled smugly thinking about her surprise and looked up to see Sarah staring at him.

"What is it?"

"You'll have to wait and see." He tried to shrug off the suspicion in her tone. He just needed to escape with her alone. Tonight could change everything.

Chapter Twenty-Four

Jonathan

The afternoon progressed as Jon planned. He and Sarah ate a late lunch on the balcony of their room alone. It was the first time in days that they were alone together for any length of time. Sarah shared her experience meeting the French journalist at the café, and Jon tried to reassure her she hadn't given away any important personal information. Christophe hadn't mentioned running into her, so she shouldn't worry about the journalist. Nothing she said would cause them problems. She didn't need to worry about such trivia. What he had planned would be life-changing.

After eating, Jon called Leslie and disappeared into the bathroom with his phone, closing the door so Sarah couldn't eavesdrop. He didn't know how Leslie was able to do what she did. He thought nothing would be available for hundreds of miles, but she was a miracle worker and well worth her salary.

When he returned to the room, Sarah was lying across the bed on her stomach, wearing just a T-shirt and her panties. She looked up from her journal when she heard him groan.

"Hmm...Oh, man...I wish we had more time. You look so hot," he said, setting his phone down on the table and stalking toward the bed, her behind sticking up perfectly just asking to be fondled.

She capped her pen and smiled up at him as she closed her journal. He sat down on the edge of the bed, trying not to look at her unconscious invitation. He didn't have time to act on it. But when she wrapped her body around his from behind and started distributing sweet, hot kisses across the back of his shoulder slow enough as to not tickle him, he almost gave in.

"I didn't know what to wear. You haven't told me where we're going yet," she whispered between kisses.

"Hmm," he groaned again. "Leslie and Nak are going to be here in five minutes," he lamented.

"There's a lock on the door," she stated the obvious and continued kissing him.

"No...Sam will be with them. He has a key. You better get dressed," he said, standing up and turning to face her.

"In what?"

"How about your burgundy dress, the one you wore yesterday on the boat...and bring a sweater or a jacket. It may be windy where we're going. I asked Leslie to pack you a bag. It's going to be an overnighter."

Sarah looked in the closet and declared, "I don't think she had a chance to pack anything. All my clothes are still here."

"She picked up a few new outfits. This is a working trip for her."

Sarah took a red-colored, flowing sundress off the hanger. It's style similar to the burgundy one he liked so much. "Is everyone coming with us?"

"Just the three of them," he declared, picking up his phone and sunglasses off the table and sliding them back into the pocket of his loose-fitting, tan cotton pants.

There was a quick rap on the door. Sarah grabbed her dress and scurried into the bathroom, closing the door behind her.

Jon sauntered into the main room and opened the suite door. He greeted the three and walked to the closet as he spoke. "Everything is set, right?" He pulled his empty carry-on bag out of the closet. "Everything?" he reiterated. He still had to pack. He was more nervous about tonight than the night he asked Sarah to marry him. It had to go just right.

"Yes," Leslie assured. "It will be perfect." She smiled at Jon and handed him the bag she had for Sarah.

Sam cleared his throat. "I've got good and bad news on the stalker." He pulled out his phone and brought up a picture of a woman, showing it to Jon. "Do you recognize her?"

Jon shook his head. She didn't look familiar.

"They caught her inside the courtyard, with her face pressed up against one of the guesthouse windows. Luckily the doors had already been secured for the evening and she only got into the courtyard."

Jon took Sam's phone and examined the picture again. The woman looked like dozens of other women he had seen before. There wasn't anything distinctive about her medium-length blond hair and brown eyes. He still didn't remember her. "Do you really think she could be our stalker? She doesn't look familiar at all."

"The good news is you probably won't recognize her. Someone hired her to sneak in and take pictures. We don't know who, but we will."

"So it's only a matter of time before we find the stalker?"

"Just a matter of time, Jon."

Sarah returned, her smiling face glowing with anticipation. The red dress flowed almost to her knees, but he knew those legs and didn't need to use his imagination for his breath to hitch.

"Great news, beautiful. They have a good lead on the stalker. It won't be long before the restraining order is written up." He knew it wouldn't make much of a difference anyway. Like paparazzi, stalkers never got what they deserved. Unless they got violent, the police couldn't do much to protect the victims, and sometimes by that time it was too late. They had talked enough in the last week about stalkers that Sarah knew this, and he didn't feel he needed to bring it up again.

∾

Once the boat was in open water, Jon began to relax. The yacht was surrounded by the beautiful blue sea, and the land was shrinking smaller and smaller from view. Jon knew they were too far out for the cameras to film them from the coast. All they would have to worry about was other boats. They were heading for a secluded side of an island that would provide even more privacy. The tall rocky cliffs of the island were impassable and would provide shelter from any watchful eyes. Jon was excited to put his plan into action. He was sure Sarah would agree and once she did, nothing the press said about Mia could hurt them anymore. As he contemplated, Sarah peered around the corner hanging on to the brass rail that surrounded the boat's edge. She had been getting her things settled down in their cabin below the deck. Sarah was laughing about something when Jon spotted her, and she had a huge smile on her face.

"What's so funny?" he asked as she approached.

"Leslie. I don't know if she was bragging or if she was making sure that I knew she and Nak wouldn't be bothering us, but she made it quite clear they would be in their room for at least the next hour," Sarah shared with a chuckle.

"Only an hour…that doesn't leave much time." He smiled and pulled her flush against his body as he wrapped his arms securely around her. "I guess we'll have to get right to it, then," he chuckled before wetting her lips with his. They continued to kiss as Jon's hands found their way up her thighs. He picked her up, and she wrapped her legs around his waist as he carried her to the large, blue, padded lounger in the center of the deck. He spun around and plopped down on the lounger with her on his lap. She squealed and clung to Jon tighter so she wouldn't topple over. He started kissing her again as his hands roamed across her body. He was so relaxed. He loved that they were outside and didn't have to worry about voyeurs.

Sarah pulled back from his kiss and eyed him questioningly. "What are you doing?"

Jon smiled at her and responded, "I thought I was being pretty obvious, especially for someone college educated like you."

"Out in the open?"

"You can leave your dress on. I'm confident I can work around it," he chuckled as he eyed her bare thigh.

"What if someone sees us?" she questioned.

Jon handed her a tall flute of champagne that he had staged next to the seating area. He raised his glass and toasted, "To our first sex tape." She glared at him as he sipped from his drink. "I'm kidding. I asked the crew to leave us alone for the next two hours. Sam is in his quarters. Leslie and Nak are busy, and there is no one in sight. Why not?" he questioned with his most enticing voice. "It reminds me of the week at your parent's lake…no one around. We did what we wanted, where we wanted."

She blushed. He could tell she was running out of resistance. She looked into his blue eyes and wrapped her arms around his neck.

"If you're sure no one will see us."

Jon's hands smoothed up Sarah's thighs until they reached her tiny panties.

"These aren't your favorite pair, are they?" he asked, tugging on her underwear.

"No," she whispered, as if she was worried someone other than him would hear her confession and know what was going to happen next.

"Good," he said as he shredded the fragile fabric between his fingers and tossed it to the floor. His hand slid over her silken skin as she unbuttoned his pants.

But just as Jon and Sarah were starting to get really comfortable, an unmistakable thrumping sound began echoing through the sky. The noise resonated all around them. They couldn't tell what direction it was coming from. It filled the air. Jon stood up and fastened his pants. Sarah straightened her dress and curled her legs up, wrapping her arms around them. They looked up at the sky and waited, hoping it would pass right by. They could tell it was getting closer. The noise was getting louder and louder.

Jon picked up the bottle of champagne and filled their glasses to the brim. There it was. A helicopter hovering about five hundred feet from them with a long camera lens, poking out the side that was pointed right at them.

Jon glanced at Sarah. She rose, picked up her goblet, and shadowed him below the deck. He held the estate room door open for her to enter first. The room was elegant with glossy wood and brass accents and definitely worth the money he was paying for it. As she jumped onto the large bed, some of her champagne slopped onto the comforter, so she reached for a tissue sitting on the shelf above the bed. He slumped down across the end of the bed as she dabbed at the Moroccan blue comforter with the tissue. Why couldn't the press just leave them alone? He looked over at her with a defeated expression. The helicopter was still circling.

"Why are we here, Jon? I know if you wanted alone time on a boat you wouldn't have brought Leslie and Nak. What's going on? I feel like you're hiding something from me again."

He closed his eyes in frustration and took a deep breath, not knowing what to say.

"You're acting weird," she stated as she crawled to the end of the bed and hovered above his face.

He opened his lids and stared into her beautiful green eyes. "Will you marry me, Sarah?"

"You already asked me and I said yes, remember?" She smiled at him and held up her left hand.

"I mean tonight…on the boat. I want to be married to you, right now," he said with desperation. He needed this. He wasn't sure if it would solve any of his problems, but feeling more bound to Sarah would definitely ease some of them.

"You are *so* sexy when you talk like that," she said, leaning down to kiss him.

Jon pulled back, and Sarah paused with a surprised look. "I mean it. I want to get married tonight on the boat. Leslie and Nak can be our witnesses."

Sarah sat up and questioned, "But I've been planning the wedding for months. All the plans are cemented. Don't you want all of our friends and family at the wedding?"

"That doesn't matter to me. I just need you," he smiled, trying to exude charm.

She examined him skeptically and questioned, "You have me. Why does it matter when we get married? What happened with the press today?"

"Why do you think something happened with the press?"

"Because we were supposed to go to that party with Isaac and Remi tonight and you whisked me away, completely avoiding the press. This wasn't planned. Did you tell everyone about our wedding plans in your interviews or something?"

"I would never do that."

"So why the rush then?"

Jon got up and lifted the window blind. It sounded like the helicopter was leaving. The thrumping was getting softer, and he didn't see it hovering. He picked up his flute and downed about half of its liquid before glancing back at Sarah. *Why was she so suspicious? Was it that obvious?* He settled on the arm of the club chair that sat across the small room from her and confessed, "The news about Mia's pregnancy broke. Her publicist confirmed it and she didn't identify the daddy. One of the journalists asked me during our interview if I was the father. He just blatantly came out with it. Then Remi stepped in and told him

I wasn't going to answer the question. That just made it worse. I could see the speculation spread on the people's faces in the room. I didn't want you to have to deal with that."

Sarah

There it was—the moment of truth. She sat up and leaned against the headboard, folding her legs in front of her. "You're not the father, are you?" She watched him expectantly.

He cocked his head and scowled at her. "How could you even ask that?"

"You didn't answer my question." She stared wide-eyed. He always avoided what he didn't want to talk about by asking another question. She wanted an answer. She deserved an answer. "You were with her the night before my accident back in December. I saw the pictures online. You never told me she was out with you. Why did you keep that from me, if you weren't hiding it?"

Jon looked down, shaking his head in frustration, and Sarah wasn't sure if he was irritated that he'd been caught or if he couldn't believe she didn't trust him.

"Are you kidding, Sarah? I barely talked to her that night. She ran into Liam and he mentioned where we were going. She just showed up. I wasn't hiding it from you. You just get so crazy about her that I didn't think—. Then you had the accident and I didn't even know what end was up. I totally forgot about her being there."

"Could the baby be yours, Jon?" Her voice was soft. She waited impatiently. He needed to answer her.

"You are really asking me this question?" He grunted and pinched his eyes together. When he opened them again, he turned and looked her squarely in the face. "No…It is not my baby. Is that clear enough?" His bitter voice penetrated her as he emphasized his point with wide eyes. "I haven't been with anyone else since I met you. I thought you knew that." A hurt expression seized his face.

Whoa. Her heart thundered. She shouldn't have asked. She wilted and stared at him. She knew it would hurt him, and she didn't want that, but she had to know.

"I just needed to hear it from your mouth. I do trust you, but you've been acting so peculiar this trip…and Mia seems to have some strange hold on you. You're keeping something from me. What's changed? Why do you want to get married so badly?"

They sat in silence for almost a minute before he spoke. "I don't know…I guess it's just this pregnancy rumor…and then seeing Amy again." Sarah could see that Amy Richardson had really thrown him off. She knew something was wrong at the premiere. Jon usually kissed his female costars on the cheek and held friendly conversations with them, even the ones he had dated. He barely acknowledged Amy, which was out of character for Jon. He didn't even stand next to her on the red carpet.

"I could tell you guys dated. Did it end badly?"

"You could say that." He glanced at his feet with apprehension. "We started filming the movie together about six months after Jack's death. I was a mess then. I knew I killed my brother and I was bent on self-destruction. I was out drinking every night at the clubs." He took a deep breath. "Then there were the women. There were a lot. Amy was just one of them. I pretty much did what felt good—to numb the pain. I hooked up with Amy, and she ended up getting pregnant," he confessed, looking at Sarah apologetically.

Holy what? Sarah stared at him for a moment, unsure what to say. They had been together a year, and he hadn't told her he had a kid. *Really?* She was pissed, or she would have been if he didn't look so distraught. *OK. That would be a hard one to confess, but they were getting married.*

"So…you have a kid you never told me about?"

"No…" He shook his head and looked down. "Amy ended the pregnancy. She never even asked me what I wanted—never gave me a choice. We were so young, and she was supposed to start filming another movie in six months. A pregnancy would have ruined her career. It's not like we were in love. With the way I was then, what woman would have wanted to share a kid with me? I was such a wreck." He paused. "She said it was her body, her choice. I've always resented her for not even asking me, though. It was my kid, too. So here I am, almost five years later, forced to face her again, and then the press accuses me of fathering Mia's baby. It just brought up all those feelings again. I don't know…"

"Did you want the baby?" Sarah asked, still searching for logic in his words.

Chapter Twenty-Five

Jonathan

Jon remembered back to that year he had tried so hard to push out of his head. He and Amy weren't just hooking up, but they weren't serious either. Like on many films, they had chemistry on set and it spilled over into their personal lives. They partied together and spent most of their time together for three months on and off set. Jon didn't know what to think the night Amy told him about the baby. She said it so casually over dinner that he thought she was joking. When he realized she was serious, he questioned, "Is it mine?" It was kind of a douche thing to say, but he wasn't even sure they were exclusive.

"Yes, asshole!" she answered without batting an eye.

He was confused. He always used a condom. How could she get pregnant? He thought he had always used a condom, but there were entire nights that alcohol erased from his memory. How could he know for sure?

"I don't know what I'm going to do about it yet, but I just thought you should know," Amy continued. They finished filming for the day without talking about it again. Then Amy disappeared for the weekend to her parent's house in New York and didn't answer his texts the whole filming break. He figured she just needed time to think, so he didn't call.

Meanwhile, Jon spent two days pondering fatherhood. It evoked some sort of change in him, as if there was hope for something more out of life—more than drinking, more than just hooking up. By Monday morning on set, he knew what he had to say to her. He didn't think he and Amy would ever last, but he was willing to try. He offered to marry her over a turkey sandwich at craft services. No matter how hard he tried to expunge Amy's response from his memory, he couldn't.

"Oh my god. Are you for real?"

It was a slap in the face that he hadn't expected.

"I'm only twenty years old, and you are not marriage material. You don't have to worry about it anymore. I took care of it. No more baby."

"What?" He couldn't believe she would just end the pregnancy without even talking to him about it. "But, it was my baby, too." The baby would have been a bright spot, someone to love him unconditionally, without judgment for what he had done to Jack. He couldn't believe it was gone.

Amy rolled her eyes. "I didn't have to think about it, Jonathan. I know I told you I did, but I'm not going to let some parasite spawn ruin my career. *My* career would end, not yours. You don't get a choice."

꙰

Jon looked up to meet Sarah's eyes. "Did I want the baby? I…I don't know. I think I was just searching for a replacement for Jack at the time—something to distract from the agony. When Jack died, I knew it was my fault, and I would have done anything to trade places with him. He was the one with the bright future. He was the one with all the talent—the A squad, the one who was going to do great things. I was second string. It should have been me that died—nobody would have cared. I did all I could to show God he had picked the wrong brother. I drank, popped pills, slept with as many women as I could.

I was angry at the world, at myself, and I was going to punish God for taking my brother. Then when I found out I was going to be a father, I found hope. Hope that I could be more than a screw-up, motivation to be better, and then that was gone as quickly as it came."

"So why didn't you tell me until now, and why get married now?"

Jon shrugged. "It's not my proudest moment." He collapsed into the seat of the club chair and dragged his fingers through his hair across the top of his head before continuing, "I thought I was over my issues with Amy. I've grown up a lot since then. Honestly…I never thought *Third Rung* would be released. No one was interested in it for so long. I thought it would just disappear, like so many movies do, and I wouldn't have to see her again. Then there are the Mia rumors. I can see how much they bother you. I just thought if we got married, we could forget about everything else, everyone else."

"I don't want to get married because of Mia or some other ghost from your past. I want it to be about us. Can you understand that?" she said, scrunching half of her face.

Jon climbed onto the bed next to her. He stared at her with guilt smeared on his face. He paused. "I want our wedding day to be *your* perfect day."

"We can enjoy ourselves on the boat," added Sarah.

"Yeah," he muttered again without enthusiasm.

"You need to stop feeling guilty about the things you can't control. I don't care about your former life. You're a good person. The past is past and you can't change it. You have to let it go. There's no other choice." Sarah leaned her head against his shoulder and whispered, "I love you, Will."

She hardly ever called him Will anymore, and it made the corners of his lips turn up slightly. He wondered how he could be so lucky. How could he have finally found someone that accepted him with all his flaws? She put up with his cracked life and hardly ever complained. He didn't think he deserved her. He knew he didn't. He wrapped his arm around Sarah and sat without speaking, contemplating his life since he met her. It had changed so much. She made him a better person. "I feel like we're already married. That's why I said you were my wife when I punched the paparazzo. It's just a ceremony, right? You're the best part of my life, Sarah."

Sarah softly kissed his cheek and snuggled into the crook of his arm. They lay in silence staring at the ceiling for several minutes until Sarah admitted with a sigh, "I hope our kids have your eyes." She ran her finger over his cheek until his dimple appeared. "And your dimple."

Jon turned to kiss her finger. That was the sexiest thing she had ever said.

He rolled on top of her, his knees straddling her hips as he ripped the Velcro cast apart and tossed it on the floor. His hand didn't even hurt anymore. Why was he still wearing it? Then he pinned her hands to the bed next to her head. She was adorable. He bent down and ran his tongue across her lower lip until she opened her mouth with a moan to accept it deeper. His lips covered her soft and supple ones.

When he sat up, breaking the kiss, he smiled and said. "I want a daughter with your eyes, your flawless skin, and your perfect little nose." He bent down and kissed her nose, her hands still pinned. "I'll be putty in her hands, though. She'll be *so* spoiled." He gathered her hands into one of his. His other hand trailed down her cheek and she smiled. Then he trailed a finger down her beautiful supple neck to her breasts. He drew a circle slowly and methodically over each one. "She will never be allowed to have these. They drive boys crazy. They'll do anything just to touch them." He kissed her where his finger had traced as his free hand found the hem of her sundress.

Sarah laughed. "You can't stop our daughter from growing boobs."

"We can't have any girls, then," he gasped as he leaned back and pulled her into a sitting position. He maneuvered her dress out from under her, and she lifted her hips to help. "Because boys are filthy…filthy animals," he declared as he pulled her dress over her head.

"Yeah, I've noticed." She chuckled as her now-freed hands slid under his shirt and ran over the ridges of his abdomen. Her pale pink bra dropped to the valley where their bodies met, and she looked up at him. "Did you do that? You're good."

"Why thank you," he accepted with a grin. "There's more." He flicked up one eyebrow and stared devilishly at her as he pressed her against the mattress. Her arms wrapped around his back, drawing him closer. His mouth focused on her neck right below her ear for several seconds, before he rolled off her, pulling his shirt off over his head as he moved. He lay down on his side next to her— her naked, and him in his cotton slacks. "What am I going to do with you?" he asked as he grazed his finger down her body with feather-like softness. He watched as her whole body quivered under his touch.

"I'm all yours. Do what you like," Sarah said with a not-so-innocent grin.

He ran his finger over her flat stomach as he envisioned her with a small baby bump. His baby. The thought of Sarah with his baby ignited his desire. "Anything I like?" he asked.

"Anything," she crooned, closing her eyes. She seemed to relax with each brush of his hand.

She pulled at his pants, and he kicked them off with his boxer briefs. As his pants hit the floor, he visualized nothing between them. She said "anything" after all. He wanted kids so badly. He knew all her weaknesses. He could get her so revved she wouldn't even notice. He was confident in his skills with her. She seemed to be made just for him. He positioned himself above her. Cupping her breast with one hand, he pressed his lips to her skin. He sucked and licked and teased before moving to the other. Her fingers entangled in his hair as he kissed down to her navel. She wriggled beneath him when his hand and lips moved lower. She responded with a soft moan to each tormenting move he made. *God, he loved this woman.* He could slide right into her and they could make a baby— his and Sarah's baby. Their love needed to be shared. He wanted so much to have children with her. He hoped their children would look just like her. She was so perfect. They would have her inner beauty, her innocence, and her optimism. He kissed his way back up her body and stared at her face.

He paused as he watched her breathing calm. She was so trusting. He wouldn't be giving her a choice. He was as bad as Amy. He reached for Sarah's champagne glass next to the bed and downed a large swig, trying to collect his thoughts. Her green eyes fluttered open, and she smiled when she saw him staring down at her. She opened her mouth as he drizzled the bubbly in until it started to splash over her lips. Then he kissed the sweet excess from her mouth and almost changed his mind. He set the glass back on the bedside table and reached for the box he had stashed there earlier. He found a foil square and held it up for her to see as he spoke. "I love you, Sarah. And my *anything* would be to not use one of these."

A small gasp escaped Sarah's throat as her muscles tensed under him. It told him all he needed to know. He brushed his fingers through her hair on the side of her face and then smoothed his thumb over the line that had formed on her brow. "I know you're not ready, so we'll use this today." He set the condom on the bed and felt Sarah's muscles relax beneath him.

He knew he would have to backtrack to get her to the point she had been, so he kissed his favorite spot on her neck, the spot that always made her moan. As his hands began to move over her skin again, he whispered, "Someday soon I want to feel you without anything between us."

He never wanted to take away her rights. For as much as he wanted to have children with her, he would never do that. He flipped her on top of him and handed her the foil square.

Jon clasped his hands behind his head as he watched the awareness bloom on his fiancé's face. She licked her lips and ran both hands slowly down his body to his navel. She smirked as if she knew exactly how much power she had over him. And oh, she had all the power in this relationship. When she touched him, his breath caught, his entire body shuttered, and he closed his eyes to savor the feel of her fingers.

A growl rose from deep inside as he grasped her hips, and the girly noise that emerged from her throat froze his hands, locking her in place. He couldn't resist her pleading eyes, though. He couldn't resist her at all. When he finally released her and she started to move above him, he realized he needed her to slow down. All the talk of marriage and children had pushed him too close to the edge. Knowing she deserved so much but that he would never last with her in control, he wrapped his arms around her and flipped her back underneath him.

"You are too sexy," he whispered, settling on his elbows above her and meshing his lips with hers. He wished she'd agreed to get married tonight. His motivation may have started out all warped, but that didn't change how he felt. He wanted her as his wife. He wanted that claim on her. He knew not all marriages lasted, but theirs would. They were meant to be together. His tongue dipped into her mouth as one of his hands smoothed over her soft body. She had told him the first time they'd made love that she'd never been pushed over the edge of desire until that night. He was the only one to ever do that for her. He could see it in her face now. The connection they had went beyond anything he could have ever hoped for. He wanted to grow old with her. He wanted so much out of their life together and he wanted to start right now.

He pulled back from the kiss and said, "Promise we'll get married soon."

She giggled the loveliest sound ever. "I promise."

Sarah

An hour later a knock on the door broke the quiet of the room. Sarah's head rested on Jon's chest, and her eyes flickered open at the sound.

"What do you need?" Jon asked as he shifted, covering Sarah with a blanket.

"The kitchen staff is asking about the evening meal, sir."

"Give us forty-five minutes."

He got up, turned on the shower to warm, and returned to Sarah on the bed. She hadn't moved. He grabbed her hand and tugged. "Come join me in the shower," he whispered in his sexy, you-can't-argue voice.

She smiled up at him, shaking her head back and forth. Her head was reeling from the last hour. With all the bad memories and the pending press about Mia's pregnancy, maybe Jon had changed his mind about having kids right away. It made sense why he had wanted a child. He was trying to fill the void left by Amy Richardson's actions. But now he's changed his mind. He only said he wanted not to have to wear a condom. He never said he wanted to make babies.

Sarah closed her eyes remembering the moment. When he said the words, she imagined it. She wanted it. Her whole body tensed, hoping. If he had said he wanted to make babies, she was sure she would have agreed. With all his hardness pressed against her, he could do whatever he wanted and she wouldn't have said no. Besides, the idea of having his baby had been growing on her, ever since the doctor had said she was healthy and there was no medical reason why she couldn't get pregnant. What was stopping them from starting their family? The wedding. They should wait until after the wedding. She wanted that. But what then? Nothing. Her hand ran across her belly as she imagined what it would be like to have a baby bump. Jon's baby bump.

It didn't matter now though. If Jon wanted to enjoy a condom-free life, they could wait to have kids. She had gotten the prescription the doctor gave her filled. The pills sat in her purse waiting for her to make the decision.

"If I have to carry you, you know we'll never make it to dinner." Jon's words broke through her thoughts.

He was staring at her. Thank god she was covered with a blanket. She took his outstretched hand to join him in the shower, and eventually they made it to dinner.

They spent the rest of the week on the boat. It was incredibly blissful, even with Leslie, Nak, and Sam there. Sarah and Jonathan found ways to sneak away. The boat docked at a smaller port a few days after they left Cannes and she and Jon went shopping, just the two of them. It seemed so normal—no one stalking them, no blinding camera flashes—just two people in love, and it felt good.

The day after their shopping spree, Sarah and Jon got their alone time on the boat's deck with no helicopters hovering and no one filming. Sarah knew they would never be able to recreate their week at her parent's cabin, but this week on the Mediterranean was pretty close, and in some ways better. Meals were prepared for them, and lightning never left them without electricity.

Jonathan had shut off his phone, and Sarah appreciated that they weren't constantly interrupted by it. Leslie had hers on for a while, but Jon refused to deal with business issues, so eventually she shut hers off too. When their week was up and they all returned for the flight back home, she wished they missed the flight.

Of course, Isaac sat next to them and started up right away.

"I had to promise them that you would do a two-week tour through Europe. It doesn't look very good for the star of the movie that won best drama to not show up for the awards ceremony. Paul Sterling wanted you to accept the award with him. The whole cast was there except you. You didn't even tell me you weren't coming back. I thought you were only going to be gone overnight. I kept expecting you to show at the last minute. Paul made some derogatory comment about you not changing. It wasn't cool just to run off with some girl and disregard the award like it meant nothing. You're going to have to do this tour. The promoters want to see that you support the film. This film is your ticket to that serious role you've been craving. If you don't back it, no one will see your work."

"It's not as if I got any awards. It was just the film that got recognized." Jon's tone showed that he felt as if he'd been snubbed. "And I didn't run off with some girl, Isaac. I ran off with my wife."

Isaac looked at Jon, his eyes the size of quarters. "Don't tell me you..."

"Not yet. But she is still my wife, and you need to show her a bit more respect." Jon smiled at Sarah and ran his thumb gently along her jawline. "I'll do the tour, if you drop the condescending tone. I'm sorry if it was reminiscent of Atlantic City dealing with Sterling, but Sarah and I needed to get away from the press. Mia's people confirmed that she's pregnant, and I knew everyone would assume it was mine."

"Is it?" asked Isaac, and Jon slammed him with a death glare. "I guess that breaks a chink in her attempt to woo you."

"You think? I'm marrying Sarah. It wasn't going to work anyway, and someday in the future, after we've officially signed the papers, we will have kids of our own."

As Jon finished his sentence, Remi joined the conversation. "Is Sarah pregnant? You have to keep me in the loop, Jon."

Jon shook his head and said, "I'll let you know."

Sarah smiled and kissed Jon's cheek as she got up. "I need to talk to Leslie," she said, though she didn't really have to talk to her. She just didn't want her fairy-tale week to end with Isaac and Remi talking business with Jon, but she realized that it already had. She saddled up to the plane's bar next to Nak and asked him and Leslie if they enjoyed the week as much as she had.

Chapter Twenty-Six

Sarah

Lunch with Mia—Sarah couldn't believe she had actually agreed to it. She'd only been home for three days, and she had to spend today having lunch with her mortal enemy. Sarah had no desire to get to know Mia better. She'd rather scrub out dog kennels in her dad's veterinary clinic for a week during an epidemic of canine parvovirus than spend an hour with Mia, and disinfecting kennels was the worst job she had ever had. The lunch date was Jon's concoction, and Sarah would do anything for Jon. So here she was wasting her valuable wedding prep time driving out to Ventura to have lunch with someone she detested.

They got seated at a booth in a secluded corner—or it would have been secluded if it wasn't so visible from the large window looking out onto the sidewalk. At least there wasn't anyone seated near them. Jon didn't want anyone to hear their conversation.

"Mia, why can't you just tell everyone who the father is? Or haven't you told him yet," Jon asked after the waitress left.

"He knows I'm pregnant."

"What's the deal then?" he exclaimed.

"Have you seen the pictures of you and me melded together? They've already named the baby. *Mia-thon*—that's what they're calling it. The fans are rooting for you to claim it."

"Great," Jon said, shaking his head.

The server appeared and took their order. When she was a safe distance from the table, Mia started up again.

"All you have to do is own up, Jon," stated Mia.

Own up? What the hell was she talking about? Sarah didn't understand.

"Even when you're as careful as you are, things can happen. Oh, but you know that." Mia grew a conniving smile. "Did Jon ever tell you why he's so vigilant about condoms? His little oops...has he told you about that? Or is he keeping that from you, too," she prodded Sarah.

What a sleazy little bitch. "He has. Jon and I don't keep secrets," Sarah volleyed back. She hated that Mia knew Jon so well, that she had carnal knowledge of him. She despised that Mia had a past with Jon because she felt Mia rubbed it in her face every chance she had. Even the fans wanted Mia and Jon together. Sarah was tired of Mia's manipulation of their life, and she wasn't going to let her have the upper hand. "We don't have time to raise your baby, Mia. We're going to have our own to take care of," declared Sarah.

Jon froze with eyes wide. He laid his arm across the back of her chair and leaned into Sarah with a huge smile. "Why didn't you tell me?" he whispered.

"Surprise, surprise. I guess it *really* doesn't matter how careful you are, does it?" snickered Mia. "Two at a time, the press will EAT. THAT. UP."

"Shut up, Mia!" Jon asserted. He looked at Sarah with a confused expression.

She returned Jon's glance, apologizing, "I mean...in the future. I'm not pregnant now…but I will be someday, after we're married."

"Oh god. Isn't she precious? Where did you find her, Jon? She doesn't want to disappoint you. You want kids, but she's not ready, is she? She wants to wait until you're married—how cute. Everybody has a baby out of wedlock in Hollywood these days. Hell, most have two before signing the papers, if they sign them at all. I guess your mommy and daddy wouldn't approve." She mocked in a little girl's voice.

"You know, I defended you. I told Sarah you wouldn't be that bad once she got to know you. I didn't realize that pregnancy would turn you into a raging bitch."

"It's been a long time since you called me a bitch. Wow, I must have really pissed you off," she chuckled. "I'm not trying to piss you off, Jon." She paused, not making eye contact. "It happened that night I met up with you at the sushi bar in December," Mia whispered. "I tried calling you when I found out, but you didn't pick up. I wasn't going to leave it on your voice-mail."

Jon stared at her, his face unreadable.

"I thought you'd own up to it. I thought you'd do the right thing. How was I to know you found someone else? That night, you never told me you were getting engaged. How was I to know? All you had to do was tell me. We've always been there for each other and now you're abandoning me, just like everyone else in my life," Mia admitted, her eyes welling up.

Sarah whimpered as she rose from her chair and took off for anywhere other than the table. She had just cleared the hostess's stand when Jon grabbed her wrist.

"Sarah, stop, please," he pleaded.

She yanked her arm free, but he grasped her shoulders, tugging her to the wall near the exit. She shrugged off his hands, but he caged her, one hand pressed against the wall on either side of her, encircling without touching.

"Would you just listen?" his voice desperate.

Why wouldn't he just let her go? She could feel the tears stinging in her eyes. He didn't need her to have a baby. Mia was already pregnant. It made sense. Everybody knew they were meant to be together. She could feel Jon's stare, but she refused to meet his gaze.

"I can't do this right now. Just let me go. I have to go."

"I'm not going to let you go. You're too upset."

She ducked under his arm and took off through the door. Sarah was aware of all the eyes on her, but she couldn't deal with this. He had lied to her. She had to get away, and she was taking the car. With her head start, she was able to get into her car and almost get the door closed before his hand slipped in and clutched the steering wheel. The tears were streaming down her cheeks. She couldn't even see straight.

"Please. I just need some time to process."

"Why are you acting like this, Sarah? Just stop and talk to me."

She threw the car into gear and pulled the door closed when Jon finally let go. A loud *thump* reverberated through her BMW, and she glanced in her mirror to see Jon staring after her, shaking his head.

Jonathan

He pounded his fist on the back of the car as she drove away. *What was wrong with her?* He couldn't understand why she suddenly took off running. What had she said? "You lied to me." What had he lied about? OK, maybe Mia *was* as bad as Sarah had made her out to be. That wouldn't cause her to make such a big scene though. He had never seen her so distraught. He slid his phone from his pocket and typed out a text to Sam.

Jon: *Can you track Sarah's phone? She took off and I don't know where she went.*

Sam: *She's not going to be happy.*

Jon: *I know, but I need to make sure she's safe.*

256

Taking a deep breath, he turned back to the restaurant. Mia was still inside. He just wanted to leave, but he still had to deal with her.

As he came through the door, the hostess addressed him, "Is there anything I can help you with, Mr. Williams? A car service? A cab?"

Shit. Jon shook his head and continued back to the table where Mia waited. He collapsed in his chair across from her. The salads had been delivered. Jon wasn't hungry anymore. Mia's sugary smile didn't help.

"I take it she isn't so keen about me having your baby."

Could Sarah have really thought he would cheat? He told her he wasn't the father. Why would she think he lied? He scratched his forehead trying to make sense of her words. "You lied to me," she had said.

"Leave it alone, Mia."

"She made quite a scene. Crazy *that* one. Unstable. You could have anyone, Jon. Hell, you could have me for god's sake. Why her?"

Jon took out his phone, ignoring Mia. Several minutes had passed since he sent the text to Sam. He should have located her by now.

Jon typed, Did you find her yet?

"You know that's rude. You shouldn't text at the table." She took a bite of her salad.

Jon bit his lip, swallowing the explosive words he knew would spill if he opened his mouth.

Sam's reply flashed onto his screen. *It looks like she's headed home. I'll let you know if she goes off course.* Jon felt the tension in his body start to dissipate. He would let her cool off and then she would stop being so irrational. She would have to know in her heart that he wouldn't cheat. He looked up at Mia, who was making her irritation obvious by the way she kept tapping her nails on the table.

"Seriously, if she can't handle a little joking around, how are you two ever going to make it? She's not resilient at all. The press is going to destroy her long before the wedding."

"You don't get it, Mia. She's my more. Sarah is the only person who truly sees me as a person, not just a movie star. She doesn't look at me as a way to raise her status in Hollywood. She doesn't see dollar signs when I kiss her. She wouldn't care if I gave up acting all together, because all she wants is for me to be happy. She accepts me for who I am. I don't have to put on a show with her. She's the most genuine person that I have ever met, and I will be marrying her. I'll leave Hollywood if I have to."

"I guess she draws her line of acceptance at you having a baby with someone else," Mia snarled before taking another bite of her dry salad.

Jon rubbed his fingers through his hair, summoning strength. "So you were saying," he slid his salad to the side of the table and glared at Mia, "you slept with one of my buddies that night at the sushi restaurant? Or was it just some guy in the bar?"

Mia rolled her eyes. "It wasn't just some guy off the street."

"Which one of my boys was it? Nick? Not that I give a damn, but we've always had an understanding about exes, a man code. It doesn't really matter, though, having a baby with you should be punishment enough."

"Where's our food? I'm starved." Mia looked around, straightening the napkin on her lap. She glanced back at Jon. He was glaring.

"You need to tell him."

"I have told him, and he doesn't want anything to do with the baby… something about his wife…blah, blah, blah. I don't even remember."

"You slept with Chris? What the hell were you thinking?"

"I wasn't looking for a commitment. A married man isn't going to tell anyone, especially you, Jon."

"His wife is nine months pregnant. What a stupid bastard." It didn't surprise Jon. It just frustrated him.

"I didn't mean to get pregnant. I was on antibiotics the week before. I didn't think they would mess up my birth control for the entire month. I guess I shouldn't have given you so much crap about wearing a condom. You were right; the pill can fail."

"Why him? He's the only one of the guys that's married," Jon asked, though he knew it was because he was married.

"We were both pretty trashed. I didn't rape him. He was very willing."

"You knew he was married." Jon stopped himself—he wasn't going to judge. "You know what? I don't want to know the details."

"He's hot, in a trailer trash sort of way. Besides, I hadn't spoken to you in months and you barely acknowledged I was there. I was just looking for some validation. Chris has always been my favorite next to you. His bod is smokin', and he's got those tribal tattoos."

"I thought my friends were beneath you."

"Oh, you remember how I like to be on top." She smiled her sucrose smile and continued, "My friend, Kiera, slums it all the time. I should be allowed once in my life."

The server interrupted, "Mr. Williams, would you like me to box the third meal to take home, or would you like to cancel it all together?"

"I'll bring it home. Thank you."

She nodded and left.

"So…what are your plans after the baby comes?"

"I'll hire a nanny. I've got until August to find one, right? I don't really need Chris to man-up. I don't want him as a partner. I'd rather have you, if you're willing."

The server delivered their meals—planked salmon with coconut-mango risotto and BBQ ribs with baby potatoes and summer squash. "I'll bring the boxed meal out when you are ready to leave." She smiled sympathetically at Jon.

"That will be fine. Thanks," he said. He wished he could just leave. He broke a potato in half with his fork and pushed it around his plate. *Why would Sarah think he fathered the baby? It didn't make sense.* He took out his phone again and, as Mia rolled her eyes at him, sent a text to Sarah. She wouldn't check the text until she got home, but at least it would be waiting for her.

Jon: It's not my baby. Mia was just messing with you. Don't be mad.

"What kind of pathetic, groveling note are you sending now? I'm starting to think they should revoke your man card." She took a bite of her salmon and looked down at her plate without a hint of humor.

"Can you drop me at the house?"

"It would make it a lot easier if you would say the baby is yours. We could write up a contract. You wouldn't have to pay anything. I don't need your money."

"Easier on who, Mia? Not me. And definitely not Sarah. The press'll slaughter me. And Sarah doesn't deserve any of this attention."

She closed her eyes fighting back tears, or maybe she was conjuring them—he wasn't sure. "It's different for men. Even in Hollywood. They say we're equal. They even stopped calling us actresses, right? Everyone is an actor now. But we're not equal. Men can be with as many women as they can manage and everyone high-fives them for their conquests. But women, once they've had more than three public relationships, they're a slut or they can't hold a man. Look at Ashley Taylor—the sweetest girl in the world, right? No guy wants to date her, though." A tear dripped down her face. "The fans would accept you. We have a past together. They won't accept me having a baby with a man that I have never dated or even been seen with. Besides, I don't want to ruin Chris's life. His wife is pregnant."

He stared at her not really knowing what to say. He swallowed the first words that came to his tongue. "Honestly, if I hadn't met Sarah, I would consider taking responsibility for the baby, but I'm trying to build a life with her." He paused and looked into Mia's blue eyes. "Being a father isn't just taking credit for conception; it's a lifetime commitment. If I were to put my name on the birth certificate, then the baby would have to be raised as if it were mine. I'd have a say in where it lived, what schools it went to and who spent time with it. Do you really want me to have so much control over your life?"

"Better you than some guy that I don't even know."

"You knew him well enough to sleep with him." Jon tried to make her laugh.

"Are you mad about that? I didn't think you would ever find out."

"I'm not mad. It's your life." He paused. He needed to be direct and tell her what was on his mind. "I know you well enough to realize that if I let you put my name on your baby's birth certificate that someday, maybe ten years from now, we would disagree on something, and then somehow it would leak to the press that the kid wasn't mine. I would lose all rights and access to a kid I had invested years of my life raising because a paternity test would prove that I'm not the real father."

"I'd never do that."

"Yes, you would. I will help you any way I can, Mia, but I can't be the baby's father."

More tears streamed down her cheeks. As she tried to recompose, Jon glanced around the restaurant, wondering how this spectacle called lunch looked to everyone who would be tweeting about it.

"I can't tell the press about Chris yet. I still have too much to figure out." Mia dabbed her napkin under her eyes.

"I'll talk to him and see where his head is. It will all work out."

She met his eyes and the corner of her lips turned up just a little.

"If you're done, can we go?" he asked. She nodded, and he waved the server over, handing her his credit card when she reached the table.

As they left the restaurant, Jon was careful not to wrap his arm around

Mia like he normally would. He held the takeout bag between them to keep a distance. He knew what the tabloids would say, and he knew how that simple act would irritate Sarah if someone snapped a picture.

The ride was long, and they spoke about Mia's next project and how she had gotten the studio to push back the filming a couple of weeks to give her more time to get back into shape after the baby was born. "I've already gained seven pounds. I'm going to be a total cow by the time I get this thing out of me."

Jon laughed at her comment. He told her that he would like to start a family with Sarah and confessed that he tried to convince her to get married on the Mediterranean. When they neared the house, Mia asked, "Do you need me to come in and tell Sarah the baby isn't yours?" Her tone insinuated that Sarah didn't trust him and would only believe the words coming from Mia's mouth.

"No. She'll be fine." He knew having Mia in the house would only aggravate Sarah. That's why they went out to lunch in the first place.

The paparazzi outside the gate frenzied when they recognized Mia and Jon in the car together. The guy in the white van that usually blocked the security camera actually got out of his vehicle to clack his lens against the windshield for a shot. Mia punched in the code and Jon tried to look nonchalant as the gate seemed to take forever to open. When the car came to a stop outside the guesthouse, Jon thanked Mia for the ride and told her he would call her after he spoke to Chris.

He pulled the door to the house closed behind him, expecting to see Sarah standing there with a scowl on her face. He shouldn't have forced her to have lunch with Mia. He sincerely thought it would go better, and she was probably pissed about the whole situation. At least she would have seen the text by now and would know that she had overreacted. He would wrap his arms around her and kiss the top of her head, and all her bitterness would melt away. She wasn't standing by the door, though.

Jon checked the kitchen as he stashed the food bag in the refrigerator, and then the courtyard before calling out to her, "Sarah. Where are you, beautiful?"

He headed upstairs—maybe she was napping. He wasn't that far behind her, an hour at the most. She wasn't in the bedroom either, so he checked the bath. She liked baths. The tub was bone-dry. "Sarah?" he called again as he spotted her phone on the bed. *If her phone was here, she was here,* he thought. Maybe she had her headphones on and didn't hear him come in. She had to be somewhere. He continued to look without success. He opened the door to the garage, not really knowing why she would be hiding in the garage, and his heart hit the cement.

Her car was gone. Her phone was on the bed, but her car was gone! Where would she go? She always had her phone with her. The visual Sarah had planted in his brain flashed into his head—her being stuffed into the trunk of her own car with her phone nowhere near her. How was he going to find her? He called Sam. "Sarah's gone. Her phone is here, but she and her car are gone."

"I'll be there in thirty minutes. She probably just ran out for groceries. Don't freak out."

Don't freak out? There was some psychotic person sending death threats, Sarah was missing, and he wasn't supposed to freak out. He couldn't call her, he couldn't track her phone, and he had no way to find her. He paced back and forth across the kitchen, stopping as his eyes brushed past the courtyard. The picture of Sarah's face as she sat under the pergola and looked up at the camera popped into his head. The cameras. He could see what happened. He'd have record of how she was taken, maybe even glimpse the face of her abductor.

Jon didn't know how he got to the security office. All of a sudden he was sitting in front of the computer, looking up at the large monitor on the wall as his fingers clicked frantically on the keyboard. He scrolled back through the gate footage until he saw Sarah's car coming in. He didn't see anyone in the car with her. He concentrated on the screen, waiting for movement—nothing out of the ordinary. He scanned and waited. With his eyes fixated on the monitor, he watched as Sarah's car drove back out the gate. It had only been twenty minutes, and she appeared to be alone. *She must have left on an errand,* he thought, as he rose to return to the guesthouse. *Why wouldn't she take her phone?*

Fifteen minutes later when Sam arrived, Jon explained what he had seen on the security tapes, and they laughed about how they had overreacted.

"Does she have her Pilates class today?" asked Sam.

"No. That's tomorrow."

"She probably just needed girl supplies or something."

Jon chuckled. "No, that's next week."

Sam passed him the "seriously, why would you know that" look.

"What? A man needs to know these things. You can't tell me you don't know when Cassandra's cycle starts."

"Not a clue," said Sam.

"Then you, my man, are not getting enough sex."

"True. That's the drawback of having children."

Jon hadn't thought about that. "Maybe Sarah and I *should* wait on having kids."

"They will definitely change your perception of life."

"As it is even without children involved, it kills me every time Sarah leaves the house. I don't think I can take it much longer. We need to find that stalker."

"We'll get some leads soon."

"What did the FBI say?"

"Pretty much what I told you already. We meet with a specialist who will help pinpoint suspects tomorrow."

"I hope it's not too late." Jon settled on the couch waiting for Sarah to walk through the door so he could apologize in person for pushing her into meeting with Mia. He shouldn't have pushed so hard for it. He just hoped they would learn to get along with each other, because Mia didn't have many female friends and with this pregnancy, he thought she needed someone she could confide in.

Chapter Twenty-Seven

Sarah

Sarah handed the hotel clerk her credit card—the one she had in college, not one of Jon's. She refused to use his money. Hoping no one would recognize her, she tossed her hair with her fingers until it hung in her eyes, veiling her face. The man standing on the other side of the counter smiled at her as he handed her the receipt to sign. With one phone call, he could tip off the paparazzi and everyone in the world, including Jon, would know where she was.

She nervously repositioned her computer bag on her shoulder and the man asked, "Can I call someone to help you with your luggage?"

"No, thank you. I have it." Sarah didn't need anyone else notifying the vultures either. She scooped up her key card as she grabbed the handle of her suitcase. She prayed she could make it to the room before the tears started again, but by the time she crossed the threshold, they were streaming down her face. What was she going to do? He had lied to her—something she thought he would never do. She dropped her bags to the floor. Collapsing on the king-sized bed, she couldn't hold her sobs back any longer. She pulled the pillow out from under the covers and buried her face in it.

She had believed him when he told her the baby wasn't his. On the boat he had looked her straight in the eyes and said it. *He was such a good actor.* She thought about the picture of Jon with his arm around Mia at the sushi bar and Mia's smug smile today when she revealed she had gotten pregnant that night. Sarah could have forgiven him for cheating, she knew that, if he had told her on the boat instead of denying it. If he had admitted the baby was his, then she was pretty sure she would have been able to get past it. But he lied, and that was the one thing she couldn't forgive.

She had to leave him. There was no other way. If she couldn't trust him, they had nothing. If he could lie to her so convincingly that she felt guilty she asked in the first place, how could she trust anything he said? She would have to find a way to move on, but she just didn't know how she would do it. In the year she'd known Jon, he'd become the most important person in her life. He was like air or food—impossible to give up. Her heart was his. How would she ever get it back?

She rolled over and looked blankly at the ceiling as she took in a shaky breath. If she cut all ties and never saw him again, it would be easier. It would kill her to look into his clear-blue eyes knowing that he lied. And if he found her, she didn't know if she would have the strength to leave. In two days Jon would be heading back to Europe for two weeks of promoting *Third Rung.* It was part of the deal he had worked out with Isaac.

After skipping the festival awards ceremony and disappearing for a week on the Mediterranean, he needed to make up for his lack of professionalism and had agreed to the promotional tour. He couldn't get out of it. If she stayed hidden until he left for the tour, she could get the rest of her things from the house and drive home. Her family and friends would help her endure this. They would make it almost bearable. She closed her lids and the haze that was covering her eyes spilled down her cheeks.

She stared up at the popcorn ceiling for hours until the tears no longer came. With her body too numb to move, her eyes finally wisped closed.

Jonathan

The sky was taking on the pink-orange haze as the sun began to drop beyond the horizon, and Jon was starting to panic again. *Why hasn't Sarah come home yet? Where is she?* Could the stalker have grabbed her after she left? Her phone. Why did she leave her phone? Maybe her phone would give him a clue as to where she went. It would have her calendar at the very least. Jon hustled up stairs and the phone bounced on the bed when he landed next to it. He slid his finger across the screen using the password he had help set up. He rolled onto his back as he looked at her pending messages. He read back through about twelve texts, all from her friends, until he found a name he didn't recognize.

Cami: I wish I had been wrong about Jon. He's such an ass. I heard about what happened at the restaurant with Mia on Entertainment News. Call me if you want to talk.

Who the hell was Cami? And why was she calling him an ass? He scrolled down the messages to the first ones pending. Nothing so far indicated anything about Sarah's whereabouts.

Alli: We're all here if you need us.

Megan: Men are dicks! Call me.

Jessica: Hey. Are you OK?

Apparently lunch with Mia had made the tabloids. *Wait a minute.* His message was still pending. She hadn't read it. She still thought he had fathered Mia's baby. *Shit.* He looked around the room and realized the suitcase she was unpacking from the trip was gone. Her computer bag was gone. She left on her own. She thought he had lied to her and she left.

His head sunk into the pillow. Sarah had to know that he would never cheat. Why would she believe Mia's innuendos? It was just talk. He had already told her the truth. She shouldn't have even questioned what his ex said. Mia was right—Sarah wasn't resilient. She must still have doubts—enough that she didn't trust him. He stared at Sarah's phone, not knowing what would happen. How would they survive if she didn't trust him? Taking a deep breath, Jon rubbed his hands over his face. There was still a stalker out there. The words from the last note burned in his mind. *She will learn to hate you, as I have.* He had to find Sarah, even if she didn't want to be found. Jon headed downstairs to see what ideas Sam would have to track her down.

Sarah

The dark room smelled of bleached fabric and lemon furniture polish. Sarah's head felt like a boulder that had been dropkicked off a cliff. She slowly sat up, negotiating the best position for her pounding head. She hadn't really thought through leaving her phone at the house. Abandoning it cut her off from all her contacts. She didn't even know her friends' numbers. She didn't need to memorize them because they were always on her phone. At the time, ditching her phone seemed like the right thing to do. All she knew was that she didn't want Jon tracking her. She couldn't face him. And she knew he would come for her if he could find her.

She reached over the edge of the bed and dragged her purse and computer bag onto her lap. She prayed the bottle of Advil in her purse wasn't empty. She shook it. There was something in it. She looked around the room, no minibar. Had she really gotten that spoiled? The plastic-wrapped cups sat stacked on the desk in the corner. She would have to drink from the tap or find a vending machine in order to take the pills. With her keycard, the Advil, and a few dollars in her hand, she headed out the door to find a bottle of water. Her day of crying tolled on her face and she figured no one would recognize her.

When she got back to the room, she settled on the bed and opened her laptop. She remembered back to when Jon gave it to her. They had known each other for months online but had met for the first time in person that day. He had gone up on stage with his friend Nick's band and sang that beautiful song he wrote for her. "I Found You" was its official name. Jon was so unsure of himself that night, so sweet. When he kissed her for the first time, it was like reality shifted and she knew nothing would ever be the same. How was she going to walk away from him? Tears pricked in her eyes again.

She had known loss before—the death of her grandmother and grandfather, but she was young when they passed and she didn't remember them. Tyler Rainer, the boy who was her first kiss, died, but she didn't really know him well. None of these impacted her life that much. Besides, she understood death. Death was concrete. It didn't have a gray area. A person was either alive or dead. This loss of Jonathan was harder to sort out.

She looked at her reflection in her computer screen. Her eyes looked hollow and empty. She felt like a tree in the coldest part of winter—lifeless and frozen. A part of her was still alive inside, but she didn't know if it would pull through to the thaw. She could stay with him, but with no trust, what kind of mediocre life would she have? Spending her life questioning everything that he did would be exhausting. She deserved better.

She thought she was in love once before Jon with her high school boyfriend Matt, but he lied to her a few times over the two years they dated—small modifications of truth, like saying he would be one place and then be spotted by one of her friends somewhere else. But she always let it go as immaturity or poor planning. When she gave him her virginity, she truly believed he loved her. It wasn't until weeks later that she found out about the other girl he'd been hooking up with. Sarah felt so betrayed at the time—not understanding how a man could love her and still cheat on her. She knew now that what she had with Matt wasn't really love—not like the love she felt for Jonathan, not anywhere close. Would she feel the same about Jon someday as she did about Matt? She doubted it. She would always love him. She just couldn't trust him.

He had been lying to her for half of their relationship. He and Mia had sex in December, and he lied to her the entire time since. How many times had he told her he loved her? A lie. Every time they made love was a lie. It was true that acting was a game of deception, and Jon was the master.

Megan was right. Some conniving scheme of Mia's was responsible for Jon's cheating. He wouldn't have done it on his own. He was with her, but somehow not in control—possibly drugged, like Sarah had been by the woman that had tried to abduct her. But Jon's guilt came from the lying, not the act itself.

She saw now that the life she had envisioned with Jonathan could never happen. Hollywood wouldn't allow it. She would never get her happily ever after with him. The numbness penetrated her body like a twenty-below-zero wind chill.

She unscrewed the cap on her bottle of water and took a sip before opening her computer. She knew people saw what had happened at the restaurant, but she wasn't sure if anyone would leak it to the press. She typed "Jonathan Williams" into the search engine and watched as article after article mentioning the afternoon's happenings popped up. Sarah clicked on the top one.

> THE ENGAGEMENT IS OFF! Did Jonathan's infidelity prove too much? Witnesses say that Jonathan Williams's teary-eyed fiancé stormed out of a restaurant in Ventura while having lunch with Mia Thompson. Jonathan chased her into the parking lot, where she sped off in her convertible, but not before throwing her half-million-dollar ring at him.

Sarah twisted the ring on her left hand. Had it actually cost that much? She would have to make sure he got it back. The knot in her throat swelled as her tears started to roll down her cheeks again. She didn't want to cry anymore. It just made the pounding in her head louder. She thought back to the night Jonathan had proposed. It was Christmas Eve, the day she got home from the hospital after her accident. He was acting so weird all through dinner. She didn't know it was because he was planning to ask her to spend the rest of her life with him. After everyone left, he carried her downstairs and made her close her eyes as he got down on one knee. He told her how much he loved her and how he couldn't imagine his life without her. She smiled remembering his gentle touch as he placed the ring on her finger. She could almost feel his breath against her skin as he kissed her that night. She ran her finger across her lips and a sob bubbled from her throat. *What now?*

She didn't know the night he proposed that less than a week earlier he had slept with his ex-girlfriend. Sarah eased the ring off and stared at it pinched between her thumb and finger. Jon always said that the emeralds reminded him of her eyes. She unfastened the chain around her neck and slid the ring onto the silver thread before reclasping it. She didn't want to lose it. *No.* She took it off the chain and slid it back on her left hand. She wasn't ready to take it off yet and if she lost it, she would never be able to repay Jonathan for it.

She glanced down at her computer. She was supposed to go to Pilates tomorrow. She hadn't been there since before the trip to France, and she really needed to work out. It was the one thing that might help her stop crying. She couldn't go, though. Jon could find her there, and she couldn't face him. The instructor would be mad if she missed without notifying the scheduler. She pulled up the studio's web page and clicked on the link. She typed out a message in the "I can't make my scheduled class" box.

I won't be able to make Cami's 4:00 p.m. class tomorrow. If you have any questions, please contact my e-mail. My phone is not working. Sorry, Sarah Austin.

She was pulling up her contacts on her computer to get Jessica's number when an e-mail notification came up on the top of her screen. It was from the studio. Great, she was probably going to lose her spot in the class. Even though she knew it wouldn't matter because she would be moving back to Minnesota, she didn't want to piss off the instructor. Three e-mails from Jon sat in the pending box as well. She wasn't ready to see more lies, so Sarah clicked on the one she could handle.

Sarah, I was sitting at my desk when your note came in. Are you OK? I heard about what happened at the restaurant. Do you want to go out for a drink and talk? Cami

Sarah sent a reply.

I'm not in the mood to go out, and I'm kind of in hiding. I don't need anyone seeing me.

OK. I'm just leaving the studio now. I'll come to you. Where are you?

Give me your number and I'll call you. I don't want Jon stalking my e-mail and finding me.

Sixty minutes later Cami was at her door with two Caboose juices, a pint of chocolate ice cream, and a bottle of vodka. She handed Sarah one of the juice glasses and the vodka as she came through the door and said, "We have to drink some to make room in the glass before we can add the alcohol."

She wasn't sure she was in the mood to drink. Alcohol was a depressant, and she didn't need to add to what was already dragging her under. Cami set the ice cream down on the desk next to the miniature coffee maker and pulled two spoons from her pocket. "And don't feel bad about the ice cream. You look like shit. Have you eaten at all this week?"

Sarah nodded and sat on the edge of the bed. She was used to her friends being so blunt; she had known them forever. They didn't need the social niceties anymore. Cami was still kind of an acquaintance in her mind. And she wasn't sure if she was comfortable with her familiarity.

Cami opened the pint of chocolate heaven and handed it to Sarah with a spoon. "You need a base before we start drinking." Cami pulled a long draw on the straw in her juice and continued, "Move over. I'd sit on the floor, but after seeing an exposé on hotel cleanliness six months ago, I'm lucky if I can sit on the bed. I won't go into details, because in this case ignorance is bliss. Let's just say I will never go barefoot in a hotel room ever again."

As Sarah scooted over and spooned a bite of ice cream into her mouth, she thought Cami was a lot like Jessica, at least as far as their germ issues were concerned.

"You haven't said a word since I came in. Tell me what happened."

"I don't even know where to start."

"Tell me what happened at the restaurant. I can see that you still have your ring, so the witnesses had it wrong."

Sarah looked down at her ring. "Yeah, that part anyway. I'm going to have to find another way to get it back to him."

Cami stood up and grabbed Sarah's drink off the low dresser under the TV, where Sarah had set it. "Drink." She handed it to Sarah. "We're going to get drunk."

Sarah drank it down about an inch and handed it back to Cami, who had opened her own lid and the vodka while waiting for Sarah. "So he's getting back with Mia Thompson?"

Sarah exhaled loudly. She didn't know what was going to happen. She shrugged. She couldn't stand the thought of Jon being with that woman. Cami handed her the clear plastic juice cup now filled to the rim. She sat down next to Sarah and looked at her with sympathetic eyes.

Sarah didn't know Cami enough to trust her with her intimate secrets, but she couldn't hold them in any longer. She spilled everything. She told her all that happened at the restaurant—how Mia kept telling Jon that she thought he would do the right thing, like she had already told him the baby was his and he was abandoning her. He had been acting like he didn't know who the baby's father was. And when Jon chased her into the parking lot, he thought she was overreacting. "That's not the worst part. Last week he told me point blank that he didn't father it. If he had just told me the truth, then I probably could have gotten over it." She sucked in a mouthful of juice and swallowed.

"What an asshat! He should have been honest with you." Cami pulled her hair from the rubber band and adjusted it back into a tighter ponytail as she spoke. "I'm so sick of guys who think women will just forgive them no matter what they do. Entitlement is rampant in Hollywood. Everyone jumps to the A team's every whim, and they act like their shit doesn't stink."

Sarah felt the corner of her lip turn up. She'd seen how some people trip over themselves trying to please Jon and it always irritated her a bit. Hell, it irritated Jon most of the time. Jon respected honesty and integrity more than a yes-man. "Jon's not one to surround himself with suck-ups, but I know what you mean. I've seen it."

"They all do it. Even my ex…" Cami stumbled with an emotion that Sarah didn't understand. "He enjoyed the attention."

"Jon likes the devotion from the fans. I mean who wouldn't? It's an incredible high. But he prefers honesty from the people he works with."

"It doesn't sound like he's too honest with you."

She didn't want to admit it, but Cami was right. Sarah scooted across the bed until her back bumped the headboard and then she set her drink on the nightstand. Stuffing a pillow behind her, she said, "Yeah, looks like it." She reached for the ice cream pint before asking, "Who is your ex anyway." Hollywood was a really small town. Sarah wouldn't be surprised if she had met him. Shoveling a spoonful of chocolate into her mouth, she hoped they could talk about something other than Jon. Her stomach was starting to churn with nausea, and she didn't know if it was the conversation, the alcohol, or the ice cream.

The look on Cami's face said she regretted Sarah mentioning her ex. She lay down on her side at the foot of the bed facing Sarah, stretching her leg so far back that it touched her red ponytail. As she returned from the stretch, she answered, "Everyone knows everyone. I don't want to say." Straightening out completely and laying on the bed, she added, "All you need to know is my heart got broken. I don't think there are any happy endings in this place. You should get out while you can and be thankful you haven't wasted years in this hell hole."

"Did that happen to you? Did you break up after years or was it your car accident that ended your relationship with him?" Sarah had a feeling it was the latter. Somehow she knew the accident had done more than maim Cami's body. It had completely destroyed her hopes and dreams.

Cami traced her finger down and then back up the straw in her smoothie. Without looking up she shook her head as if defeated and said, "The accident wrecked my life."

Sarah waited for her to elaborate, but she just continued to shake her head in silence.

"Any guy who would leave you because of a couple of scars and a career change isn't worth the effort."

Cami dropped her head to the bed and balanced her lidded cup on her flat stomach. Sarah wondered if she could see her toes when she was lying down. Weird thought, but she couldn't help it. She was feeling a slight buzz from the vodka, which was a good thing, Sarah thought—anything to distract her.

"Are those real?" Sarah asked, pointing at Cami's breasts.

"Do they look real?" Cami cupped them like they were her favorite thing in the world, her glass still balanced on her flat stomach. "I got them when I moved here. I thought they would help my career. They're one of my best assets, don't you think?"

"Nah. Physical assets are never anyone's best asset." Sarah thought about how the plastic surgeon had wanted her to have an "augmentation." She liked Jon's reaction. He had probably seen enough to spot the fake ones at first glance.

"On some people they are," said Cami.

"Like Mia Thompson. There is nothing redeeming about her personality." Sarah paused, wondering if she could trust Cami or not. She had already shared so much. "I'm pretty sure she drugged Jon to get pregnant. He never would have slept with her otherwise."

"Really? They used to date. He probably just thought he wouldn't get caught," she said before taking another sip of her smoothie.

"No. Jon is really careful. He always uses a condom. It's like he's obsessed with them. Even Mia commented about it."

"Well, he obviously forgot or he wouldn't have fathered the kid."

"Honestly, I think she tricked him somehow."

"Men don't need to be tricked into having sex with women like Mia Thompson." Cami raised her eyebrows, suggesting that Sarah was stupid if that was what she really thought.

Sarah decided to drop that line of conversation. Maybe she was being stupid, naïve. She started spooning the chocolate heaven it into her mouth again.

Cami smiled and asked, "What are you going to do now?"

"Jon leaves for a promotional tour in Europe the day after tomorrow. He can't get out of it. He has to go. He'll be gone for two weeks. I think I'll just stay hidden until he leaves and then go back to the house, get the rest of my stuff, and then drive back to Minnesota."

"What if he changed the locks, and you can't get into the house to get your stuff?"

"He wouldn't. He's not like that. He wouldn't want to hurt me."

"Seems like he already has."

"He wouldn't want to hurt me any more than he has already." Sarah thought about what Jon must be thinking. "He's probably freaking out right now."

"He should have expected that you wouldn't just let him get away with lying to you."

"No, he's freaking out because a crazy person is stalking us. It's killing him not to know where I am or that I'm safe."

Cami laughed and got a huge smile on her face. "Good. He deserves to suffer."

Sarah was definitely feeling the effects of the vodka. "I guess." She didn't really want Jon to suffer. He had already had enough suffering for a lifetime. She just knew she would never be able to leave if she saw him. Tears pilled in her eyes again. She couldn't help it.

"Sarah, are you crying? That bastard doesn't deserve your tears. You have to leave him. He doesn't respect you. People like him are incapable of thinking of anyone but themselves."

She wasn't sure if she agreed with that generalization of Jon, but he couldn't have been thinking about the girl he was going to propose to when he was sleeping with Mia, so maybe Cami was right.

"So will your parents let you live with them. I doubt my dad would let me move home. It wouldn't fit with his young image to have a daughter in her midtwenties. He thinks he's twenty years younger than he is since he's remarried."

Sarah hadn't thought about where she would stay. "My parents haven't even changed my room since I left. I'm sure they'd let me move home, but I have a house." She hadn't thought about it, but the house was a graduation present. She could live there. No. She couldn't. It would be too painful and it wouldn't be right to keep such an elaborate gift. Besides, it would always remind her of Jon, and that would make it impossible to live there. "Jon bought it for me for graduation, but I can't keep it."

"Why? If it was a gift, it's yours. Legally it's yours. Same goes for that ring. If he asks for them back, you just tell him to go to hell."

Sarah leaned back on her pillow and closed her eyes, thinking about the look on Jon's face when he gave her the house. His whole body was glowing with anticipation of her reaction. He wanted her approval so badly that he was buzzing with electricity. When he told her the house was hers, theirs, she couldn't believe it. He had planned it for months without letting it slip. Leslie had scouted it out and arranged the purchase. It was mostly furnished, but Jon had picked out the bedroom setting and some of the accessories throughout the home. He bought the house so they could visit her family anytime they wanted and have a place to stay. He always tried to make her happy. She missed him.

"I'm not like that. I don't want his money."

"Why the hell not? He screwed his ex and then lied about it. You are too good for him. You have to get over it. He'll be moving on and what will you be left with? Nothing. Take all you can get, I say."

He screwed his ex and then lied about it—Sarah needed to remember that. He was a liar and a cheat, just like her last serious boyfriend. Only Jonathan wasn't like Matt. He was her fiancé, and that made it worse. The alcohol was fuzzing up her head, and she didn't want to think about Jon anymore. "I can't talk anymore. Let's watch TV."

Cami picked up the remote and began flipping through the channels. "Oh my god. We have to watch this." She stopped channel surfing. "It's one of my favorite shows. See the guy with the blond hair? He is such a bastard. He makes Jonathan look like a freaking superhero."

Sarah broke out laughing. She couldn't stop. There were tears in her eyes, but she was laughing. Cami was so funny. It felt good to laugh. She sat up shaking her head. *Whoa, the room is spinning.* She couldn't believe Cami just said that. "That blond guy is one of Jon's best friends. He's actually a nice guy." Sarah started laughing again. Liam *was* a really nice guy.

"So Jon-a-thon is friends with Liam Nordstrom. I should have remembered that." Cami's words were as slurred as Sarah's.

That was funny. Sarah laughed even harder. How would Cami have known that? She probably followed the tabloids.

"What?" Cami stared at the screen as if it would explain Sarah's laughter.

"His brother Jack used to call him Jon-a-thon. Whenever he and Jack would compete as kids, Jon would just keep going and going. He never gave up until he won. Jack used to say competing against Jon was like running a marathon. That's why he called him that. That's what Jon said anyway."

Cami started laughing. "You're funny."

"Jack died." Sarah didn't know why she said that. Maybe it was because Jon hadn't. He kept going even after his brother's death. He never gave up. Sarah wondered if he would give up on her.

Cami stopped laughing. "I hate Jonathan."

They definitely had drunk too much. Cami didn't even know Jonathan. If she actually knew him, she'd love him. Everybody did.

"You are so drunk," Sarah said as she got up. "You're going to have to stay here. I'm not letting you drive." She looked back as Cami rolled over, burying her face in a pillow. "I'm not sharing my toothbrush, though," she added, trying to find humor in their state. *Jon always found humor.*

After she finished getting ready, she crawled into the bed next to Cami, who was already asleep.

~

When Sarah awoke Cami was sitting on the end of the bed tying her cross-trainers. She had a life to get back to, while Sarah didn't. Sarah sat up and watched as Cami pulled her red hair back into a knot on the back of her head.

"I made some coffee, if you're interested." She pointed to the small coffee pot on the table near the window.

"Thanks."

"I've got to get to the studio, but if you want me to go with you to get your stuff from the house, I can go. When's he leave?"

"Early tomorrow morning. I could use some support. Could you do it around ten?"

"I think that will work. Do you want me to come over tonight?"

"No, I think I'll need some rest if I'm going to be driving for three days."

"I'll pick you up here around ten tomorrow, then."

"Thanks, Cami. I really appreciate your help."

"No problem. You're doing the right thing. That bastard doesn't deserve a second of your time. You're going to be so much better off without him."

Sarah pulled on a smile, though it was completely fake. "I'll see you tomorrow."

After Cami left, the day dragged and dragged. Sarah knew she needed to contact her family. They would be worried about her, especially if Jon called looking for her. What if Jon hadn't called? What if he didn't even care she'd left? Sarah paused as she thought about that for a minute. No, Jon would be looking

279

for her. She opened up her laptop to her contact list. She could call her friends from the hotel line to let them know she was OK, but what would she say to them? She lay on her stomach staring at the computer screen for a half hour unable to summon the courage to call anyone. Maybe she'd do it after her body had finished metabolizing the vodka from last night and her head felt a little clearer. She flicked the TV on instead.

Chapter Twenty-Eight

Jonathan

Sarah had been gone for two days, and he wasn't any closer to finding her than he was the day she walked out the door. *She walked out the door.* Why was she so stubborn? Jonathan knew that Sarah chose to leave him. He didn't know what happened to her after she left, though, why she hadn't called or at least replied to his e-mails. He even tried messaging her online with no response. Lunch with Mia must have thrown her over the edge. She must have realized Hollywood wasn't worth the trouble—he wasn't worth the trouble. Still he needed to know she was safe. And he didn't. He couldn't even think straight. How was he supposed to leave for two weeks of touring Europe when he didn't know if Sarah was safe?

The meeting with the FBI yesterday hadn't shed much new insight into the identity of the stalker, but they did work up a profile—a profile that didn't fit anyone he knew. The words chosen in the letters indicated the stalker was a woman. The FBI was positive about that. Paris Borel, the website manager who had abducted Sarah in January, was the first person to come to mind, but she was in a women's detention center for six more months. Then she would be released on parole. Her sentence was so lenient that he thought the judge was joking when he heard it. Apparently she wasn't considered a threat to anyone but him and Sarah. Besides, she had never been to the house. The agency felt that the stalker had definitely been at the house over a period of time, not just once. Jon racked his brain. Ex-girlfriends would be the obvious place to look, but Jon couldn't think of any that he had really hurt enough to turn them into stalkers.

He called Isaac again.

"We made a commitment, Jon." Isaac didn't even say hello. "You said nothing would keep you from it, and after what you pulled at Cannes, you better uphold your word. You can't wait around for Sarah to grow up and figure out what she wants. You have a responsibility to these people, to your fans. You can't blow this off."

Jon shook his head, no words coming to his lips. He collapsed onto the couch and put his feet up on the ottoman table as Isaac continued.

"You've done everything you can to find her. The rest is up to her."

"What if it's not her? What if it's the stalker?"

"I know this isn't what you want to hear, but no one else is going to tell you."

"What?" Jon's voice was severe.

"If the stalker has her, there is nothing you can do anyway." He paused like he was regrouping. "The chances of her being abducted again are nonexistent. You have to get that out of your head and do your job." Then Isaac's tone changed as he added, "She's just trying to get your attention. You know that, right? All women do it before their weddings. Your two weeks away will give her a chance to get over her wedding jitters. You'll come home exhausted from the tour, and she will be here waiting for you. It's probably just what you need—some time away from each other. Hell, you've been joined at the hip since you got engaged. Give her some space."

"It just doesn't sound like Sarah." Jon remembered how he thought she had left him in January when she was actually drugged and shoved inside the trunk of a car. He was wrong then. Was he wrong now? He watched her leave on the security camera. She wasn't abducted this time. She left on her own. And they hadn't gotten any more letters from the stalker. The contact at the FBI said the letters' frequency would most likely escalate before any direct contact was made by the stalker.

"In your first interview…where is it?"

"London."

"You let it slip that you're not the baby's father. You know that's all the press wants to talk about anyway. That way you're keeping your commitment to the film and at the same time you're letting Sarah know you didn't cheat on her. The producers will be thrilled that you bring in so much publicity for the film, and you get what you want. Screw Remi. I know she wants you to keep that info to yourself, but you're no good to anyone if you can't do your job. I'll deal with her. Sarah will come crawling back the second she hears your announcement. You'll see. You just make sure you're on the plane. The rest will fall into place."

Isaac was right. If Sarah was avoiding him, it was just because she thought he cheated and then lied to her. It wasn't because she was abducted again. It couldn't be. He ended the call with Isaac as Leslie walked in with her bags.

"We're sending the bags over tonight. They'll be here to get them in about an hour. You're packed, right? Or do I need to pack you?"

"What did the car dealer say?" He'd get packed, but he needed to know what Leslie had found out first.

"You're not packed at all, are you?"

"I will be. What did they say?"

"They said they weren't able to locate her car. Either the LoJack wasn't working properly," she hesitated, "or the car had been chopped up for parts and it had been disabled."

Just as he was starting to accept that Sarah left on her own, this was thrown into the loop.

"They couldn't verify that it has ever worked. It's supposed to help you find the car if it is stolen. What he said doesn't apply in this situation. We'll find her. She's just upset about Mia. I know you don't want to, but I think one of us needs to call her friends or her parents to see if she's contacted them. You'll see she's fine and we can leave on the tour guilt-free."

"I'll do it," he said, taking his phone out. "I should have done it yesterday." He pulled Jessica up on his contacts and headed toward the stairs. She would be the first person Sarah would contact.

"What did you do to my best friend? She won't even answer her phone."

"Hey, Jess. I'm fine. Thanks for asking." He swallowed and added, "I didn't cheat on her. I'm not the father of Mia's baby."

"Are you sure?" she said in a bitter voice.

"Yep. I'm sure."

"Then why is she so upset?"

"Have you talked to her? Can you tell her I didn't lie to her?"

"Did you not hear me when I said she's not answering her phone?"

"Sarah left her phone at the house and took off. I haven't seen her since lunch with Mia." He may as well tell her. She'd sent texts alluding to the restaurant incident. Besides, Jessica could tell Sarah and all this would resolve before it got worse. "I was hoping she called you. I don't know how to get a hold of her. I tried messaging online, e-mail. I even tried to go to the website where we met, but it was shut down." He hoped that wasn't an omen.

"She hasn't spoken to anyone here. We thought you and she were working out your problems and she didn't want to talk to anyone about it. You know how she gets when she's really upset."

"Yeah. She runs away and won't talk." She did it when she was mad about

Craig following her to Pilates. He thought back to when they were dating. The only misunderstanding they had when they were dating happened because Sarah shut down and didn't ask questions about what he meant by the word *break*. He meant a break from seeing each other not a break in their relationship. She never asked. She just assumed the worst and shut down. That's why it was so easy for him to believe she had left in January. He never thought she was abducted because it was more likely that she just needed time to herself to cool off. He stood in the bedroom doorway, staring into the room. It felt so empty without her. "If you hear from her, tell her what I said and that I love her, OK?"

"I will."

"Thanks, Jess." He ended the call, feeling worse than he did before making it. He held his finger to his temple as if it were a gun and blew that thought from his head. How could he even think that her leaving him was worse than her being kidnapped by a stalker? It *was not* worse. She had to have gotten his e-mails by now. She knew he wasn't the baby's father and she was still punishing him. She must not have been as strong as he thought. He turned around in the doorway as Leslie found her way to the second floor.

"Anything?" she asked.

He shook his head.

"They haven't heard from her?"

"No, but when she's really upset, she doesn't want to talk to anyone, so it didn't surprise Jessica. I think Sarah just needs time to check her e-mail. She'll come around." He lied. Jon doubted this mix-up about him sleeping with Mia was the real problem. Sarah didn't trust him. She didn't even give him a chance to explain. She ran off before he even knew why. She obviously had doubts about him or she wouldn't have been so quick to believe Mia's innuendos. That was the real problem. For the first time since he proposed, he doubted Sarah's love. He didn't know if he could fix it, and it probably meant their relationship would end up a casualty of Hollywood.

Leslie pushed past him, walking into the closet, and he followed. "It doesn't look like you packed at all." She reached up and pulled down a medium-sized bag, setting it on the floor. Then she grabbed the bag for his suits. He just couldn't put his head around his new revelation. Without trust, he and Sarah wouldn't make it. He would lose her. He didn't know what more he could do. He closed his eyes, pushing down the thoughts in his head and burying them deep inside his core.

"Where are the suits that Grant sent over? You're going to need all of them. How are you supposed to pack sixteen unique outfits in one bag? I hate these stupid tours. Oh…Here they are." The suits were hanging on one end of the closet, and Leslie carefully stuffed them into the garment bag. "You've got to get packed. The car is coming for the luggage, and I'm not packing your underwear."

He took a deep breath and blew it out, trying to clear the fog in his head. He watched Leslie as she pulled his gear together. She knew how much Sarah meant to him. She knew all that was at stake, yet she kept moving him forward. He stepped to the T-shirts stacked on the shelves and pulled out about ten of them, handing them to Leslie. He didn't really care which ones he brought. He spent the next fifteen minutes helping pack, making sure he had underwear and his man kit. Then he hefted both bags downstairs, setting them next to Leslie's. He'd done all he could. Maybe leaving would be the best thing for him. He wouldn't have time to think once the tour started—two weeks with sixteen countries and no time to breathe.

Chapter Twenty-Nine

Sarah

The house was eerily quiet as Sarah and Cami entered. They wouldn't have to be there long. Just long enough to grab the essentials Sarah hadn't grabbed the first time she left, and then Cami would drive her back to the hotel. She'd be home in a few days. It was funny how this house felt like home to Sarah. She looked around the room. The Dali pencil sketch that Jon bought for her in France hung by the front door. And there was Pedro—the green, animatronic monster staring back at her with his big, bulbous eyes. She smiled thinking about all the times he had caught her and Jon making out in the living room. Jon used to give him a voice, a deep raspy voice, and Pedro would make suggestive comments between Jon's kisses. "Hey, gorgeous. Why don't you leave that wannabe and be with a real monster." He'd kiss her neck and then add, "You know…once you go green, you never go back." She shook the raspy voice from her head. She had to get her stuff and get out or she would change her mind, doomed to live a life of mistrust and frustration. She headed toward the stairs.

"I'm going to use the bathroom," said Cami.

Sarah raised her hand to point her in the right direction, but she was gone, as if she already knew the way. Sarah made her way up the stairs, knowing it would be the last time she would see the room she and Jon used to share. Her phone was gone, so she knew Jon had gotten her message. *Thank god he wasn't here.* She took the suitcase from the closet, laid it on the bed, and walked back to the closet. She unhooked as much of her hanging clothes as she could carry in one trip and brought them to the bed. She knew she couldn't fit all of her clothes in her car, but she was going to bring as much as she could because Jon would have no use for them. She laid each item flat in the large suitcase and then removed the hanger. She figured it was the fastest way to pack them without too many wrinkles.

After she had all of the clothes she could fit in the bag, she zipped it closed and sat on the bed next to it. She reached into the drawer of the bedside table and pulled out the lacquered wooden box—her engagement ring's box. It would be easier if she just left the ring here. She wouldn't have to worry about how she would get it back to Jon. She would leave it on the bed like her phone and he would find it when he got home from Europe. She twisted the gorgeous ring on her finger. Why was taking it off so hard? She had to leave him. He lied to her. She couldn't marry a liar.

She heard Cami coming up the stairs and knew she would argue with her if she saw what Sarah was doing. She would tell her she was stupid for not keeping the ring. Sarah quickly slid it from her finger, placing it in the box. She didn't have time to think about it. She didn't want to have to defend her actions to Cami. She knew what she was doing was right. There was no way she could keep it. She stuffed the box under Jon's pillow and sat up as Cami stepped through the doorway.

Sarah looked up and met her eyes, hoping she hadn't seen her put the box under the pillow and wouldn't notice the missing ring. But they weren't Cami's eyes staring back at her. They were the glacial blue, almost colorless eyes that could melt her into a puddle. She froze as her heart stopped.

"Did you really think I could leave, not knowing you were safe?" His tone was hurt, as if she was inflicting so much pain he could barely speak. "I understand the phone. I know why you left it, but you got my e-mails."

She had gotten the e-mails, but she couldn't bring herself to read them. Twenty-three e-mails in total sat in her inbox, unopened. Her eyes still locked on his, and she somehow felt relieved by his presence. It was the opposite of what she wanted, but being near him felt so calming and right. Her voice abandoned her and she nodded.

"And you're still leaving? Why?" His eyes flicked to her naked left hand and then back to her face. He forced his fingers through his hair, taking a deep breath, his jaw hard and fierce.

Why did she feel like she was in the wrong? He was the one who cheated. He was the one who lied. "You cheated on me and then lied to me." Her voice was small and mousy. She wished she sounded more confident.

Jon stared at her for a moment and then his whole body language changed, as if he owned the room and everything in it. Which he did. "You never read them, did you?" He took a step closer. "Why don't you trust me? I've never lied to you."

"Really?" His declaration pissed her off enough for her to find her words. She'd heard it from Mia's mouth. He was lying to her right now.

He took two more steps toward her, and the corners of his lips turned up. He was laughing at her. He knew all he had to do was touch her and she would never be able to leave. *What a bastard.* He knew. She slid the heavy suitcase from the bed and stood it up on the floor, ready to bolt out of the room if she needed. She had to leave before he got too close. She glanced at the door wondering if she could make it out before he reached her.

"The baby isn't mine, beautiful." He took another step forward, and she breathed in his clean, masculine scent.

"Why did Mia say that you needed to claim it? Why would she expect that if it's not yours? She said it happened the night you were with her. You were there; I saw the pictures."

"I was there that night, but I didn't sleep with Mia. My buddy Chris did. It's his baby. Please don't leave." He wrapped his arms around her and pulled her against his body.

"It's Chris's," she whispered, confirming his words in her mind. He kissed the top of her head. "But Mia said—"

"She was just messing with you. She would like me to claim it. The fans aren't going to accept her having a baby with someone they've never seen her with. It would be easier for her if I said it was mine, but I'm not going to. That wouldn't be fair to you or our kids."

"Our kids?"

"You can't leave. We're meant to be together, Sarah." He cupped his hands around her face and stared into her eyes. "I will never lie to you, beautiful."

His eyes were so sincere. What was she thinking? The fact that he lied was the hardest part for her to swallow. She never really believed it was true. That's why she had such a hard time leaving. Her heart knew. His lips brushed hers, so gentle and sweet that her eyes started to tear up. And when his tongue pushed into her mouth, all she could do was surrender. His hand slid to the back of her head, pulling her in closer. He scooped her up in his arms, holding the kiss. He nudged the suitcase out of his way and set her on the bed. He pulled back and stared at her with a look she couldn't decipher.

"My friend Cami is here." Her eyes darted toward the door. As much as she wanted him, she didn't like the idea of someone walking in on them.

"This won't take long." He jumped over her, landing on the other side of her on the bed. Then he climbed on top of her and pinned her hands above her head with one of his hands.

"Seriously, the door is wide open."

"I'll be really fast. I promise."

"Is that…a good thing?"

He leaned down, meshing his lips to hers again. Then he sat back, straddling her, and brought her left hand to his eye as if he needed to examine it closer. "I have issues with this." He flipped open the box that had been under his pillow. Sarah hadn't even seen him retrieve it. He slipped his index finger through the ring, plucking it from its case and dropping the box next to her. Then he slid the ring onto her finger. "It's yours. It will always be yours. Please don't take it off again. He kissed her hand and then the ring, like he had the first time he slid it onto her finger. He kissed her lips once more before rolling off and lying next to her. "I told you I would be fast." He smiled and then glanced at the door. "I want to meet your friend Cami. What's her last name?"

"McCall or Mathis or...I'm not really sure. It starts with an *M*. She told me once, but you know how bad I am with names. I can't ask her at this point. I'm surprised you don't know. She's great, though. You'll love her."

"I'm pretty sure she hates me. She called me an asshole in a text she sent you."

"She's just a little anti-Hollywood, but she'll like you once she gets to know you."

He grabbed her hand as she stood up and pulled her back onto the bed with a grim expression. "Sarah, we still need to talk."

"I know. I'll tell Cami I don't need a ride back to my car and then we can 'talk' about anything you want." She stood up again, he followed, and they headed downstairs together in search of Cami.

"Cami?" called Sarah. They looked around but didn't see her. Sarah opened the front door wondering if she went outside. "Her car is gone," she told Jon. Some friend she was. When Jon shows up and Sarah potentially needed Cami the most, she disappeared. "She must have heard you come in. I guess she just couldn't deal with conflict." She'd send her a text and explain everything after she talked to Jon.

Jon held the door open for her, his expression said he meant business. She walked inside and found her way to the couch. His face was so serious when he sat next to her that she couldn't fathom what he was going to say. His ice-blue eyes burrowed into Sarah's and made her nervous. She folded her legs up next to her, leaning her body closer to him, hoping their closeness would change his demeanor.

"Why don't you trust me? I've never lied to you."

"I do trust you."

Jon shook his head as if he didn't believe her, while his eyes searched the air above her head. "I told you I wasn't the baby's father." He combed his fingers through his hair across the top of his head and then added, "Then Mia insinuates it's mine and you automatically assume I lied. You believed her over me. That's not trust."

He was right. Why would she believe anything that woman said? "It's just Mia. I can't be around her. I just can't. She's a horrible person. I don't even know how you could have dated her."

He tucked a strand of her hair behind her ear, his hard jaw softening. "I need you to trust me. You can't believe others over me. There will always be someone there to push doubts into your mind, but I need you to trust that I will never lie to you. It doesn't matter if it is Mia, your mother, or the damn president of the United States, I will always be the one telling you the truth. Got it?" He kissed the side of her head as he wrapped his arms around her.

"Yes." She leaned against his chest, listening to his heartbeat and breathing in the clean scent of him. There was nothing more comforting to her than being in his strong arms, and she almost blew it.

"Now, we have to get you packed. I'm pretty sure we can get a flight out tonight and still make tomorrow's premiere. We'll have to sleep on the plane, but…"

Sarah stared at him for a long second wondering how she could tell him. She had already hurt him so much. Then she just blurted it out. "I can't go to all those premiers. I have nothing to wear. I wasn't planning on going with you before and there is no way I'm going to be red-carpet ready."

"Well, you have to come now. You've tortured me for the last two days; don't make me spend the next two weeks without you."

She sat up and turned to face him. "I'm supposed to have a dress fitting on Thursday. I finally found the perfect shoes for the wedding and now we have to get the hem right. And besides the girls are coming in on the weekend for their fitting. Leslie had to reschedule, but I can't ask all of them to change too. I'm sorry about the last two days, but I can't go. Blame Mia."

"Yes, you can." His eyes lit with the challenge. "And we can find clothes along the way. The first stop is London. We can pick up what you need there."

"You said you would barely have time to eat on this trip—that you wouldn't have time for anything but the premieres and sleep. Were you lying?"

"Noo," he drawled.

She could tell he caught the sarcasm in her voice because he smiled.

"The time will be really tight, but you could miss the first premiere and go shopping." He looked at her wide-eyed, pleading. "You don't have to go to any of the premieres, just come with me."

This was going to be harder than she thought. She wanted to be with him, but she was so tired of being on show. "Between graduation and Cannes, I haven't been home in a month. I want to be with you, but I don't want to go. I wasn't planning on going and the girls are coming in." The last two days had mentally exhausted her and she really didn't think she would fare well on the trip with Jon. "I need a break. I promise I will be here when you get home."

"I'm not going then."

"You have to go." She knew he had to go.

"I know." He paused. "I don't want to go."

"I know." She entwined her fingers with his. "Raul and Craig were planning on being here with me when you left. That doesn't have to change. I'll drag them everywhere I go. I promise."

He watched her for several seconds without saying anything and then took out his phone. "I've got to let Leslie know you're safe and get a flight out. At best I'll have a couple of hours with you." He kissed her forehead. "I'm going to let it slip during the first press junket that Mia's baby isn't mine. Remi will be mad, but Isaac said he would handle her. By the time I get home the press shouldn't be bugging us anymore about it."

Sarah knew Remi wanted to let the baby speculation play out as long as possible and that she had told Jon to avoid the subject during interviews. She said that before the incident with Mia at the restaurant, though. Sarah wondered what was going to happen to Chris and Toni when it came out that Chris cheated on her. "Does Chris know he's the father?"

"Yeah."

"I feel so bad for Toni. Does she know?"

"I have no idea. I haven't talked to Chris yet. I need to call him before I leave, just to warn him I'm renouncing paternity." He turned to her, his eyes clear and earnest. "I don't know why people cheat. I guess life isn't black and white. Why Chris would risk everything he has with Toni for one night with Mia is beyond me. That's just not how my brain works."

"I'm glad." She smiled and ran her fingers through his hair. He closed his eyes as if relishing her touch. "Don't think I'm selfish, but I'm just glad I'm not her."

"He's cheated on her before, but I thought he had it out of his system. He probably figured Mia would never tell anyone and Toni would never find out. He's always been hot for Mia."

He groaned as he stood up, and she could tell he just wanted to freeze time. He pulled her into his arms and slid his hand down her back as his lips met hers. His tongue skimmed the inside of Sarah's mouth, sending a shiver raking through her body, and she pressed her body against his. She snaked her hands under his T-shirt, and he pulled back.

"I've got to call Chris and then I need to get some sleep, but you're coming with me to bed." He smiled the mind-blowing smile of his, and Sarah was sure they wouldn't be sleeping. "You should probably call Jessica. She's worried about you."

"You called her?"

He held up his hands as if to say he had no choice. She used the pad of her index finger to smooth the line between his brows. Before she headed upstairs, she kissed his cheek. When she was halfway up, she realized she didn't know where her phone was and asked, "My phone?"

"Plugged in by your side of the bed." A tentative smile inched across his face.

She liked that he kept it plugged in. It meant that he expected her back. He had more faith in her than she did. As she continued her ascent, she tried not to think about what she would be doing right now if he wasn't here to stop her from leaving. She couldn't imagine life without Jon. She was glad she didn't have to.

Jonathan

While Sarah made her call to Jessica, Jon took out his cell and called Chris. He had been putting this off. He needed to know Sarah was safe before he could make the call. Chris was going to be the father of Mia's baby. Holy hell. *How was he going to survive?*

"Hey, Will. What's up?" Like most of Jonathan's high school friends, he called him Will.

"Not too much. I'm heading to Europe today to promote a movie. Just thought I'd call and chat before I left. Liam said your band is playing at the Sasquatch next week. Wish Sarah and I could get up there to see you. Maybe we can make it to the next one."

"Yeah, should be a good time. Toni won't be able to make it either. She's just about ready to pop."

"I can't believe you're going to be a dad."

"Me neither." Chris sounded excited.

"Is everything OK with you and Toni?"

"Sure, we're fine." Chris paused. "I'm going out for some air, babe," he said, but not to Jon, and Jon heard a door click closed. "Why do you ask?"

"Sarah and I had lunch with Mia a few days ago," Jon started, and Chris fell silent, even his breathing had stopped. "I'm getting crucified in the press and I just wanted her to tell Sarah that it wasn't my baby. The whole 'Mia is pregnant with my baby' debacle has really been messing Sarah up. I don't think she can take much more of it," Jon said with a knowing tone. It wasn't that he was passing judgment on Chris; he just wanted him to know how he and Sarah were being affected.

"Sorry," Chris said softly.

"What the hell were you thinking?"

"Well…it was just the one night, and I didn't think she'd get pregnant, let alone keep the baby if she did. She never came off as a pro-lifer. What the hell?"

"That's not the point. Did you forget you're married?" Jon paused and took a deep breath. He hated the judgment in his tone. He had no right to judge. "Does Toni know?"

"I don't know how to tell her. It will crush her, especially because it's Mia. Toni's never cared much for her."

Chris and Toni had been together for years so Toni had been around when Jon and Mia were dating. Jon hadn't noticed any animosity between them then. Maybe it had something to do with Chris's obvious attraction to Mia, though. Jon had seen it before, but most guys reacted that way around her.

"Well…you better start groveling for her forgiveness. And do it fast. Mia is a loose cannon. She'll tell the press at the least convenient moment, especially if she feels slighted by you. *Right now* she's not talking, but tomorrow, on my trip, I'm going to spill to the press that I'm not the father, so that may change quickly."

Chris muttered a string of curses. "What an F-ing nightmare."

"Just wait until the press gets a hold of you."

"Great," Chris baulked.

"Get ready for the ride. Your name is going to be scrolling across the bottom of the screen on the E! channel, and your picture will be plastered on the aisles of the supermarket. Welcome to the paparazzi feeding frenzy, man. Not so good for your marriage, but it won't be all bad. The band will benefit. You just have to make sure they know you're the drummer in Invasion. It will give you a ton of free publicity. Mia's got a huge fan base, so I suggest you get on her good side."

"I've just been worried about Toni. I need to get that sorted out before I can take on the press or Mia."

"Groveling. I think it's your best bet."

"Thanks. I was planning on waiting until the baby comes, because I don't want to miss the birth of my first son and honestly I don't know if she is going to forgive me this time. I guess I need to move it up."

"All you can do is try." He felt bad for him. People make mistakes, but some were more forgivable than others. "So Toni's having a boy."

"Yep, the pictures were really clear. He's well endowed, just like his daddy." Chris chuckled halfheartedly.

"You better hope Toni doesn't cut yours off," Jon laughed, plopping next to Sarah on the bed. She was off the phone and just staring at the ceiling when he walked in. He wondered what she was thinking. He held his hand over his phone and mouthed, "He's going to tell her."

"She'll put my dick in the deep freeze and I'll never get it back," Chris moaned. "I mean it. She's hardcore."

"You better hope that's all she does," Jon said, and they both laughed. "Not that I don't enjoy talking about your frozen junk, but did you get fitted for your tux?" All the other guys had. He had talked to each one while Sarah was gone. But he just couldn't bring himself to call Chris until he knew Sarah was OK.

"Yep, last week. You really ready to take the plunge?"

"Beyond ready. I tried to get her to elope weeks ago."

"You're going to spend the rest of your life with her?" Chris asked, as if he didn't believe it was possible. "Only her?"

"That's the plan."

"You can't tell me that when you were filming the last Demigod movie you didn't hook up with Rachael Marrero. It was all over the press."

"I didn't get with Rachael." His hand snaked around Sarah's waist as he flipped onto his side. "I know people in Hollywood who need that kind of open relationship and it works for them, but that wouldn't work for Sarah and me. The cheap thrill of hook ups doesn't do anything for me. I'm over it. Sarah is all I want." He squeezed her, hoping she was listening closely. "She's genuine and doesn't treat me like I'm a movie star. I love how normal she makes me feel. She keeps me grounded. You'll probably crave normalcy too, after the press gets a hold of you."

Sarah smiled at him and took in a deep breath. God, he had missed her. "I've got to head out in a couple of hours and there's a few things I need to take care of before I go. I'll talk to you when I get back and you can let me know how things went." He said his good-byes and as he set his phone on the bedside table, he began regretting taking time to call Chris. He knew he needed to do it, but it was Sarah's time he had used.

He stared into her gorgeous emerald eyes. Her lids were slightly swollen and he knew she must have been crying a lot during the last few days. "Are you going to be OK when I leave?" He tucked a tendril of hair behind her ear so he could see her face better. He wasn't sure when he would have to leave. Leslie hadn't gotten back to him yet.

She nodded, putting her hand on his chest. His reaction to her touch was immediate. No other woman could do that to him. He wanted her so badly, but he didn't know if she still needed to talk more. He stroked the side of her face with his thumb as he studied her. Did he really deserve someone so sweet? She smiled and tugged at his T-shirt. *Guess she didn't need to talk.* He pulled it over his head with one hand just as his phone started vibrating. As he reached for the phone, he kissed her nose and said, "Hold that thought." It was Leslie. She had set up a flight for him to catch in two hours. That meant, at best, he would have an hour with Sarah. And he was going to take full advantage of it. He ended the call and turned back to Sarah.

"We've got an hour."

She groaned with disappointment, and he knew they were both on the same page. His lips were on hers within seconds. She tasted *so* good. He couldn't believe he almost lost her because of a misunderstanding. Sarah squirmed as he consumed her mouth. In what seemed like a blink, Sarah had shrugged out of her clothes. He hadn't realized she had done it until her hands yanked on the waistband of his shorts. *The girl was motivated.* He kicked off his shorts and flipped onto his back, pulling Sarah on top of him. He loved that she was still wearing her bra and panties. She knew how much he enjoyed relieving her of them. She smiled devilishly at him as he scanned her body. Man, she was beautiful. At least he would have this visual of her to get him through the next two weeks. Then, in five weeks, she would officially be his wife.

Chapter Thirty

Sarah

As Jon rolled the tinted window down and his beautiful blue eyes beckoned her, Sarah's breath caught in her chest. He was really leaving. She'd wasted so much time brooding over Mia Thompson's lie and now he was going to be gone for two weeks. Tears pricked in her eyes as she leaned in through the opening and he pressed his forehead to hers, still fixing her with his eyes.

"Be safe," he whispered. "I love you."

She smiled because he always said those words when he left without her, whether it was to the store, a business meeting, or on a flight. She knew the *I love you* was his way assuring his last words to her were meaningful just in case something happened to one of them. It was kind of morbid, but who could blame him after all he had been through? He kissed her lips forcefully, sucking in her bottom lip as if he wanted to devour her, and when he pulled back, she knew he had to leave.

"Be safe. I love you, too." She tried to smile to tell him she would be OK, but she was sure it came off looking like she was going to vomit. The window rose, and the car inched forward as Sarah turned toward the house. She wiped the tears before they ran down her cheeks. She and Jon had never been apart overnight since their engagement. At least until she disappeared two days ago, and in her mind two more weeks felt like two months.

She regretted not believing in him. She didn't know what was wrong with her. She kept making mistakes. She had always relied on her intuition, but lately it wasn't working. First she believed Megan was selling her to the press when it was really Chase. That was the only way Sarah could explain Liam's press leak. Though it could have been anyone involved in the intervention, and it may never truly be revealed. Then she trusted a complete stranger, who ended up being a journalist, just because he pretended not to know who she was. She still hadn't seen the fallout from that. And finally she believed Mia over Jon? Maybe she was going crazy—probably stress induced.

She didn't really feel like doing anything except sulking and hating Mia, but her car wasn't going to drive itself home. She needed to pick it up before dark. She took her phone out of her pocket and sent a text to Craig, who most likely had been watching the good-byes on the security cameras. She waved at the camera as she passed it by the front door.

Fifteen minutes later, she sat in the passenger seat of Jon's car as Craig navigated the 405. She didn't know much about Craig. He was the quiet one on the security team—serious and analytical. Sarah wasn't sure if she had ever had a conversation of any substance with him before, and it didn't seem like today was the day that was going to change. She knew Raul better. He had a playful, positive way to look at every situation, and his teasing personality clicked with Sarah's right away. But Craig's serious demeanor made her uncomfortable.

She leaned into the leather bucket seat and typed out a text to Jessica letting her know she was OK.

Sarah: *Jon left for Europe. It's not his.*

Jessica: *He told me.*

Sarah: *I think I'm going crazy. What was I thinking? Do you have time to talk?*

Jessica: *I'm with your mom, probably not the best time. I'll call you in a little bit.*

Sarah: *You didn't tell her what happened, did you?*

Jessica: *No. She's clueless.*

Sarah: *Good. I don't want her to know I had doubts.*

She stared at her phone wishing Jessica had more to say so she could feel less awkward about the silence in the car. She waited an entire minute before calling Cami. It was pretty rude of her friend to abandon her when she needed her the most, and Sarah wanted an explanation.

"Hey. I just wanted to let you know it's not his kid. I misunderstood what Mia had said. And I was wondering if you were OK. You disappeared so quickly. Did you get sick or something?" Sarah didn't really believe she got sick, but it was a more polite way of approaching the conversation than asking, "Where the hell did you go?"

"No. I heard you arguing upstairs, and I figured you didn't want me there to witness all your dirty laundry."

When she put it that way, it sounded like the most decent response to a bad situation, not abandonment. "Thanks. We worked it out. He's not a cheater. It's my issues with trust that caused the problem."

"Maybe subconsciously you know he's a bad person and that's why you don't trust him."

"If you knew Jonathan, you'd never say that. He's the most kind, loyal, and honest human I know."

"He didn't put Mia in her place, and he lied to you about the stalker. You didn't even know about it until Mia told you."

Sarah had told her about the stalker on the car ride to gather her belongings from the house.

"He was just trying to protect me. He didn't want me to worry. It's probably just some psychotic fan."

"What if it's not, Sarah? What if the stalker is someone Jonathan hurt, not a fan, and he comes after you?"

"I'm tough. Besides, I have security with me all the time now." Sarah looked over at Craig, who was pretending not to hear her conversation. His face was stern without expression. "In fact, I'm sitting in the car with Craig right now on the way to pick up my car from the hotel."

"Oh." Cami sounded surprised. "Jonathan's left already?"

"Yeah. He just stayed to make sure I was safe, but he couldn't get out of the tour. He'll be gone for two weeks."

"We should get together while he's gone. What are you doing tomorrow?"

"I have a dress fitting, but I'm free tomorrow night."

"We're going out. I'll text you the details."

By the time Sarah got off the phone, they were pulling into the hotel parking lot.

"Where did you park, ma'am?" Craig drawled.

She smiled. He always called her ma'am or Miss Sarah. He told her once it was because of his southern upbringing. Sarah wasn't used to such formality. People in Minnesota just weren't so respectful, especially to people who were younger than them. "On the side there." Sarah pointed. She had parked out of the view of the street just in case Jon sent out a search party looking for her car.

He circled around her car once and then parked about five stalls down, leaving the car running. "Stay in the car," he said tersely. Then he reached down and grabbed something off the floor, stuffing it in the back of his jeans as he closed the door behind him. When he passed in front of Sarah, she saw the butt of his gun sticking out of his waistband.

What had he seen? Sarah strained in her seat to see her car, but a huge vehicle blocked her view and she couldn't even see Craig anymore. A chill ran through her. She clicked the door lock to make sure no one could get in and listened nervously for a clue as to what was happening outside. After several minutes Craig crossed in front of her, a piece of white paper pinched between two fingers, and she unlocked the doors. He set the paper on the backseat, locked the doors, and started to back the vehicle out of its parking space.

"You're scaring me. What's going on?"

"I'm sorry, ma'am. I don't mean to frighten you. We won't be able to pick up your car at this time." He fastened his seatbelt as he pulled to the parking lot exit.

"Why? We're right here. Did someone slash my tires or smash my car? What's happened?" Sarah craned her neck to see her BMW, just catching a glimpse. It looked fine. "Just tell me."

"I have to get you home. I'll get Raul to deal with your car."

"Craig, just tell me what is wrong with my car."

"I have to talk to Mr. Williams, ma'am."

"You need to tell me right now or I'm jumping out and walking back to see for myself."

"That wouldn't be advised," he said, and Sarah swore the car sped up.

"Why wouldn't it be advised?" She just wanted to know what was wrong.

"Because you would get hurt, ma'am. I'm driving too fast for you to exit safely, and the traffic is particularly busy in this part of town. Even if you were able to land safely, you would most likely get hurt by another vehicle."

"I bet you would lose your job, too, if I jumped."

"Yes, ma'am."

"Just tell me, please."

"There was a message from the stalker on your windshield. Your car isn't safe. I'll have it inspected before anyone drives it."

The stalker found her? How could the stalker have found her? Sarah looked to the backseat, where the paper sat that Craig had so gingerly handled. She wanted to reach for it but knew it may have the stalker's fingerprints on it. "What does the note say? I'm going to see it eventually. You may as well tell me now."

He pulled the car to the curb and took out his phone. He messed with it for a minute before handing it to her. On the screen was a picture of a white piece of paper. She enlarged the picture so she could read the words: LEAVE HIM OR YOU WILL DIE TOO!

The font was Times New Roman. Sarah recognized it. "This could be from anyone. It's not distinctive at all. Any of the ten thousand teenage girls who want to marry Jon could have recognized me and put it on my car. Why do you think it's from the stalker?"

"On the bottom of the page, the embedded article fits with the stalker's other notes. It's from her."

Sarah scrolled down the photo. When she had enlarged it, she must have cropped out the article. The title read: JACK WILLIAMS KILLED BY HIS OWN BROTHER.

There was even a picture of the accident. Holy crap. That was severe. The print on the picture was too small for her to read, but she would look it up when she got home. She handed his phone back to him, and he started driving again. She didn't know what to say. The stalker followed her to the hotel and was threatening her. Part of her was pissed the stalker could be so manipulative, and part of her was bone-chillingly scared.

When they got back to the house, Sarah sat down on the couch, pulling her legs up and draping her arms around them. She felt small and defenseless. She wished Jon wasn't gone. She needed her fiancé's warm, protective arms around her. She needed him to tell her she was safe. She glanced up and caught Craig watching her. He had his phone in his hand, his expression torn.

"If you want, I can stay at the guesthouse tonight. I don't have to be in the security office as long as I have the tablet so I can track the cameras."

Sarah nodded immediately. She didn't want to be alone in this huge estate with him all the way over at the main house. He left to retrieve the large tablet from the security office, and Sarah flicked on the TV. Even with the extra-loud drone of the commercials, every noise in the house seemed amplified—the buzz of the air conditioner turning on, a creak from somewhere upstairs. When she heard the kitchen door opening, she knew it was Craig but still felt the need to scoot down so the back of the couch hid her head. He nodded as he came around to face her and sat down on the chair. He propped the tablet up on the ottoman table and turned to her.

"Give me your phone, ma'am."

She unlocked it before handing it to him and watched him as he fiddled with it for several minutes. When he handed it back, two new icons appeared on her main screen. An icon of a chain with oversized links sat in the upper right corner and one of a canned air horn like she'd seen used as a noisemaker at football games sat in the lower right corner.

"You push the one with the chain and your phone will immediately alert my phone. Our phones will be linked, and I will be able to hear you even if your phone's mic is muffled because it is stuffed in your pocket." He took out his phone and pressed several buttons on it as well before returning it to his pocket. "The app strengthens the signal. This one," he pointed to the air horn icon, "is used for distraction. Push it."

Sarah tapped the picture on her screen and her ears curled into her head trying to escape the loudest horn, she had ever heard, blasting from her phone.

"You can use it to get noticed in a crowd if you feel you are in danger or if you just need a distraction to get away. The longer you hold it, the longer it sounds. Sometimes all you need is a second of distraction to make an escape. Both apps will work even if you are on the phone or have other programs running on your phone."

Sarah tapped the chain and an alarm blasted from Craig's pocket for just a couple of seconds. He didn't even have to touch his phone before she heard their voices echoing from it.

He pulled his phone out and said, "See. Only I can break the connection." He tapped his phone and the echoing stopped. "That way, the stalker won't be able to break our connection. Stalkers are a lot like terrorists." He sat forward in his chair, resting his elbows on his knees with his hands clasped and outstretched as he met her eyes. "They learn enough about you to strike fear in you, but the more prepared you are—the better you know who they are and what motivates them—the more control you have. We're prepared. There's no one getting into this house." He typed on the tablet for a second and Sarah heard the house's security system arm.

Just then her phone went off, startling her so much she practically jumped to her feet.

"Hey, Jess." She inhaled and blew it out her mouth trying to slow her heart rate. "You are not going to believe the week I've had."

"First you have to tell me, did you really…really throw that gorgeous ring out the car window? I didn't have the guts to ask Jon."

"What do you think?" Sarah couldn't believe her best friend believed the tabloid.

"I don't know. Hollywood turns people crazy."

"Does it make them stupid?" Sarah paused. "Wait, don't answer that. No, I'm not crazy or stupid. Though I may be a little crazy." She was rambling incoherently and knew it. "It's still on my finger." She stopped herself before she said any more.

"Good. I would hate to see that beautiful work of art lost."

"Do you want to hear about my week or not?"

"All right. I'll shut up. Tell me."

Sarah shared all that had happened at the restaurant with Mia and how she stupidly believed Mia over Jon. "She's so damn manipulative. She actually wanted Jon to claim the baby as his because it would be easier for her fans to accept than her having a baby with a guy she's never been seen with, especially because he's one of Jon's buddies." Sarah looked over at Craig, sure he heard every word she said, but he pretended not to be listening. She wasn't going to leave the room, though. She was still too shaken up about the stalker. Privacy was overrated.

"Oh my god! One of Jon's buddies slept with Mia? Was it Nick?"

"No. It's not anybody you've met."

"Is Jon pissed?"

"Honestly, I think he feels sorry for the guy. He called him before he left just to warn him that he's going to tell the press he's not the father."

"And you're still letting Mia come to the wedding after all that?"

"I think I have to invite her or the press will say that I'm jealous of her and wouldn't invite her because I see her as a threat to my marriage. If she comes to the wedding, then they won't have anything to say." She paused and backpedaled. "Well, that's not true because they will just make something up. But if she comes, I'll look better in the tabloids."

"You *are* the better person, Sarah."

"Thanks. I try. Anyway, I have to tell you what else happened. After the restaurant incident, I went to a hotel and disappeared for a couple days. I convinced myself I had to leave Jon. At the time, I believed he had cheated on me and lied to me about it. I can't be with someone I can't trust. You know my issues. Well...my friend Cami came and stayed with me the first night. Remember the punishing Pilates instructor that I told you about?"

"The one whose class you never thought you would get into and then a spot mysteriously opened up two weeks after you applied?"

"That's the one. One woman told me she waited eighteen months to get into her class. The only reason she got in was that another woman's husband died and she was too grief-stricken to notify Cami that she wasn't going to make it to class. Cami gave her position away with full knowledge of why she didn't call."

"Harsh."

"You think? I heard the waiting list is a mile long. I don't know how I got in, but I wasn't going to question it. She's a really good instructor, and I'm always rung out when I leave her class."

"Maybe she's hot for Jonathan."

"She doesn't seem like the type to give a celebrity preferential treatment. Actually, I could see her do just the opposite—not letting you in because you're a celebrity. She seems to hate actors in particular—jilted by some guy a few years ago. She reminds me a little of you, though—definitely obsessive-compulsive with her germ issues. Which is good. At least I know I won't catch any nasty diseases from the Pilates equipment."

Craig looked up from the tablet for a second and Sarah could tell he was paying attention to her conversation. Maybe he still hated Cami for helping her escape to Caboose Juice that day. If Sarah had known about the stalker, maybe she wouldn't have been running from his protection. She wasn't going anywhere today.

"It turns out she's really great. She brought me back to the house to give me moral support. I hadn't grabbed all my stuff when I left the first time, and I figured I'd just sneak in and get the rest before driving back to Minnesota. I thought Jon had left for Europe already, but he was over at the main house. His mom is visiting his dad on location in Toronto for the week, so I didn't think anyone would be home. I was wrong."

Craig picked up the tablet and was fiddling with it.

"Hold on a sec." Sarah watched Craig. Pressing her phone to her chest she asked, "Did you see something?"

He shook his head. "No, ma'am."

Sarah let out the breath she had been holding and returned her phone to her ear. "Cami heard Jon and me arguing upstairs and left because she didn't want to invade our privacy. Most people would have recorded every word and then sold it to the tabloids. At least I don't have to worry about that with her."

"Speaking of selling you to the tabloids, I think Megan is talking to Chase again. She was on the phone with someone yesterday and she wouldn't admit who it was."

"Seriously? I don't have the bandwidth to deal with her and him anymore. Don't tell her any of this stuff with Mia, OK? Just in case she gets back with him. You can tell her Jon's not the father, just not any of the details."

"OK. I won't. So what happened after Cami left?"

"Jon was pretty mad I believed Mia over him. I hurt him so badly, and I didn't even have time to make it up to him before he left. I mean we only had an hour. There's only so much you can do in an hour. He left to catch his flight, and then Craig took me to get my car from the hotel. And this is where it gets freaky. The stalker found me at the hotel and left a note on my car that said, 'Leave him or you will die.' Can you believe that?"

"Wow."

"We left my car there in case the brake lines were cut or it was rigged with explosives and now I'm just holed up at the house. The worst part is that Jon is on his way to London."

"Are you going to tell him?"

"It doesn't matter what I do. I'm sure Craig has already sent a text to Sam. Jon will know by the time his flight lands."

"The fact that the stalker found you at the hotel and could pick your car out of all the other cars in the lot, that's pretty scary."

"Yeah, I'm not leaving the house for the next two weeks unless I absolutely have to leave. We'll have to stay in while you guys are here. Is that OK?"

"We're not there to see LA anyway. We're there to see you…and get the dresses fitted."

"Thanks. I can't wait until you come." Sarah paused. She hadn't thought about what would happen if the stalker tried something when her friends were visiting. What if one of them got hurt? She'd never forgive herself for putting them in danger. Maybe that was how Jon felt. Besides not wanting Sarah hurt, he would feel as if he was to blame. She needed to girl-up and not let Jon see how much the stalker affected her. It would only make him feel guilty for something he couldn't control. Just like the ten other guilt-trips he's imposed on himself.

"Hey, Jess. I haven't slept in days, not since the restaurant incident. I'm exhausted. Can I call you tomorrow?"

"I've got my study class for my nursing boards until four, but we can connect any time after that."

"Talk to you then."

Sarah turned to Craig and asked, "Would you mind doing a sweep of the upstairs just to appease my nerves?"

"Not a problem, ma'am."

She followed him upstairs and listened as he opened the closet door in the music room. Then she tailed behind him as he entered her bedroom. She watched anxiously as he checked the closet and the bath and got down on his hands and knees to look under the bed. He stood up and met her near the door. With a slight grin on his face, he said, "All clear."

She didn't care that he thought she was being paranoid. She had a right to be. It wasn't every day someone threatened her life.

"Do you think Jon will come home because of the stalker's note?" Even though she didn't want Jon to shrug his obligations, she didn't want to be alone for two weeks.

"It's hard to know, but I wouldn't recommend it. If you let stalkers manipulate you, then it empowers them. Most are narcissists who crave to be in charge, in control, and want others to see them as influential. If you let them gain that advantage over you, then it may escalate the stalking, bringing it to a more dangerous level. It's best to be smart, careful, and not let them know they have power over you or your actions."

Sarah let his words sink in. She nodded slowly, trying to convince herself that she believed what she was about to say. "Then he should finish his tour. I'll be fine here. We can't let the stalker know that he has power."

"It's a she, ma'am. The stalker is female. That's what the FBI said."

"Then *she* is not going to have control over me." She walked deeper into the room and Craig exited, closing the door behind him.

∽

It was 5:00 a.m. when the text came in. He would have just stepped off the plane in London and was likely being swept off to the premiere right away. She knew he would freak out.

Jon: Are you awake?

Sarah: *Yes.*

A minute later, her phone vibrated with a call. She was in bed, but she hadn't slept all night.

"I'm sorry, Sarah." His voice was soft and dripping with remorse.

"What do you have to be sorry about? This is not your fault." She was a bit frustrated that he always blamed himself for all the problems in the world.

"Are you all right? Craig said you were pretty upset."

"He's exaggerating. I'm fine." *Stupid Craig*. Why did he have to tell Jon that?

"I can come home if you need me, but the FBI said we shouldn't cancel major happenings or the stalker will feel empowered."

Crap! He wasn't coming home.

"I heard. Besides, you need to do the tour. People are counting on you." She wanted him home, and she hoped he could see right through her words.

"Whoever this stalker is, we'll find her. I can't imagine any woman that I've pissed off enough that she would threaten you."

"If she wants me to leave or die, then she just wants you for herself. See, you didn't do anything wrong. She just wants what I have."

"Well, she's never going to get me. You're stuck with me until death do us…" He paused as he realized what he was saying. "You're just stuck with me. Forever. Are you sure you're OK?"

"I'm fine. Just go back to work. The girls will be down next weekend and Cami is around."

"How do we know Cami's not the stalker?"

"She's not. She owns a Pilates studio. She has a life. She doesn't need to obsess about ours. I think it's Mia. She wants me out of the picture so she can get you back."

He laughed, making it clear that wouldn't happen. "You better get some sleep, beautiful. I'll talk to you after the premiere. I love you and stay safe."

"You too." When the line went dead, she clutched the phone to her chest as if it were Jon and took a deep breath. Two weeks was a long time, but she would have to make it through without him.

Chapter Thirty-One

Sarah

As Sarah and Raul drove out the front gate to meet the wedding planner, and Sarah's favorite hair and makeup stylist at the designer's studio for the dress fitting, Sarah looked a little closer at the vehicles parked on the street. Just a beat-up car and the white van. Could the stalker be on the street in front of the house? She had never really thought of that before.

This morning after Jon's premiere finished, she and Jon had a lengthy phone conversation about the insight the FBI provided about the stalker. He wanted her to know all the facts. They said it was a woman because of the words chosen on the letters.

"But maybe the stalker intentionally made himself sound like a woman to throw them off," Sarah questioned.

"They know how to spot that. The FBI also said the stalker has been in the guesthouse before, because she mentioned specifics about the soundproof walls in the master bedroom and how no one in the rest of the house would hear the screams."

"What? Is that even true?" Sarah asked.

"I didn't want to mention it before because it sounds sleazy. I didn't have it put in. Jack did. The guesthouse wasn't remodeled until I was a freshman in high school. My parents didn't want to deal with the expense if they weren't going to use it, but they changed their minds by the time Jack was seventeen. He was practically living in the guesthouse by then, so they decided on a remodel in hopes of keeping him under their roof a little longer. Jack put up his own money to have the bedrooms upstairs upgraded to acoustic-grade insulation. That's why the music room is so great. If the door is closed, no one can hear me play."

"So the stalker knows more about our house than I do?"

"No, Sarah. She just knows the bedrooms are soundproof. I don't remember who I've told about the acoustics, but that little bit of information narrows the search and will help us find her."

"That means the stalker is probably an ex or a hookup that you told about the soundproof qualities of our bedroom so you could have loud, sleazy sex with her."

He groaned at her words, then said, "Please don't go there. You know I have a past and I am far from perfect. You make me want to be a better person, beautiful. You are my present and my future, and no one else matters. Besides, the only person I ever want to have loud, sleazy sex with is you. And we won't get to do that until after the wedding. You realize that, right?"

"What are you talking about? You'll be home in thirteen days." As the words passed her lips, the dates clicked into place. "You don't get home until after our month of celibacy starts. Great! Just great." She paused, shaking her head. He could have reminded her before he left. "We don't have to do it. It's just something I read in *Cosmo*."

"No, we're doing it. I think that not having sex for the month before the wedding will make the honeymoon that much sweeter. And I'm committed to making our honeymoon as sweet as possible. And pleasurable. And…"

By the time she got off the phone, Sarah was feeling a little more relaxed. Jon had reassured her that Craig and Raul's experience dealing with insurgents in Afghanistan had trained them better than anyone to deal with a stalker. Spotting the note on Sarah's car was just an example of how aware they really are. Sarah had to agree. She was amazed that Craig saw the note at all. She would have thought that it was a flyer for a band or a club and probably wouldn't have even looked at it.

Raul smiled his easy smile as they pulled into the private underground parking lot. He was a little quieter than usual this morning. Building security monitored who entered and exited the parking garage, so Sarah knew the stalker wouldn't be able to tamper with the car today. They still hadn't gotten her car back yet. Craig had arranged for it to be towed to a garage where a mechanic could take a look at it and a bomb-sniffing dog would be employed as well. Sarah wasn't going to be driving it anytime soon, so it didn't matter how long the inspection took.

Four hours later Sarah was on her bed in her soundproof room looking at the pictures on her phone. The fitting had gone well. The shoes Nicole had ordered were perfect with their pearled-sequins straps and heels that were just the right height. And best of all, Deidra was able to work up an intricate updo that dreamily complemented the veil and then captured them in pictures on Sarah's phone so it could be recreated on the big day. Sarah stared at them now, wondering how every detail was going to magically fall into place. The fitting had definitely kicked up her nerves about the wedding and pushed her thoughts about the stalker into the background.

As she clicked back through the pictures for the twentieth time, her phone buzzed with a call. She checked the ID hoping it was Jon, but she knew he was either sleeping or on another flight by now.

"Hey, Sarah. Are you ready for a night on the town?"

"Cami. I don't really feel like going out tonight. Could we take a rain check?"

"No way. We are going out and you are going to tell me what happened with that jackoff of a man you live with."

"He didn't lie to me. We kissed and made up. End of story."

"How do you know he didn't lie to you? Did Mia Thompson admit it wasn't his baby?"

"No. I trust him."

"Well, that's your mistake right there."

Sarah rolled her eyes. "I know who the real father is. It's not Jon."

"Is he an actor, too? Because they're professional liars, all of them."

"You used to be an actor."

"But I'm not anymore. I'm picking you up at ten. Wear something skimpy. We're going clubbing."

Cami ended the call, leaving Sarah shaking her head. There was no way she was going anywhere without Jon in something skimpy. The press would be all over it. The fact that she and Jon hadn't been spotted out publically together since the restaurant incident already had the tabloids believing she and Jon had called it quits. She didn't want to feed the frenzy by showing up at a club without him. Besides, she didn't want to leave the house—there was a stalker leaving death threats on her car.

She sent a total of four texts to Cami over the next few hours telling her she was staying home. When she didn't get a single response, she assumed Cami had gotten the message. She didn't expect her to show up at the gate at 10:00 p.m. exactly. Raul called her cell to notify her, and she almost told him not to let her in. Instead she met her by the door in her yoga pants and tank top.

"You're not going out in that. That's social suicide." Cami smiled. "I'm kidding. I got your message. What do you have against going out?" She reached into the backseat and pulled out a basket with alcohol and mixers.

"Where should I start?" Sarah answered as she opened the door and held it for Cami to pass through. She followed Cami into the kitchen and watched as she started unpacking the flavored vodka and two kinds of diet soda.

"I hope you ate dinner, because I didn't bring any food with me."

"I have food." Sarah pointed to the refrigerator. "Are you hungry?"

Cami shook her head as she reached into the cupboard and pulled down two glasses. "Tell me what's going on with you. Jonathan just left? After he tortured you, making you think he fathered Mia's baby, he just left? What a douche."

"It was my fault. He tried to tell me it wasn't his, but I didn't listen. And he had to go on this tour."

"Anybody with his status in Hollywood doesn't have to do anything he doesn't want."

"It's not that simple." Sarah blew out a breath. "The promotion is for a movie that won a bunch of awards at Cannes. Jon skipped out on the awards ceremony. He wanted to spend time with me alone. And the media blew up at him, saying he only supported big box office films that made him money and that he thought he was too good for an indie film. The fans and the filmmakers were upset because they thought he was going to be there to accept the awards and he wasn't. He could just ignore the press, but that's not really a good career move in this climate. I can't expect him to skip the tour just because of a misunderstanding. Besides, he can't change his plans because that's what the stalker wants him to do."

"What do you mean? Did you get another note?"

"The stalker left a note on my car."

"Oh my god! Did you freak out?"

"Yes. Wouldn't you? I completely lost it. My car was at the hotel. I haven't even gotten it back yet. How did the stalker know it was mine?"

"What did Jonathan say when you told him about it? I mean, he was gone by the time you went to get your car."

"I don't know. I didn't tell him. One of the security guys did." Sarah still wasn't sure if it was Craig or Sam who broke the news to Jon.

"Knowing how protective he is of you, I would imagine he was completely devastated." Cami handed Sarah a mixed drink, smiling as if she was enjoying their conversation. "I can't believe he didn't turn the plane around and come home to guard you himself."

Sarah had thought that's what he would do too. "We're not supposed to make any changes to our scheduled activity. The FBI says that it just empowers the stalker. It makes her feel as if she has control over us." Sarah wasn't sure if it was the FBI or just Craig that came up with that theory, but it was easier to defend if it was the government.

"You didn't tell me the FBI was involved. I didn't think they got involved unless there is cyberstalking or the stalker used the US mail."

"Maybe Sam knows someone, or maybe it's just that Jon is a high-profile figure. I don't know how they got involved." Sarah took a sip of her drink and tried to motion Cami to join her outside in the courtyard.

"Can we just sit in here?" Cami asked, veering into the living room.

"Sure." Sarah followed her and planted herself at one end of the leather couch.

"What did the FBI say?" Cami asked, sitting in the oversized chair next to Sarah and setting her drink on the table between them. "I mean, Jonathan must be pretty shaken if the FBI is involved."

"They said it was a woman and that she's been in the guesthouse before." Sarah didn't want to go into detail about how they knew the woman had been in the house. "It's probably an ex or a hookup of Jon's, though he said he hasn't really had any hookups since he moved in here. It's probably Mia Thompson. I'd like to catch her red-handed with one of the stalker notes."

"You seem so cavalier about this whole thing. What's wrong with you?"

"It bothers me. I bring a bodyguard with me when I go out, but other than that what can I do about it? Nothing I do is going to change anything."

"I would be so pissed at Jonathan for not cancelling his plans and coming to rescue me. I don't know why you're not mad at him for putting you in this situation in the first place." Cami stood up, visibly irked, and stormed to the counter to refill her glass.

Sarah pulled her hair back in a loose ponytail to get it off her neck. She didn't really want any more drama right now. She was still so unsure of how she felt about the note on her car. She really wasn't in the mood to be drinking and hashing out her horrible week. She just really wanted to go to bed.

"Are you ready for a refill?" Cami called from the kitchen. Then, within seconds, she was crouching down in front of Sarah, her eyes wide. "There's someone at the back door," she whispered.

Sarah instinctively ducked and then looked over her shoulder toward the kitchen door. "It's just Raul. He always checks in before he sets the alarms for the night." Sarah had been expecting him. Cami stood up and plopped back into her chair, her drink sloshing in her glass. The door closed, and Raul appeared. His perma-smile immediately put Sarah in a better mood.

"Are you feeling any better?" he asked, and Sarah nodded. "I'm just going to check upstairs, and I'll be out of here." He stood by the stairs in jeans and a button-down shirt with his sleeves rolled up.

"Thanks." He didn't usually check the rooms upstairs, but Craig must have told him how upset she had been last night.

"Does he live here?" asked Cami, and Sarah couldn't tell if she was interested in dating him or what the expression on her face said.

"Yeah, pretty much. Both he and Craig, the guy I was hiding from at the studio, are staying here while Jon is gone. Why? Are you interested? He's kind of cute, isn't he? I think he has a girlfriend, though."

"He *is* hot. There is no doubt there. I'm just surprised that even with Jonathan gone, you're still stuck with his entourage."

She shrugged. She wasn't going to complain about her security detail anymore. Sarah changed the subject. "Are you dating anyone? You never mention your love life."

"I am seeing someone, but he's more of an acquaintance that I sleep with."

Sarah laughed at Cami's confession. "Do you think it will turn into more?"

"I don't know. I'm so busy running the studio and he's a computer genius, busy doing what computer geniuses do."

"How did you two meet?"

"At the studio. He took one of my classes. He might be a nerd, but he keeps his body hard."

A voice from the stairs interrupted the conversation. "Everything looks good up there. Let me know when your friend leaves," said Raul as he hit the last step. He cleared his throat as if he was uncomfortable with what he was about to say. "If you want, I can stay at the guesthouse tonight."

Cami burst out laughing. "I guess you *don't* mind the security detail as much as you let on. Dark, gorgeous man keeps you warm while Jonathan's away. You can't beat that. It brings a whole new meaning to the title *bodyguard*. Don't worry; I won't tell Jonathan about your arrangement."

Sarah looked at Raul, smiling as she rolled her eyes. "It's not what it sounds like. I was a bit freaked out last night after finding the stalker's note on my car. Jon's folks are out of town and won't be back until it's almost time for Jon to return. This is the first time Jon and I have been apart this long since I moved in, and I was scared," said Sarah, and then she explained how Craig had stayed downstairs at the house last night to calm her nerves.

"I can stay with you if you want. We can do another slumber party like we did at the hotel." She pointed to Raul. "And he *is* welcome to join us as far as I'm concerned."

Sarah smiled. "I'm sure he has better things to do than to babysit us. Are you sure you don't mind staying with me, Cami?"

"No, it will be fun. Besides, I think I've drunk too much to drive anyway."

"Thanks for the offer, Raul. Cami can keep me company, and I can set the alarms in here when we go to bed."

"I'll be in the security office if you need me." He gave Sarah a nod and left through the front door, locking it behind him.

"It's too bad he was so busy." Cami guzzled her drink and got up to refill her glass. "You're not keeping up, Sarah. I feel like I'm the only one committed here."

Sarah started to wonder if she was serious about a three-way with Raul. She hoped she wasn't. "I'm trying not to waste the calories on nutrient-hollow foods. I have to fit into a wedding dress. I can't afford empty calories."

"Vodka and diet Sprite, you can't get lower calorie than that. No excuses, Sarah." Cami took Sarah's glass from the table next to her and filled it to the rim. Handing it back to Sarah, she said, "You need to finish this just to catch up."

Sarah took it, knowing she wouldn't finish it. It wasn't just the calories. She just wasn't in the mood to drink. She took a sip and set it on the table.

"I can stay with you this week if you want. My geek is out of town anyway, so my nights are free."

"That would be great. My bridesmaids are coming in from Minnesota to get their final fittings for their dresses over the weekend. If you would stay with me until they come in, I would really appreciate it. I can't drink every night though, OK?"

"Sure. We can find something else to do. When is the wedding anyway?"

Sarah cringed at her question. Should she tell her? Should she not? "It's next month." She decided to be vague. Technically it was next month, but it was more than a month away.

"You must be insane. Days ago, you were leaving Jonathan because he cheated on you. You make up with him and then hours later he leaves to travel Europe. Someone threatens your life, and he doesn't even seem to care. Are you sure you want to marry this guy?"

Sarah took another sip of her drink. "Yes. I want to marry him."

"You know, I read this article once about how Jonathan didn't even feel bad about killing his brother. It said he was jealous of all the roles Jack was getting and it was a relief for him not to have to compete with his brother anymore. There were pictures. They look so much alike, and Hollywood is only so big."

"You can't believe everything you read."

"The article had a ton of examples. It was obvious the information was from an insider, probably someone in his family sick of how smug Jonathan was. He started back to work right away like he didn't even care that he killed his brother."

"He didn't kill Jack. It was just an accident. A paparazzo spilled his motorcycle right in front of him. What was he supposed to do?"

"Sarah, he was driving the car. He could have swerved the other direction and hit a parked car, but instead he pulls into oncoming traffic in front of a giant SUV. It couldn't have been an accident. Nobody is that stupid."

Really? Sarah couldn't believe her ears. "He was nineteen years old. Jack's death destroyed him. You don't know what you are talking about. Just because you read some misguided tabloid doesn't make you an expert on his life."

"You're right. I just don't understand how someone could do what he did and still live with himself."

"He struggles with it every day." Sarah hoped it was just the alcohol talking and Cami didn't really believe what she was saying. She couldn't deal with this kind of discussion for the rest of the week. "You really should at least meet Jon before you pass judgment on him. We can do lunch sometime, or better yet, he makes this awesome chicken curry, and he's not bad at Italian either. He could cook for us."

"OK. That would be great." Cami looked around the room and then asked, "How secure is this place? I mean your stalker's not going to be able to get in here while we sleep, is she?"

"There are camera's everywhere outside and alarms on the doors and windows. I can't imagine how she would get in."

They talked security for a few more minutes and then turned on the TV and caught a rerun of Liam's show. By the time it ended, Sarah just wanted to go to bed. She lent Cami one of Jon's T-shirts to sleep in, and while Cami fell asleep quickly on the other side of the large bed, Sarah wrote a couple of pages in her journal. It always helped her sleep if she dumped her thoughts onto the paper before bed. Though it was comforting having a live person within screaming distance, she missed Jon.

༄

Sarah opened her eyes as the buzzing began a second round. She reached out and seized the offender off the bedside table, unplugging it as she swiped her finger across the bottom of the screen. She didn't even look to see who was making the call. She just wanted the noise to stop. She sat up and whispered, "Hello."

"Hey, beautiful. Did I wake you?"

She glanced at the unmoving mound on the other side of the bed and stood up, trudging into the hallway before answering.

"Maybe." She didn't want to wake Cami.

"I'm sorry. I've completely lost track of time. I think we're in Zurich. The street signs have lots of umlauts on them anyway and it's not Berlin. What time is it at home?" Jon's voice exuded energy.

She pulled the phone away from her ear to check the time. It had to be early; the sun wasn't even up. "Eight minutes after four."

"I didn't mean to wake you. I could let you go back to sleep."

"No, I'm already awake. Let's talk. How did last night's premiere go?" She rubbed her face as she stood up and walked down the hall to the music room. She may as well utilize the soundproof walls. She closed the door before settling on the mustard-colored sofa and snuggling into the throw blanket off its back.

"I'm right at that tipping point where I can no longer sit through the movie. I've seen it so many times. I know I'm supposed to pretend that each premiere is the first showing, but I think the subject matter of this movie just hits too close to home for me with Jack's death that I can't stomach it anymore. I'm going to try to sneak out after the screening starts tonight so I don't have to watch it again."

"You could put your earbuds in and listen to music."

"That's a good idea. I may have to use that. How are you doing? Are the boys taking good care of you?" He called them boys, though they were older than him.

"Yeah. They've been great. Cami is going to stay with me until the girls come on the weekend. It's nice having someone else here."

"That's great. When I get home, we'll have to take her out to dinner to thank her."

"I told her you would cook for her."

"I could do that. Hey, what did your e-mail mean?"

"What e-mail?"

"The one you sent last night. Who is she? And what was her choice?"

"I don't know what you are talking about. I didn't send you an e-mail."

"It says it was from you. It has your e-mail address on it."

"What does it say exactly?" Sarah sat up as an icy chill ran through her body.

"It says, 'She made her choice.' That was all that was written. You didn't send it?"

"Cami was here last night. We had a couple of drinks, we watched some TV, and we went to bed. I didn't even have my computer on, and I didn't send anything from my phone."

"Could your friend, Cami, have gotten a hold of your phone?"

"Why would she? Besides, I was with her the whole night. She fell asleep before I did and she's still sleeping. Do you think the stalker hacked into my e-mail? And what does that mean, *she made her choice?*"

"I don't know. Are you sure Cami fell asleep before you?"

"Yes. Also, all my stuff is password-protected. How would she have logged on? She doesn't know my passwords."

"I'm going to talk to Sam and see what he thinks. I'll call you later, after the premiere. I love you, Sarah. Don't think about it too much. Maybe it was just a glitch in the e-mail delivery system."

"OK. I love you, too."

The call ended, and of course Sarah couldn't stop thinking about the e-mail. She snuck back into her bedroom, grabbed her journal, and made her way to the kitchen table. There was no way she could go back to sleep at this point.

Sarah had just finished starting the coffee when Craig opened the kitchen door, punching in the code for the alarm as he stepped inside. She glanced up at the clock, not saying a word. 4:47. She hadn't even opened her journal yet. Jon must have been more worried about the e-mail than he wanted her to know.

"Good morning," Craig said, as he shifted the computer monitor and laptop in his hand. She smiled as he added, "I'm going to be working from the guesthouse today. I'll set this up in the office and then I'm supposed to look at your phone."

"OK. The coffee should be ready in a couple of minutes."

"And, Sarah, let me know if you're planning on going anywhere. I have to go with you when you leave the house."

"Always," she said, opening her journal and grabbing her pen.

The rest of the week progressed without another e-mail. Cami left for the studio every morning and came back to the house every evening. They hung out and watched movies together, and Cami showed her some really effective exercises for her thighs and butt. Sarah wondered if Megan did them and deliberately never shared them with her friends just so she could keep her "best ass" title.

Feeling really comfortable with the way she and Cami were getting along, Sarah asked, "I know the acquaintance you sleep with is coming back into town today and you're going to be busy over the weekend, but you wouldn't be interested in coming back here for a couple of days after my friends leave, would you? I've gotten used to having you keeping me company." Sarah looked at her with her best puppy dog eyes.

"How could I say no when you are so good at making salad from a bag?"

Sarah chuckled. "I promise I will go to the grocery store and get some more food before you come back."

With Raul and Craig both eating their meals at the house, and the fact that groceries hadn't been bought since before lunch with Mia, the refrigerator was looking a little barren. She needed to buy groceries before the weekend or she and her friends wouldn't have anything to eat. The thought occurred to her that she could send the girls out for groceries. They wouldn't mind. *Was she really that scared to leave the house?* She needed to get over it. Besides, she wouldn't want anything to happen to *them*. What if the stalker hurt them? The FBI had been notified about the e-mail, but nothing had come of it yet.

That afternoon, Sarah fabricated enough courage to get groceries with Raul, and she even went to Pilates. It felt good to get back into her normal routine and by the time the girls arrived, she had stopped some of her obsessing over the stalker.

During the weekend, she shared all that had happened with Mia and the stalker. She didn't care at this point that everyone but Megan believed Megan was back together with Chase. It just felt good to be able to vent to her friends. Being with the girls helped her truly relax for the first time since the restaurant debacle. They hung out at the pool, and it felt like old times. The girls even convinced her to go out to lunch after the dress fitting, and she started to almost feel prestalker normal.

But as Sarah watched the driver load each of the girls' bags into the car's trunk to take them back to the airport, she could feel the comfort her friends had brought her stripping away. They hugged their good-byes and her friends got into the car. Sarah waved toward their fleeing Town Car, just as a white Audi pulled up to replace it. She didn't recognize the vehicle, but it had to be someone they knew because Craig had opened the gate. The door opened and a woman stepped out. For a heartbeat Sarah feared the worst. The stalker was a woman after all. But when she spotted Remi's black, razor-cut hair sticking out in all directions, she didn't know what to think.

"I'm not the stalker, Sarah. Jon said you were handling this, but your face says otherwise." Remi started walking toward the house as Sarah followed.

"I'm fine." She scowled. "Did Jon send you to check on me?"

"No, but he knows I'm here. I have something to show you. Are you sure you're all right?"

"My bridesmaids just left for Minnesota and I already miss them. That must be what you see." Sarah tried to brighten her expression as she trailed her through the door.

"Maybe." Remi glanced around the living room shaking her head. "I can't believe that you put up with this tiny guesthouse. Tell Jon to buy you a decent place to live."

Sarah laughed. "I like the guesthouse. It's cozy. Besides, Jon bought me a huge house in Minnesota."

"You're not planning to live in that house, are you? Jon said you were staying here."

"You just want us to buy a big house here to keep us close by."

"That's partially true. But this place, it's embarrassing. *My* house is five times this size," declared Remi as she walked into the kitchen and sat down at the table.

"I guess it's the soundproof master bedroom. I just can't part with it."

Remi looked at her in confusion and patted the chair next to her. "Come sit."

Sarah wondered what brought Remi all the way here when Jon wasn't home. Remi pulled a large manila envelope from her bag and set it in front of her.

"Read the e-mail first. It came to the office yesterday. I was going to forward it to you, but Jon said your e-mail had been hacked. I printed both the English and French versions."

Sarah opened the envelope and pulled out the magazine spread, before reading the attached e-mail.

Sarah,

I just thought you might like a copy of my article going out in the magazine this week. I really adored our talk at the café in Cannes.

Enjoy!

—Christophe Laurent

She browsed the article uncertain what she would find. When Sarah finished, she was in awe. She couldn't believe he had written such a complimentary article about *her*. It cited her short story that was published while she was in school and the screenplay she was in negotiations for selling. Somehow Christophe knew about the bidding war that had occurred but didn't mention that the war was most likely due to the fact that Jonathan playing lead was part of the package. She laughed as she read the last line. "Jonathan Williams better keep her happy or another man, namely me, is going to swoop in and steal this gem of a woman."

"Wow. I can't believe he wrote that," admitted Sarah.

"I'm going to get quotes of the English version out as soon as the mag hits the stands."

"Maybe everyone will stop hating me."

"Nobody hates you, Sarah."

Sarah glared at her, trying to emphasize that she didn't believe her.

"You can't let the haters get to you. You're a target right now, but that will calm down after the wedding. And you seem to have made a fan in France without anyone's help. It will get easier, I promise."

"Thanks, Remi."

Chapter Thirty-Two

Jonathan

He rolled his head on his shoulders, back and forth, trying to relieve the muscle knot tightening between his blades. Jon hated these tours. The constant travel, the rigid schedule and the lack of sleep were all taking tolls on his body. He understood this kind of expedition for big box office films like *The Demigod* series, but this little indie film was only going to be released to a limited number of theaters, let alone countries. He felt a bit sorry for the promoters. They were never going to recoup the cost of this tour in ticket sales. Maybe he was the one he should feel sorry for, though. He was the one being abused. He tried to remember his fans were his motivation. Some of them had waited outside in the scorching heat for days just to catch a glimpse of him. He wanted to give them a good show—sign their autographs and take pictures with them. They were the reason he was here torturing himself.

He reached back and dug his fingers deep into the muscles of his neck, desperate to alleviate the pain. The hotel that they were heading to supposedly had an extensive exercise facility and he was going to use it. He really needed to work out. It had been days since he had a chance to lift weights or let loose on the treadmill. Maybe they had a rowing machine. That would help. It wasn't just his body that needed the release; it was his mind, too. Every time he closed his eyes, his thoughts drifted to Sarah.

It's not that he didn't trust his security team back home. Craig had spotted the stalker's note on Sarah's car after all. It was just that the thought of Sarah's life being threatened was like being eviscerated and then dragged across a giant cheese grater by his intestines. She meant more to him than his own life, and he was stuck on the other side of the world repeating shallow sound bites while he posed for pictures with people he didn't even know.

"I'm going to get a massage. Do you want me to set one up for you, too?" asked Leslie, looking almost as exhausted as he felt.

"Nope, I'll pass." He shook his head. "It doesn't matter how professional the massage starts out, I always get propositioned."

She looked up from her phone at him. "I can schedule it with a dude."

He rolled his eyes. "You think that matters. Male, female...I always end up in the same awkward situation. No, thanks. I'm going to work out, get a hot shower, and catch a nap. Maybe Sarah can release some of my tension in my dreams."

"Yuck! Don't...I just ate. It hasn't even been two weeks. You're not going to make it to the wedding night."

He smiled. "We'll make it. Honestly, all I want is to hold her in my arms."

"Piff," Leslie snorted. "Really. You can't stop talking about her body."

"OK. That *was* a lie. But I *would be* satisfied if I could just wrap my arms around her. I can't wait until we get home."

"Our contact at the FBI wants to meet with us when we get back. They have a picture of the person that put the note on Sarah's car. It's not a great shot because her face is blocked by a hat, but they want us to see if we can identify her. It was from the hotel's parking lot cameras. I'll set the meeting for the day after we get back, just to give us a day to relax," announced Sam.

"Sounds good. I can't wait to put the whole stalker ordeal behind us." He looked over at Sam and added, "I know that even if we figure out who it is, it probably won't make the stalker go away. She can keep on stalking, but at least we'll know who to stay away from. I couldn't have told more than a few people about the walls in the guesthouse, but I don't remember who I mentioned it to and who I didn't. I felt as if I was giving out contact names to the CDC to prevent the spread of STDs when I talked to the FBI last. I'm glad Sarah wasn't there. She doesn't need to know all the dirty details about my past. You wouldn't believe how intrusive their questions were. I guess my honesty is worth it if it helps find the stalker.

"Have you ever had to do that before—I mean, give names to the CDC?" asked Leslie with a dropped jaw.

"No. Have you?"

He turned back to Sam and asked, "Did Raul and Craig say how Sarah's weekend with her friends went? Did the girls keep them busy with their exploits?" Jon chuckled to himself imagining all the trouble Sarah and her friends got into.

"No. Raul said they were homebodies all weekend, hardly went out at all."

"Oh." That was worse. It meant Sarah was too freaked out by the stalker to enjoy her friends' visit. "Is Sarah doing all right? She seems fine on the phone, but I've always had a harder time reading her when I can't see her face."

"She'll be fine. We'll be home in two days." Sam checked his phone and met Jon's eyes. "I hope the facility has free weights. I can never get a good workout on those machines."

"I think they do. It looked pretty good sized," added Leslie.

The car slowed as it pulled up to the hotel. A dozen people stood behind a velvet rope barrier watching the car expectantly. "Do you have a pen, Leslie?"

"There goes our work out," proclaimed Sam, handing Jon a black Sharpie.

"It won't take that long. We have a couple hours," said Jonathan.

"You're just encouraging more people to come stalk you," added Leslie.

That was a poor word choice. "We're only here for a night."

The door opened and he followed Sam out. The crowd screamed as he approached, and Jon dragged a smile onto his tired face. With Sam at his side, he motioned that he would sign autographs. It didn't matter that he didn't speak the same language, miming was universal. Leslie checked them in, while Jon stayed, posing for pictures and signing his name.

When it came time to leave for the premiere, there were twice as many people behind the rope, just as Leslie had predicted. Unfortunately Jon didn't have any time to give them, and he felt badly to disappoint them.

The red carpet and the screening went smoothly. As they headed back to the hotel, relief encompassed him. It was their last stop, and they would be catching a flight home in the morning. The crowd was growing outside the hotel and as much as he hated disappointing his fans, he just couldn't muster enough energy to sign any more autographs. When Sam told the driver to go around the block and pull into the back entrance by the kitchen, he smiled. Sam had read his mind.

Overall the tour ran smoothly. He and Amy Richardson even found a way to be cordial to each other. The last few nights they posed for pictures together, exciting the crowd into believing the movie's love interests could be more than just coworkers. It was good for ticket sales and his job. *It's called acting for a reason.*

He hit the shower first, trying to wash the entire tour down the drain and put it behind him. The hot water burned as it ran over his muscles, and yet it was just what he needed. The next stop was home. And Sarah. Jon couldn't wait. He'd told the press point-blank in London that he wasn't the father of Mia's baby. It hadn't come out as smoothly as he had hoped, but at least the press was clear that the baby wasn't his and that he and Sarah were still getting married. He turned and the water spray doused his face. Sarah. Anytime his eyes closed, he envisioned her. Just the thought of her awoke his aching body, stirring places only she could quench. He'd spent this entire tour planning their wedding night. Sitting through screening after screening of the same film provided ample hours for him to think about how he could pleasure her on their honeymoon. *That thought wasn't helping.* He was going to save all his energy for the wedding night like they had planned. He ran his fingers through his hair to wash away any lingering soap and shut the water off. He toweled off and slipped on his last clean pair of boxer briefs. Steam rose from his heated skin in the air-conditioned room. He collapsed on the bed and clicked the TV remote.

His phone beeped with a notification of an e-mail from Sarah. What was she doing up at this time of the night? It must have been three in the morning at home. His stomach twisted as that thought sank in. Somehow the stalker had hacked into her e-mail. She'd changed her password, but that didn't mean it wouldn't happen again.

All that discomfort you forced Sarah to endure having those scars removed, and you'll still never get to see her in a bikini again. It seems pointless and cruel. But that's not new for you.

What the hell did that mean?

He quickly clicked on the embedded video. As his heart hammered violently, he watched the camera pan around the courtyard at his house and focus on a dark spot in the pool. Sarah rose out of the water, ran her fingers through her hair, pulling it from her face, and then, with a smile, she waved. The video cut to black with the words *the end.* Jon's stomach began to retch.

Chapter Thirty-Three

Sarah

Sarah sank into the bucket seat, the leather hot against her back. It was the first time since her car accident in December that Sarah had enough confidence to wear just a sports bra and yoga pants out in public. It was as if the plastic surgeon had done a voodoo ritual and her scars magically became invisible…well, practically invisible. She dug in her bag and plucked her T-shirt from the bottom. It was one thing to work out in a sports bra, but something completely different to wear one into a juice bar.

"It's a shame you got your scars fixed for nothing. Jonathan won't even get to see you in a bikini." Cami glanced at Sarah's bare stomach before pushing the button to start the engine.

"What are you talking about? He'll be home late tonight." Sarah pulled the T-shirt over her head, before adding, "I bought four new bikinis for the honeymoon. One of them is really tiny. I mean, seriously small, like Miley Cyrus's bikini small. But it is so cute I just had to get it and I know Jon will love it. I'm not sure if I can wear it in public, though. I'll show it to you sometime and you can give me *your* opinion." She was still burning off the adrenaline from the workout, and she felt as if the energy was causing her to blurt out her every thought. She buckled her seatbelt before taking out her phone and typing a text to Craig, just to let him know they were headed to the Caboose Juice.

"Let your bodyguard stew. He doesn't need to know where you are every minute of the day. He has LoJack on your phone anyway. He'll figure it out." Cami pulled out of the back parking lot toward the Caboose Juice three blocks away.

Sarah hit *send* and tossed her phone back into her bag. "No really...I'm OK with it now. Ever since that note was left on my car, I don't have a problem with just shooting them a text or bringing them with me when I go out. It helps me feel safe. Do you know if the Berry Bloom smoothie has raspberries in it? I was going to try it the last time I was there, but I'm not a big raspberry fan."

"I'm not sure, Sarah." Her voice sounded irritated.

What had she said? They rounded the corner, and Sarah watched as they passed the bright red-and-white juice café. "There was a parking spot right in front. Didn't you see it? If we go around the block, it *might* still be there."

"You know...I changed my mind. I'm not really in the mood for juice. We're just going to go for a drive."

"I was really looking forward to getting an energy boost. Would you mind? I'll run in really fast."

"I don't think so, Sarah." Cami's voice sent a shiver up Sarah's arm.

"That's OK. I'll just get out here and walk back." The car was stopped at a light a couple of blocks from the Caboose Juice. Sarah reached for the door handle, but when she pulled on it, the door didn't open. She tried the window, but it didn't budge either.

"I had it installed last week. Child locks are usually only in the backseat, because it is too dangerous for the little munchkins to be next to an exploding airbag, but I gave the guy at the garage a sob story about how my grandmother

340

had Alzheimer's and kept trying to open the car door while I was driving. I told him how scared I was that she would get hurt. I guess I'm still a decent actor. It's amazing what you can get done if you just ask. Just look at you." She looked over at Sarah and smiled. "I asked you to come without your bodyguard and here you are. All I had to do was ask." Cami turned back to the road, gripping the steering wheel tighter as she pressed the accelerator.

Oh god! What had she done? Sarah needed to get out of here. She needed to distract Cami. Her phone was in her bag. If she could unlock it and push the button for the panic app that Craig installed on it, she could alert him to her predicament. It would connect her phone with his and he would be able to hear the conversation in the car. He said she could use it anytime she felt threatened. At the time, she thought he was just trying to placate her. He said it could save her life. She hoped he was right.

"Why are you doing this, Cami? I don't understand," asked Sarah, pulling her bag onto her lap and positioning it so she could slip her hand inside without being too obvious. "I thought we were friends." They clearly weren't friends. Cami had been using her to keep tabs on Jon. She'd been stalking her this whole time, tormenting both her and Jon.

"Yeah. That's the hard part about this. But there was really no other way to get you into a car alone with me."

"Why do you want me in the car with you so badly?"

"That will be revealed in time," she said with a worried look on her face, as if she hadn't worked all the details out yet.

Sarah slowly inched her phone to the edge of her bag. This was going to be harder than she thought. She needed to unlock her phone, and she couldn't even see the screen or the fingerprint scanner. She turned, pretending to look out the window, and then skimmed her eyes down the sports car's door. The glossy wood panel reflected the light from her phone like a mirror. She swiped her finger, but it didn't work. Her fingers were shaking so badly that her print wasn't registering correctly. She couldn't remember her alternative password. Ever since she got the phone, she'd only used the print scanner. She needed to calm down.

"What do you have against me anyway? Did you used to date Jon?" She took a deep breath and tried the scanner again.

"No. I never dated him, and I didn't want to hurt you. It's just what has to happen."

Sarah's phone screen opened, filling with icons, and she tapped the picture of the linked chain. "Cami, you sent us all those threatening letters and now you have me trapped in your silver Audi. What do you want with me?" Her voice was starting to shake. *Was she too obvious with the description?* She needed to tell Craig what road they were on or at least a landmark or two, and she needed to calm down so she could think.

"You're my ticket to paying back Jonathan for ruining my life."

"How did Jon ruin your life? You don't even know him."

"I never dated him, but I know him. He took my life from me. He stole everything I loved."

Cami wasn't making sense, and Sarah needed to make sense of this. "How did he do that, Cami?"

"I was engaged once. We didn't have the rings, but he had asked me. Then Jonathan killed him. He killed my Jack. He was jealous of his brother, and he drove into oncoming traffic on purpose. He stole the only man I've ever loved. He left me maimed and unable to do the job I wanted since I was a little girl. He took everything from me. Don't you see? Now I am going to take everything he loves from him. Payback's a bitch." Cami's gaze turned to obsidian—hard, rigid, and dark.

Sarah's breath faltered. She knew she couldn't reason with her. She was insane. Tears trickled down Sarah's cheeks. She had to hold on until the police caught up with them. They had to find her soon. There was LoJack on her phone. They had to be on their way.

"Why are we getting on the Ten? What are you going to do to me?" Why hadn't she just stabbed or suffocated her while she slept. She could have poisoned her a hundred times. Why did Cami want her in a car?

"I'm just looking for the right opportunity. You see, we have to be going fast enough for my plan to work." She sounded perky and amused now, as if her day couldn't be any better.

Cami's words tightened the growing knot in Sarah's chest. She tried to suck in a breath, but no air could get through. Cami was going to crash the car. "If you crash the car, you'll get hurt, too."

"Here's the deal, Sarah. I might get banged up, but you'll be dead. Do you want to know why I'm so certain?" She didn't wait for a response before continuing. "Because I disabled the airbags on your side of the car, even the side ones. I learned how on YouTube. And your seatbelt, it's hanging by a thread inside the door. I cut it. As soon as there's any pressure on it, it will snap. You'll go flying into the windshield. You'll be dead and Jonathan will be devastated. Besides, I don't even care if I die. What does it matter anymore?"

Sarah wiped her hand across her eyes. No one was going to be able to save her. If the police came after them it would just make Cami crash sooner. She needed to get a hold of herself. She stared out the window searching for an out.

"I wish I could see Jonathan's face when he realizes what he let happen to you."

Sarah didn't want to think about that, and she wasn't going to validate her words with a response. "Tell me about Jack. What was he like?"

"It's not going to work. I know what you're trying to do, and I'm not going to change my mind. But I guess you should know what kind of person your fiancé killed." Cami was starting to weave in and out of traffic, passing the slower cars and gaining speed. "Jack was a strong man, a good man. He wasn't scared of anything. He had this way of talking that made you believe everything he said. He didn't act as if he was better than anyone else. He was just who he was."

"He sounds a lot like his brother." Sarah wanted to remind her that there

343

was a connection between them.

"He is nothing like Jack," Cami spat.

The conversation wasn't helping. Sarah took a shallow breath. It was all she could muster. *Where was the highway patrol?* They were here any other time someone was speeding. Couldn't anyone else see that she was in trouble? Sarah looked around the car for something she could use to break the window. There was nothing. It was the cleanest car she'd ever seen. Cami probably had it detailed for the event.

"I heard that Jack rescued some kids from a burning car once. It sounds as if he was a good person. I don't think he would want you to hurt me. That doesn't sound like something he would allow."

"You don't know him."

Not, 'You didn't know him.' She was speaking as if Jack was still alive.

"I know he saved Liam Nordstrom's dog from some kids who were trying to drown it. He cared about others, even dogs. Would Jack want you to kill me to punish his brother? He loved his brother. It doesn't sound like a plan he would agree to. And I haven't done anything to deserve this. I don't think Jack will forgive you." Cami had to be thinking she and Jack would reunite in… heaven? Otherwise what was the point of all this? Cami's face scowled, but Sarah could tell she'd hit the mark. The car began to slow. Slow enough to give Sarah hope.

She glanced up to spot a sea of red lights in front of them. Maybe it wasn't her words. Even if it was just circumstance, Sarah needed to seize the moment. She knew she had to find a way to disable the car so it couldn't move. She reached into her bag and hit the icon for the air horn. The loud blast distracted Cami for just a second, but it was long enough for Sarah to grab the steering wheel and crank it to the left, Cami's side of the car. Sarah hunkered down as low as she could in her seat and braced her free hand against the dashboard in front of her as they hit the cement barrier and only Cami's airbag exploded. White powdery smoke filled the car, blasting Sarah back against her seat just as the impact of the crash propelled her body forward. Time seemed to slow as Sarah felt her seatbelt tethering her to her chair. She expected it to give way any second as Cami had described, but the sharp pain across her breastbone informed her that it wasn't going to let her go.

Sarah waited for more vehicles to join the party as flashbacks of her accident in December flooded her head. She remembered how just as she thought it was over, she felt the jerk of another car joining the pileup and causing her to hit her head again and again on the flattening airbag. Sarah didn't have any protection, except the strap across her chest that was holding for now.

When the pounding on the window started, Sarah finally let her body relax. A man in dark clothes wrenched on the door handle. Sarah shook her head. "I can't open it." She felt as if she was yelling, but the words sounded muffled in her ears.

"Stay back." His words were muted, too. He motioned that he was going to break the window.

She looked over at Cami to gage her reaction, but she was slumped away from her and she couldn't see her face. Sarah covered her eyes as the glass shattered into a million pieces and then crumpled to the floor. Gloved hands pulled back the rest of the window as if they were peeling a giant hardboiled egg. When the opening was wide enough, Sarah lunged for the outside without success. Then she reached over with shaking hands, pushed the release on the seatbelt, and untangled herself from it. She looped her hand through her bag's handle just as strong arms stretched inside the car, grasping her under her arms and pulling her from her seat.

Chapter Thirty-Four

Jonathan

Her limp body curled over his chest like a fitted T-shirt as he nuzzled his face into her neck. She felt *so* good in his arms. He was never going to let her go.

"Sir. Sir. We need to check her over. You are going to have to let us do our job," a woman's voice to his left demanded. It was like a broken record in his ear, and he just wanted it to stop.

Sarah's head began to slowly shake no, and he squeezed her tighter in his arms, if that was possible, ignoring the woman.

"Jonathan, the EMT just wants to make sure she is all right. And we need to get out of this fish bowl, sir." Craig's voice cut through the haze as his hand touched Jon's arm.

Jon looked up at the parking lot of cars on the expressway, spotting at least five cell phones sticking out the windows of various vehicles. He followed Craig to the ambulance and climbed into the back, before seating Sarah on the gurney. She was safe; that was all that mattered. Her hand clutched his arm as he pulled back. "I'm not leaving."

"I'm fine, Jon. I just want to go home." Her voice was barely above a whisper.

"I'll take you home as soon as we know you're not damaged." He was trying to be cute, but the second the words left his lips, he realized what he said. Whether her body was injured or not, this experience had damaged her. What was wrong with him? Why had he taken this innocent girl and turned her into a circus attraction. He watched as the EMT ran through her checklist. His hand dropped slowly to his side when Sarah was asked to extend her arm for one of the tests. He wanted her hand back. He needed it back.

"Sir, are you all right?" Craig asked. He was just outside the ambulance, and the expression on his face said, "You should sit down."

Jon was in a haze. He hadn't slept for two days, not since before the last e-mail from the stalker. Camille Moss, or whatever her name was now, was the stalker. Why hadn't he thought of her? She'd been in the guesthouse when Jack lived there. She knew about the soundproof walls because Jack told her. He thought she had moved on, left Hollywood, and gone back to Michigan after Jack's death. He didn't know Sarah's Pilates coach Cami was really Camille. No wonder she disappeared when he intercepted Sarah at the house. She didn't want him to recognize her. Then he left for his tour, leaving Sarah alone with the one woman she feared the most. He shook his head.

"Jonathan, do you need to sit down?"

After he got the stalker's e-mail and watched the video of Sarah in the pool, he assumed that the stalker had been in the house and Sarah wasn't afraid of her, but he wasn't sure. The video could have been filmed with a high-powered lens. He called Raul right away and told him not to allow anyone into the house. He told him to make sure that he or Craig stayed with Sarah at all times. Jon shared the stalker's e-mail and asked who'd been in the house. He gave him a list—just her friends from Minnesota, Remi, the cleaning lady, the pool guy, and Cami.

He'd never dated a Cami. How would she know about the soundproof qualities of his bedroom? It just didn't register. Sarah was already so scared of the stalker he couldn't tell her about the video. He got on the first flight out. He needed to be with Sarah. He needed to protect her. His entire flight he imagined finding Sarah floating in the pool facedown—a swirl of red water trailing from her body. He'd seen it in the movies a hundred times.

Since his flight got in early, instead of going back to the house to wait for Sarah, he decided to go straight to her workout class to meet her. He was waiting with Craig outside the studio for her to finish when Craig got the text that she was heading to the Caboose Juice with Cami. He figured this was his chance to meet Cami. He'd walk in on them as they sipped their juice and surprise Sarah. That's not what happened, though. Everything quickly turned ugly, and as he listened to every horror forced on Sarah broadcasted from Craig's phone, he sat powerless to save her. He knew if he made his presence known, Cami would just act that much faster to complete her plan. So after he and Craig caught up to Cami's car, they hung back waiting for the right moment. He hadn't thought about crashing the car as a solution, but when he saw Sarah reach for the steering wheel, he knew his brilliant fiancé had a plan of her own. She saved herself.

He looked over to Sarah, and she reached her hand out to his. Her touch seemed to bring him out of his daze. The EMT's radio buzzed several times, but Jon didn't hear what was being said. Then the woman assessing Sarah announced, "I'll be there by the time you get her out." She turned to Sarah. "If you have a private physician." Then she looked to Jon. "I would suggest getting checked for a concussion. I don't see signs of it, but that doesn't always matter. Since we're the only ambulance able to get through the traffic out there and the helicopter is tied up further down I-10 at the accident that caused this one, I have to go help with the driver. She's in worse shape. You're welcome to stay in here, or if you have another vehicle, you can try to make it out of this parking lot."

Jon nodded, and the woman left, grabbing a black duffel bag as she jumped out of the vehicle. He bent down, kissing Sarah on the top of her head. "Are you ready?" He didn't ask if she wanted to stay. He knew the answer.

"Jonathan Williams. Someone said that they saw you pull a woman from the crash, and I just thought it was one of those fake celebrity sightings. But you Williams boys must have hero in your blood."

Jonathan glanced over to the uniformed officer standing next to Craig. The man extended his hand and added, "I'm Chip Nelson, highway patrol. I met your brother once in a very similar situation, when he pulled those kids from that burning car. If he hadn't helped them, they surely would have died of smoke inhalation."

Jon met his hand with a smile and shook, the man's grasp firm.

"I'm sure you heard that story a hundred times." A sincere smile beamed from the officer's face. "Now let's get your story."

Jon's expression fell. Did he really need to do this now?

"If you want I can give a statement, and you and Sarah can go sit in the car," said Craig. He apparently was learning to read Jon's mind.

"No. I am going to need a statement from all three of you. But if you have a vehicle, we can do it in there."

When they finally got off the freeway and made it home two hours later, Jon had fallen asleep with Sarah tucked against his chest. The sweet tinkle of her voice saying his name woke him. It was the most beautiful sound. She looked up at him with her sweet smile, and he couldn't help but wrap his arms tighter around her.

Chapter Thirty-Five

Sarah

To say she was traumatized by what Cami had done to her was putting it mildly. The first two days following her fallout with the Pilates instructor Sarah couldn't leave the house. She couldn't walk out the door, not even into the courtyard, without a paralyzing fear erupting from her stomach and spreading to her limbs. She'd never experienced that kind of irrational anxiety until then. Jon had shown her the e-mail with the video of her in the pool, and the thought of Cami filming her and using it as a tool to terrorize them ruined the tranquility of the pool area for her. It was no longer her favorite place. She hated that someone she considered her friend could turn out to be so evil. *Sick*, she reminded herself. If she thought of Cami as being ill, it was easier to handle.

As the weeks passed, it got easier emotionally for Sarah to leave the house. With Jon constantly glued to her side, she knew that if someone tried to hurt her, they would have to answer to him and Sam, or Raul, or Craig. She didn't see the downside to having an entourage anymore; the more the merrier.

She worked through her anxiety quickly because she could see the pain on Jonathan's face every time she hesitated in a doorway. Not wanting to add to his insurmountable guilt, she pushed through her fear, and it got easier.

Now Sarah's problem wasn't leaving the house, it was escaping the press when she and Jon left. The paparazzi were unyielding. The very public crash and rescue on 110, along with the impending wedding, placed her and Jon on the top of every entrepreneur with a camera's priority list. Because they didn't live in a gated community, yet, and there was no foolproof way to escape the paparazzi at the end of the driveway, except wearing a disguise or hiding on the floorboards of the car—which they had done last week—when Leslie offered to pick up a few groceries on her way over, Sarah graciously accepted.

Sarah sat at the breakfast bar in the guesthouse, trying to mentally file all that had happened to her in the past year and all that was ahead with the wedding. Cami survived the accident, but Sarah didn't know how severely she'd been hurt. Jon said Cami had been hospitalized for a psychiatric evaluation in Michigan, near where her father lived. Sarah was still working to figure out her feelings about the whole nightmare. She'd stayed off the Internet and avoided the E! network, hoping to miss the tabloid analysis of it all.

Leslie plopped a magazine down on the kitchen table next to Sarah. For a second Sarah thought it might be the French periodical with the article about her, but when she noticed how thin it was, she knew it had to be a weekly. She rolled her eyes in disgust. "Why would you bring that rag into our house? Don't you think that we've seen it all?"

"Just thought you might be interested in this one, and don't hate the messenger," she replied as she began unpacking the canvas grocery bag. "I'll put the groceries away. I didn't get much, just a couple of things to tide us over until we leave."

Sarah flipped the magazine over and scanned the cover. It was a picture of her and Jon kissing at Cannes. It looked like it had been taken with a high-powered lens. "Oh god!" She stared at the headline in disbelief: JONATHAN & SARAH EXCLUSIVE: AN INSIDER SHARES ALL THEIR SECRETS FROM

THEIR FIRST DATE TO THE AISLE.

"Has Jon seen this?"

Leslie shrugged.

Sarah said a little prayer as she opened the glossy pages of the magazine. As long as the wedding's location wasn't leaked, it would be OK. More pictures taunted her from the colored spread—a picture of Jon singing on stage at the concert, another one she hadn't seen before from her private graduation party. There was one of the Pilates studio and a fourth picture of her family's cabin. Sarah examined the photos carefully. *Damn it!*

She settled onto her stool and began to read. The article claimed a source close to the couple revealed that the two first met on the Internet and that Sarah didn't even know Jon's true identity until the night of the concert where Jon sang her the infamous birthday girl song. The couple spent the night of the concert together in a posh Minneapolis hotel, but the pair didn't consummate their love that first night. They waited until the week after the concert, when the couple disappeared to Sarah's family's cabin in northern Minnesota.

Sarah stared at the article, shaking her head in disbelief. No one knew this. It had never come out before, and now the world knew. Her parents would see it. She was sure they suspected she and Jon slept together at the lake, but to have it printed in a magazine for all their friends to read…that was a whole new level of embarrassment, for both Sarah and her parents. Even Pastor Brian and Nana would see it. A lump formed in her throat and tears clouded her eyes.

"Oh god!" she said again as she brought her hands to her head in frustration. It had to be one of her friends leaking the information. They were the only ones who knew, besides Jon. Her instinct was to call her friends and ask for their advice, but it was one of them that leaked it. Who could she trust? Not them. She didn't want to call her mom, either, not yet, though she knew she would have to give her parents a heads up about the article if they hadn't already seen it. She turned to Leslie and asked, "Did you read this?"

"Yep," she answered quickly as she put the last bit of groceries into the refrigerator.

"Jon always said this would happen, but I didn't believe him. How could this happen?"

"It's not that big of a deal, Sarah. It didn't mention the wedding's location. So the world knows you and Jon had sex. Oh, how shocking," Leslie said sarcastically. She flipped her hair back and rolled her eyes as she spoke.

"That's not the part that bothers me. It bothers me that the article specifically states we didn't on the night of the concert. That bothers me."

"Why? You wanted people to think you did?"

"No…Only three people knew we didn't on the night of the concert…four people." She shook her head. "Only four people—Jessica, Megan, Alli, and my brother, Jeff."

"You and Jon knew," said Leslie, "and I knew."

"Really? Jon's got a big mouth."

"Jon told one person and you told four. Who's got the big mouth?" Leslie chuckled as she opened the fridge again and took out a bottle of juice.

"You didn't tell anyone, did you?" asked Sarah.

"Nope. I signed a contract. I can't say anything, or Jon can sue me. He would probably just kill me, though. Then he wouldn't have to hassle with the lawyers."

"So it had to be one of those four that leaked it."

"Or sold it," added Leslie.

Sarah looked at her, exasperated. "What am I supposed to do now? I don't know who to trust. Do you think one of them was just talking too much, or do you think that," she swallowed, "someone actually knew what they were doing?"

"Your friends don't seem stupid, Sarah. They know what's at stake. The backstory about how you and Jon met would have brought a good chunk of money. The wedding date and venue weren't revealed, but that doesn't mean it wasn't leaked along with the other, and the two together could fund a small country."

"Why wouldn't they reveal it if they had the information?" Sarah asked, but realized the answer the second the words left her lips.

"Because they want exclusive pictures that would bring in even more money."

Sarah didn't know what to say. She thought her friendships could withstand the money temptation.

"Jon's dad, Zander, has a sister Jon hasn't spoken to in years, Aunt Mara. She lives in Van Nuys. She sold a story about how Jon didn't regret the accident because he was jealous of Jack. It really hurt Jon. She made up all kinds of other stories too and sold them over the year after Jack's death. There was just enough personal information in each story to give them some credibility. Jon finally figured out it was her and confronted her. She denied it, but when Jon and his dad cut off all communication with her, the stories slowed and eventually stopped."

"His dad's sister?" she questioned. She'd never heard of Mara. She definitely wasn't on the wedding guest list.

"As far as Jon is concerned, she's dead. She hurt him so badly that I don't think he will ever forgive her. He already blamed himself for Jack's death. He tortured himself enough on his own that he didn't need the world condemning him as well. It was pretty bad—so bad that I didn't know if Jon was going to survive.

"What made you think that?" It was kind of a strange thing to say.

"He was drinking a lot, out at the clubs every night. There were always women around. His life was utter chaos, pretty destructive. That's when the media started labeling him as a man-whore. He kind of was, but never as bad as they made him out to be. Then one day he missed a call time and almost got fired from the film. Isaac tracked him down and got him to the set. He was a couple of *days* late, though, and the director really raked him over the coals. If they hadn't been so deep into the film, they would have replaced him." Leslie drank some juice from the small bottle and added, "I didn't work for him then, obviously, or that never would have happened. After that incident, he realized he had to take some control over his life and he stopped going to clubs. He stopped drinking in public. It just fed the problem…and he's never missed a call time since."

"He was filming *Third Rung*, right? With Amy Richardson?"

"Yeah, she broke up with him the day before he disappeared. I guess he wasn't ready to see her at work the next day. I don't think he was very serious about her. It was just a combination of all the pressure he was under. Everyone has a breaking point," concluded Leslie.

"Hmm…" Jon admitted that he never told his parents about the baby, so Sarah wasn't sure if Leslie knew. She didn't want to explain the details, if Jon hadn't told her. She could imagine how alone he felt. He was dealing with the loss of his brother, the one person he confided in the most, and the loss of the baby that Amy had aborted. With someone feeding the press, he couldn't trust anyone. No wonder he was so messed up.

"The clubbing…the girls—I just assumed it was his way of working through the death of his brother. I didn't realize someone in his family was selling him out and making all his problems worse. I've never heard of Aunt Mara."

"She's dead," Leslie said with a chuckle. "Jon's a pretty forgiving guy, but I think once someone crosses that line, it's hard to forgive."

Just then Jon walked in, setting his keys and phone down on the counter and opening the refrigerator. "Forgive who?" he asked.

"Aunt Mara," answered Sarah, scrutinizing his face for a reaction.

"I don't need to forgive her. She's dead," Jon said matter-of-factly as he pulled a gallon jug of milk out and set it on the counter. Sarah looked at Leslie with a questioning expression. Jon poured the milk into a glass and placed the jug back in the fridge before continuing, "Why are you talking about her?" He glared at Leslie.

Sarah held up the magazine, flashing Jon the page with the picture of the cabin. He joined her at the breakfast bar and exclaimed, "Damn, I was hoping we could use your parents' lake home later this summer." A look of disappointment crossed his face. "I guess that's out now."

"It gets worse. Here." She handed him the magazine, flipping to the cover.

Jon skimmed the cover and then opened it to the article. When he was finished reading, he looked up into Sarah's eyes with a wary face. "Well, at least we know for sure." He scratched his face as if contemplating what to do. "Do you think the venue got leaked?"

Sarah shrugged. She didn't have a clue how they could know for sure whether the wedding information was sold or not.

Jon tapped his finger on the picture of the cabin. "So…is Megan the Aunt Mara?" They both knew that the information in this article was knowledge that was never shared on a phone, in an e-mail, or in a text. It was information Sarah shared with her friends in person a long time ago.

"I don't know. I can't believe any of them would do it."

"It had to be one of them." He said it a little too unemotionally, as if he expected it all along.

"I know it wasn't Jessica or Jeff. Jessica complained about someone calling the house, making Mom all upset. They said they were from *People Magazine*, but they weren't. They wanted to interview with Mom and Dad about what it was like to have a daughter engaged to a mega star. Did you know they discontinued the house phone? We had that number all my life."

"A mega star?"

"Is that all you got from my whining?"

"I'm sorry they had to sacrifice their landline. Destruction follows me everywhere I go."

"It's OK. Even Mom admitted the only people who called that line anymore were political parties and universities looking for alumni donations. I think they were happy to get rid of it." She didn't want him to feel responsible for the treachery. It was one of her friends. She had to accept that. "So how do I confront them? What should I say?"

"Be honest with them. Tell them how much the betrayal has hurt you, how much trouble it's caused. Hopefully one of them will confess to it."

"And if they don't?"

"Then we play detective. This kind of information is worth some coin. Do any of them have more money than usual? Or are in need of money?"

Sarah thought about Jon's question. She didn't think any of her friends were in such dire need for money that they would stoop this low. Jeff and Jessica were always talking about needing money—for their wedding and for a down payment on a house—but she was certain they wouldn't sell her out. Besides, she'd told Jessica much more than the other girls, and none of what she had shared with her alone had been leaked. "It wasn't Jessica."

"If you don't think it was Jessica or Jeff, then what about Megan? We never really found out how Liam's information about his brother's intervention got leaked. We kind of just dropped it when you found out the guy who gave her the new phone put a stalker app on it. How did the press end up with the story? I think she's the most likely candidate. Maybe she hooked up with the connections he already set up, or maybe she's back with him."

Megan's ex, Chase, was definitely unscrupulous enough to sell the wedding story to the press. But Megan would have had to have gone along with it, and Sarah didn't think she would do it. Megan was never one to sell out for money. She had a couple of offers for graduate fellowships in the fall—a full ride at Princeton and one at UCLA. Both offers had stipends, but she still wasn't sure if she would take either of them. She didn't feel obligated to the schools just because they were willing to pay for her education. She never acted like she needed money. She was always satisfied with what she had. Even though she didn't seem to need money, Chase used to be able to talk her into anything, and maybe he had talked her into this. She could have been selling them out all along and that's why she never complained about needing cash. Sarah's mind was spinning.

Then there was that picture, right there in the magazine. Sarah remembered posing for it. It was at her graduation party with all her friends and family at the house she got for her graduation. She and Jon stood in the center with Alli, Jessica, and Jeff encompassing them. Sarah could see the house in the background. Over Jon's head perked bunny ears from Sarah's cousin Ronnie's two-and-a-half-year-old daughter's fingers. Someone, probably her dad, was holding her up behind Jon, enabling the photo bomb. She didn't remember who took the photo at the time, but Megan was the only one not in the picture. She must have been the photographer; otherwise, she would have been in the picture.

Tears started to prick in Sarah's eyes. She couldn't help it. How could she do this to her? They were like sisters. She thought Jonathan was the only one who could break her heart. She was wrong. This betrayal felt as if she was literally being stabbed in the back, and each line in the article was a twist of the knife. Had all they had been through over the years meant nothing to her?

"Maybe Megan is the culprit. But how will we know for sure?"

"You won't unless she confesses. We have to confront her. We need to find out if she told the press when the wedding is. If the media knows the date and the venue, then we need to add even more security to assure the wedding doesn't turn into a circus." Jon wrapped his arms around her, and she melted into him. The comfort of his protecting embrace was just what she needed.

Chapter Thirty-Six

Sarah

Bitterness burned in Sarah's blood the more she contemplated Megan's betrayal. She'd spent the entire night—a long, sleepless night—going over the evidence in her mind. It had to be Megan. It all started with her. Jessica had said that Chase had been back at the rental house several times in the last week. Maybe he was helping with the sale to the tabloids. They were probably working together. She could never say no to him before. What made Sarah think she could do it now?

Sarah knew she wouldn't have time to fly to Minnesota and talk to Megan in person. She and Jon were supposed to be leaving for the Caribbean tomorrow. They had rented an entire island for three weeks—two weeks before the wedding for prep and one week after for the first phase of their honeymoon. They were going early to help with the groundwork just because they could. Sarah still hadn't finished packing yet.

She needed to call Megan and tell her she knew it was her and that she wasn't going to put up with the deception any longer. She needed to uninvite her to the wedding. She turned the phone over and over in her hand as Jon wrapped his arms around her from behind and rested his chin on top of her head.

"It has to be done, Sarah. I'm sorry she had to be a casualty of our life," said Jon in a firm but sorrowful voice. He leaned down and kissed her cheek, but his comfort did nothing to prevent the swell in her eyes and throat. She grasped his hand that was around her waist and squeezed it before pulling away.

"This isn't your fault. She did this. It was her choice." Sarah slid her finger across the phone's screen and made the call. As the phone was ringing, she strode to the counter where the magazine sat displaying the evidence.

"Hey, Megan. I was wondering if you saw the latest tabloid about Jon and me." Sarah's hand shook as she spoke.

"I saw it yesterday. I couldn't believe it. How did they get all that?"

"Why don't you tell me?"

"You're blaming me for this?" Megan's voice sounded surprised, but yet not.

"I just want to know what you told the press about the wedding. Is the date and location going to show up in next week's issue?"

"I didn't tell the press anything about your precious, exclusive wedding. I just don't get why you assume I'm the culprit."

"Where do I start?" Sarah paused and looked down at the magazine, trying to remember the most damning evidence. "The article quoted a source close to me as saying I was terrified Jon was the father of Mia's baby, not because he would leave me, but because she would always have her clutches in him. It stated my exact words—the words that I told you."

"We all talked about how nervous you were about Mia's baby and how manipulative you thought Mia was. Jessica, Alli, and I all talked about it. I shared everything with them. I'm sure Jeff heard it all, and your mom, too. Why am I the only one ever accused of selling information to the tabloids? Is it because of Chase? Well…I've talked to Chase and I'm not convinced he was selling you out. He showed me his stock portfolio and his bank account online. He doesn't need the tabloid's money. He's got more money than he knows what to do with."

"Maybe he just did it for fun then."

"Or maybe he bought me the phone because he cares about me and it had nothing to do with you and Jon. Not everything in the world revolves around you. You act like you're the only ones who have a life."

"No, we don't have a life because someone keeps selling us to the press… Megan. What about that picture you took at my graduation party? You were the only one that wasn't in the picture, and it's right there…in the magazine."

"What picture? I don't remember taking any pictures. I don't have any pictures from that party on my phone. If you think I would do that to you, then you don't know me. I can't believe you think that of me."

"What else am I supposed to think when all the evidence points to you? How could you tell them all my personal information? I told you all that stuff in confidence. You knew how important it was to me to keep it from the press. You ruined everything."

They sat in silence for several seconds. Sarah knew she shouldn't have expected Megan to admit it.

"Alli says you're always sneaking off to talk to someone in private. What, you can't talk to the tabloids in front of your housemates? I'm not the only one who thinks it's you. Alli and Jessica have both told me you've been really secretive since Chase has been back in your life. And then there's that whole ordeal with Liam."

"OK…you caught me." Megan's voice rang of sarcasm.

"So you admit it?" Sarah's voice shrilled.

"I've been talking to Chase…But just because I talk to him does not mean that I talk about you…and he never asks. I'm not the one that leaked the story about your week at the lake or any of the other crap. It wasn't me. I don't know who's been doing this to you, but if you truly believe that I'm involved, then we're not friends."

"Well, that's obvious. A friend would never hurt me like you did," resounded Sarah.

"I don't need to listen to your accusations anymore. I hope you and Jon have a wonderful life together," she shrieked, and the phone went dead.

Tears spilled down her cheeks as she turned to face Jon. "That couldn't have gone any worse."

"I guess we should just prepare for the worst-case scenario with the paps. We'll tighten security. It will all work out, Sarah." He placed a finger on each corner of her mouth and pushed up to make her smile. She looked into his gorgeous blue eyes and knew it would be OK as long as she had him. She forced a smile, and he pulled her against his chest, kissing the top of her head.

Even if she had a normal life, she could have still lost Megan as a friend. People drift in and out of each other's lives all the time. Life is fluid, ever changing. This was just a change that would take some time to digest.

Chapter Thirty-Seven

Sarah

Most of the guests had arrived yesterday, but the wedding party, her and Jon's parents, and a few select people had been on the island for almost a week. Activities had been organized to keep the visitors busy until the wedding tomorrow. The happenings included snorkeling, parasailing, fishing, and of course just hanging out on the beach or at the pool. If inclined guests could even take mamba lessons.

The wedding party spent most of the afternoon, yesterday, snorkeling as a group and then joined the other guests for a traditional island barbeque on the beach. The bridesmaids and groomsmen, their significant others, and a few friends had stayed out talking and drinking until the sun began to peak over the horizon. It reminded Sarah of weekends at her parents' lake cabin with a big group of friends telling stories and laughing in front of a fire near the beach. Someone had brought an acoustic guitar and since most of the groomsmen were musicians, there had been a lot of singing, too.

She tried not to think about who was missing from the group and why. It just made her stomach churn. Her cousin Ronnie would be filling Megan's spot. The bridesmaids' dress designer and her assistant flew in last night and would be fitting Ronnie into Megan's dress this afternoon. Sarah wondered how it was going to work since Ronnie and Megan's body types were completely different.

This morning, the twisting and turning of Sarah's stomach had awoken her after only a couple of hours of sleep, and she dragged herself out of bed, not wanting to wake Jon as well. He lay gorgeously clueless to the growing agitation inside her. Sarah couldn't pinpoint what was bothering her, but something was wrong. She could feel it. She'd sensed it the whole week. She'd barely been able to sleep or eat. She thought she'd concealed it from everyone, but then at the beach party last night as she unconsciously pushed her food around on her plate, Jon whispered in her ear, "You have to eat or your wedding dress is going to fall right off you. You need to leave me something to grab on to on our wedding night."

Sarah ate what she could, not only to appease him, but because he was right. She didn't want her dress sagging in all the wrong places. She tried to put the feeling of dread behind her. It was probably just nerves—the normal nerves every bride gets worrying about the *world* hearing how she face-planted on the white carpet as she walked down the aisle to meet her movie star groom. *Every bride went through that, right?*

With her hair pulled back in a ponytail and a coffee and flip-flops in her arms, Sarah walked along the beach until the rocky cliff jutted out of the water and ended the sand. Being alone on the beach didn't bother her. She'd been on the island for two weeks and had gotten really comfortable with the high level of security provided here. She lifted the lid of her coffee and blew on it, wishing the liquid caffeine would cool enough for her to drink it, before turning around and heading back toward civilization. The cool sand squished between her toes as she walked, and it helped distract her from thinking about all that could go wrong if Megan leaked the wedding's location to the press.

Sarah noticed a few people trickling out of the resort lobby, making their way to the pier where the snorkeling boat was docked. An ATV passed her pulling a large rake, picking up debris in the sand from last night's party. She had seen it working earlier, but now it was moving farther down the beach. She reached the bench that marked the path for the shortcut through the thick foliage to the large wooden pavilion where the reception and dance would take place. She dropped her flip-flops to the ground, sliding into them, and followed the path until the structure stood in front of her.

She peeked inside and stepped onto the wooden floor. At the far end, a raised platform teamed with band equipment waiting to be set up, and she spotted the long table reserved for the wedding party near the dance floor. In front of her, a woman and a man covered folding chairs with sophisticated linens, transforming them into elegant pieces of furniture, while still another worker distributed them to the tables. She glanced up as someone came rushing toward her.

"Sarah, you're supposed to be sleeping. We've got this." Her wedding planner's voice perked through the air.

"I can't sleep, Nicole, and I didn't want to wake Jon, so here I am."

Nicole ran her thumb under Sarah's eyes as if trying to discern whether she hadn't removed her makeup last night or if there really were dark bags under them. "You're going to need to take a nap today, and hot coffee is not a good drink in this tropical climate. It will just dehydrate you."

Sarah took a gulp of her coffee quickly as Nicole reached for it to pull it out of her hand. She needed the caffeine, not to stay awake, but to prevent the headache she would get without it.

"What you need is a big bottle of water to help get rid of those bags under your eyes." Nicole grabbed Sarah's wrist and led her to the front of the pavilion. She reached into a box on the floor and pulled out a bottle of water, handing it to Sarah. "It's not cold, but you need it more than I do."

Sarah grasped it against her chest. "Are you sure the flowers will be ready?" she asked, unscrewing the bottle cap and taking a sip of water. Nicole had been concerned about the viability of the flowers during shipping.

"Of course…I talked to the florist an hour ago." She tapped her index finger against the walkie-talkie clipped to the flap on her electronic tablet. Sarah knew it was inconvenient to use the radios to communicate, but the security specialist thought it was the best option since cell phone use was prohibited for the weekend.

"Everything is going to be perfect," she continued. "You just need to sit back and enjoy. Don't worry about anything. I've got it under control."

Sarah spun, admiring the way everything seemed to be coming together. The tables looked beautiful, and the lanterns had been hung perfectly. A flash or the sun's reflection caught Sarah's eye from across the pavilion. Alli stood on the edge of the reception area near a clump of vegetation. "Nicole, I need to take care of something. Are we good?" she asked.

"Yes, everything is good."

Sarah rushed off to meet up with her friend. She didn't expect to see her for several more hours, so she was curious why Alli was up so early, and what was that flash? She wove her way through the white linen-covered tables and chairs until she met up with the redheaded woman. "So…what's going on?" asked Sarah.

"I was hoping to catch up with you. I thought you might need some help. Your mom said you were freaking out," she answered, nonchalantly stuffing her phone into her purse.

"No, Nicole and her staff have it all under control," she said as she waved her hand in front of her. Sarah needed to talk to Alli somewhere more private. Now. She didn't want anyone overhearing their conversation. She thought quickly about where they could talk and stated, "There are a couple of last-minute items I could use help with inside, though. Come on." She led her friend under the tree canopies that trailed to the resort's hotel, through the large glass and wooden doors and up the stairs.

When she got to the presidential suite on the second floor, she opened the doors wide, propping the door open with a wrought iron pineapple next to it for just that purpose.

"It's been so warm in here that I like to keep it open when I can. I don't think the air conditioning is working very well," she lied. Sarah peered into the open bedroom door hoping Jon was inside, but he must have gotten up while she was out. She took a deep breath and asked, "Help me figure this out, would you? I've got something new...my ring, my dress...pretty much everything I have is new. I have these gorgeous earrings from Jon's mother." She opened a blue velvet box to reveal two stunning white gold and diamond pendulum earrings. "She got them for her tenth wedding anniversary. They're my old and my borrowed, but I haven't figured out what to use for my blue yet. Any ideas?"

"Gosh...I don't know. What's blue? I thought everything was supposed to be white."

"There has to be something blue, or the whole wedding will be cursed... as if it hasn't been already," she stated sarcastically. "My mom had some ideas, but I can't remember any of them. I should have had this figured out before we left, but that whole ordeal with Megan really threw me off. May I borrow your phone? I saw you still have it, and I really need to get this figured out. Jon's got mine, and my mom is one of the few people that got to keep hers."

"Um...yeah...Let me unlock it for you." She pushed several buttons on the phone, bringing the phone key pad onto the screen and then handing it to Sarah.

"You know...I'm so messed up about the leaks to the press. I don't know which end is up lately," she said as she maneuvered her way to the photo gallery on the smart phone. She gasped when she found what she was searching for. The bottom of her stomach dropped, and her heartbeat quickened. Sarah knew she had made a terrible mistake. She planted her feet firmly on the floor as she gathered her courage. "Why are there pictures of the wedding pavilion on your phone?"

Alli looked stunned, her mouth frozen open, but not moving.

"You don't have to answer, because I know the reason. Tomorrow the security will be impossible. Security is going to be hunting down any electronics and you wanted to make sure you got the shots, so you came today when security isn't as strict. How could you do this, Alli?"

"You're so paranoid. Do you hear yourself? They were just for me. I want to remember your wedding. It's going to be so spectacular. I wasn't doing it to hurt you," she claimed, almost looking innocent. "Just give me my phone back." She reached for it, but Sarah pulled away with the phone still in her grasp.

"You almost had me convinced, but it all makes sense. You were the one to point the finger at Megan. You made sure all the evidence led to her and Chase, but you were the one selling Jon and me out...weren't you?"

"It wasn't me. I was just taking the pictures for myself. I wasn't going to sell them."

Sarah continued to search through the phone's photo gallery, spinning to escape Alli's outstretched hand. "I should have known it wasn't Megan. She never did admit to selling information and if she had done it, she would have. She always owns up to her mistakes. Even when they are awful, she owns them. I suppose she never told you about the nonrescue dog. Of course, she didn't, that lie never came out in the press."

Sarah flashed Alli another photo on the phone they both knew was leaked to the tabloids. "This one made the cover of *CM*. It made me look like an alcoholic slut. I don't drink anymore when I'm out because of that picture. You set that picture up. I didn't even want to take it, but you insisted. You made Megan take the picture, but with your phone. You knew that all I would remember was that Megan snapped it," she accused. "And look, here's the picture of me and that guy at the fair. That was like a year and a half ago." Sarah held up the phone just out of Alli's reach. "Jon asked me which one of my friends snapped it, but I assured him that none of my friends would ever do that to me."

"Just give me my phone back."

"How could you do this to me? We're best friends."

Sam popped his head into the room where Sarah and Alli stood. "Sarah, are you all right?" he asked in his deep voice.

"Yeah…I found the real culprit who was making our life hell. It wasn't Megan after all. I was wrong." She handed Sam the phone. "Could you go through this and erase anything that is about Jon and me?"

"That's my specialty," Sam proclaimed as he began searching the phone.

"I just want to know why? How could you betray us like that?" questioned Sarah.

"When we were at your house in April, Jake said you have to feed the press just to keep your name out there. If you don't, people forget about you and you don't get the top roles. Any press is good press, right? Isn't that what the saying is? I was just doing Jon a favor. You said yourself that getting married may stifle Jon's career. So what if I was making some money off it. Everybody wins."

"How does everybody win?" Sarah couldn't believe what she was hearing. "You saw how the media ruins people. How your parents, your professors, and everyone around you reacted to those kiss pictures with Jake," Sarah squealed in frustration.

Alli was silent for a pregnant moment and then said, "They said they wouldn't release the article until after the wedding."

"So they lied to you. What a surprise." Sarah was anything but understanding at this point.

"You know, it was your fault my parents stopped paying for my schooling. They saw what a bad influence you were. They didn't want their doctor daughter to be best known for partying around Hollywood. They told me if I stayed away from you, if I broke all contact, they would continue to help pay for it. You were right when you told me I was an adult and my parents needed to accept that. As an adult I was looking at two hundred thousand in student loans. Do you know how little a resident makes? It's barely enough to get by and after my residency, who knows what the health care system will look like. I'd be in debt forever."

"If you needed money, all you had to do was ask."

"I couldn't ask you for that kind of money. That's just not something you do. I knew my parents weren't going to give in, and I didn't want to ruin your big day. We've been friends forever. I didn't want to disappoint you. I couldn't do that to you. So I found another way to pay for it, where nobody got hurt."

"It hurt me. Everyone knew my personal business. They knew where I would be. They stalked me. Jon got arrested because of you. It terrified me to leave the house, because I knew someone would be taking pictures of me all day long. I could never relax. I can never relax. I always have to have my A game on. It's exhausting. It hurt me. You saw the footage at the airport. You don't think that whole incident didn't damage me for life? Our wedding…Did you tell them about our wedding?"

"You knew what you were getting into when you left with Jon. You knew what it was going to be like. I thought you expected this, accepted it. I never meant to hurt you, Sarah."

"It's not the intent. It's the impact—psychology 101. It doesn't matter what you meant to do. You knew what you were doing, and you saw what it was doing to me. I told you everything I had to deal with. I trusted you, and now I don't think I can ever trust you again. You need to go. I don't want you here."

"You don't mean that. Look what I gave up for you."

"It doesn't seem like you've given up anything. You made it look like Megan was the one who was selling us out. You don't care about anyone but yourself."

"Sarah, you left us. You didn't care about us anymore. All you cared about was Jon and your new celebrity life."

"That's not true and you know it." Tears were building in Sarah's eyes as she looked away from Alli. "Good-bye, Alli." Sarah glanced up to meet Sam's face. "Can you have one of your team make sure she's escorted off the property? I don't want her wandering around taking pictures of the wedding."

"Yes…Sarah." He gently touched her shoulder. "I'll take care of it myself."

"Thanks," she whispered. She was trying to stay composed. It was stressful enough to get married, but now she had wrongly accused one of her best friends of selling her out to the paparazzi. She lost two lifelong friends in a matter of a couple of weeks. Sarah didn't know if she would ever forgive Alli, and she didn't know if Megan would ever forgive her. Tears dripped off Sarah's chin, staining her cotton dress, as Alli left the room with Sam.

She could feel thick sobs bubbling out of her throat as she tried to suppress them. Sarah felt awful. Her whole body was numb, like she was compensating for all the emotional pain by getting rid of all physical senses. There was nothing left. She stood in the room crying. The door was open, but no one walked by. She was alone, more alone than she had ever felt in her life. With her wits depleted, she looked around the room at all her belongings staged for tomorrow, dazed. Tears streamed off her face. She should have known. Everything was ruined. She may as well call off the wedding. Her bridesmaids were gone. The press most likely knew the wedding was this weekend, and it wouldn't be long before helicopters and yachts would be circling the island. Everything they worked so hard to keep private would be exposed. What was she thinking? Was it worth all this to keep their life private?

Sarah slowly climbed onto the king-sized bed. *I just need a nap*, she thought. *Everything will be better after I get some sleep.*

Jonathan

Jon slipped inside the door where Sam asked to meet. It was about as far away from the bridal party's suites as the resort allowed. Alli sat in the upholstered chair next to a small table. She stared blank-faced like an accused prisoner.

"So you located our Aunt Mara," Jon stated as he entered the room. Alli looked up, but didn't meet his eyes.

"Yep. She has about four hundred photos on her phone. I gave her the choice though to let me have her phone or I would confiscate it for evidence." Sam held up the phone, showing a photo of Jon carrying Sarah to the water's edge with his hand caressing her butt as the group partied around them last night on the beach.

"No doubt this one would have made it in with the wedding photos. It would have brought enough to buy a new car."

"Text me that one, would you?"

"You got it, boss." Sam smiled and focused his attention back on the phone.

"Allison, Allison, Allison...what should we do with you?" Jon ran his fingers through his hair in frustration. She shrugged and looked to the floor. "The problem is all the guests agreed to the security stipulations when they sent in their RSVP. You signed yours. I know because I personally looked at every single one. You wouldn't have been allowed on the island if you hadn't signed it. Do you remember the nondisclosure agreement? It was spelled out clearly—the requirement that stated you needed to turn in all electronic devices when you got on the plane."

She still stared at the floor in silence, but Jon could see her shoulders rising and falling as if she was crying inside.

"Normally I wouldn't even get involved in a situation like this. I would let our security team and the lawyers handle everything. You see, I've been through this a hundred times. It doesn't even upset me anymore. We prosecute the offender, and the lawyers suck up any money that the tabloids paid. You remember that line in the contract where you agreed to pay all the lawyer's fees. The contract is solid, and the person who leaks pictures or information ends up with nothing."

Her sobs broke the silence, and he sat down on the chair across from her, pausing for a moment as he decided how to proceed.

"What does upset me, though, is how this whole ordeal affects Sarah. I'm sure she's heartbroken over this. You were one of her best friends, and she never believed me when I told her one of you girls would betray her. She was confident it would never happen. Yet, here we sit." He strummed his fingers on the table in contemplation like he imagined the lawyer that he would be playing this fall might do.

"Jon, I never meant to hurt anyone. I just needed money for school. My parents cut me off, and I didn't know what else to do. Please just let me go. You've got all my pictures. I won't do it again."

"I know you won't, Alli. Because in an hour or two a lawyer will come in and talk to you about a new contract that I'm going to have you sign. You're going to tell him about all the photos and information you've already leaked so we can do damage control. If more information comes out that you forgot to disclose to the lawyer, we'll prosecute you, so you need to be thorough. The new contract will be more stringent and include more restrictions, but the lawyer will explain it. The most important amendment will be that you will never contact Sarah ever again. You will avoid gatherings that she is likely to attend, never call her, never text her, and never say another word about Sarah or me to anyone. You will be dead to her.

"You might ask, 'Why would I sign another contract?' Well, here is where it gets interesting. I'm going to pay you to sign the contract. How much did you say she needed, Sam?"

"She told Sarah two hundred grand." Sam held up another picture that made the tabloids a couple of months ago.

Jon exhaled loudly as he met Sam's eyes. "I will give you three hundred thousand dollars if you abide by the contract and Sarah never has to be reminded of what you did to her. If you don't sign it, we will prosecute you to the full extent of the original contract and you will end up with nothing. Everything we've talked about will be in the contract and the lawyer will explain it. The money will alleviate any false guilt Sarah may have about your situation and put a barrier between the two of you. She is too forgiving for her own good." He stood up and pushed in his chair. "I need to go check on her. Your accommodations are comfortable here, but there will be a security guard posted outside your room to ensure you stay put. You are not being held against your will, but if you leave this suite, you will be escorted to a plane and the deal is off. Good luck with your life, Allison."

He headed up to his and Sarah's suite. What more could go wrong? At least they caught her before the wedding. Sarah's eyes were closed when he dipped the mattress and his arm wrapped around her waist. She was so beautiful. He couldn't wait to be alone with her on the honeymoon.

"Sarah," his sweetest voice whispered, "are you all right?"

Her weighted lids opened just a crack. As she reached her hand out and touched his face, a slight smile blossomed on hers. "You were right. We should have eloped," she said in a slow, sleepy voice.

"I know, but the wedding *is* tomorrow. We don't have to wait much longer."

"I can't do it. We have to cancel. Can you tell everyone?" Sarah pleaded with her eyes still closed. She was adorable.

"It's too late to cancel, baby. We're in the homestretch." Jon kissed her cheek.

"It wasn't Megan. It was Alli. I was wrong, and I need to apologize. I'm sure she won't talk to me. I was so awful to her. She must hate me," she admitted in a slow drawl.

"I'm sure she'll forgive you. It will work out." He trailed his fingers through her hair. "Sarah, did you take any pills or anything to relax this morning?"

She shook her head back and forth sluggishly on the pillow.

"Open your eyes and look at me," he begged. He was starting to realize something wasn't right with Sarah. "Can you open your eyes?"

"My stomach hurts," she confessed without opening her eyes.

Jon sat up on the bed and took out his phone. He found the number for the concierge and pushed *send*. He ran his hand over her arm as he spoke.

"This is Jonathan Williams in the presidential suite. I need you to send the doctor to my room as soon as possible."

"Right away, sir."

Jon turned to Sarah and kissed her forehead. She felt really warm on his lips. He ran his fingers through her hair and declared, "The doctor is on his way. We'll figure out what is going on with you, Sarah." He pressed his cheek against Sarah's. "I love you. It will all work out, beautiful," he whispered.

A quiet rap on the door to the hall shot a tinge of relief through his chest. "That was fast." He got up to open the door but was surprised when he saw Kate standing in the doorway.

"Come in." He backed up to allow her entry.

"Is Sarah sleeping? She asked me to meet her. I have her blue. It took me forever to find. Do you think it would be OK if I woke her?"

"Kate, don't get upset, but…" He walked through the large suite to the bedroom as he spoke and then turned to Sarah's mother. "Sarah's not feeling well. I've called the doctor, and he should be here any minute."

"What do you mean she's not feeling well? I talked to her two hours ago. She sounded fine."

There was another knock on the door. "I'll explain in a minute. That's the doctor." He walked back across the large living area and opened the door as Kate entered the bedroom suite. He knew what Kate was thinking, but he didn't have the energy to expend on defending himself right now. Instead he opened the door and greeted the short, dark-skinned man who spoke in a British accent. "She's in here." He led the doctor to the bedroom.

"I found her on the bed. She has been dealing with a bunch of wedding problems this morning and I thought she was just lying down for a quick nap. She hadn't slept well last night. She was talking to me at first, but she seemed really tired and now I can't get her to respond." Jon moved out of the way but sat on the bed next to Sarah's head as the doctor approached.

Kate was already positioned on her other side when the doctor opened his clichéd black bag and took out his stethoscope and a few other tools.

"What is her name?" he asked as he sat on the edge of the bed and positioned his instrument around his neck.

"Sarah," Jon and Kate said at the same time.

"Sarah, can you hear me?" She did not open her eyes, but she made a quiet guttural sound. The doctor touched his hand to Sarah's forehead and then moved it to her throat, holding two fingers against her neck as he monitored his watch. Then the dark-haired man lightly pinched the skin on the center of

Sarah's chest. He paused and watched her skin sink back into its normal shape before reaching for Sarah's hand and pinching the top of it as well. With Sarah's hand still in his, he pinched the skin again, only this time deliberately hard, twisting the skin until Sarah yanked her hand away.

Jon glared at the doctor in alarm and questioned, "Why would you do that?" He was starting to wonder what country this doctor was licensed in and if the island had another doctor.

"I wanted to make sure she has an appropriate response to pain. Did she take any medication or say anything when you spoke to her?"

"She denied taking anything. I believe her. She barely takes Tylenol since her narcotic overdose in January." The doctor seemed unfazed by Jon's words, but calmly asked, "Does she or has she ever had a drug problem?"

"No," Jon clarified. "Some crazy woman drugged and abducted her in January."

The doctor checked her eyes with a small flashlight and then listened to Sarah's heart as if it was normal for someone to be abducted. As Kate began a complete explanation of the kidnapping incident, he brought a finger to his lips and the room fell silent. When he finished listening, he pulled the stethoscope from his ears and asked Jon, "Did she say anything else?"

"Her stomach hurts."

"Is she pregnant?" the doctor asked.

"I...I don't think so," Jon answered, taken aback by the question. With all he'd seen, it was possible.

Kate looked at Jon with a questioning look.

"She's not," Kate said. "She's been on the pill since May. She's not one to forget to take medicine."

Jon stared at Kate in disbelief for just a moment until he was able to erase the expression from his face. *Why would Sarah not tell him that she was on the pill?* It didn't make sense—unless she was afraid to tell him. She knew how much he wanted kids. Was he pressuring her too much, or was she afraid he would just *accidentally* forget about something that had become second nature to him? He couldn't let Kate know Sarah kept secrets from him, so he nodded in agreement.

The doctor pushed his fingers deliberately deep into several spots on Sarah's abdomen—her lightweight cotton dress providing no barrier.

"You're right. She's not. She doesn't have appendicitis either or she would be on the ceiling when I do this." He applied pressure to the right side of Sarah's abdomen. "She's most likely just dehydrated. I can see it by the way her skin has lost its elasticity. The nearest hospital is an hour by plane. We could bring her there and run a few more tests, but I think all she really needs is some fluids. I'm going to start an IV on her to get her rehydrated and she'll start feeling better."

Jon ran his fingers through Sarah's hair and sighed in relief. He looked up, smiled at Kate, and then focused on the doctor's actions. He was digging in his bag again. The doctor plucked out the supplies he needed, laying them on the bed next to Sarah—a bag of liquid, a package of clear plastic tubing, tape, a couple of sterile pads, iodine swabs, a rubber tourniquet, and a needle. The doctor assembled the IV, running the liquid through the tubing.

"Oh, crap!" Jon exclaimed under his breath when he saw the needle break Sarah's skin. "Sorry. It's just that Sarah hates waking up with IVs in her arm."

"Hook this over the top of that picture," the physician instructed Jon as he handed him the fluid bag. When he was done affixing the small hook attached to the bag over the top of the art, the doctor adjusted the flow and asked, "Does this happen often?"

"No. Not often, but this will be the third time she's has woken up with an IV in her arm in the last six months. She's not going to be happy about it," Jon admitted.

"Then I will secure it well with tape," chuckled the short, dark man. He ripped off two more pieces of tape and smoothed them onto Sarah's skin. "She will pop up in an hour or so, feeling much better. You will see."

"So we don't have to cancel the wedding? She'll be fine?" Jon asked.

"Absolutely, she just needs some rest and fluids. She'll be fine by tonight."

Jon kissed Sarah one more time on the cheek and looked to her mother. "Kate, would you stay with her for the next hour? I have a few items to take care of before tonight."

"Sure. I'll be here." She sat down on the bed next to Sarah and gave him a reassuring smile.

"Thanks. I won't be long." He headed out the door. First he needed to find the guys and talk to Liam. And then he needed to find Liam's dad and get him to write up the new nondisclosure agreement for Alli to sign. He hoped he could get it all done in an hour. On the first floor as he exited the elevator, he bumped into Leslie.

"Just the person I wanted to see," he said as he wrapped his arm across her shoulder.

"What now? We're supposed to go parasailing in a little bit."

"This won't take long. Besides, the parasailing guys will be out there all day. And since I'm the guy paying them, I'm sure I can get you into a different time slot. I need your help."

He followed her up to her suite as he explained what had happened with Sarah and everything that had led up to it. Then he asked her to help with the paperwork and the flights, while he talked to Liam and Liam's dad.

⁓

He found Liam down by the beach with the rest of the groomsmen and pulled him aside to talk in private. After all Jon's explanations and pleas, Liam still seemed a bit leery of what he was asking of him.

"Today?"

"It has to be today. The wedding's tomorrow. You are the only one who can pull this off for me. I need you, man." Jon begged with wide eyes.

382

"You seriously think I can make this happen?"

"If anyone can, it's you."

"Only for you. Only for you." Shaking his head, he took the envelope from Jon's hand. "I hope this works."

"You and me both. Do you know where your dad is? I've got to see if he can work some lawyer magic and write up a new NDA for the real defector."

"Last I heard Jim was hitting the golf course with Isaac and Zander."

"Thanks. Good luck."

"I'm going to need it."

Jon took out his phone. There were very few people who were allowed to keep their cell phone on the island, and two of them were golfing with Jim. Isaac lived with his phone practically glued to the side of his head and Jon knew it would be impossible for him to come for a long weekend without it, so Jon didn't have the heart to take it away from him. And Sarah felt it was demeaning for the bride and groom's parents to have to surrender their electronics. So Zander also had his phone.

"Dad, is Jim Nordstrom with you?"

"Yes. And I'm kicking his butt for the first time in my life. You should have seen it. He got bogged down in the sand on the sixth—four strokes. It was classic. I thought he was going to blow a gasket. It's been a while since we've played, but he's as competitive as ever."

"Can I talk to him? I need help with some legal issues." Zander handed the phone to Jim repeating what Jon had told him.

"Jon, don't let your dad BS you. I am still below par and miles under Isaac and Phillip." He paused, and Jon could hear the smile in his voice turn serious. "What kind of help do you need?"

He gave him a brief summary of the situation with Alli and told Jim what he needed in the updated nondisclosure agreement.

"If I can connect somehow with my office, I could have it ready fairly quickly. There *is* Internet somewhere on the island, right?"

There was a computer in the security office and there had to be one at the registration desk. There must be service on one of them. "I'll see what I can come up with."

"The groom needs my help. It looks like I'm going to have to forfeit," Jim said as he handed the phone back to Zander.

"Son, we're on the seventeenth hole. Can't this wait? I'm winning. Let us finish our game."

"That's fine." Jon knew his dad would be utterly disappointed if he missed his one opportunity to beat Jim on the golf course. "Just give me a call when you're done." Jon figured they would be done in the next half hour, and he needed some time to secure a computer with Internet anyway. *Two down, twenty million to go.*

Next he headed to the resort's concierge's office to enlist help with the computers. The woman assured him that even though the Wi-Fi to the rooms had been disabled at the request of Jon's security, she would have a landline with Internet available for Mr. Nordstrom in a private office. Jon thanked her and headed toward the elevator.

There was something he was forgetting, but he couldn't place what it was. He called his assistant.

"Leslie, I talked to Liam and Jim. The concierge is setting up an office for Jim to use to write up the new contract. What am I missing?"

"The dresses. I already took care of it, though. I think you're done."

"Thanks. I'm going to check on my wife."

"She's not your wife until the wedding," Leslie laughed.

"She's my wife," he muttered to himself. "Have fun parasailing, and give Nak a big, sloppy apology kiss for me."

She laughed again.

He ended the call as he stepped onto the elevator. He couldn't wait for this whole ordeal to be over. He pushed the button and closed his eyes, leaning his head against the elevator wall.

"Hey, big guy."

Her voice shrilled in his head like nails on a chalkboard. He ran his fingers through his hair and clinched his fist as if he was going to pull out the clump in his hand. When he opened his eyes, Mia was staring contritely at him.

"I've been looking for you. This whole no phone thing is stupid. I feel naked without my phone."

"What do you need, Mia?" He couldn't keep his frustration out of his voice.

"Since you obviously don't want me here and Sarah for sure does not want me here and my baby's daddy is here with his wife and new baby, I feel a bit unwelcome. If it's OK with you, I think I'll head back to the mainland today and skip the ceremony. With me as big as a cottage, it's not like I can party with you and your boys anyway."

He smiled at her. She was being overly dramatic as usual. He felt bad, even though everything she said was true. When it came down to getting the invitations out, it was Sarah who insisted Mia get one. He thought she most likely didn't want to be blamed by the press for not allowing Mia to come.

"I've been voted off the island, but I still need your permission to leave, because no one is allowed to leave until Sunday evening. Someone told me you shut down the airport."

"Not exactly," he confessed. "There's a flight leaving for Minnesota in a couple minutes and another in a couple of hours, but after that you're here until Sunday."

"Well…I'm obviously not going to make the first one. But book me on the second one?" She met his eyes. "I'm sorry I can't stay. I know this day means a lot to you. I just know my limits."

"It's OK, Mia. Let me know when the baby comes." The elevator opened, and he stepped out, blocking the door so it couldn't close before they finished their conversation.

"I'm hoping it will come early—maybe this weekend while Chris is at the wedding with no phone. He says he wants to be in the delivery room. Screw him. That's not going to happen."

"I'm glad you two are working this parenting thing out." He smiled at her.

"I'm not really supposed to be flying. The changes in air pressure can bring on labor."

The devilish look on her face made him laugh inside. He figured the fact that Chris and Mia were even talking was a miracle. Jon knew that if it was his kid, she'd demand he was there for every agonizing minute of labor.

"I love you, Jon. Good luck tomorrow."

Despite his frustration with her, he still wanted the best for her. He leaned in and kissed her cheek. "Thanks. I'll let the concierge know you'll be on that flight." He smiled and waved as she disappeared behind the closing doors. *Even Mia was growing up.*

He headed down the hall to the presidential suite, making the call to the concierge about the flight for her as he walked. He figured he had better take care of it before it slipped his mind.

Jon hurried his way through the empty suite to the bedroom where he'd left Sarah hooked to the IV. The door was closed, and Jon slowly opened it, hoping not to wake her. Sarah was still sleeping, and Kate sat in the wingback chair across from the bed.

Jon collapsed on the loveseat, sinking into its plush fabric. "Has she woken up yet?" he whispered.

"No, but she's moved around a little bit." Kate set her phone on her lap facedown, as if readying for a long intense conversation. "So what's going on?

What happened this morning?"

Wow, he never realized how much Sarah sounded like her mother.

"I think she just hasn't been eating right and drinking enough water. She's so worried about looking perfect in her dress. At least she hasn't been juicing or doing colonics. She's just been so busy that she forgot to hydrate. And we were out in the sun most of the day yesterday."

"That's not what I meant. I'm sure she'll be fine. David stopped by and checked on her and he thought she looked dehydrated as well. She probably needs the rest, too. What happened with Alli? You mentioned something had happened with Alli."

He explained the day's events to Kate, leaving out the part about the money. He figured Sarah could tell her if she wanted her to know.

"Oh my. That's a lot to deal with. How are you holding up?"

"I can't wait to put this all behind us and start our married life together."

Kate looked at him pursing her lips as if deciding whether to ask another question or not, tucking her auburn hair behind her ears nervously. "You didn't know she was on the pill, did you?"

Taken aback by her question, he took a deep breath and let it out. He didn't want to lie to his mother-in-law, so he chose his words carefully. "I knew she wasn't ready for kids." *Oh hell.* He may as well confess. "She hadn't told me. How could you tell?"

"You may be an actor, but I'm a mother and a photographer. I know faces. And yours said you were totally caught off guard."

Jon ran his fingers through his hair and looked down at the hem of his shorts, not wanting to meet her eyes.

"I think she just needed to feel in control. She's only twenty-one. Besides, accidents happen all the time. Condoms are so unreliable. That whole mess with Mia Thompson could have been avoided if..." Kate trailed off.

Was he seriously sitting here talking condoms with his mother-in-law? What was wrong with him? This had been one of the weirdest days ever. Jon was certain condoms had nothing to do with Mia's problem. Maybe if they'd used one, but that wasn't the case. His mind flittered around, trying to catch up with the day's events. So Sarah wasn't ready to have kids. He could accept that. He looked over to Sarah on the bed. She was angelic, beautiful. And hell, not having to wear a condom on his wedding night had to be the best wedding gift ever. Sarah was probably going to surprise him with it. He closed his eyes and blew out a breath. He didn't need to be daydreaming about the wedding night with Kate in the room. *How was he going to get out of this conversation?*

"You're right, Kate. We have plenty of time to start a family," he said, though he didn't know if it was true. Ever since Jack's death, he didn't believe in timelines. He relied on the here and now, but he could wait for Sarah to be ready. He would wait. His phone buzzed in his pocket, and he silently thanked God for the out. "I've got to take this. Will you stay here?"

She nodded and he exited the bedroom before answering the line.

∽

Forty-five minutes later, after meeting with Jim, Jon was back with Sarah. He opted to lie on the bed next to her instead of starting another conversation with Kate, and his mother-in-law excused herself from the room politely. Jon wasn't trying to be rude. He just really needed to be closer to Sarah. Her being unconscious on the bed with an IV in her arm was starting to be too déjà-vu. He needed to wake her just for his own sanity. The groomsmen wanted him to rehearse the song before tomorrow, and he was supposed to meet them in Nick's suite at 5:30 p.m. He wouldn't be able to go if he wasn't 100 percent sure Sarah was all right.

He pushed a strand of dark hair off her face and kissed her forehead. Her beautiful emerald eyes fluttered open, and he couldn't help the smile that spread across his lips. "Hey, beautiful. I was worried about you."

She looked confused, but he could tell his presence comforted her. That was until the IV tubing caught on the bedding when she moved her arm. Sarah lifted her head, looking down at her arm, and then swore, something she rarely did. "What happened now?"

He laughed. She looked so lost. "You haven't been drinking enough water. You need to take better care of yourself." Jon smiled because it wasn't the first time he had said that last sentence to her. "I didn't cancel the wedding, so you need to get better by tomorrow."

Chapter Thirty-Nine

Sarah

Sarah had been waiting for her bridesmaids too long, and her patience had all but disappeared completely. The breakfast buffet had been delivered to the balcony of her room, and Sarah was worried it would get cold and soggy before her friends arrived. She was supposed to be having breakfast with the girls—everyone except Alli, *the betraying bitch*. And Megan. She wouldn't be there either, but that was Sarah's fault. How could she have been so wrong? Her stomach twisted, and she wasn't sure she could get any food down when everyone arrived. How could she have said those things to Megan? If she could do anything to change what she said to her, she would. But Sarah knew she couldn't do anything about it now, not the day of her wedding. Maybe someday Megan would forgive her. They could go out for coffee and laugh about the entire ordeal, but it wouldn't be happening today.

She and Jonathan had slept in separate rooms last night, and that was probably a mistake because she didn't sleep well without him next to her. They spent the evening until just before midnight under the stars with their friends, listening to the waves of the ocean lap against the shore while they sang around a huge bonfire. It was easier for the both of them to be surrounded by people than to be alone together. They not only gave up sex for the last month, which ended up being five weeks because of Jon's mandatory *Third Rung* tour in Europe, but they also decided to uphold the tradition of the groom not seeing the bride until the ceremony on the wedding day. And somehow not being able to see him made this breakfast even harder.

"Finally," Sarah muttered as she heard the girls at the door. When she pulled the door open, Jessica and Ronnie walked into the suite, followed by Leslie and Megan. *Oh my god!* Megan was there. Sarah reached out, wrapping her arms around her and gushing, "Oh, Megan, I'm so sorry. I'm so very sorry. I should have known you would never be as awful of a friend as I am. Will you ever forgive me?"

"I'm thinking about it." Megan rolled her eyes and smiled as she pulled out of Sarah's grasp.

"You're really here. I can't believe it. Did Jon call you?"

"No. Honestly, I was so mad at you that I don't think a phone call would have gotten me here. Jon sent Liam. He came to my house with flowers and a handwritten apology letter from Jon. Liam was so damn sweet when he showed up I couldn't resist him. How could I say no? That groom of yours is dangerously manipulative."

Sarah, with a smile beaming on her face, met Megan's eyes. "I'm just glad you're here. It wouldn't be the same without you." She grabbed her hand and squeezed it. She couldn't believe Jon arrange it. "Come on. The food's getting cold." It probably wasn't getting cold. There were warmers under it, but it would taste better if they ate sooner rather than later. The girls followed Sarah to the balcony and sat down on the cushioned chairs.

"So what did Liam say to you?" Leslie asked as she pulled out her chair.

"I'd rather not say, but it was incredibly sweet. I couldn't resist him." Megan sat and crossed her legs as a light blush crossed her cheeks. "It's not important."

They ate breakfast, and Sarah shared the story about Alli. She explained how Jon had convinced her to sign a second nondisclosure agreement, leaving out the payoff amount. Sarah just shared that he gave her some money to leave them alone and sent her off on a plane to Minnesota.

"I didn't know where she went until I ran into your mom yesterday. She was supposed to meet Jeff and me to go parasailing, but she never showed. I just figured she found something better to do. You know how she is," admitted Jessica. "I should have seen the signs. She'd been too gossipy lately. And she always asked me what you said when I got off the phone with you. I just can't believe anyone would sell you out. Why would she do that? What could she possibly get out of it?"

"Two weeks ago, she mentioned she was thinking about not going to medical school. Maybe she was worried about paying for it. Her parents have been really unreasonable ever since those kiss pictures came out," said Megan.

"She told me her parents weren't going to pay for her schooling. She needed the money to finish her degree," Sarah added. She scooped a spoonful of eggs onto her plate and took a sip of her mimosa. She didn't want to talk about Alli anymore. She tried to communicate that to her friends without words, and Megan was the one who caught on.

"So are you ready to marry your movie star?" said Megan, following Sarah's lead with dishing up the eggs. "Where are the circling helicopters and the scuba-diving paparazzi?"

"Don't even say that. I'm pretty sure the island's government's been bribed."

"Really?" asked Ronnie. "Can you do that?"

"I don't think they actually bribed anyone, but there's security maintaining a perimeter around the island." Sarah looked to Leslie for confirmation, but Leslie just smiled as if maybe the government had been bribed. She thought it was a joke when Sam had mentioned it.

The conversation came easily after that, and it felt as if Sarah had never unjustly accused Megan of selling her out. Sarah loved that Jon had been able to fix her mistake and that Megan was able to get past it. Soon Kate joined them to get ready for the ceremony—three hours of hair, nails, and makeup.

At first it seemed as if they had all the time in the world, but then too quickly Sarah was being helped into her dress. She felt like a princess as the silken fabric slid over her body. But when the photographer started snapping pictures, Sarah's nerves tightened in her stomach. Pictures of her and Kate, pictures of her and the girls, even a picture of her and the wedding planner Nicole. Then Nicole was rushing them out of the suite and down the large staircase.

Sarah spotted her dad waiting nervously in his black tux by the large cluster of palm trees that marked the procession's starting point. He offered his arm and Sarah latched on, clinging to him. More pictures and then the music started. Her mother was escorted by Jon's groomsman, Hayden, down the white carpet to her seat. He winked at Sarah as he turned, and she smiled back at him. She hoped her anxiety wasn't apparent to all those around her.

"You look beautiful," announced David with a smile. "I can't believe my little girl is all grown up."

"Thanks, Dad. I love you."

"If you want, we can take off for the beach." His eyes sparkled with amusement as he cocked his head toward the beach.

His joke loosened the tension and she began to relax a little. "Nah. I've got this," she said, resting her head on his shoulder as the girls began their procession down the carpet. One by one, each of her friends disappeared. Then the music slowed and the violins joined the brass and keyboards in a more jazzy rhythm. Her father led her beyond the cluster of trees into the opening. The crowd was all standing and facing her, nearly overwhelming her, but she found Jonathan's glacial blue eyes and locked on.

She concentrated on the gorgeous guy in the perfectly fitted tux who was waiting for her on the other side of the gauntlet of people and with each step, she was a little closer to him. The music and the faces disappeared and all she saw was the man she knew she was meant to spend the rest of her life with. Finally her father kissed her cheek and slid her hand into Jonathan's. Jon appeared so calm, as if it was just another day, but she could see the raw emotion in his eyes, and it made tears glaze her eyes as well. He leaned in and whispered in her ear as their fingers intertwined. "I'm glad you could make it. I've been waiting my whole life for this moment with you."

Sarah almost broke out bawling, but she swallowed the knot in her throat and turned to face the pastor. The warmth of Jon's interlaced fingers spread through her, and she thought about all that led them here. She thought about how Jonathan had flooded her heart with love and forced her to take notice. She thought about how with just a touch he could make all the monumental problems in her life seem miniscule. And whatever problems they encountered in the future, they would face them together. She loved this man more than she ever believed she could love another human being.

Minutes later, their vows had been recited, rings had been exchanged, and the pastor's voice rang out loudly, with only the quiet waves lapping the shore in the background. "I now pronounce you man and wife. You may kiss the bride."

Jon turned toward her, cupping her face in one hand while his other hand curved around the small of her back pulling her in. His lips touched hers tenderly for just a second before he pulled back and whispered, "I love you, Mrs. Williams." Then he dipped her back as his mouth covered hers, his tongue gently dipping in. The reverence in his gorgeous blue eyes bled into her soul, and she couldn't help the ferocity of her return kiss.

Chapter Forty

Sarah

Sarah spotted her gorgeous man across the candlelit room. He was talking to Uncle Phillip. She and Jon tried to connect every fifteen minutes since the big dance number, but with every guest demanding a chunk of their time, it was getting harder to do. She'd made her rounds with her relatives and danced with just about everyone at the party.

The boy band-esque dance number Jon and his groomsmen performed earlier had blown her away. When Jon pulled her onto the dance floor and motioned for her to sit on the chair in the center of the floor with all the men dancing around her, she didn't realize to what extent she would be embarrassed. Jon's voice mesmerized her. It was such an unexpected treat to hear him sing. He and Nick must have spent months composing the beautiful words and music and then choreographed it with all the guys. Sarah was overwhelmed. When Jon handed the mic to Nick and the groomsmen formed a crescent, shielding her from the audience, she didn't know what to expect. That's when Jon got down on his knees in front of her, lifted her dress, and retrieved her garter with his teeth. His hands were not gentlemanly, and Sarah was sure everyone watching could tell by the blush of her face.

He stood, opening his jaw, and the garter dropped to his hand. "Just a taste of what I have planned for tonight." His words made her gasp, and she blushed even more. When the men's shield opened to expose them, Jon reached for her hand, pulling her into his arms for a kiss, all the while he spun her garter on his finger. Nick threw him the mic, and Jon sang the closing line. "All my love for you, Sarah."

Now as she watched him from across the room talking to his uncle, looking completely innocent and refined in his tux, she wondered how much longer they would have to stay at the reception. Her eyes locked with Jon's, and she watched as he excused himself before bee-lining for her. He offered his hand, and she followed him onto the dance floor. He pulled her against him.

"I've wanted to touch you all day. I have thought of nothing else since the preacher proclaimed you my wife. But there are too many people around." He kissed the spot on her neck that always made her melt into his arms. "And I don't want to share you anymore. Can we leave yet?" Jon asked before closing his eyes and letting his lips gently whisper over hers. "I'm ready. Please be ready." It was as if he could read her mind.

"I just have to say good-bye to our folks and the girls, and then we can go." She was definitely ready.

"Let's just go. They won't even notice we're gone." He kissed her again. "Wait..." He gripped both her shoulders and pushed down slightly as if securing her to the floor. "I'll be right back." He strode up to the MC and took the microphone. "Sarah and I would like to say goodnight to everyone. We appreciate you coming and hope you enjoyed the celebration. You are welcome to stay as long as you like, but my wife and I have other plans for the rest of the evening. Goodnight." His smile lit on his face, with his dimple dipping into his cheek.

Jeers from the crowd roared as Jon's eyes met Sarah's, one of his eyebrows raised questioningly. She smiled at him. His gaze never left her when he handed the microphone back to the MC. As he stalked back to her like a predator coming in for the kill, her stomach dropped with anticipation.

"Shall we go?" He held out his elbow like a gentleman for her to loop her arm through, and when she did, they walked arm in arm to near the resort entrance where a car was waiting. The driver in white gloves, top hat, and tails opened the door. As Sarah climbed in, Jon helped by hoisting her dress for her. "I'm glad you left this on, but I can't wait to strip you out of it," he uttered only to her. She had made the choice to stay in her gown the entire day. She wanted to make the magic last as long as she could. After all, she would never have another wedding. This was her one and only.

Jon nuzzled next to her and wrapped his arm around her torso, tucking his long fingers under the edge of her bodice under her arm. As he drew her in closer, his hand slid deeper beneath her gown, resting lightly on the top of her breast. She looked up at him, but he stared out the window innocently as if the circles he started drawing with his finger were on her hand and not the sensitive tip of her breast. She took a deep breath and rested her head on his chest, deciding that if he wasn't going to admit what he was doing, she may as well just enjoy it.

They drove twenty minutes in silence before the road narrowed. Tall tropical plants lined the street as it twisted and turned like a maze. Eventually the road ended, looping in front of a small cottage. Small really wasn't the right word. It was about the size of the guesthouse if it only had one floor. It was a beautiful sandalwood color with a flagstone entrance and intricately carved heavy wooden doors that looked like they had been reclaimed from an ancient ruin.

Jon waited for the driver to get out before sliding his hand from Sarah's dress. He kissed the top of her head as the driver opened their door. Then he stepped out, offering her his hand. After she emerged from the car, he slid his hand behind her knees and lifted her up against his chest. He carried her without effort through the now-open wooden doors all the way through the master bedroom and through a second set of glass doors. He set her on a huge, round lounge bed on the patio facing the ocean.

He leaned over her, sucking her lip into his mouth. His breath hummed as he pulled back. "Don't move." His eyes, almost colorless in the moonlight, pinned her to the bed as he turned to go back inside the house.

She sat up, propping her elbows behind her for support, and took in the picturesque cove. Tall rock cliffs rose on either side of the small bay, completely cutting it off from the rest of the island. It looked impassable on foot, and that comforted Sarah. The waves lapped with a soothing roar, and the clean salt air awakened her. It was so beautiful.

The water trailed out endlessly, and down the center of the bay, the moon reflected its luminous tail. Her eyes followed the light to the stars singing in the night's sky, millions of them dotting the darkness. A warm glow of a dozen waist-high candles flickered in the warm breeze along the edge of the veranda. The candles reminded her both of the night Jon proposed and the night in the blackout of the rainstorm when they first made love. This place couldn't be more perfect.

She could hear him when he came back out, the rustle of his pants maybe? Sarah turned, and he was standing in the doorway watching her. He'd changed out of his tux and was wearing a pair of white cotton pants that flapped in the wind as he stepped out of the doorway. No shirt. No shoes. Just the pants hanging low on his hips. With every one of his glorious muscles catching the moonlight, he prowled toward her.

A smirk drew on his face as he passed her one of the two goblets in his hand. "Drink up, beautiful."

"Water?" she questioned before taking a sip. The ice water did nothing to soothe the burn that was growing inside her.

"I want you fully aware of what I'm doing to you." He drew a mouthful from his goblet and swallowed slowly. Only Jon could make drinking water look sexy. "I thought about an energy drink because you're going to need stamina for what I have planned, but I prefer your natural state."

He wasn't even touching her and he already had her body's full attention. She took another sip from her glass before Jon grabbed it from her hand, setting it with his on the table next to the lounger.

"Thank you for leaving this on." He bent down, pinching the hem of her dress between his fingers. "I've been fantasizing about pleasuring you in this dress for over a month. Every time I closed my eyes on my tour of Europe, all I saw was you in a white dress, this dress. It's just like I imagined. And now I get to live it."

With a glint in his eyes, he lifted her dress and let the breeze catch it, ballooning it up until the air slowly dissipated. His smile looked both innocent, like a child unsure of himself, and devilish, as if all his evil plans were coming together. He leaned forward for her hand and guided her to the edge of the lounger. *God, he was gorgeous.* He was hers. No one could take this from her—not the media, not Mia, not Alli, and not a crazy stalker. This was her and Jon's moment and she would never share it with anyone else. Jon pulled a pillow from the seat next to her and dropped it on the patio in front of him before collapsing on his knees.

Now eye level with her, he clasped her face in his hands and gently brushed his lips against hers, soft as the breeze. Pulling back and starting over again and again, each time he came forward, his pressure on her lips grew until he pushed into her with his tongue. Sarah gasped, her heart racing. He could do more with just a kiss than any other man had ever accomplished with her body. Her hands moved to his bare chest as he trailed his tongue down her neck. The heat radiated off him, warming her deep inside. She wanted nothing more than to lose the dress, but Jon seemed so enthralled by it she couldn't deny him.

As his mouth moved over her bodice, his breath burned through the satin fabric. His hands followed, cupping her breasts, and a small moan slipped from her throat. As his lips moved down her, he softly pushed her back against the cushion and all she could do was submit to his touch. He kissed her side where her scars used to be and then found his way to her navel. Her eyes closed as he

401

lifted the hem of her dress. His hand grasped her thighs, pulling her closer and then smoothed down her silken stocking to her ankle. He unbuckled the strap of her sandal with ease and then started the process at her thigh again for the other leg as the first shoe fell to the ground, the motion slow and sensual. Back at the top of her thigh again, he unfastened the buttons of her garter and rolled her lace-topped stocking to the tip of her toes, following his touch with his lips, before moving to the second leg.

"Be patient," he scolded as her muscles tensed. He could obviously tell what she wanted.

When his fingers slid under the edge of her panties, she moaned. She knew what was coming. Jon could push her over the edge with just his touch. Sometimes he would do it two or three times before the main event. She wondered what his plans were for this night. She was ready for the main event right now. *Right now.* Her panties soon joined her shoes on the patio floor. As the scruff from his day's beard brushed against her inner thigh she realized it was definitely in her best interest to let him carry out his plans. But she couldn't even lace her fingers through his hair in this position with him under her gown. She clutched the blanket beneath her as he teased her, and too quickly she hung perched on the edge ready to jump. "I want you." Her words came out breathy and barely audible.

"You have me, beautiful. I'm your husband."

She could hear the smile on his lips. He knew what she meant.

"I need you, all of you," she begged. And she did.

He pulled the white satin off his head with a smile and said, "Oh? We'll need to get this dress off then." He offered his hand and pulled her up, spinning her around to deal with the tiny buttons down her back. He kissed down her back as each button opened, exposing more skin. When he reached the last one, she heard the distinct sound of his zipper. He lifted her skirt again and pulled her back against him. Her body screamed for more as she felt him pushing into her, but just as she thought she would get what she was begging for, he grasped her hips, freezing in place.

"I *so* want you right now, but I want to see your face." She could hear the hesitation in his deep husky voice, his hands still locking her in place. Then he took a deep breath and stepped back, dropping his grip as he let out the breath he'd been holding. "Let's go for a swim."

A swim would be good, she thought. It would refresh her and give her a chance to regain her composure. She nodded as her dress fell to the ground with a soft thud. She stepped out of it and Jon laid it over the back of a nearby chair. When she turned, her eyes met his face. He looked so confident, so beautiful. If she had been there without him, she would have felt bare, too vulnerable, but with Jon, she felt strong. No one could hurt her. She glanced out over the water, the walled cliffs providing privacy to the lagoon. She knew Jon would never take her in the open water naked if there was any chance someone would see them. She didn't need to ask—she trusted him completely. She took his hand, and he led her across the warm sand to the water's edge. The salt water lapping at her toes seemed so gentle compared to the hard sprays on the other side of the island. The waves were rhythmic but not overpowering. It took little effort to walk out into the current, and very quickly she was submerged enough to cover her chest.

Jon turned her to face him and then kissed her forehead. "You are the most beautiful woman I have ever seen, both inside and outside, and somehow I convinced you to marry me. I'm the luckiest man in the world. I get more." His dimple-laden, heart-stopping smile lit his face. And her heart did stop. He didn't give her time to respond to his words before his lips covered hers. He lifted her off her feet so he wouldn't have to lean over so far and then wrapped her legs around his hips, positioning her just right—all while his tongue plunged into her mouth, soft and gentle.

When he pulled back, he was no longer smiling. He stared into her eyes, burning into her core.

"I love you, Jonathan Williams," she whimpered as she draped her arms around his neck. The words didn't seem strong enough. She wanted him closer, *so* much closer. His hands caressed her backside, and his lips kissed down her neck, settling on one of her breasts. Her body arched back, giving him better access as he moved to the other one. He held her in his arms with ease. She could hardly breathe. Intensity radiated off him, and she knew that of all the women he had been with, she was the only one to experience this with him. She alone got to see him this raw, this exposed. She alone was his more and he hers.

The groan he made when he pushed into her almost set her off—let alone all that came with it. The passion splayed her. Maybe it was the month of celibacy, or maybe it was just the fact that they were man and wife; she didn't know, but there, in the water, under the stars, they were one. Jon turned. His body, his gorgeous naked body, catching the waves as the water headed for the shore. He stared into her eyes while the rhythmic push and pull of the water did most of the work, slow and gentle but more than she could have imagined.

"I'm never going to get enough of you, Sarah Isabella Williams."

His words set it in motion. His blue eyes burned into her as her entire body released. He held her in his arms, watching her as she fell apart around him. And when she finally took a breath, he crushed her to his chest and held her even tighter.

"God, I love you." His words came out gasping, and Sarah could barely hear them above the sound of his heart in her ear. They stayed that way for several minutes, until Jon slid her to her feet and crouched down in the water saying, "Climb on my back and I'll carry you to the beach. We're not done."

His promise sent goose bumps down her arms and legs. She wasn't going to argue. She was lucky her knees held when he set her in the water. She clung to his muscular back, and he tucked her legs around his waist. The warmth of his skin heated her as he carried her to the lounger.

It was a miracle that they had found each other. She never dreamed when she first spoke to him online that he was such an incredibly giving man. She never dreamed that she would fall in love with him or that he was famous. The way fate had somehow drawn them together was unexplainable.

When she settled back on the large, round lounge bed, she immediately missed the heat of his skin. He spun to face her, and the light of the moon glowed behind his head, giving the Adonis standing over her an angelic glow. She stared up into his darker-than-usual blue eyes, his face as serious as Sarah had ever seen it, and she wondered if she was dreaming. When he pressed her into the cushion, his eyes penetrated her with so much raw emotion she could feel his presence in every cell of her body. Heat radiated from him like never before. Every thrust, every touch, every tease tightened her insides. She felt as if they had never been closer. How could this be so much better than anything she had ever felt before? Jon had always been amazingly good, but tonight somehow he brought it to an entirely new level.

Closing her eyes, she clutched him like a lifeline, hoping she wasn't leaving marks on his back but not being able to control herself. Every movement brought sounds to her throat she couldn't suppress. He teased her with his lips and ground against her so perfectly. Sarah could hear the pleading in her moans as he pushed her to the edge again.

"Look at me, Sarah," he demanded.

She strained to focus, trying to follow. His piercing gaze tensed every spring inside her as he took her hands and pinned them above her head, interlacing his fingers with hers. *She was so close*, and he always knew somehow. Stretched out above her, he moved tenderly but controlled. She arched against him, feeling each one of his muscles contract with every plunge. Then, suddenly, he stilled with the most gorgeous sound she'd ever heard as he claimed her with his eyes, and she could feel him pouring into her. It set her off, and she was right there with him.

Chapter Forty-One

Jonathan

How many dreams had he had in the last weeks about this moment only to wake unable to exact his desires on the warm, supple body lying next to his? It had been hard, very hard, but after five weeks of frustration, abstaining from Sarah was definitely worth *this*. Being with his wife was better than he ever imagined. He covered her lips with his and dipped his tongue into her mouth. *WOW*. She was incredible. He rolled off her and collapsed on the bed, closing his eyes and waiting for his vision to become normal again.

She reached down and touched him. He couldn't believe she was ready for more.

"You are insatiable. That was the most mind-blowing sex I have ever had. Give me a minute to catch my breath," he panted. With his eyes still closed, he trailed his finger across the tip of her breast to pay her back for the zing she had given him. "I won't need much time though, thanks to your magic little fingers electroshocking me."

"You're not wearing a condom." Her voice was soft and satiated, and it made him smile.

"I know." *Why should I if she's on the pill?* He should have talked to her, but he didn't want her to feel bad about keeping it from him. This was a much better way to open the discussion. He turned on his side propping his elbow against the lounger to see her face.

"You always wear a condom."

He cocked his head smugly as she stared back with a stunned expression. "I'm pretty sure you enjoyed my performance. Two times, mind you. But I'm not keeping score. Besides, I know you're on the pill and have been for months. Your mother told me."

"Jon—"

"I'm not mad. I just wish you would have felt like you could tell me how you were feeling. We need to be honest with each other."

"But—"

"Just let me finish. I'm sorry I made you feel as if you had to hide it from me. I know that when I get something into my head it's hard to argue with me. I don't mean to pressure you into having kids."

"But—"

He kissed her lips to silence her. He needed to get this out. She didn't need to apologize. "It's just, now that I've found you, I can't wait to have them. Ever since Jack's death and then this crap with the stalker, I just feel so temporary, like my life could end tomorrow. I want to get to experience everything with you. I want to cram as much into our life together as I can, and kids are part of that for me. If I die I want to know part of our love will live on. That's why I want kids. I finally figured it out. It doesn't have anything to do with anybody but you and me. I know you're not ready and I can wait. But if you are on the pill, there is no way I'm going to use those damn condoms. I'm glad we waited until our wedding night, though. It was *so* worth the wait. Life-changing. Best.

Lovemaking. Ever!" He looked at her wide-eyed for her response.

She blushed and looked away from him. "I lied."

"You lied about what?"

"I lied to my mother about being on the pill," she laughed. "I told her how you wanted children right away and how I wasn't sure if I was ready. Then she lectured me on how it was my body and how I should be in control of it. She kept bringing it up, and I was tired of talking about it, so after I went to the doctor, I lied to her. I told her I started the pills and she hasn't brought it up again."

He squished his eyes together. "Fuck!" He buried his head next to her ear and whispered, "I'm sorry."

"I'm not." She turned and kissed the side of his head. "I don't want to wait. That's why I never started them. I couldn't think of a single reason to put it off. We'll make it work, just like we've done with every other part of our life."

He crushed his lips against hers, not able to control himself. He didn't deserve her. Ever the optimist, Sarah could turn dirt into sunshine.

After a minute or so, she pulled back. "Do you want to go again?"

"Hell yes," he admitted before mashing his lips back to hers.

❧

Four months had passed since the wedding, and Jon's next film was in full production. He and Sarah sat in the dirt perched on the side of a hill looking down into a ravine where all the cameras and the crowd's attention were focused. Lighting towers blared false sunlight against the Texas Hill Country's dark sky, and though they weren't far from the shooting, they were in shadow—inconspicuous.

Jon leaned in and stole a quick kiss before saying, "Let's do this now." The look of dread on her face spoke more than any words. "Come on. I only have forty-five minutes before I have to be back down there." He pointed to the ravine below. "That doesn't give us much time," he pleaded.

She lay back, flat on the hill, obviously forgetting about the scorpions and spiders surely lurking within inches of them. She pleaded up at him with those gorgeous green eyes he couldn't resist. "You are not playing fair," he muttered.

"Well…it's your fault."

She was manipulating him. She knew him so well, but he couldn't let her win. "Really?" he said calmly. "Because I remember someone asking if I wanted to go again. I'm only human. I can't resist those words from your luscious lips." He dragged his finger from her lip to the top of her abdomen. *Two can play at this game.* "And you're the one who lied to your mother in the first place. That's what got us into this," he continued. He leaned down and kissed her stomach, then ran his hand over the hard, round, barely there bump. If they hadn't been surrounded by a hundred people, he would have found better use of his forty-five-minute break.

"We can just text them a picture," he said as he took the phone from Sarah's hand, pulled her sweatshirt up, and took a selfie of him kissing her belly. "They'll figure it out."

As she glared at him, he typed, *The rumors are true,* and pressed *send.*

"We can't take it back now," he laughed. "They were going to find out at Christmas anyway when you didn't drink wine with dinner."

Her phone began to buzz within seconds. "I hate you. You know that, right?" she said, shaking her head. He kissed her on the lips once quickly before she answered the call. Jon knew she didn't hate him. She just wanted him to make the call.

"Hold on, Mom. Let me put you on speaker." *Ouch. She knew all the tricks.* "Jon's here, and we're near the filming, so no screaming, OK?"

"How far along are you?" Her mother's voice was almost a whisper.

Jon patted his chest to tell Sarah that he had this question. "Four months, Kate. And Sarah is sucking it up like a trooper. All those months of throwing up and she hardly ever complained."

Sarah rolled her eyes at him.

"Oh, honey. You were sick. Why didn't you tell me?"

Jon smiled at Sarah because he knew he had successfully dodged the question about birth control.

"We wanted to wait to make sure the baby took. I didn't need the extra stress of worrying about how to deal with the questions if something happened. But now that we're past the first trimester, we thought we better tell you before the press outs us," said Sarah with a confident smile.

Jon smiled back and massaged her shoulder, trying to convey that she had chosen her words well.

"I thought you were on the pill. How did this happen?"

Sarah banged her head sideways, one, two, three times against Jon's shoulder while she held her thumb over the phone's microphone. "I knew she wouldn't let it go." She moved her thumb.

"I guess it was stress, Mom. You're happy for us though, right? Because I'm excited about the baby."

"Of course I'm happy for you. What kind of question is that? When are you due?"

"Mid-April. Will you tell Dad?"

"Don't you want to tell him yourself?"

"No. It was hard enough telling you," said Jon.

"I'll tell him," answered Kate. "This is wonderful news. It needs to be shared, and we'll have to plan a shower for you when you're home."

"Thanks, Mom. Jon's got to get back to filming soon. I'll call you tomorrow. Love you."

"Love you, too. And take good care of my grandbaby. Oh, that sounds so weird."

"We will," said Jon as he leaned down and kissed Sarah's belly again. He couldn't get enough of touching it.

"So what do you think your parents will say when we tell them?"

"I already told them. Auhh," he grunted as the back of her hand slammed into his stomach, hard. *Damn.* "I guess it's not a good time to tell you that besides Leslie, Nick, Liam, and Isaac know, too."

She shook her head in disbelief. "You wouldn't let me tell Jessica, and you blabbed to all those people?"

"I had to tell someone. You're having my baby." He couldn't stifle the smile on his face as he rubbed away the pain on his abdomen.

"Is that why your dad has been so nice to me? He sent that big bouquet of flowers—my favorite, pink peonies. It's gorgeous. I couldn't figure out why he was sending me flowers."

"I think the pregnancy might have something to do with it, but I'm pretty sure he's buttering you up because he wants your help rewriting the dialogue on the screenplay for his next film. He asked me if I thought you would have time before Christmas. I told him he would have to ask you and give you credit on the film." He knew Sarah would be excited. His father was a tough person to please, and if he trusted her, she would have to know how good of a writer she was.

"Well, if I get my name in the credits, I will," she said with a smile.

He couldn't resist her lips any longer. He pressed her into the dirt and covered her mouth with his. He didn't know what his life with Sarah would bring, but she would always be his more—the one who made life worth living.

The beginning

Sneak Peek

at Schussler's Next Novel

Between Friends

I hand the cashier my card, and the hair on the back of my neck stands on end. I know what it means—he's here. I can sense it. Scanning the tables in the coffee shop, relief trickles through my limbs. I don't know what is wrong with me. Maybe it's my lack of caffeine. I take a relaxing breath to calm my insides, and then I hear it.

"Hey, babe."

The sound pierces my spine, and I freeze as a chill spreads across my skin. *Damn*. I haven't heard that familiar voice in almost four years, but it still burns in my mind. I know I should pretend I didn't hear him. I know I shouldn't turn around, but I can't stop my body. His bright blue eyes and that cocky half smile almost knock me to the floor. God, he looks good, better than I've ever seen him. Our eyes meet, and I'm completely gone.

My body would jump him right here in the coffee shop, if not for the little control my mind still possesses. My world cultures professor stands three spots behind him in line. I struggle to put up my wall quickly and smile, but he knows me so well. Those eyes could always read me. It's like we're back in his Ford pickup in high school and no time has elapsed. I move down to the end of the counter to wait for my latte, trying to put as much physical distance between us as I can.

"We should catch up," he calls to me as he pays for his coffee.

My breath hitches, and I know he heard it because he chuckles. Damn my professor for being here. "I have a few minutes right now," is all I can squeeze out as I try my hardest not to let my body win. *Limit our time together. Do it now and never again. In public—always keep it in public.* I grab my skinny latte off the counter, hoping he will decline.

"I've got all the time in the world for you, Meg," he says with that smile.

He pulls out a chair at a nearby table, spins it around, and straddles it. He crosses his arms over the top of the chair's back and stares at me as I hang my purple jacket over the back of my seat.

"Your coffee is ready," I remind him, and he lifts his chin in acknowledgment, like he always did. When he returns to the table, he pulls his sweatshirt off over the back of his head, in the sexy way that always meant "get ready, Meg," and turns his chair back around before sitting down. I know it is a mistake to be here without my friends for support. They are my backbone when it comes to Chase Maxwell. If my girls were here, they would tell him where to shove that beautiful face of his. I should just get up and walk out the door right now. Why does my body react to him? No one else does this to me. I'm always in control, except with him.

"Short hair suits you," he says, raising his chin again.

"What does that mean?"

"Relax, Meg. It's a compliment. I like it. It's feisty. You really need to learn to accept compliments."

I am impressed with what comes out of my mouth next. "It's just you I have a hard time believing."

Then he looks at me with those blue eyes and says, "Don't hate me. I never meant to hurt you."

"But you did," I say. *I can do this*, I think for a second, until he reaches out and touches my hand. The goose bumps shoot up my arm. I can tell where he is looking, and I'm grateful for the thick sweater I'm wearing. I quickly pull my hand back, tucking it away on my lap. Here we go again.

"You left me, remember?" he says, his blue eyes penetrating mine.

"You gave me no choice." I don't want to rehash this, so I'm relieved when the text from Alli buzzes on my phone. It gives me an out. I can tell him that I have to meet her. I'm sure he remembers how neurotic my roommate is about being on time. I set my phone on the table, readying my excuse—big mistake. Always good with his hands, he snatches it off the table and quickly punches in his number to send himself a text.

I stand up and slide my jacket back on. I hold my hand out for the phone. "I need to go," I say as convincingly as I can.

"No, you don't," he replies, looking up at me. He's the only one who can see through my walls. How does he do that?

"I just want you to know. I went through rehab. I'm clean."

I look at him skeptically.

"Have been for two and a half years," he claims. "I miss you, Meg. I gave up all my old friends after treatment. You weren't one of my drug buddies, and no one knows me like you. I just want to talk. You've got my number now. I have yours. Let's talk."

I nod, and that cocky smile appears again. God, I hope I can handle this.

As I leave, I consider dropping my phone down the storm drain on the way to the bus stop, but I just can't. Part of me has wanted to run into him. I knew I would someday. I ran into his younger brother last summer. His dark hair so different from Chase's, but his eyes were the same and it threw me off.

He carried a toddler in his tattoo-sleeved arms, and the boy had Chase's eyes, too. His brother hugged me like I was his long-lost sister, and we chatted on the sidewalk for an hour. He told me then that Chase had gotten into rehab but didn't offer his number or a way to contact him, and it took everything I had not to ask. I told myself then that being clean didn't matter, but when I see him now, I don't know what to think.

I finish my coffee waiting for the bus and toss my empty cup into the garbage can on the sidewalk. The late February wind bites up my short ski jacket as I peer down the street hoping to spot my bus turning the corner. Instead, I see Chase jaywalking across and getting into a bright yellow sports car. It's not a make I recognize—too expensive. He must be selling drugs instead of using, or maybe he's turned to pimping.

The bus comes before he pulls out of his parking spot, so I don't get a closer look. The heat on the bus is stifling and such a change from outside that I unzip my jacket to get some balance.

My phone goes off in my pocket, and I pray it isn't Chase. I need more time to recover. The text is from Peterson.

U R coming to the game tonight, right?

I totally forgot about the game. Dylan Peterson and I have this standing date for the Gopher basketball games. His younger brother plays, and his family has a block of six season tickets. His parents don't go that often and even when they do, Peterson always brings me. He calls me his lucky charm. Every game I've missed, the team lost; and every home game I've attended, they've won. I can't explain it. I think it's just a coincidence, but Peterson swears it's me. I don't mind; I like basketball, and it's free. I reply: *What time are you picking me up?* He probably is placing a bet and wants to make sure my plans haven't changed.

Dylan: *I'll be out front at three thirty.*

Me: *Why?*

Dylan: *I owe U dinner, remember?*

Me: *Yeah, I remember. You're supposed to cook it. R U cooking?*

Dylan: *No time. We have a game tonight.*

Me: *At least your culinary skills won't kill me.*

Dylan: *That's what I said. See ya soon.*

Peterson and I have been seeing each other off and on for a while now—mostly off. We met at a basketball game, and that is really all we have in common. He's a big guy who played football in high school and lives in a frat house off campus. He's entertaining to hang with and kind of like one of my brothers, only bigger and not an asshole. We don't have a serious relationship and we both date other people, but during basketball season we pretty much only see each other. It's just an understanding we have, not that it would upset me if I caught him out with someone else. It wouldn't. And he doesn't have any claim on me, but dating someone else would complicate game night. It doesn't matter to me. I don't get serious with anyone anyway, not since Chase broke my heart.

❦

Peterson picks me up, and we meet up with four of his buddies at Keane's Pub for dinner. I get a burger and fries, and of course, Peterson eats most of my fries. Why do guys always assume that a girl is too full to eat her fries? Give me enough time and I can finish them.

My mom used to say that my metabolism would slow down someday and all the food I eat would find its way to my thighs. It hasn't happened yet. I can still eat what I want, and she didn't stick around long enough to say, "I told you so," so it doesn't matter what she thought. Maybe I'll be lucky and not have to spend my life eating nothing but lettuce.

When we get to the game, Peterson plants a kiss on my lips before the first buzzer. The kiss is full of excitement and anticipation and part of his ritual. He's very superstitious and very predictable. We watch the Gophers annihilate the Huskers with a forty-six-point spread and talk player statistics most of the game. Statistics is the reason I like the game. Statistics is my thing. I especially like basketball because of the sheer number of points scored in a game. The ratios are less subjective, more concrete.

Most guys don't know that I have a gift with numbers. They hear that I'm an education major and think that I'm just some sweet little innocent that likes children. They don't know that I can whip their butts at poker or blackjack because I count cards, or that I know more about sports statistics than they do. I don't usually share that my second major is math and that I've been offered a fellowship for my doctorate. It just intimidates guys. They would much rather think I'm some hot little blond teacher. They don't need to know. Dylan Peterson knows, but he doesn't want to share the knowledge with his friends. He would much rather keep me to himself and pick my brain during basketball season.

Peterson gives me a fist tap and then dips me back for our end-of-the-game kiss. He's so predictable. He rights me and squats down so I can climb onto his back. I slip into my jacket and jump on. He folds my legs around his waist and carries me out of the stands, showing no strain as we head up the stadium ramp. I know he can bench press three of me. He likes to brag about it to his buddies. When he gets us out into the cool night air, he drops me to the sidewalk and tucks me under his arm to keep me warm. He really is sweet, like a giant teddy bear.

We head back to his place, where the usual Friday night party is in full swing. Games aren't usually on Fridays, and I don't always see Dylan on nongame nights, so I've only made a couple of the house parties this spring. A year ago, my roommates would have met me at the frat house, but now I'm on my own with Peterson. My closest friend, Alli, is trying to maintain her grades until her acceptance letter for medical school comes. She's applied to four schools, but her first choice is right here at the University of Minnesota. I know she'll get into the U. Her father and mother are legacy med students, and her grandmother teaches at the medical school. Alli could get in through nepotism alone, but the fact that her MCATS were pretty close to perfect doesn't hurt either. Alli doesn't come out anymore. Maybe she'll revive her social life after her acceptance letter comes. My other besties have already found the loves of their lives and aren't motivated to go to a party with a bunch of drunks anymore. Jessica is practically married to Jeff—all she needs is the ring. They've been together forever, it seems.

And Sarah, she snagged a famous Hollywood hottie on the Internet a year ago and already has her ring—four karats according to the tabloids. She moved out to LA to start her new life. I'm left here, stuck in limbo, so broken that I'm sure I'll never find someone to love.

Acknowledgements

First, thank you to all the wonderful readers who continue to follow my work. You inspire me to keep writing. Thank you, Cathy, Mary, Stasia, Crystal, and Ann for beta-reading *Between the Lies*. I appreciate your honesty and enthusiasm. You keep my writing on track. Thank you, Christy, for proofreading at the end when my eyes began to blur. You saved me. Thank you to my editor, MNG, you are a crucial part of the book process and I appreciate your knowledge and diligence. Thank you to all the women at WOW (Women on Writing). You are a fantastic resource and just a great group to hang with. And finally, thank you to my husband for your patience, and for always believing in me. Without you, I would not know true love and this book would have been impossible to write. You are my more.

About the Author

Susan Schussler loves the happy endings found in fiction because they inspire real-life dreams. Growing up the youngest of eight children, she quickly developed a strong understanding of and respect for others' points of view. There are many facets that make up an individual, and she learned this early in life. Since then she's gathered degrees and worn more than her share of career hats, but her passion has always been writing fiction. She draws upon her hectic childhood and the diverse individuals that she's encountered throughout her life to formulate her characters and story lines. Find her online at **www.susanschussler.com** and discover insights into her characters in her blog, *A Life Outside the Books.*